A
DEEPER
DARKNESS

A DEEPER DARKNESS

J.T. ELLISON

MIRA®

MIRA

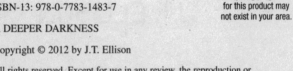

Recycling programs for this product may not exist in your area.

ISBN-13: 978-0-7783-1483-7

A DEEPER DARKNESS

Copyright © 2012 by J.T. Ellison

For questions and comments about the quality of this book please contact us at Customer_eCare@Harlequin.ca.

www.Harlequin.com

Printed in U.S.A.

For Scott Miller, who encouraged me to believe in this story, and, as always, for Randy.

In loving memory of
David H. Sharrett II
"Bean"
June 29, 1980–January 16, 2008
Private First Class—U.S. Army
101st Airborne Division
Bronze Star, Purple Heart
Victim of Friendly Fire

PART ONE

"The most terrifying fact about the universe is not that it is hostile but that it is indifferent; but if we can come to terms with this indifference and accept the challenges of life within the boundaries of death—however mutable man may be able to make them—our existence as a species can have genuine meaning and fulfillment. However vast the darkness, we must supply our own light."

—STANLEY KUBRICK

CHAPTER ONE

Washington, D.C.
Edward Donovan

Eddie Donovan didn't like crowds. Crowds were unpredictable, dangerous. Crowds held a multitude of malcontents, any one of which could be the death of him, in the most literal way. He was surrounded by people, and sweating. Despite the aviator-style Ray-Bans perched on his nose, the sun shone brightly in his eyes, making it harder to see. Even in his car he felt unsafe.

Donovan, formerly Major Edward Donovan, 75th Ranger Regiment, couldn't help himself. He scanned the pedestrians incessantly as he looked for a place to park. Susan said she'd meet him at the carousel behind the Smithsonian and they'd walk the girls over to the Tidal Basin together. He'd thought it better for her to get off at the Smithsonian Metro stop and cut through the back streets, where there would be fewer people, but she'd insisted. The day was fine, spring sun yellow and sharp, and she wanted the exercise. The girls needed it, too—the more they got during the day, the easier it was to put them down at night.

He was running late. He finally found a spot on Seventh. He pulled in, dropped a handful of quarters into the meter and took off at a jog, down the Mall, away from the Capitol.

They weren't alone in their planned endeavor. It seemed every family in the Washington metro area, plus oodles of tourists, had decided to meet on the Mall and walk down to the Tidal Basin to see the cherry blossoms. There were hundreds of jolly people milling about.

Police ringed Independence Avenue, wary and watchful. Despite the beautiful day, terror threats were always paramount in law enforcement's mind, especially when it came to large gatherings. Just plain common sense was needed. But for a former Ranger, the authorities' lack of common sense was teeth-grindingly aggravating. As he moved swiftly through the crowds, Donovan spotted at least five points of ingress, holes in the watch. Of course, this was his world now, his job. He was a civilian in clothing only—his mandate was to protect. Only his paychecks were printed and signed by multinational corporations instead of the U.S. government.

The Gothic spires of the Smithsonian appeared to his left, and the music of the carousel floated to his ears. He spotted Susan, her blond hair up in a ponytail under a Redskins baseball cap, matching aviator Ray-Bans on her face. She looked like an incognito movie star, daintily lean and trim, and for the hundredth time he congratulated himself on landing her. She was the daughter of his former mentor, the man who'd shown him how to be a soldier. A good man now rotting under a white stone at Arlington, lost not to battle, but cancer, like too many others who'd served in Vietnam and Korea. The last thing Stewart had asked was for Donovan to take care of his little girl, a mission Donovan was only too happy to undertake.

Susan spied him and a smile spread across her face. Alina and Victoria—Ally and Vicky—were attached to either end of Susan's arms like limpets, dragging her forward. He smiled in return and crossed the remaining few feet to them, grabbing the baby, Vicky, by the waist and swinging her up onto his shoulders. The five-year-old squealed in frightened pleasure, and Ally smiled indulgently at her little sister. In a perfect imitation of Susan, she crossed her little arms and said, "You know she just ate, right, Dad? You do that and she might throw up."

Eight, going on thirty.

"I've been barfed on before by lesser women." He swung Vicky around his shoulders, the helicopter, they called it, and she laughed and laughed. Her giggles were infectious, and soon the whole family chimed in. Donovan felt his heart constrict. This—making his daughters and wife laugh—this was sheer perfection.

Vicky attached herself to his back like a monkey, and they started walking west.

"How are you, chickens?" he asked.

"We're fine," Susan answered. "I got the oil changed on the way to the Metro—apparently we need new wiper blades."

"They always say that," he muttered, and she smiled.

"I know. The danger of sending a woman to do a man's job. I told them I'd let you know and the kid looked at me like I was an idiot. Have you eaten? I packed us some sandwiches. Vicky had half of hers already, she couldn't wait. I thought we could stop in front of the monument and have a little picnic."

"Sounds great."

It sounded like a perfect chance for a sniper to pick them all off one by one, but he wasn't about to share that with Susan. She was hardly delicate, his wife. After years of being the daughter of a soldier, then the wife of one, she was battle-hardened herself. But once the girls had come along he'd felt an overwhelming need to protect her, to keep her ignorant of all the dangers surrounding them.

It only took a few minutes to get to the grassy knoll the monument rested upon. Donovan stared at the obelisk, shaking his head. He'd lived in the District his whole life, yet had never gone up in the monument.

For a time it had been under renovation, and, of course, September 11 meant it had been closed, and the elevators didn't run except for visiting dignitaries. But it was back open now, more than a symbol of the geographical heart of Washington, D.C. It was a symbol of power. Phallic. Soaring. White marbled. Like a flawless compass pointing north, not to the magnetic pole, but to the heavens. To the only real masters of the brethren beneath.

He really needed to schedule a time and take the girls. He'd heard the view was amazing.

They found a spot on the hill and settled in, the buffalo-checked stadium blanket warm underneath them, both girls serious about eating their sandwiches but shivering in excitement, like racehorses in the gates. Donovan understood their anticipation, but for different reasons. He wanted to get down to the cherry blossoms and take their stroll, watch the festivities and go home. Get them out of harm's way. Home was the only place he could truly relax. These milling masses of people were too much for him. He chided himself—marking time was one of his worst faults—but blamed it on the crowds. And the feeling that something was wrong. He'd learned the hard way never to ignore his gut.

Ally was staring at him, and almost as if she could read his thoughts, set her half-eaten sandwich on the plastic bag and said, "Can we go, Mommy?"

"Finish your sandwich, baby."

"I'm done. Look, Daddy's done, too."

"Eddie," Susan scolded. "Eat."

He glanced at her, then to Ally. With a sly grin, he shoved the rest of the sandwich into his mouth. Ally responded with giggles and tried to do the same, wedging the Wonder bread sideways, smearing peanut butter on her cheeks. Vicky, now eating Cheerios from a sandwich bag, proceeded to upend the plastic into her mouth, spilling little Os down her shirt. She looked festooned for a party, and Donovan laughed out loud.

"Finished," they cried together, and Susan shook her head at them.

"I didn't think I'd ever raise such savages. Fine. Fine. We can go."

They stood, wiped the girls down, tidied their things. Susan folded the blanket and tucked it into her backpack.

"Carry Vicky," Donovan said, lifting Ally into his arms. There was no way he was going to chance losing one of them in this crowd.

They strolled to the Tidal Basin, where the cherry

blossoms were in full bloom. Some had already begun to fall, slowly dying on the ground, creating a blanket of pink-and-white fairy-tale snow. The girls oohed and aahed, wriggling like puppies in their parents' arms. Donovan and Susan set them down and they immediately rained themselves in the crushed petals.

Susan snapped photos, immortalizing their antics.

They were down by the paddleboats when Donovan's cell phone rang. There was only one reason for Donovan's phone to ring today, of all days, the day he'd arranged to take off in order to spend time with his family, as if they were regular people, in a regular world.

"Shit," he said.

"Daddy, you owe a quarter!" Ally said.

Fumbling in his pocket, he pulled out a quarter and handed it to her, then, ignoring Susan's basilisk glare, answered the phone.

He recognized the voice immediately. "We need to talk."

"Now?"

"Yes."

He clicked the off button on the cell and glanced at Susan. He resisted the urge to close his eyes to avoid forever being turned to stone, instead bent close, as if talking tenderly might help.

"Honey, I'm sorry. I have to go. You and the girls have fun, and I'll see you at home tonight."

"Eddie, you promised them." She flung her hand to the right, where Ally was studiously avoiding his gaze, showing her sister the intricate bark of a weeping cherry tree.

"Don't do that, Susan. Please."

"You promised me," she said, softer this time.

He heaved a breath in, his mind already five miles away. He didn't do guilt. Guilt was for the weak. Susan rarely pulled it on him, either. He couldn't help himself; his tone changed. He straightened up, the calm, cool demeanor back in place.

"I said I was sorry. I'll be home as soon as I can."

He leaned in and bussed her mouth briefly, then went to the girls.

"Daddy has to run an errand, chickens. But I'll see you at home tonight. Why don't we have…pizza!"

They danced in little circles, all disappointment forgotten. "Pizza, pizza, pizza!"

If only everyone were so easily swayed.

He gave them each a quick kiss, touched Susan on the cheek in apology and started off at a quick jog down Wallenberg toward Maryland, looking for a cab. His car was parked all the way back by the Air and Space Museum, on the meters at the top of the mall. It would be quicker to get a ride.

He was in luck. Within moments he caught the eye of a turbaned man who swerved to the curb to pick him up. The cab smelled of evergreen and cumin, and something else, that indefinable scent that all D.C. cabs seemed to have. Maybe it was fear. Or power. Or greed. Or envy. Regardless, it insinuated itself into the very fabric of the city.

He slid in the back. "Corner of Seventh and Independence, please."

The cab darted from the curb, and deposited Donovan at his car five minutes later, having only been stymied by a single motorcade.

Eddie jumped in the Audi and took off toward Constitution, then swung back around and headed down toward the Navy Yard. The radio was tuned to 101.1, a song by one of his favorites, Nine Inch Nails, playing. He turned it up and tapped his fingers in time on the steering wheel.

The sun shone in the corridor today. Streams of people walked down to the Nationals stadium for the season opener. Baseball and apple pie coupled with naval history and pastel row houses.

Happy.

Safe.

But there was something Donovan had learned from hard experience.

Appearances could be deceiving.

CHAPTER TWO

McLean, Virginia
Susan Donovan

When the doorbell rang, Susan wasn't surprised. She knew something was wrong. Something had been wrong all afternoon. It began the second the phone rang in Eddie's pocket, and had chased her the rest of the day—onto the subway, to the car, to their local Jerry's for the promised pizza, to the driveway, which stood empty, devoid of Eddie's Audi, to the empty answering machine, dinner, the girls' baths, story and bed. Chased her like a snapping dog down the stairs, to the kitchen for a glass of wine, and, with that innate sixth sense, to the powder room medicine cabinet for a prophylactic Ativan before following her, snarling, to the couch, where they both waited in the dark.

She paused for a moment, hoping it was a mistake, that a neighborhood kid had run by the house and rang the bell as a prank, but no, there it was again, low and insistent, and the beast that waited with her screamed in silent agony.

The wife of a soldier knows to respect those feelings of dread. She becomes so attuned to the nuance of the night air that she can smell her man's sweat, even when he's six thousand miles away, humping it through an explosive-laden desert. A missed email or phone call signals the worst, and silence predominates until the news is spread.

A doorbell. So innocuous. For regular people, the signal of good things, happy things. Packages from the postman and Girl Scouts selling cookies, friends of daughters coming for playdates. But for a soldier's wife, the doorbell is the harbinger of death. A one-way path to sheer, aching numbness.

Stop all the clocks, cut off the telephone. Prevent the dog from barking with a juicy bone.

She took a last sip of the wine and went to the door. Glanced out the glass. Recognized the black uniform of a Metro D.C. beat cop and the rumpled brown suit of a plainclothes detective. A third man joined them, some sort of preacher. He wouldn't be needed. Susan didn't believe in the same God she used to. Not after the things Donovan had told her about what men did to one another in the name of freedom, the whispered confidences late in the night, when sweat still glistened on their bodies and tears coursed down his face.

Her hand was on the knob. She realized she had a cut, the thin flesh on the dorsal joint opened just below her ring finger. Blood was seeping from the wound. When had that happened?

She turned the doorknob without taking a breath, knowing it was useless. He was gone. She'd never breath properly again.

"Mrs. Donovan?" The plainclothes detective held up his shield. Gold. A man of rank.

She didn't speak, merely nodded. God, she was tired. So tired. She only caught bits and pieces of the conversation. She was floating, on her first date with Donovan, him all flashy in his dress uniform, the usher at a friend's wedding. It was always such a joke to them both that they'd met at a wedding, for Christ's sake.

"Ma'am, can we come in…"

"I'm sorry to have to tell you…"

"Shot…carjacking…"

"Notification…"

"Identification…"

Amazing how many "-tions" there were in death. Deletion. Cancellation. Subtraction. Consolation. Elaboration. Coordination. Motion. Action. Caution. Cooperation. Reaction. Resignation. Sensation.

"Mrs. Donovan, can we call someone for you?"

She came back then, looked into the earnest, sad eyes of the detective, who said his name was Fletcher.

Susan shook her head, and the blackness consumed her.

CHAPTER THREE

Nashville, Tennessee
Dr. Samantha Owens

Dr. Samantha Owens, head medical examiner for the state of Tennessee, checked her watch, then hurried down the forty-foot brown-carpeted hallway to the prep area for the autopsy suite. As head of Forensic Medical, the suite was her home. A place she knew as intimately as her own body. She had four medical examiners, eight death investigators and six techs on her staff, all hand-picked, all excellent. And since her conference call had gone long, she was keeping them waiting.

Sam spent a minimum of four hours a day in the suite, overseeing autopsies, for the most part, though she liked to put herself in the rotation at least once a week to keep her skills sharp. The exceptions were unique or difficult cases, or especially high-profile homicides. Those were always slated for her scalpel. Though she'd never talk about it, Sam was one of the finest forensic pathologists in the country.

She was already dressed in scrubs but stopped before

the doors and geared up the rest of the way. Booties, cap, an extra mouth shield. Gloves. The heavy-duty Marigolds that could take a slip of a knife and not get cut, followed by two pairs of regular electric-blue nitrile.

She used her shoulder to push open the door. The stainless-steel cart that housed her knives waited for her.

Sun streamed through the skylights, cheering the place up a bit. The job was hard on everyone. Death was the most natural part of life, but it took a special kind of person to live with it day in and day out. Autopsy was brutal, but necessary. There were good days and there were bad. Then there were the excruciating ones; those that saw children were always the worst. But any unfortunate death could cause tightening around the mouths and eyes, quiet glances, extra gentleness.

So anything she could do to keep her teams happy, she did.

But today wasn't going to be one of those days. She could tell. When she entered the room, there were genuine smiles. The radio blared Van Halen.

I'm hot for teacher.

"Okay, team, what have we before us today?"

Stuart Charisse, her favorite tech, came forward with charts. "Four guests, Dr. Owens. Two unattended deaths, a probable coronary and a possible suicide by overdose."

Sam went to the computer on the far side of the room and looked over the information on the guests, then nodded to her team, a signal for them to get started. The ballet began, Y-incisions done on all four bodies almost in unison, with Sam tapping a pen against her leg like a conductor.

They worked quickly, efficiently, and when the first tech yelled, "Chest's ready," she started her own dance.

She was just beginning the dissection of an aortic rupture on their cardiac guest when the suite phone rang.

Stuart turned down the radio and answered it, mumbled a few things she couldn't make out, hung up and came to Sam and stood quietly.

"What's up?" she asked, not taking her eyes off the board.

"Um, that was Ann."

Ann was one of Sam's top death investigators.

"And...?"

"She's bringing in a...a drowning."

At the word, the room went silent. Sam froze. There was a pause of at least four heartbeats before Stuart lightly touched her shoulder.

"Dr. Fox is already here. He's handling the remains they found yesterday, from the dig in the lot off Demonbruen. That skeleton. He can finish up. I'll just go get him."

Sam bit her lip and swallowed down the nausea.

Breathe, Sam. Breathe.

"Hold on. Let me just finish here," she managed. She made her final cut a little more forcefully than necessary, read off her findings to Stuart, then went to the sink, washed her knives and left the suite. Behind her, the din resumed. She hoped they weren't talking about her but assumed that was wishful thinking.

Out of sight from her team, the rabbit hole opened

and dragged her into the abyss. She hated how her world could turn on a dime. Still. Would it ever end?

She stripped off her gloves and washed her hands methodically at the sink outside the autopsy suite, *one Mississippi, two Mississippi, three Mississippi, four.* The washing had become a shrivening of sorts, a way to find forgiveness for the act of mutilation that was a postmortem.

She didn't know when she'd started thinking of it that way. She'd been a forensic pathologist for fifteen years, starting in the morgue straight out of her residency. It was safe, and comfortable, and she was damn good at her job. She made a difference. She answered the unanswerable, for both loved ones and the police. That should be enough.

But lately she'd been drawing back. Not looking forward to coming to work. Cringing as she dissected the organs. Not wanting to identify stomach contents. It wasn't like she'd ever been breathless in anticipation to start the day—it was a job, after all, and a difficult one—but she'd begun dreading waking in the morning: the alarm blaring in her ear, the five-minute shower to wake up, the cup of coffee from the brown mug, the organic cornflakes from Trader Joe's, the obligatory makeup and hairdryer, slipping into her trousers and tank, a cardigan and pearls, soft loafers on her feet, a dab of perfume, then the twenty-minute drive from the dark house across town to Forensic Medical.

The bodies, one after another, stacking up like cordwood in the cooler, waiting for her to ferry them across the river Styx with a slash of scalpel and a signature on a page.

She'd actually seen a body with a coin in its mouth

once, payment for Charon, and forevermore felt herself allied with the age-old euphemism: Death comes for us all.

It just comes for some sooner than it should.

Rote. Her life was only safe when it was a metronome.

Five Mississippi, six Mississippi, seven Mississippi, eight.

She turned the water a little warmer and rinsed, taking care to remove all of the residue, because she'd developed an allergy to the industrial hand soap the state provided, and when it was left on her skin her hands turned red and flaked. At least, that's what she told herself.

She turned the sink off with her elbow and used the harsh brown paper towels to dry off. A flash of light from the suite indicated the morgue garage doors were opening. She did not look.

It was understood among the staff.

Sam didn't post drownings.

Not anymore.

Into her office for a moment, to gather her purse and keys. She needed to go home.

Numb.

It was better that way.

She didn't go straight home. She drove for hours, aimlessly, around Nashville, seeing but not seeing.

The Batman Building looming high over the city, the focal point for miles around. The Capitol, stately on its hill, flags flapping in the breeze. The persistent bottleneck where the three highways kissed. The leafy greenness that turned to woods and farms five miles from downtown. A storm was brewing, rain billowing in from the west. Sam shivered. Rain meant something else to her now.

She avoided those areas that had been ravaged during the flood.

Her town. She'd grown up here, lived and loved here. Lost everything here. She loved it still, but the emptiness was all-consuming.

The house was quiet when she finally arrived, dark. She'd forgotten to turn on the front lights again. Her answering machine had a blinking light. She set the mail on the counter, poured two fingers of Laphroaig and hit Play. The voice that spilled forth was unusually subdued.

"Sam, dear, it's Eleanor. When you have a moment, would you please call me? On my cell phone."

Click. The empty hiss of dead air filled her kitchen.

Eleanor.

Sam rubbed her forehead with her free hand, then took a sip of scotch. Her pulse picked up. She had a terrible feeling, one all too familiar.

Eleanor Donovan was a friend from D.C., the mother of one of Sam's few boyfriends, the boy she'd dated during medical school at Georgetown. Twenty, fifteen, even ten years ago, a message from Eleanor would have filled her with alarm. Concern that she'd always stowed away, hidden from everyone around her. But now, no. Donovan was out of the military. There was no reason to worry about him anymore. Admitting she was worried about Donovan was paramount to admitting she'd loved him, once—something she wasn't ever willing to do. Her feelings for Donovan were private. Something just for her.

And, of course, for Eleanor, Donovan's too-percep-tive mother, who'd seen the emotions coiled in Sam's gut as if they were naked on her face.

If Sam was being honest with herself, her ties to Nashville were the death knell for her relationship with Donovan. She had another waiting at home, a man she'd been with for years, a man she was taking a break from while she attended medical school because it would be "healthy." She wasn't supposed to fall in love with someone else. That wasn't a part of the deal. Dating, dinners, maybe even a little sex, all sanctioned. Love, no.

Hearts are traitorous things—fickle, capricious and certainly not under the thumb of the rational mind. Sam was astonished to find she had no control over hers.

Eleanor had known all along. She'd been kind enough never to speak of it, but calmly, generously, kept Sam in Donovan's sphere with monthly phone calls, little updates disguised as "keeping in touch." Sam knew he'd finished his third tour as an infantry officer in the Middle East, Afghanistan this time, was married with two girls and had finally left the service and taken a job as a security consultant in D.C.

She picked up the phone and dialed Eleanor's cell, that voice in the back of her mind, her sixth sense, roaring in her ears: *something is wrong.*

Just like two years ago.

One ring, two, three, then Eleanor finally answered.

"Thank goodness it's you, Sam. I have some bad news."

"What's happened, Eleanor?" Sam heard the tremble in her own voice echoed across the line, the older woman's wavering slightly more. She already knew what the next statement would be.

"Sweetheart, Eddie's been killed."

The words floated into the air in the dark house, shimmering in the gloom, and Sam realized she'd neglected to turn on the inside lights, too.

Rote.

Eddie was dead.

Now they were all dead.

She managed to draw a breath.

You are normal. Nominal. Capable.

She resisted the urge to go to the sink and wash.

"Oh, God, Eleanor. How?"

"He was murdered, Sam. A carjacking, at the Navy Yard."

"But he was always so careful…." The Donovan she knew was careful. Perhaps the latter Donovan wasn't. Maybe he was careless, and took chances he shouldn't have.

"He *was* careful. Susan, his wife, said he'd gotten called to work. But it was a safe area. Hasn't had a shooting in years. He was shot in the head."

Eleanor broke off with a sob.

"Eleanor…"

Sam heard a ragged breath, realized she was holding her own.

Oh, Donovan. What happened?

"I'm okay. It's been a horrible couple of days, but I'm managing. I always knew this could happen when he was overseas. I never expected it once he was home safe. But, Sam, I have a favor to ask. I will understand completely if you say no. I can't imagine it would be an easy thing."

"What do you need, Eleanor? You know I'll do anything I can."

The older woman sighed, and spoke softly, as if imparting a terrible secret.

"I need you to come up here and redo his autopsy. I don't believe the police are telling me the whole truth about what happened to my boy."

CHAPTER FOUR

Nashville, Tennessee
Dr. Samantha Owens

Sam was surprised by how clinical her own voice sounded.

"I'm sure the medical examiner did everything right, Eleanor. The police in D.C., too—they see this all the time. I could look over the report—"

"No. Sam, listen to me. The police are saying this was a random shooting. They have no suspects. They aren't closing the investigation, but they practically told me that finding his killer is like looking for a needle in a haystack. I don't believe that, not for a second. Eddie was working on something. He was withdrawn, quiet, distracted. I don't believe he was gunned down by some random drug dealer. I think he was deliberately ambushed and murdered."

Sam sat at the kitchen table, her scotch forgotten on the counter.

"Eleanor. You have no proof. You can request a

second autopsy from a private pathologist—that's your right. But think about what you're saying."

"Think about what *you're* saying, Sam. How could you even doubt me? That man was as edgy as a newborn foal. He was always on alert—that's what made him such a good soldier. He saved too many lives to count because of that nervous edge. I can't believe for a second that he'd let his guard down. He never has. The war changed him, Sam. He wasn't the same man you knew."

Eleanor's voice softened. "If you can't do it because of what happened, I truly understand. But something isn't right here. Eddie was so aware, so *on,* all the time. I can't imagine he'd allow himself to be ambushed by a thug."

She's right, Sam. You know that. Donovan was the cautious one. He was the one who held back when you were willing to plunge headlong off the cliff with him, run away and forget the world. He held back.

And now he was dead.

"I'm not an investigator, Eleanor. All I can do is look at the facts the body reveals."

The body. Jesus, Sam, he was your lover, and you're referring to him as the body.

"Call it a mother's instinct, Sam. Please."

A mother's instinct. Possibly the strongest force of nature in the known world. Sam knew what that was like, once. She shoved her emotions back into their cage, locked the door and sighed.

"All right, Eleanor. I'll be up there in the morning. Call the homicide detective assigned to the case and tell him to all stop, that you're requesting a secondary protocol autopsy be performed by a private pathologist. We'll see if your hunch is correct."

"Thank you, Sam. So much. I can't begin to tell you how much."

She hated this. Hated it like hell.

"Just be prepared for the truth, Eleanor. Sometimes it disappoints us all."

Sam hung up the phone and stared off into the distance. Memories rushed at her like starved wild animals, all competing for her attention, tearing away bits of her skin. Donovan on Key Bridge, the wind blowing his sandy-blond hair into her eyes as they kissed, the lights of D.C. spread before them. The look on his face when he came to tell her he was reenlisting. Slow dancing to Dire Straits' "Romeo and Juliet." The horror she'd felt when she realized he was ending their relationship. The pride she felt when she saw him in his uniform the first time. Their first date, at Charing Cross, the wonderful Italian food, then running down the street to Nathan's for a nightcap, a new band called Nirvana blasting from the speakers.

With the lights out, it's less dangerous....

All that emotion, tucked away for so long. She had a moment of nausea, swirling in her stomach, overwhelming and immediate. She bolted for the bathroom. Got sick. Slid to the floor by the toilet, put her arms on her knees and buried her face in them. Stayed curled on the floor of the bathroom for an hour, fighting with her mind.

She finally rose, exhausted. She'd wrestled the demons back into their rightful place. Her eyes were dry. Tears were unfamiliar to her. She hadn't been able to cry for a very long time.

Numb.

One Mississippi. Two Mississippi. Three Mississippi. Four.

She went to pack.

Donovan. You bastard. You weren't supposed to die, too.

CHAPTER FIVE

Washington, D.C.
Georgetown
Jennifer Jill Lyons

There was a light on in the house across the street. The top floor. A single window glowed behind the drawn blinds. Shadows—one, two—moved past the light.

Jennifer set her book in her lap and watched. She wasn't supposed to be awake. It was nearly 2:00 a.m. But she couldn't sleep. She was too excited. Tomorrow was her sixth birthday. Today, actually. She was already six, but it wouldn't count until 6:25 a.m. That's when she was actually born, took her first breath. At 6:25 on the dot there would be cake for breakfast, a family tradition, and tonight, a small party with her cousins and siblings. She'd asked for riding lessons and hoped that her mother would allow such a thing.

She wondered about the people across the street, why they were awake so late, as well. Perhaps they had a birthday tomorrow, too?

The light went out. Darkness crawled across the

street, deafening and slick, and she was suddenly afraid. There was a brief spark in the window across the street, triangular, flashing out, then gone. Like a shooting star.

Moments later, she saw a shadow move around the corner of the house and walk away up the street. Something felt bad. "Mommy!"

Feet shuffled, and her mother's warm, cinnamon scent preceded her into the room.

"What's wrong, sweetie? Did you have a bad dream?"

She gathered Jennifer into her arms. The tattered paperback fell to the floor. Her mother picked it up and sighed deeply.

"Jennifer Jill, how many times have I told you not to read that gruesome stuff in the middle of the night? *Ghost Story?* That's not a book for a girl your age, even if you can read it. Did your brother give it to you?"

"Yes, Mommy. But, Mommy—"

"No. None of that. It's just your imagination, all stirred up. Get back in bed and go to sleep."

"But, Mommy, I saw—"

"Jen, honey. Stop. It's late."

Jennifer knew that tone. It was the one that made her close her mouth and climb into bed. There would be no more comfort from her mother tonight.

"Good girl. Do you want me to leave the closet light on?"

"Yes, please. Night, Mommy."

She let her mother kiss her briefly on the cheek and watched her leave the room, flicking on the closet light as she left. Jennifer rolled over, wondering. The flash was like a shooting star, there one moment, gone the next, quick as a blink. What had made a shooting star in the room across the street? Who had made it? Maybe it was from the tip of a wand, like in Harry Potter. She wished she could have that kind of power.

A star.

Her voice was soft, a gentle singsong. She'd gotten herself to sleep this way many times before.

"Star light, star bright, first star I see tonight. I wish I may, I wish I might, have the wish I wish tonight."

CHAPTER SIX

Georgetown
Detective Darren Fletcher

Darren Fletcher hated when the schedule rotation put him on the overnight shift. He was supposed to get off at 6:00a.m., but it never failed—nights there was a murder, and that was more often than he liked, he always got the call around 4:00 a.m. Which meant that after spending ten hours on he'd have to pull another five or six. Yes, it was overtime, but he was a creature of habit. Losing sleep made him cranky.

And he was cranky right now. It was 4:13 in the morning. He was nursing a rapidly cooling cup of coffee from the Dunkin' Donuts down the street, and staring into the empty eyes of a dead man.

A man who had three eyes, if you wanted to be specific, because he'd been shot cleanly through the forehead, with an accompanying shot to the chest.

Kill shots.

Fletcher had no idea which was the fatal injury, though he was willing to guess it was the head, because there was a tidy pool of blood under the man's chest and neck, which told him the body had been dropped with the chest shot, the bullet to the head delivered as the coup de grâce. The man had crumpled into a nice heap, his right leg bent under him as if he were trying to turn and flee.

There were no obvious contact burns on the man's skin or clothing.

So he'd been surprised, whether by an intruder or a conversation gone terribly wrong.... Fletcher would have to figure that out.

The dead man's driver's license identified him as Harold Croswell of Falls Church, Virginia. He was thirty-nine, five feet ten, a fit one-eighty, brown on brown. Organ donor, though it was too late for that. Maybe his eyes, those brown, murky eyes, could be given for corneal transplant.

Fletcher winced and looked away. He'd signed his own donor card, but the idea of someone taking his eyes freaked him out.

The soft voice of his partner, Lonnie Hart, interrupted his thoughts and he turned, grateful for the distraction.

"Not a smash and grab. I can't see anything disturbed outside this room. Do you think this is his place, and he just hasn't gotten the license updated?"

"I don't know. Maybe," Fletcher said.

"It's kind of weird downstairs. Fridge is empty and the temp's turned down. There's no mail. The whole house is spotless. No dust, vacuum cleaner tracks in the carpets, fresh TP rolls in the head. Looks like someone's out of town for an extended period. And it's clean. Bet you dollar to doughnuts we won't find any prints."

"No shell casings, either. This guy's smooth—shoots a guy and cleans up after himself. A pro."

"Don't know how he'd have time for all that. M.E. said liver temp shows the body's only been here for a couple of hours."

"Fresh meat. Who called it in?"

"No idea. Where's the patrol?"

"Probably downstairs. I sent him to run the sheet."

"Let's go talk to him."

They trooped down the stairs. Fletcher spotted the patrol he'd talked to when he arrived, standing at the open front door. The sun wanted to come up, but the sky was fighting the light. Maybe there'd be storms today. Who knew. Fletcher had stopped worrying about the weather long ago. It wouldn't change his ability to do his job, or the inevitable outcome for the victim.

"Detective." The patrol greeted Fletcher seriously. His name tag designated him B. Jimenez. He turned to Hart, smiling, looser. Hart was the buddy, Fletcher was the boss. Good cop, bad cop. Had to happen like that out here on the streets. At least, that's what Fletcher told himself.

"How's it, Lonnie?"

"Benito. *Bay-neat-toe.*" Hart thought he was funny. "How's it hanging? I didn't realize you were here. Thought you worked days—who'd you piss off?"

"Price you pay for greatness. Gotta do some scut. I'm taking the sergeant's exam next month."

If Fletcher had a dime for every time he heard that... The exam was easy to take, hard to pass and even harder to land a slot if you did pass. Budget cuts always meant lower personnel levels, and everyone wanted to move up. Move up or move out.

"Good luck with it. So what's the story here? Detective Fletcher would like the rundown."

Jimenez squared his shoulders and pulled out his notebook, and Fletcher shot Hart a look. Hart just grinned.

"Yes, sir. Call came in to 9-1-1 at 2:15 a.m. Said there was a body at this address. Dispatch put it out at 2:17 a.m. I was closest, rolled up on the house at 2:32. Officer Gefley was with me. There were no lights on in the house. The front door was unlocked. We swept the premises, found the body on the second floor in the front bedroom. I checked the decedent's pulse, found none and called it in. Came downstairs and waited for the rest of you to show."

"Who made that initial 9-1-1 call?" Fletcher asked.

"Hell if I know. Sir."

"Let's find that out," Fletcher said, and Hart nodded. He turned back to Jimenez.

"What was the neighborhood like when you arrived?"

"Quiet. A few cars parked on the streets. No one walking around. It's like that here usually, this late. This early. Now, a few streets west and you get the spill-off from the bars on Wisconsin and M, the Georgetown students wandering home or back to campus. It's got folks stirring at all hours. But over here, they settle in and go to bed like good little boys and girls."

"So why's he dead here? What's special about this place?"

"Well, the name Emerson is on the box. Could be family, or he was house-sitting or something, though the place was awfully clean for that. That's all I got. I'm leaving the detecting to you fine gentlemen."

Smart-ass.

"Did you smell anything when you got to the house?"

"Sir?"

"Detective work is more than just what you see, Jimenez. Did you smell anything?"

"Naw. Just blood, and shit. The usual."

"Stop for a moment and think back. Close your eyes."

Jimenez frowned, but complied, and Hart rolled his eyes in response.

"Mumbo jumbo," he whispered, but Jimenez's eyes shot open.

"Cigarettes. I smelled cigarettes."

"Fresh or old? Stale?"

"No, sir. Fresh. Definitely."

"Did you observe any cigarette butts or ashes on the premises?"

"No, sir. But Crime Scene will be looking at everything."

"Excellent, son. Thank you. You can get back to your post now."

Jimenez sauntered off looking pleased with himself, no doubt thinking he had made a good impression. Fletcher watched him go.

"All right. Let's do it. Lonnie, you pick. Body or house?"

Hart shrugged, the overbuilt trapezius muscles of his neck flexing. "House."

"Fine. I'll go find out what I can about Mr. Croswell there. If you get a chance, can you track down that call? In this kind of neighborhood, you'd think someone might have heard or seen something, even if it *was* the middle of the night."

"They're all out there now."

He pointed out the door, where a small crowd had formed.

"Let your buddy Bay-Neat-Toe start talking to them. He seems keen to help."

"You're the boss." This was said without rancor—Hart had been his partner for eight years now, and they both liked the setup. Hart was an excellent cop, one hell of a detective and seriously lacking in any ambition to rise above his current post. Fletcher, on the other hand, couldn't wait to get out of Homicide. He was five years from his twenty, and counting down every second. He'd take a promotion, push papers, ride a desk, anything to get out. He'd seen too much. Been in this position too many times. It wears on a man. If he's sane. And Fletcher would like to think he was, after a fashion.

He watched Hart talk to Jimenez, saw the young man's eager smile and shook his head. He'd been like that once. Full of piss and vinegar, titillated by his proximity to evil. So certain he could make a difference. Not unlike the gaggles of twentysomething college graduates that flooded the city each May, buffed and polished to a high shine—no more jeans and sweatshirts, but dark blue wool suits, crisp white shirts and red power ties for the lads, skirts and dresses over the knee, nipped at the waist and lightly shoulder-padded for the lassies. Drinking venti coffees, staring at their handhelds, talking earnestly over single malts and pitchers late into the night at the various Capitol Hill watering holes. He watched them on his way home, on his way to work, and marveled at their hope.

Hope that wouldn't alter this empire of dirt. D.C. was immortal: the more things changed, the more they stayed the same. Even Icarus flew too close to the sun. But in D.C., the sun moved out of the way for the chosen ones, only singeing them around the edges in punishment. Nothing ruined a career in D.C. except for the obvious: a dead girl, a live boy or pictures of your junk all over the internet. Still, no one was ever totally destroyed. Even in death, the vanquished took on mythic qualities.

Confident things were well in hand, Fletcher shook off his melancholy and went back to the stairs, looking for anything out of the ordinary. The house was too clean, the scene too quiet. Soon the body would be moved, the cleaners would arrive, mopping the blood, replacing the carpet in the bedroom, and things would go back to normal. Normal. As if that could ever happen. More than likely, the owner of the house would decide to sell, unable or unwilling to stay behind where a life had been lost, and the thread of the day's events would be gone in the ether. Empty, the house would collapse in on itself little by little: first the paint flaking, the porch sagging, a roof leak or two, until one of the many polite neighbors got upset and grouched to the owners, who by now were in Florida, paying a fresh mortgage, allowing the bank to foreclose on the property they couldn't sell.

It was his job to find the answers before the trail was dead and gone. He didn't need another cold case cluttering up his desk.

Crime scene techs crawled all over the second bedroom, dusting for latent prints, attempting to lift electrostatic footprints from the hall, accumulating the evidentiary elements that would be needed down the road to prove the identity of the murderer. Even the tiniest bit of matter could solve a case, and no tech wanted to be the one who missed it.

Fletcher let them work. He leaned against the wall and pulled out his iPhone, searched for Harold Croswell, Falls Church, VA. It would be just the first of multiple computer searches through multiple databases, but why not start with the easiest?

Bingo. With the treasure trove of information the internet could yield, detecting was sometimes made easier.

Facebook. MyLife. Twitter. "Hal," as he was known, was married, with three kids and two dogs. Great. Notification would be fun.

"We're all done here, sir." A freckled worker, laden down with bags, flagged him down in the hall. "M.E.'s gonna move the body now."

"All right. Thank you. Who's on this morning?"

"Lurch." The tech grinned at him. "Have fun."

"Great," Fletcher groaned.

"You are talking about me, I presume."

Amado Nocek emerged from the hallway. He was cadaverously pale and extremely tall. Fletcher always thought he looked like some sort of translucent praying mantis, hands rubbing together in glee over the dead. They called him Lurch behind his back. He would suck them dry if they tried it face-to-face, but he knew what they said. In the manner of all great men, Nocek ignored their ignorance.

Fletcher shot the tech a look. "Of course we aren't talking about you, Dr. Nocek. How have you been?"

"I am fine. Suffering from a malady I've not yet been able to discern, but it involves a great deal of mucus." He proved his point by sniffing hard and long, his reddened nose closely resembling a proboscis. When the insect invasion came, Nocek would be flying in the lead formation.

"Keep that cold to yourself. When will you do the post?"

"You'll have to call the office. We had a rash of deaths this week, and I'm afraid we've fallen behind. Some of that is my fault. The illness I alluded to has precluded me from working for the past few days."

"Will you let me know?"

"Of course. It will probably be Friday at the earliest. I intend to send out engraved invitations. Do you need a plus one?"

"Yes. Detective Hart will be attending, as well."

"Fine. Fine. I'll see to it. If you will, I'd like to return to the office of the chief medical examiner now. *Justitia omnibus.*"

He wandered off and Fletcher didn't know which to shake his head at, that Nocek didn't call it the OCME like everyone else, or the obscure reference to the motto for the District of Columbia: justice for all. Like that happened. Especially in a homicide case.

Fletcher reached in his pocket for fresh nitrile gloves and went back into the bedroom. Watched them load up the body. Yawned, and made peace with the fact that he wouldn't be getting any sleep any time soon. Decided to go help with the canvass, after all.

And damn it, the coffee was cold, too.

CHAPTER SEVEN

Nashville, Tennessee
Dr. Samantha Owens

Sam was astounded by how expensive it was to book a plane ticket without advance notice. Eleanor had insisted on paying, had given Sam her credit card number. Still, she didn't want to bilk the woman. She finally gave up on that notion and settled for convenience: a flight that landed at Reagan National at 11:00 a.m.

She turned off the computer, went to her bedroom and got ready for bed. Set the alarm, even though sleep was out of the question. Picked up a book from her night table. She had no idea what it was or what it concerned. She tried to read, but the words kept blurring. She gave up after half an hour and shut off the light. Laid there in the dark, listening to the house creak around her. She should get a cat, something soft and furry to sleep with her. She'd like a dog, but she was allergic.

Her thoughts coiled around themselves. She let them.

This morning's call about the drowning. Her flight from her responsibilities. If she'd just come home earlier, she'd have gotten the message from Eleanor sooner and could have flown to D.C. tonight.

If she hadn't been so selfish two years ago…

They might have escaped.

Water. Bullets. Hearts.

She rolled onto her side, punched her pillow to fluff it up.

She had to find a way to cope. This was her life now.

Smiling eyes, soft kisses, the breeze across the bridge.

Her house was too quiet. She missed them.

Missed them all.

Donovan.

There she was, back to exactly what she was trying to avoid thinking about—Donovan.

It was no use. It was too fresh for her to compartmentalize and hide away. She wouldn't escape him tonight.

She went back to the computer and looked up the online stories again, the same ones she's stared at when she got off the phone with Eleanor. They were sparse on details, long on color. Donovan was the twelfth carjacking victim in the District so far this year. He was driving through an area that wasn't well known for violence; the community organizers were in a frenzy. That was it for the crime. The rest was local hero stuff. There was a lengthy history of his time in the service, which brought all the horrible feelings Sam had stuffed into the boot heel of her heart back to the surface.

Donovan had enlisted out of high school, done his tour in Desert Storm, then came home and went to college. Sam met him the first week of med school. He was part of her Gross Anatomy team of first-years. They took turns egging each other on to make that first cut into dead flesh, learning the depersonalization skills that were so vital to their intended career paths. But then the war started again, and he got noble, started entertaining the notion that he wanted to go back in, this time as a Ranger. He would be a tough guy, infantry. On the front lines. Leading the 11 Bang-Bang into battle. And if his medical training could help save lives in the bargain, so be it.

She couldn't shake him from his path, which seemed to her a death wish: infantry sustained the highest number of casualties in a war. She had to admit, part of her was so hurt when he chose the military over her that she let him walk away. The night on Key Bridge, when he'd kissed her, said he loved her, then told her he was leaving and broke her heart in two.

She could have promised to wait for him, but she knew that would be a lie. She had another, one who loved her desperately, one who wanted her home, wanted to share her life. One who put *her* life plans first, who called daily telling her she was missed. One she'd already committed to. In truth, even though heartbroken, Donovan reenlisting gave her permission to move back into her life the way it was originally meant to be. Donovan was simply a diversion on the road.

She told herself that, and eventually came to believe it. Mostly. She pushed the feelings down into a tiny deflated ball, flat and meaningless, a spot of black on an otherwise perfectly red and juicy heart.

She turned off the computer, careful to check that the surge protector was on, then went back to her bedroom. Shadows danced across the walls as she moved, slowly, numbly, to the bed and lay down. Got up and washed her hands. Lay down again.

A different woman might have been tempted to open up the closet door, drag out that brown box she kept—the before box—and look through for a picture she knew was in there.

But she didn't. Samantha Owens wasn't the type of woman to look back.

She kept telling herself that. If she repeated it enough, it might even come true.

Relief came a few hours later, when the alarm began to buzz. Shower, coffee, cornflakes, a relatively quick drive across town. The airport wasn't crowded, the lines for security mercifully short. She glided through—apparently women weren't being X-rayed this morning, only the men—and had plenty of time to grab another coffee from the Starbucks.

She lined up dutifully when her time came, got on the plane, sat and pulled the bottle of Purell from her plastic bag. She rubbed the antibacterial gel into her cracked palms, and remembered the last time she was supposed to fly. Their vacation had been a spur-of-the-moment thing, and she realized she'd never called the airline to let them know they weren't coming. She may even have a credit. She'd have to check. It went into her mental database of things to do that she'd never really remember, the file that flitted through her life like little birds hopping up and down the branches of the river birch in her yard. She told herself that she remembered the things that mattered. That made her strong. It got her through.

The flight landed, bumping her back to reality. Another chunk of time gone. She gathered her things and left the plane. She managed to avoid eye contact with the people around her. It was better that way. She couldn't seem to look at anyone these days without imagining them pale and chilled, arms spread akimbo, a hard plastic block under the third thoracic vertebra, spreading the chest wide for her scalpel. It always bothered her when television crime shows, which purported to be accurate, showed bodies at autopsy under sheets with the block under their necks. Then again, normal healthy people didn't want to know the details of what happened when Sam took over their loved ones' lives.

At the end of the hallway, before she got to Baggage, there was a driver with a sign that read OWENS in chicken-scratch black marker. Kind Eleanor, no doubt. Even respecting the name, unlike so many others. Eleanor understood what it was like to lose. Sam had dropped her husband's name. It was too much of a reminder.

Not everyone agreed with her choice.

She had no bags—just the overnight case she'd slung together with two changes of clothes in it; she didn't plan to stay long enough to need more. Swoop in, do her due diligence for Donovan and get home.

Home.

As if she knew what that was anymore.

She let the driver take her carry-on, followed him out of the terminal to the curb.

It was overcast, cold and rainy, typical Washington spring weather. She got settled in the back and watched as the driver silently pulled into traffic and pointed them toward town. Within moments she could see the Washington Monument, the best orienting spot of any city in the world. The Monument meant center west, the Capitol exactly 1.2 miles east up the National Mall, and the city tidily moved from those points outward on a fine grid. Lettered streets went east to west, numbered streets went north to south, states went at an angle through the city. Four quadrants—northeast, northwest, southeast, southwest—delineated by time, race and society. Independence Avenue and Constitution Avenue were the main thoroughfares along the Mall, and the whole city was ringed by parkways and freeways, parks, trees, monuments, bridges. It was hard to get lost downtown. Just look over your shoulder, see where you are in relation to the monument, and change course as needed.

It was a beautiful city, one made more so in spring, when the delicate pink-and-white cherry blossoms took over.

Sam could see them across the Potomac and the Tidal Basin opposite the parkway, like puffy snowballs suspended in midair. They were at their peak, but the cold rains were causing them to wilt. A pity, though they matched her mood. They'd be jubilant tomorrow or the next day, when the sun returned to the sky.

The driver took the exit for Key Bridge and ferried her across to the edges of Georgetown. Eleanor lived on Q Street, just up from the old haunts Sam and Donovan used to frequent. They were stopped at the light in front of one of them right now: Dixie Liquors, a building that had been the source of every kegger she'd attended during school.

Sam realized she was smiling. Funny that the thought of upside-down keg hits brought her right back to a freer, easier time. Maybe it was just being out of Nashville. Then again, she had always loved D.C.

By the time the driver deposited her at the front door to Eleanor's elegant Georgetown Federalist town house, she could almost feel the weight starting to lift from her shoulders. Like her wings might eventually unfold again, curling lush and firm from her back, where now they lay dormant, desiccated husks that felt like they would never bring her flight.

Fine time for optimism, Sam. Standing on the door-step of your dead lover's mother's house.

The house hadn't changed on the outside—three stories of rust-brick and black shutters, a welcoming red door and two dormer windows peeking out onto the street. Classic. Unending.

She raised her hand to knock, but Eleanor must have been waiting. The door opened and the older woman launched herself into Sam's arms.

It felt good. To be touched. Even if mournfully.

"Oh, Eleanor, I am so, so sorry."

Eleanor gave her another squeeze, as if she knew Sam needed that extra bolstering, then stepped back. Her hair had long since gone gray, but was colored in D.C. denizen style, an ear-length bob lowlighted with stormy streaks that gave depth to her silver. Her eyes were blue and moist; she'd lost weight since Sam saw her last. God, what had that been, eight years ago? No, just five—Sam had been back for her reunion, and had met Eleanor for coffee.

Right when Donovan was headed into Kirkut.

"You look like hell. Come on in. I've made some tea."

Dear Eleanor. Never able to lie, even decorously.

"That sounds lovely."

* * *

They took their tea to the pristine kitchen's island, where blue-and-white-striped cushions softened the iron café stools that stood in readiness. Vivaldi's *Winter* played softly on the house speakers.

Eleanor settled herself on the cushion.

"Was the flight okay?"

"Fine."

"Did you eat?"

"No. I wasn't hungry."

They drifted into silence. Sam watched Eleanor expectantly. The dam would break soon enough. She was right.

Eleanor shook her head.

"They found him bleeding on the corner of Seventh and L Southeast, at that nasty little market. The car must have drifted off the road a bit, like his foot was on the gas. It ran into the signpost, they found paint in the scratches. The car was taken from that point, there were skid marks leading away. They dropped his body out the door like he was trash. He was dead quickly, they did tell me that."

Eleanor's tone was surprisingly matter-of-fact. Sam was impressed.

"No one saw anything?"

"Hardly. Nothing reported. They interviewed people from the neighborhood, but nobody saw a thing. The detective talked to Eddie's boss at work, Rod Deter. He claims he didn't call him to come in, doesn't know who would have, because he had taken the day off. The last incoming number on his cell phone was from a blocked number. The detectives think it was a disposable cell of some kind."

"So it could have been anyone calling. And the autopsy?"

"Gibberish. They'll issue the final report in a few weeks, once the toxicology is complete. I had to go by what the detective said. He was shot once in the temple. They said at close range. There was shattered glass all over his body."

"Left or right temple?"

"Right."

"So the shooter was on the passenger's side of the car?"

"That's what they said. Glass on his clothes, glass in the street."

"They haven't turned up the car yet?"

"No. I assume it's in parts by now."

"And his wife?"

Eleanor met Sam's eyes then.

"Devastated. She's done a good job at pretending otherwise, simply to get the girls through. And the planning…well, you know."

Sam did.

We can bury them all together, if that's what you want. They're small enough….

She swallowed more tea.

"Susan is none too happy with me calling you, that's for sure. She wants to get him in the ground and get the girls' lives back on track."

"That's understandable."

Eleanor's voice rose an octave. "It's unconscionable. Doesn't she want to know the truth?"

Sam put her hand on the woman's arm. "It's entirely possible that she does know the truth. Eleanor, you're going to have to give me more to go on than this. Why do you think this is more than a simple carjacking? You said he was working on something?"

Amazing, how they were both talking around him. As if saying his name would cause him to reappear, insubstantial and transparent, to stare at them sadly. It might, at that. The name of the dead is a powerful beast indeed.

Eleanor deflated. "Oh, Sam, maybe it's just wishful thinking. Maybe I can't accept the fact that fate decided his time was up. But something is nagging at me. It just feels wrong. It feels all wrong."

She drank some of her tea, then set the cup down on the counter.

"How are you, Sam? You've gotten entirely too thin, but that's to be expected. I did, too, when Jack died."

Sam's hands were tightly clenched in her lap. She noticed how red they were, how worn.

One Mississippi…

No, no, no. Not now. Not here. The two worlds must not be allowed to collide.

Normal. Nominal.

Sam couldn't help herself. She couldn't escape it. She picked up her teacup and sloshed a bit over the edge, over her fingers, onto her blouse.

"Damn it. Look at that."

She rose from the stool, apologetic, and started the water running as quickly as she could. Felt the anxiety slink away, content to retreat into its dank hole.

One Mississippi. Two Mississippi. Three Mississippi. Four.

Eleanor watched her silently. She felt the woman's eyes boring into her back. Sam gazed out the window to the small garden planted in the backyard. Saw a flash of white, heard giggling. She turned the water hotter.

When she felt marginally cleaner, she made her way back to the stool and sat.

"I'm fine, Eleanor. Let's talk more about…Eddie. When did you see him last?"

Eleanor squinted her eyes at Sam, but let it lie. Thank God. Sam was only one woman and, in her mind, not a very strong one, either. She couldn't manage everything, all the emotions and sadness and fears and hopes, for herself and Eleanor, too. She just needed to keep treading water, and the whole world would keep spinning. At least for another round of sunsets.

"He was over here last week, with the girls. Sunday dinner. Susan wasn't feeling well, so she stayed home. We had a roast, watched some movies. A typical Sunday afternoon."

"And?" Sam prompted. "Come on, Eleanor. What aren't you telling me?"

Eleanor chewed on her bottom lip for a moment, then stood and went to the far side of the kitchen. She opened a drawer. Sam could see it was the junk drawer. Everyone had them. She immediately thought about what was in hers: batteries, scissors, take-out menus, twisty ties, pliers. A small pink barrette.

Nausea roiled in her stomach, she tamped it down. *Stop it, Sam. Now isn't the time.*

Eleanor crossed the kitchen and handed Sam a folded piece of paper.

"You're right. There is more. This is why I wanted you here, Sam. I just remembered it yesterday. Right before I called. I'd put it in the drawer and with everything that happened…"

Sam took the proffered note. The paper was simple, thin, torn from a spiral-bound notebook, folded in thirds.

Sam unfolded the note carefully. On it were four words, written in all caps:

DO THE RIGHT THING

CHAPTER EIGHT

Georgetown
Dr. Samantha Owens

Evidence. This was evidence. They shouldn't be touching this. This was an open threat.

"Eleanor, do you have gloves?"

"Winter gloves. Not the kind you're looking for, I expect."

She'd diminished in the few moments Sam had spent staring at the note. Gone from a strong, self-assured mother to a frail old woman. As if she knew that she was right.

Sam laid the note on the counter carefully.

"Where did you get this?"

"It's not mine. Eddie brought it with him to lunch. 'For safekeeping,' he said. He wouldn't tell me where he got it, or when, or what it meant, just asked that I keep it hidden. So you see, it couldn't have been random. I know he was murdered."

"Did you tell the police?"

"No."

Sam whirled on her.

"Why the hell not? They need this information. This creates more than reasonable doubt that this wasn't a simple carjacking. You withholding the note…" She trailed off. She'd been about to say that withholding the note could have given Donovan's killer time to get away, but laying that blame on Eleanor wouldn't be fair. It was foolhardy, keeping the full truth from the police, but not life-ending.

Eleanor sat heavily on the stool. Her face was haggard.

"So he *was* murdered? It wasn't random?"

"Eleanor, I don't know. I can't say right now. But I'd like to get a chance to look at the autopsy notes right away, see if there's something they may have missed. What's the name of the detective working the case?"

Eleanor had prepared a file folder that had all the information Sam would need stowed inside. The gesture made Sam sad. Eleanor had spent years on the Hill as the legislative director to several Virginia congressmen and had hated retiring.

Old habits die hard.

She handed the folder to Sam. A business card was paper-clipped to the front.

"Darren Fletcher. And he seemed none too happy to be dealing with the case."

"Some cops aren't the most friendly, that's for sure. Tell me, what else did Eddie say about the note? Was he frightened? Annoyed? Secretive?"

"He just said he didn't want Susan seeing it."

"He didn't want me seeing *what?*"

Eleanor and Sam both jumped. A petite blonde

woman stood at the entrance to the kitchen, arms crossed defensively, staring at them both.

Sam had never met Eddie's wife, nor seen pictures, but this had to be Susan Donovan.

"Grammy! Grammy! Grammy!" Two little girls ran into the room. Eleanor immediately dropped to her knees and gathered them to her bosom. Sam forced herself to swallow, stay still. Every muscle in her body fired. She wanted to run as far away from the girls as possible. She gritted her teeth and looked out the kitchen window so they wouldn't see the sudden tears in her eyes.

The petite woman came all the way into the kitchen, removed her sunglasses. Sam gathered her self-control and met Susan's eye. She could see why she wore the glasses, despite the fact there was no sun to be seen. The woman's eyes were red and swollen, devoid of makeup, with dark circles underneath. On closer inspection, Sam saw her hair was dirty, unwashed for two, maybe three days.

"Who are you?" the woman asked.

"I'm Dr. Samantha Owens. I am so sorry for your loss." Sam resisted the urge to stick out her hand, like they were at a social mixer.

She was glad she didn't. The woman gave her a quick, hateful glance.

"Oh. It's *you*. *Our* loss, don't you mean, Doctor? Considering how well you knew my husband."

"Susan," Eleanor cautioned. "Little pitchers."

That was enough to stop the woman's attack. She glanced at the girls. "Go watch TV in Grammy's room, okay, chickens?"

In the weary way of children who know the adults

need to converse, they detangled themselves from their grandmother's loving arms and silently melted away. Sam had seen that resigned maturity happen with children forced to grow up too quickly many times before. It was as if Death knocked on their doors as he passed and told them to behave, or they'd be next.

She tamped down her annoyance with Susan Donovan and tried again.

"Yes, he was my friend, too. But we hadn't spoken in years."

Susan regarded her warily, then dismissed her entirely, turning to Eleanor. "What didn't Eddie want me to see?"

Eleanor hesitated a moment, handed her the note.

Susan read it, flipped the page over, shook her head. "What is this?"

"I don't know, dear. Something Eddie gave me for safekeeping."

"And you didn't tell me about it? You showed *her* instead?"

Her.

Sam nearly burst out laughing—when she was growing up, and her father was telling stories, he sometimes referred to Sam's mother as *her*. Laura would always retort, "Who's her, the cat's mother?"

The cat's mother.

"What's so funny?" Susan was glaring at her.

"Nothing," Sam said, sobered. "A memory, from my childhood. It's really nothing. Susan, truly, I am sorry. Eddie was a good man. He loved you very much."

"If you didn't talk to him in years, how do you know all that?" Susan was starting to look dangerous—ready to cry or scream, or fly apart at the seams. Sam recognized the look and realized she needed to tread carefully.

"Eleanor has been kind enough to share occasional updates with me."

Susan froze, unable or unwilling to acknowledge the perceived transgression from her mother-in-law. She changed the subject instead. "What exactly is it you plan to do here, Dr. Owens? Did my mother-in-law explain that I will not give my permission for a second autopsy? *Professionals* have done their jobs. There's already been enough damage to my family. We can't bring him back."

Sam turned on her medical examiner persona. She'd heard this argument too many times to count from a victim's loved one, usually in denial of a primary autopsy. "Don't you want the person who did this to see justice?"

"Of course I do. But knowing won't change anything. Eddie is still dead. Cutting him open again won't bring him back to life."

Sam understood that. She understood it more than Susan could possibly know. She tried another tact.

"I hate to mention this, but if he *was* murdered, and not randomly carjacked, you and the girls could be in danger, as well. Are you willing to risk their lives, too?"

"That's one hell of a low blow. And the only person who doesn't think this was a carjacking is Eleanor."

"And me. This note feels real. And if Eddie was purposefully targeted, the danger to you and your family is a reality, Mrs. Donovan. Unfortunately, I see my share of violent crime. I've been a victim of it myself. So I understand that sometimes, when the primary target is neutralized, and the end game has not been played out, the ones closest to the victim are also at risk."

"You're just trying to scare me. You hateful woman."

Sam did laugh then, albeit humorlessly and briefly. "I may be. But when it comes to protecting your children, I trust that you can put your ego aside for one minute and think about them."

"That's enough!" Eleanor snapped. "We can't be squabbling like this. Susan, please. Let Sam do her job. Let's put all our minds at ease." Eleanor softened her tone. "At the very least, give your permission for Sam to look over the autopsy report and speak with the medical examiner. There's nothing intrusive about that."

Susan pulled at her ponytail. Sam could tell she was embarrassed by her outburst. Susan struck her as a woman who didn't like to lose control. Sam understood that, too.

"Fine," Susan said at last. "Look at the notes. But after that, I trust you'll go back to your life in Tennessee and leave us to bury our dead."

She swept from the room, calling for her daughters.

Sam shared a long look with Eleanor. "You could have warned me that she hates me."

Eleanor began to tidy up their tea things.

"She doesn't hate you. She's just afraid of what you might find."

CHAPTER NINE

Georgetown
Maggie Lyons

Jennifer was just blowing out the candles on her cake when the doorbell rang.

Maggie Lyons waved her hands over the table to dissipate the smoke, kissed her daughter on the top of the head and said, "Hold on a minute, sweetie. I'll cut it for you in a second. Let me just see who's at the door."

She tried to ignore the outpouring of cries followed by naughty laughter that emerged from the kitchen as she left, knowing full well the wolves had descended and there would be a mess when she returned. But that was fine. It was her baby's birthday, and they were all a little hopped up on sugar and excitement. By the time she got back, the boys would be covered in icing. As would the table. And Jennifer.

The porch light was still on. She'd forgotten; she flipped the switch into the off position. Through the beveled glass of the front door, she could see two men in suits standing outside. One was about six foot, with brown hair cut close to his head. The other was shorter, squat, a bodybuilder. His arms stood out from his body almost at angles.

Cops.

What had that fool done now?

She pulled the door open, frowning. The taller of the two nodded at her.

"Ma'am? I'm Detective Darren Fletcher. This is Detective Lonnie Hart. We're with Metro P.D. We need to ask you a few questions. Mind if we come in?"

She smiled in apology, slipped out the door and pulled it closed behind her. She knew what this was about. Her jerk of an ex-husband, who had turned from a fine, upstanding young lawyer into a degenerate alcoholic who liked to bust her around when he didn't get his way. At least he was paying the child support again—though she knew his firm had garnisheed his future earnings to make that happen. They didn't need the scandal, wanted her kept quiet and comfortable so she didn't sue. Like she would—but that wasn't the point.

"Can we do this out here? I don't want the kids to hear."

"Sure." Fletcher studied his notebook. "You're Margaret Lyons?"

"Yes, I am." She heard the weariness in her voice. God, they had all fallen so far. "So what did Roy do now?"

Fletcher's eyebrows creased, and the shorter man, Hart, chimed in. "Who's Roy?"

Maggie leaned against the column. "My ex, of course. He's a frequent flyer with you. Gets delinquent on his support payments. Likes to get into fights. Isn't that why you're here?"

"Oh," Fletcher said. "This isn't about him. At least, I don't think so. It's about the homicide across the street."

"The *what?* Someone was killed? Here? Who?"

She straightened up and looked past the two men, finally registering the multitude of police cars that were parked down the street. Man, she needed to get some more sleep. How did she miss this? And she was shocked the kids hadn't noticed. Granted, they were all in the kitchen, which faced the garden, enticed with birthday cake, but one of the boys usually grabbed the paper for her in the morning. She glanced down. The paper was still on the porch. She felt a flash of anger.

God, Maggie, get it together. Someone's dead and you're worried about the kids' chores.

The detective was talking again. She tuned back in.

"Yes, ma'am. Happened overnight, sometime between two and four. We're just checking to see if you heard or saw anything strange last night."

"Whoa, whoa, whoa. Who's dead?"

Fletcher looked at Hart, who nodded imperceptibly.

"His name is Harold Croswell."

Maggie felt the wind leave her body, an exhalation she hoped the detectives didn't notice.

She shook her head. "I'm not familiar with him. Where did this happen? I mean, which house?"

Fletcher pointed over his shoulder to the Federal-style brick town house across the way.

"But that's Mrs. Emerson's place. She's in France for the spring and summer."

"So the house was vacant?" Fletcher asked.

"It's supposed to be. She travels quite a bit. A widow.

A merry widow. George Emerson, that's her husband, died three years ago. She's been lonely, says travel helps."

Fletcher shifted and she realized she sounded like an idiot. That wouldn't do.

"God, I'm sorry, I'm babbling. Maybe this man was a friend of hers. She's had a string of boyfriends. Amazing, really, a woman of her age keeping that pace."

"He might have been a bit young for her," Hart said dryly. "Do you have contact information for Mrs. Emerson?"

"No, I'm afraid I don't. She has a housekeeper, though. She'd probably have all that."

"Regular housekeeper?"

"Yes. Daily when she's home, weekly when she's out of town." She smiled apologetically. "Sure would be nice. I work full-time, trying to make partner, and with the three kids, and Roy... Well, things are a bit of a mess."

"You know when the maid was here last?"

"Um." Maggie thought about it. "Yesterday morning, maybe."

"This is a nice neighborhood," Fletcher said.

"Yeah, it is. I've lived here my whole life—my parents left me the place when they passed. But it's not the kind you'd expect people to be murdered in."

The detectives were silent for a minute, just watching her. She hated how cops made her feel guilty, even when she hadn't done anything wrong. Maggie heard the kids' screaming laughter, the decibels leaking out through the closed door.

"Listen, I've got to go. It's my daughter's birthday, we're having cake. Is there anything else?"

Fletcher shook his head. "No, ma'am. Here's my info.

If you remember anything, please give us a call. Thanks for your time."

She took his card and went back inside. Shut the door, then turned the dead bolt. Debated telling the kids, decided against it. Keep them in the kitchen, away from the scene. They'd be fascinated and horrified, wanting all the details, then would have nightmares. Like Jen had last night. She really needed to smack Bobby for giving her that book. But they may be more cooperative… No. Better to keep them in the dark.

She dropped Fletcher's card on the table by the door and steeled herself for what she had to do next.

She never even thought about what Jen had said to her, that small, scared voice in the dark. All she knew was as soon as they had their cake, she had to get them all out.

She'd read about Donovan's death. A carjacking. On the surface, a senseless act. But now, three days later, Croswell had been murdered in a house right across the street from her very own?

The message was clear. One could be chalked up to a mishap. But two?

The tiniest frisson of fear cruised down her spine. She shook it off. Pulled open the hall closet door and grabbed her bug-out bag, plus the smaller pack she had for the kids.

Fucking past. She was never going to escape it, was she?

CHAPTER TEN

Washington, D.C.
Detective Darren Fletcher

The door to the house closed behind them, and the sun popped from behind the clouds, dumping warmth and brightness on their shoulders. Fletcher slid his sunglasses out of his breast pocket, put them on against the sudden glare.

Hart put his notebook away and sighed. "So. Make that thirty people who didn't see a thing. Either they're all telling the truth, and this killer's a ghost, or someone's lying."

"Or they didn't see anything out of the ordinary, which means we need to be looking at suspects that fit into this neighborhood's profile in particular."

They walked out to the street.

Fletcher glanced back at Maggie Lyons's house.

"Hey, Hart. Was it my imagination, or did she flinch when I said Croswell's name?"

"Mmm, I don't know if I'd call it a flinch. But she did react."

"Yeah." Fletcher let that run through his mind. "We should probably find her ex, see if he knows anyone that matches Croswell's description."

"Look into her, too?"

"Mmm-hmm."

"Don't overstate it or anything. So, Fletch, what's next?"

Hart looked tired. He and Jimenez had been canvassing all morning. Fletcher had only joined up for this last house so he could drag Hart with him to the notification.

"We go to Falls Church and see Croswell's wife."

"Super. Can't wait." He yawned widely and Fletcher did his best not to follow suit.

They grabbed coffee at the Starbucks on Wisconsin. Fletcher had worked on the task force that investigated the triple murder case there in '97. Talk about a town losing its innocence. He was a green detective then, partnered with a lumbering guy named Jim Kennedy. Kennedy taught him most of what he knew about homicide investigation. Kennedy had dropped from a massive coronary in 2004. He missed him.

Traffic was starting to build, the morning rush hour already under way. Luckily they were going against traffic—the vast majority of commuters were trying to get into the District, only a few were driving out to the suburbs. Most of those workers took the Metro, anyway, which was easier, cheaper and much, much faster. Like New York, D.C. was a walking city for those who lived in its borders. D.C. parking operated on a sliding scale of seniority and importance—the daily ho-hum dwarves and environmentalists took the Metro, the midlevel management and government workers carpooled, paying through the nose for monthly passes to the parking lots, which weren't overly plentiful. Those who garnered a bona fide parking permit were on the high end of the feeding pool, able to drive by themselves into town, park at a premium spot and parade into their buildings, high on self-importance and exhaust.

For the thousandth time, Fletcher wondered why he'd chosen to set down roots in D.C. of all places—the most impermanent, intransigent, imitation place in the world. Teeming with tourists and power-hungry suits and senseless deaths, he sometimes lost sight of the city's beauty, the fact that his parents met, married and loved there, the fact that the food was on par with any city in the world, and the sports weren't too bad, either. He'd spent the past fifteen years in a small row house on Capitol Hill, a surprisingly quiet street kitty-corner to the Longworth Building. In his tiny front yard was a sculpture of an angel that he left in front of the recycling trashcan. He liked the way the white marble reflected off the blue plastic. It reminded him of why he was a cop—harmony and beauty marred by rubbish.

He'd had a string of women in and out of the house—some staying longer than others—though he always managed to chase them away. He had an ex-wife, too, and a son who he didn't get to see nearly enough, since his son's bitch of a mother had managed to convince a judge that it wasn't safe for the boy to be alone with his gun-toting homicide detective father for more than one weekend a month. Fletcher hadn't helped the situation at the beginning by having to reschedule regular days because of crimes, and Felicia had taken full advantage of that. She wanted to move away, had finally convinced the judge that it would be better for Tad to be in another, cleaner, quieter environment. They'd made the move to Rehoboth Beach, Delaware, last year, and Fletcher saw even less of his only child. By the time he was free to spend time with the boy, Tad would be grown and stressing over a family of his own.

His ex wouldn't speak to him outside of the grunted hello if they accidentally saw each other during their infrequent child exchanges. And now that Tad could drive, Felicia never came near him. She hated him with a passion.

Maybe it was for the best. Maybe Felicia was right—he was poison. He wasn't a good man. Good men didn't cheat on their wives and stay out late with strangers. Good men didn't drink too much scotch and lose interest in their chosen career paths. Good men didn't—

"Earth to Fletch."

He glanced to his right, where Hart was pointing to the light. "Buddy, light's green. Has been. Where the hell were you?"

"Felicia."

"Ah. Enough said. Let the self-flagellation continue. I'll stay quiet."

He flipped Hart the bird. "Sit and spin."

Hart did his best breathy Marilyn. "Oh, Daddy, can I?"

They both started to laugh. Count on Hart to drag his ass back from the doldrums. He really needed to think about taking that prescription the station shrink gave him at his last annual evaluation.

"Sorry, man. I'm just tired."

"Join the club. I think that's it on the right."

The house was a standard rambler, brick on the

bottom with blue siding and a carport to the right. This area of Falls Church was established, heavily treed, an older neighborhood. Three houses down a McMansion preened, full of itself and its newfound glory. Land was at a premium in D.C., so folks were buying smaller, older houses, razing them and building huge manors. Safe neighborhoods became safer, property values started to rise and folks like the Croswell family, in their comparatively tiny '70s bungalow, were either going to get on board, or get out of the way. Life has a way of marching on, whether you want it to or not.

Inside the chain-link fence, two miniature schnauzers showed off, frolicking in the dewy grass. The family was up. Fletcher wondered if they were missing their patriarch yet, if they had a sense that things were wrong. Or whether he was about to blindside yet another family.

God, sometimes he really hated this job.

They parked and went to the door. The bell wasn't working, so Fletcher knocked. Knocked again. A woman answered, small, brown-eyed, dressed in scrubs, briskly rubbing her wet hair with a towel.

"Oh. I appreciate you coming by, but we have our own religion." She smiled sweetly and started to close the door. Fletcher put his foot in the crack to stop her and held out his badge.

"Ma'am, I'm sorry. Detective Fletcher, D.C. Homicide. My partner, Detective Hart. May we come in?"

She stared at him, the look he'd grown so accustomed to. Denial, fear, hate, worry, all crowded into a single glance. He could see her mind whirling.

"Is it Hal?" she asked quietly.

"Yes, ma'am. Please, can we come in?"

She swallowed audibly and nodded. Dropped the towel at her feet, opened the door all the way for them.

"Living room," she managed, pointing. "I'll be there in a second. I must... The baby."

She disappeared around the corner. Fletcher nodded at Hart, who followed her, saying, "Ma'am? Mrs. Croswell? Let me help you."

Fletcher heard the woman stumble, curse and fall, was glad Hart was there to catch her. Denial. The first step down the tumbling path called grief. She'd tried to run away from the news, as if not talking to them would make it all just go away.

Hart led her back into the living room, got her seated on the couch. "Kids aren't up yet," he said to Fletcher.

"Ma'am, we need to ask you some questions. But first, is there anyone we can call to be with you?"

She was mumbling, whispering almost to herself, and Fletcher heard, "Sister. Number. Refrigerator."

Hart took off for the kitchen, and Fletcher got Mrs. Croswell to focus on him. She was slipping into shock—too upset even to cry.

"Ma'am, when was the last time you heard from your husband? Where was he supposed to be last night?"

She was having a hard time focusing. "Denver. But you're with Metro. Was it a heart attack? Before he got on the plane? He texted me that he was getting on the plane, would call in the morning. I go to bed early."

"No, ma'am. It wasn't a heart attack. He was found in Georgetown. I'm sorry to say he'd been shot. Do you have any idea why he would be there? Why he would lie about where he was supposed to be?"

"He never lied. Hal never lied to me. We always told the truth."

Obviously not. Fletcher scratched his forehead, rubbing at the headache that was trying to take hold. Hart came back in the living room.

"Sister's on her way."

Croswell's wife was starting to grasp the situation, and her lips were trembling. Hart had brought water back from the kitchen with him. He handed the glass to Mrs. Croswell.

She drank, greedily, then set the glass on a coaster. Neat and tidy. Her eyes grew vacant.

"Mrs. Croswell?"

She snapped back to Fletcher, the words spilling out, frantic to be heard.

"Betty. My name is Betty."

"Betty, do you or your husband know anyone by the name of Emerson? George or Tina Emerson?"

Her eyes were still blank. "No. Hal went to Denver for a conference yesterday. A reunion. His old army buddies were getting together at some aerospace thing. A few of them work for Lockheed Martin now, they were trying to get Hal in front of their bosses. He's been in and out of work since he got back from his last tour of Iraq. He mustered out two years ago. He had a rough time over there."

"Was he injured?"

"Not on the outside, nothing that wasn't healable. It was…"

She broke off, and Fletcher knew immediately. They'd seen this on the force, with the soldiers who'd returned to their jobs.

"PTSD?" he asked.

She bit her lip as if not wanting to betray a secret, then it all came out in a flood of words and tears.

"Yes. Flashbacks, and insomnia. Rage. He gets angry with me for no reason. But he's been so much better this past year. He's on medication. He's been seeing a counselor, one outside Veterans Affairs. She's really helping him. He's getting so much better."

Present tense. That always killed Fletcher. At what point was it acceptable to start thinking about your husband, wife, son, daughter, sister, brother, mother, father in past tense? Never, and that's when the guilt started its all-consuming fury.

It was also a valuable tool he used to divine relationships to homicide victims. The loved ones who immediately went to past tense needed a closer look. They almost always were involved. Their minds had already made the leap to a world that didn't have the person in it anymore.

He moved Mrs. Croswell to the bottom of his suspect list and, with a sigh, started prying into her never again safe and quiet life.

CHAPTER ELEVEN

McLean, Virginia
Susan Donovan

"Now I lay me down to sleep, I pray the Lord my soul to keep. If I should die before I wake, I pray the Lord my soul to take. God Bless Mommy, and Grammy, and Uncle Tim, and Fluffy.... Mommy?"

"Yes, sugar bean?" Susan was used to Ally's questions during bedtime prayers. Ally was her little philosopher. Vicky, on the other hand, merely said the words and closed her eyes contentedly, drifting off to sleep before Susan could ever get through a page of a bedtime story. Then again, she was younger, and quieter. Ally was just like Susan, but Vicky had Eddie's personality—quiet, contained, simmering. And sleepy, even at her early bedtime. Eddie was a morning person. As long as she'd known him, he'd gone to bed early and gotten up with the dawn. He blamed it on too many years being dragged out of his rack by commanding officers in combat zones.

Eddie's voice echoed in her ear. "Wakey, wakey, eggs and bakey!"

She shut her eyes for a moment, savoring the memory.

Ally was the night owl. She always found some pressing topic to discuss just as she was going to bed, something to turn over in her head as sleep approached.

"Mommy, is it okay to bless Daddy? If he's in heaven, will he know? Will he hear me?"

Susan opened her eyes and swallowed the rising gorge that threatened to gush all over her daughter's pink Hello Kitty sheets.

"Of course he will, sweetie. You can talk to him in heaven any time you want. He may not answer, but he hears you."

"Like God? And baby Jesus?"

"Like God and baby Jesus. Exactly like that."

"Good. God bless Daddy." She snuggled deeper into her sheets. Susan pulled the blanket higher, tucking it under Ally's arms. It was silent for a moment, peaceful, with nothing but Vicky's quiet, breathy snores coming from the bedroom next door.

"Yes, sugar bean. God bless Daddy. Now go to sleep. Mommy has to make a phone call."

"Night, Mommy." Ally settled into her pillows, her eyes still wide. Susan knew her little girl would lie there for at least another thirty minutes, but tonight she wasn't going to nag at her. She kissed her on the forehead and turned on the night-light, pulled the door nearly closed behind her.

She went down the too-quiet stairs and poured a glass of chardonnay. Took a big gulp and called the number Eleanor had given her this afternoon.

The voice on the other end of the line was soft and mildly surprised.

"Susan?"

"Hello, Dr. Owens."

"Is everything okay?"

"No. Nothing's okay. I want you to find out what happened to him. You have my permission to conduct the second autopsy."

There was a whoosh of breath on the other end of the line.

"Thank you, Susan. I'll do my best."

"Am I really in danger?"

"I don't know for sure. But I'd take precautions if I were you. Just in case."

"Dr. Owens?"

"Yes?"

"I'm sorry you had to go through this, too. Good night."

Susan hung up the phone, drank some more of her wine. When the glass was empty, she crossed the kitchen to Donovan's office. It was time to get some answers.

Georgetown
Dr. Samantha Owens

Sam felt her breath hitch in her throat.

Eleanor had fixed up the guest room for her. It felt so strange to be sleeping under this roof again, after all these years. And there was no way the woman could have known that Sam and Donovan had made love for the first time in this very bed, with its hearty scrolled wrought-iron headboard, when Eleanor and Jack Donovan were out of town.

Do beds have memories? Can they recognize the feel of a body that's been in them before? She'd shied away from lying down, but finally gave that up as foolishness and settled in on the downy white comforter.

Maybe she shouldn't have had that last bit of scotch.

She sat up and peered into the glass. There was a minuscule drop left over. She upended it and let the musky iodine scent fill her nostrils.

Maybe she should have another.

She slid off the edge of the bed and went to the door. Eleanor was in the other wing, on the other side of the house. She wouldn't know, much less mind. Though Sam doubted Eleanor dulled her pain with scotch and hand washing.

It was just… She knew it was irrational, but she was afraid that she would infect others with her bad fortune. It seemed to be happening all around her.

It was humiliating. Embarrassing. At work she could easily cover it up—after all, she dealt in blood and flesh and ran a clean shop, so no one blinked twice unless she became frantic about it.

But out here, in the real world, people noticed. Eleanor had watched her like a hawk since she arrived, weighing, assessing. Worrying silently.

Sam needed to get back to Nashville, back to Forensic Medical, where her quirks could be chalked up to legitimate hand cleaning, and the people around her knew when to avert their eyes.

She felt the sweat pop out on her forehead. She had to do it. She had to do it now.

She set the glass on the bureau and went into the

bathroom, turned on the water in the sink. It was as if she'd summoned the urge. Summoned it right into her room, into her body.

She scrubbed, and hated herself a little more. She'd have to take the pills soon. Her willpower wasn't enough when she was out of her routine, out of her element. It was pointless, anyway. The empirical part of her mind knew that. She couldn't bring them back. Nothing she did would change that.

One Mississippi. Two Mississippi. Three Mississippi. Four.

She stopped counting at forty. Her breathing was back to normal. The ball of pain in her chest eased a bit. Their faces weren't crowding her eyes.

She turned off the water and dried her hands.

Susan Donovan's call brought mixed emotions. Overwhelming relief, to start. Then a strange kind of guilt, the pervasive revulsion for her job that had been circling her lately. As obsessed as she'd been with the man's inner feelings for her, she never thought she'd find herself actually looking inside Donovan.

She grabbed a robe from the bottom of the bed, shrugged into it. She definitely needed another drink.

CHAPTER TWELVE

Washington, D.C.
Dr. Samantha Owens

It was a morgue. That's about as much as Sam could say about the OCME. It wasn't shiny and flashy like her office back home, with its beveled skylights, pristine, landscaped acreage and views of downtown Nashville. This morgue was old and dingy, housed in the basement of a redbrick building that had been a part of D.C. General Hospital for years. And, strangely, only a few blocks from where Donovan had been killed.

She was met at the front desk by an extremely tall man with a hitch in his gait. She figured he had some sort of osteoarthritis or a minor congenital dysplasia, something that could be fixed by a total hip arthroplasty, or perhaps even the lesser hemiarthroplasty if one had the time and inclination to be off your feet and away from work for a while. This man didn't strike her as the sitting-around type.

"Dr. Owens, I presume? I am Amado Nocek, assistant chief medical examiner. It is truly my pleasure to meet you."

"And you, as well. Italian?" she asked.

His face lit up, making his homeliness more appealing. "Hungarian on my paternal side, Italian on my maternal. You have a good ear for languages, I presume?"

Sam smiled and shook his hand. "Not really. I knew an Amado once. He was from Naples."

"A beautiful area. The land of the Sirens." He put a large, bony hand to his chest. "'Winged maidens, virgin daughters of Gaia, the Seirenes, may you come to my mourning with Libyan flute or pipe or lyre, tears to match my plaintive woes; grief for grief and mournful chant for chant, may Persephone send choirs of death in harmony with my lamentation, so that she may receive as thanks from me, in addition to my tears, a paean for the departed dead beneath her gloomy roof.'"

Sam looked at him in surprise. "Euripides?"

Nocek gave her a wide smile. "Very good, Dr. Owens. Most around here would not understand such things."

"We read *Helen* in school. She was always a favorite of mine."

"As she is of mine. Her words are fitting, I think, for a day like today." He gestured to a door and she followed him through, the familiar scents of cold and chemicals and death meeting her. She immediately relaxed. Home. She felt more at home among complete strangers dead than she did in her own house.

Nocek began to gather familiar blue-and-white garb. "Why do you wish to repeat the postmortem examination on this particular shooting victim, may I ask?"

"You may. The victim's mother is a personal friend. She isn't convinced the shooting was random."

He glanced at her, as if assessing how proper it was for her to be the one running this secondary protocol, but instead of saying anything, smiled sadly. "Ah. If only that were the case. We try to find understanding in that which is not understandable. It is human nature."

"Yes, it is."

"Well, then. We have prepared the body for your arrival. Will you require assistance? I personally would be happy to lend my expertise."

"Thank you. I would like a second set of eyes. Did you do the initial post?" Sam asked, setting her purse down on the counter. She washed her hands—*one Mississippi, two*—trying hard not to count aloud, then dried off and took the proffered gear from Nocek's bony grip. Booties, mask, hair cover, gloves. She got the pieces in place quickly, actions born of repetition.

She hated every minute of this.

"It was not my day to work. I will not be influenced by the previous autopsy."

"Excellent." Sam would be. She'd see the incisions, the already dissected organs in their plastic shroud, the crusted blood that dried upon contact with the air. She'd look at the body of a homicide victim, and do everything in her power not to see Donovan. Her Donovan.

She took a deep breath, ignored the interested look Nocek gave her and nodded briskly. "I'm ready when you are."

Nocek was already dressed for the autopsy suite: he simply slipped a new mask around his neck and pulled gloves from the box above the stainless-steel sink. Without speaking, he held the door for her.

Blessed Mary, full of grace. Give me strength.

She bit her tongue to contravene the overwhelming compulsion to get her hands under running water.

The body was on the first table, nearest the door. There was a buzz of activity—unlike the Nashville office, D.C. didn't have the luxury of finishing up the day's four or five posts at noon. There were so many more deaths, so many more murders, that the machine churned all day long and well into the night.

The staff was more extensive, as well. Nocek murmured names to her as they passed, each person finding a reason to swing by and see the pathologist who'd been called in to question, or affirm, their work.

Sam nodded and half smiled a few times, but her mind was captivated by Donovan.

The moment she saw him, she had to force back the tears that sprang into her eyes. He was so...dead. She saw death on a daily basis, but this, this ripped out her heart.

She swallowed, surprised to feel her stomach roiling.

She shouldn't have come. She didn't want her last memory of him to be this. This abomination of him. Of them. He wasn't supposed to die like this.

Breathe, Sam. One Mississippi. Two Mississippi. Three...

She shut her eyes. Disassociated. She could do this. She owed it to him.

Her heart rate dropped, and her clinical mind took over at last. She looked on Donovan as objectively as she could.

It was him, and yet it wasn't. Her Donovan had never looked so slack, so pale and insubstantial. Her Donovan didn't have wide black stitches holding his tender flesh together, one on each side of his chest, another above his groin, tied in the middle, nor the quickly apparent scars on his torso and arms. Shiny, knotted, tightly stretched flesh. Burns. No one told her he'd been burned in Iraq. Or shot, for that matter.

Damn Eleanor. Glossing over the truth. As if Sam wouldn't have been able to handle the news.

Damn her eyes. And damn Donovan, too.

She resisted the urge to brush his hair back from his blanched forehead. He had a bit less of it now, a slightly receding hairline that she was sad to see. When they'd sewed him up they'd gotten it slightly crooked. Only she would notice it, though. Or maybe Susan.

Nocek was looking at her strangely, his insect head tilted to one side as he tried to decide what was wrong with the situation.

She swallowed and met his eyes.

"Shall we?"

Nocek nodded. He stepped to the body and cut the twine that held Donovan's Y-incision together. *Snip. Snip. Snip.* The fancy stitching that closed the flesh entirely would be done by the undertaker after the embalming. For their purposes in the M.E.'s office, to send the body to the funeral home, they simply threaded the needle through in the three places: midsternum right and left, plus a stitch from the bottom of the incision, spots that pulled the flayed flesh back together, then tied the twine in a knot. Brutal and utilitarian. The first time Sam had seen it done she watched in horror, sure the twine would tear and the skin would fly back open, but flesh was surprisingly tough and the method quite effective.

The field was quickly revealed, and Nocek pulled

the slimy plastic bag that contained the victim's organs from the abdominal cavity.

The victim. Good girl, Sam. Maintain your distance. Do not personalize this.

Nocek gestured to the bag. "Do you wish to redissect? I can do it if you'd like to observe instead."

"No, that's all right. I'd like to get my hands on everything, if you don't mind."

"Not at all. I will read to you the measurements that were taken as we go through the organs."

Sam ignored the little voice screaming in the back of her head and settled into work, the routine. A secondary postmortem was not easy. Decomposition had begun in earnest. And without seeing the organs in situ, having the standard reference points to go on, it was slow, sloggy work. The previous M.E. had been good, though; the remaining organ sections were large enough to work with, hadn't been chopped into little pieces. Sam had been at this a long time; once she started, she found everything she needed without too much trouble.

His liver wasn't enlarged. His heart looked beautiful, with only the barest minimum of cholesterol plaque lining the valves. She sectioned off a fresh piece of lung from the upper lobe, cut it into a triangle—a trick she'd been taught to keep the upper and lower lobes identifiable after they were placed in the formalin-filled organ container. Upper lobes were triangles, lowers were squares. If she needed to pull the jar from evidence to take a second look at the organs from her own posts, she could easily identify which was which. Donovan's lungs were hard to cut, much tougher than what was normal.

"What is this?" she asked, under her breath. The

bronchioles were covered in scar tissue, developed foreign-body granulomas.

"Sand," Nocek said. "From the multiple military engagements in the desert. All of the soldiers we are unfortunate enough to see have this in their bronchial trees, deep in the tissue. They breathe it in and it settles. They practically drown in sand over there."

Nausea hit in the pit of her stomach again, hard and sudden, and she felt the edges of her world crumbling.

Don't do it, Sam. Don't even think about it.

She imagined herself at the sink. The washing was the only solution.

One Mississippi. Two Mississippi. Three Mississippi.

"Dr. Owens, are you feeling all right? You've lost your color."

She opened her eyes. Got her breathing under control.

Normal. Nominal.

"Yes, I'm fine. Forgive me. I didn't eat breakfast."

She refocused on the section in front of her.

This is Donovan, Sam. Donovan. Not Simon. Don't do this now. Not now.

Sam swallowed down the rising bile and used the back end of her scalpel to scrape away some of the grit.

"I've..." Her voice was weak, broken. She coughed, cleared her throat. "I've seen this before. We get soldiers from time to time, as well. Usually 101st Airborne. But..."

"What is the matter, Dr. Owens?"

"Call me Sam, please." She used her gloved finger to roll some of the granulomas. "I meant this. This looks like a more recent irritant. He's been back over three years. This has been caused by a recent inhalation. But how can that be?"

She had Nocek's interest now. Both lungs were put on the dissection board. They each took a side and began to cut. A few moments later, he held a sliver of tissue up to the light, turning it to and fro.

"You are correct, Doctor…excuse me. Sam. There is old scar tissue from the sand, but there is also newer, fresher areas of irritation, in the air sacs. See here, in the central tracheobronchial tree? It's barely visible, but it's there."

"Yes. I see it."

He moved to Donovan's head, took up a small swab, directed it up the left nostril. He pulled it back and examined it. "And a minuscule amount here, in the maxillary sinus cavity. And more irritation to the trachea. This is certainly a more recent occurrence."

He snapped the swab into a tube, then laid his long-boned fingers across his chest. "We must have these tested immediately. The presence of the penetrating gunshot wound may have misguided our initial examination. As head of the department, I take full responsibility."

Nocek looked pained. Sam felt bad for him. It was an easy miss.

"Well, I appreciate that, but before we go jumping to conclusions, let's finish and see if there's anything else left to find."

CHAPTER THIRTEEN

McLean, Virginia
Susan Donovan

Susan glanced at the clock, saw it was 10:30. Damn it. The morning had gotten away from her. She'd been sitting at the kitchen table, lost in thought, for the better part of two hours. A cup of coffee had gone cold and scummy at her elbow. The papers were spread before her: a copy of Eddie's will, the investments, insurance and bank statements. Since he'd returned from overseas, she'd let him handle the finances. It gave him a sense of control. Now she had to see where they stood.

She got up and dumped the coffee in the sink, poured herself a fresh cup. Skipped the milk and sugar. The sugar tasted wrong somehow, cloying and overpowering. Poisoned by memories. Eddie had drunk his coffee black. She would do so, as well.

The war had changed him. She knew how difficult it had been for him over there, and how hard he tried to fit back into the fabric of their lives once he returned. Warriors home from battle often slipped into depression, felt alien to their own lives. Without that purpose, that daily rush of adrenaline, the overwhelming courage it took to go back out on the roads, day after day after day, knowing someone was waiting to kill you, many foundered. There were no enemy combatants waiting in the bushes outside Safeway. But after years of being on guard, of not knowing if your next step was your last, they didn't know any other way to live.

Eddie had managed rather well, considering. There were others who didn't. There'd already been one suicide from his old unit. When Eddie heard, he'd locked himself in the study for hours, refusing to come out until Susan threatened to call the police. She understood when he tried to push her away, and knew she had to do everything in her power not to let him. When that happened, bad things followed.

Susan was still a part of the support group for their unit, for the women whose husbands continued their tours of duty overseas. She wanted out. Dear God, she wanted out. But she had so much experience, so much to offer these young wives and fiancées and girlfriends and mothers, that she didn't feel right leaving. Eddie may have left the Army, but the Army never leaves the family.

Now that he was gone, she'd have the excuse.

She should check in on the Listserv, if only to say thank you. The flowers they'd sent were dead now, wilted in their plastic homes, but the donation confirmations were still pouring in. They'd both been very active in the Wounded Warrior Project—and many of their friends had honored Eddie's memory by giving to the organization. She knew everyone was hoping and praying for her. She knew it. Even if she'd rather they forget she existed so she could crawl into a hole and never come out, she knew they cared.

They'd want the details on the service. Susan had spent too much time at Arlington National Cemetery. She knew exactly what to expect. And the women she'd comforted would attend by her side, walking the rows of white marble, the grass green and soft beneath their feet, the ground around them under constant disturbance, to his grave site. They'd hold her fingers, trapped in their own, and hand her tissues for her dry eyes. Just like she'd done when their husbands were being put in the ground.

When the calls started, Eleanor had stepped in and organized everything. She had taken care of parceling the food; Susan wouldn't have to cook for weeks. Thank God Eddie made her buy that freezer. He'd decided he wanted to be a hunter one year, and they had no room for the spoils, so they'd bought a wide, deep white freezer secondhand and found a spot for it in the garage. He'd filled it up with meat from his kills. She understood his sudden impulse. He'd spent so many years with a gun in his hands that he didn't know what to do with them empty. Hunting was an outlet, much more than just exercise and fresh air.

Venison. Another thing she'd have to give up. Like the sugar. Gone like her husband.

She wondered sometimes, what exactly he'd seen over there. He'd given her bits and pieces, enough to paint a rather gruesome picture, but there were still nights when he'd wake, crying out, and she could see the carnage reflected back in his wide, blank eyes. Demons followed him back from every tour. But he'd made it through every time. Damn it, they'd made it through.

And now this.

What the hell did the note mean? *Do the right thing.* It implied he'd done something wrong. Her husband wasn't the type to do bad things. It just didn't make sense.

And why hadn't he shared it with her? What was he trying to hide?

Susan sat back at the table and stared at the stack of papers. She needed to be alone. To take the girls somewhere, be quiet and simple for a while. Away from this town, which had killed Eddie in the end, after all.

The phone rang. She didn't want to answer it. But the caller ID was familiar. St. John's Academy. The school they'd chosen for the girls. Even though they weren't Catholic, they'd both agreed that children needed structure, discipline and respect. St. John's promised that kind of character building, in spades.

Heart in her throat, she clicked the talk button.

"Mrs. Donovan, this is the headmaster. I'm afraid I need you to come by my office and retrieve Alina."

Retrieve. The word registered. Thank God. Ally wasn't dead. Would she be able to ever get a phone call again from an institution and not assume the worst?

"Is she ill?"

"No. She's fine. We can discuss this when you arrive. Can you come now?"

"Yes, of course. I'll be there in ten minutes."

"Mrs. Donovan, I hope you know… Well, we are all so very upset by your loss."

"Thank you, Headmaster. And thank you for the flowers." Susan glanced at the arrangement the school had sent, already wilted and brown, the heads dropping off the lilies onto the kitchen counter. "They're lovely."

"Of course. We wanted… That's neither here nor there. We'll see you shortly."

Susan gathered up her purse and keys, thankful for the distraction. The headmaster's crisp, no-nonsense voice hinted at something, though Susan was damned if she could figure out what.

The phone began to ring again as she left the kitchen. She glanced back over her shoulder at the caller ID, saw a familiar number. Betty Croswell. Well, it was just a matter of time before the wives started seeking her out to find out about the service.

Later, she thought. *I'll deal with that later.*

CHAPTER FOURTEEN

Washington, D.C.
Detective Darren Fletcher

After the grueling talk with Betty Croswell, Fletcher had Hart drop him at his house and crashed for a few hours. Without sleep, his mind wasn't going to work properly, anyway. He woke from his nest on the couch with a sore neck, waded through a month's worth of *Washington Post*s stacked on the floor as he stumbled toward the kitchen, passed by a year's worth of books he hadn't had time to read stacked on the tiny dining room table. The kitchen was still decked out in 1970s avocado appliances and speckled linoleum.

But it served its purpose: a semiclean space to house his coffeemaker.

He started the coffee brewing and found a clean cup.

He needed a maid.

And a decorator.

And a very large trash compactor.

Despite the fact his case had kept him out all night and half the morning, he liked that it now had a wee bit of intrigue. A husband off the rails, obviously lying to his family, made for interesting investigating. It was better than that carjacking he'd caught a few nights ago. That upset him. Guy just minding his own business jacked at a stoplight, then dumped on the street. A freaking war hero, at that. Managed to survive three tours and saved God knew how many lives before coming home and biting it because some junkie needed to drive out to Prince George's County to get a fix.

The world was a seriously fucked-up place.

He opened the refrigerator, found the remnants of a Cinnabon he'd neglected to finish and tossed it in the microwave. He didn't want to think about how old the pastry was. Sipped on the coffee, leaned against his counter. Massaged his stiff neck.

Military.

A war hero carjacked in Southeast. A PTSD mess shot in Georgetown.

Connected?

Naw.

The microwave dinged. He pulled the slick wax paper out, dumped the half-eaten and very hot bun onto a paper plate, and carefully gnawed.

Military.

Hmm.

He set the plate on the counter and went to his office. Flipped open the laptop. Searched the obituary for the carjacking victim, Edward Donovan.

The obit wasn't vague, that was for sure. He'd served his last tour in Afghanistan in the 75th Ranger Regiment, Bravo Company.

Fletcher had managed to remember to charge his cell when he came in, zombified from his all-nighter.

He didn't use a landline anymore—what was the point? He speed-dialed Hart, who answered on the third ring.

"I'm sleeping. Go away."

"What unit did Croswell serve in?"

"Fuck I know?"

"Humor me."

Fletcher heard groaning, then sounds equating movement—sheets ripping back, feet on the floor, heel strikes on the teak hardwood Hart's wife had insisted they pay extra for that their Labrador's nails tore to shreds in a week. Fletcher hated to say *I told you so* to Hart—it wasn't his fault. He'd had to capitulate to the wife. That's what you did if you wanted to stay married during a renovation. In its favor, the teak had looked nice at the beginning.

Page flip. That would be Hart's notebook.

"The 75th Ranger Regiment, Bravo Company. Served last in Afghanistan."

"Fuck me."

"Really, I'd rather stick it to Ginger. She's got better equipment for that. Prettier than your nasty—"

"Shut it. The carjacking last week? Guy was in the same company."

Hart was quiet for a second. "Uh-oh."

"That's what I thought. I'm going in. See if there's a ballistics report on the Donovan case yet. I'll flag Croswell's to be compared."

"Without a weapon…"

"You got a better idea?"

"No. You really think they're connected?"

"Who knows? But I got three hours of sleep, sunshine. I'm raring to go."

Hart groaned. "I'll meet you there."

CHAPTER FIFTEEN

Washington, D.C.
Dr. Samantha Owens

Sam scrubbed up after Donovan's post, feeling vaguely uneasy. The rest of the morning had gone smoothly—no surprises. The gunshot wound to the right temporal lobe had crossed through his brain and lodged in his left ear canal, causing an unbelievable path of destruction along the way. His poor, beautiful, brilliant mind, shredded and destroyed. The bullet had certainly caused his death.

But the lungs were vexing her. How did he get fresh sand in his lungs? Eleanor hadn't mentioned that he'd been back to Iraq. She supposed it made sense—after all, he did work for a defense contractor now. But the fact that he'd been within the week before he died nagged at her.

Nocek saw her out with a promise to get the mass spectrometry on the sand ASAP, and took her cell number in order to call with the results. It shouldn't take more than a couple of hours to get their answer—

Sam assumed the sand would be a biological and eco-
logical match to Iraq or Afghanistan. Wherever he'd
been in the past week. Wherever he'd snuck off to and
lied to his family about.

She needed to find out where he'd gone. And why
he'd want to hide that fact from everyone.

She slid behind the wheel of Eleanor's Mercedes and
turned over the engine. Let the cool air-conditioned
air flow over her. She'd come damn close to losing it
inside the morgue. Too close. She knew the minute she
let things come out she'd be broken forever. If she could
just hold it together a little longer. Just get through the
next few days, then she could go back home, to her rote
little life, and continue on.

If her existence could be called living.

A living hell, perhaps.

She thought of Susan Donovan then, and her heart
broke. No one should have to know how it felt to lose
the one you love. Sam wouldn't wish that on her worst
enemy.

Focus.

Donovan.

Sand.

Lungs.

Shot.

Why him? What was it about his car, at that particular moment, that had drawn in some crooked stranger?
He'd obviously not gone along with the plan, fought
back in some way. Which would be typical of Donovan. Though she'd seen no bruising, nothing that indicated a struggle. So it wasn't a physical altercation.
She imagined that the man had drawn a gun and asked

for the car, Donovan had refused and the suspect had shot him.

That didn't work. If they'd had words, the window would be down. So why was there glass all over the body?

Besides that, who had sent the note to Donovan in the first place?

Too many questions. She needed to speak to the detective in charge of the case. Eleanor had given her his name, as well: Darren Fletcher.

Sam pulled out his card and dialed the number.

After three rings, a rough, abrupt voice said, "Speak."

"Fine, then. Woof."

The man started to laugh, a genuine, infectious sound, and she smiled to herself. At least she still had a sense of humor. Not everything had been taken from her.

"Nicely done. Who is this?"

"Dr. Samantha Owens. I'm a forensic pathologist, and chief medical examiner for the state of Tennessee. I've just done a secondary autopsy on Edward Donovan. I'm told you're the detective of record on the case."

He paused for a moment, measuring his next words. She imagined him thinking why the hell he was being asked this obvious question, and if answering in the affirmative was going to get him into a world of hurt. She heard an exasperated sigh.

"That's right. What can I do for you?"

"I'd like to go over your case notes, if I may."

"And why is that, Dr. Owens? Do you have something new for me?"

A stronger note of aggravation in his tone now. She had no time for posturing. She'd dealt with plenty of cops in her day, knew exactly what tone to take in return.

"He was still shot to death, if that's what you're wondering. Listen. Humor me. I flew all the way up here from Nashville as a favor to his mother."

He heaved a sigh. "Fine. When do you want to meet?"

"Right now. If that's possible, of course."

"By all means. I have nothing better to do."

She poured on a tiny bit of Southern. "I know you're terribly busy. I won't waste your time, I promise."

"Fifteen minutes. M Street. You know where we are?"

"I'll find it."

He hung up.

Well.

Her next call was to Eleanor, who answered on the first half ring, completely breathless. Sam felt guilty. Eleanor had been waiting all morning for news. She should have called her first.

"Sam?"

"Hi, Eleanor. We're finished."

"Did you find anything?"

Sam imagined Eleanor sitting at the counter in her pristine, gaily decorated kitchen, an untouched teacup at her elbow, waiting, so alone, for Sam to call. She didn't want that.

"I did. Why didn't you tell me Eddie was overseas recently?"

Eleanor paused for a second, then said, "Because he wasn't. He hasn't been back for three years. He'd never go willingly, either. He despised that place. Why in the world would you think he'd been back over there?"

Sam was quiet for a moment. "Do you want the details?"

"Please, Sam. I didn't ask you up here for tea."

"He had fresh irritations in his lungs that mimics the scar tissue he built up from his tours."

It was Eleanor's turn to be quiet. "I'm confused. What does that mean?"

"There's a common phenomenon that's cropped up in soldiers who serve in the Arabian Peninsula. Because of all the sand, it's embedding in their lungs. Add to that natural situation the fact that the air over there is tainted—they burn their trash, computers, plastic—those things put chemicals in the air that people breathe, and you have a mess. Soldiers are coming home with asthma, bronchial conditions, the works. Eventually there will be a high incidence of lung and skin cancers in those who served. But in the here and now, with this finding in Eddie's autopsy... Forensically, it means that sometime in the past few days before his death, he breathed in sand. Tests are being run to determine where the sand came from. As far as the investigation into why he died, I have no idea. Not yet. But something isn't right."

She heard the tone in her voice, grimly determined. She was on the hook now. She couldn't walk away and let it rest. She was going to figure out who killed Eddie, and why. Eleanor must have heard it, too, because she began to cry.

"Oh, thank God, Sam. I knew there was something more to this."

"It's too early to know anything for sure, Eleanor. Once we find where the sand is indigenous to, we'll know much more. I'm heading over to meet with the detective on Eddie's case right now."

"You'll stay in touch?" Eleanor sounded old and

weak. A lioness who's been guarding the den for too long without feeding herself, exhausted and famished.

"Of course. Why don't you lie down for a bit? Doctor's orders. I'll call Susan and let her know."

"Sam, why don't you let me."

Sam understood the question immediately. Susan Donovan wouldn't want to hear that Sam had been right.

"Of course. But then, a nap. Promise?"

She got off the phone and put the car into gear. Fletcher's office wasn't too far away. She wondered how much information he'd been holding back from the family. And what surprises that information held.

CHAPTER SIXTEEN

Washington, D.C.
Detective Darren Fletcher

Fletcher accepted a cup of coffee from Hart, who looked like a rattlesnake woken from a too-short bath in the sun.

"They found Edward Donovan's car."

Fletcher stopped the cup on its way to his mouth. "Donovan's car?"

"Yeah," Hart said. "Up by Branch Avenue in PG County, near the Safeway in Clinton. Someone torched it."

"Really?" Fletcher allowed himself a contemplative sip of coffee then. Only one reason a suspect torches a car—they think they can erase evidence. Often times, they were right.

"They found a casing, too. Under the front seat—.9 mil."

"But no gun?"

"No gun."

"Donovan was shot with a .9 mil."

"Yep."

"Curiouser and curiouser."

His phone buzzed. He hit the speaker button.

"Speak," he said, briefly amused as he remembered the response from that Southern belle, Dr. Owens. No one had ever barked before.

"Fletch. Chick here to see ya."

"Dr. Owens," he corrected. "Send her up."

He mashed the button to turn the speaker off.

"Who's Dr. Owens?" Hart asked.

"M.E. from Tennessee."

"Huh?"

"The carjacking's mother, remember her? Battle-axe called in a second M.E. to do another post."

"Why? She doesn't trust us?"

"Apparently not. Who knows, though. Maybe she was on to something. You know this is starting to look like too much of a coincidence."

There was a soft knock on the door, and he broke off. Standing in the doorway was a most attractive woman. Willowy, with shoulder-length brown hair, light brown eyes the color of aged scotch from a sherry barrel, a perfect mouth. Jesus, she was inspiring him to poetics and she hadn't even spoken yet. He felt a ridiculous pull in his groin. She was just his type.

The mouth smiled, pleasant and polite, but it didn't reach her eyes. She looked at once like a child and a woman, all rolled up into a basket of certainty laced with doubt. Pain. That was pain he saw there. Of course. He should have recognized it immediately. He'd seen enough to last a lifetime.

He was immediately intrigued. Who, or what, had damaged this stunning woman?

"I'm Dr. Owens. You'll be Detective Fletcher?"

Fletcher nodded once and gestured for her to come in. Hart almost knocked his chair over getting to his feet. He was uncharacteristically tongue-tied. Fletcher threw him a lifeline.

"This is Lonnie Hart, my partner."

"Good'ta meet'cha," Hart finally blurted out. Fletcher bit his lip. Hart was a sucker for a Southern accent.

"Thank you," she said, and sat in the chair across from Fletcher's desk. "I appreciate you seeing me on such short notice."

Her voice was soft, cultured, with hints of bougainvillea and sweet tea. Fletcher had been to Nashville before, a long weekend with his son. He'd been struck by how cosmopolitan the city was, while at the same time so very Southern. He'd liked the way they talked, so open and friendly, with those tiny inflections and knowing smiles that screamed: *You're a Yankee, brother, and don't you forget it.*

"Not a problem. Did you find anything interesting on your secondary post?"

"Actually, yes. Sand in the victim's lungs. Fresh sand."

Fletcher pulled open the file on Edward Donovan, flipped to the autopsy report. "Says here that's most likely attributable to the time he served overseas. He was stationed in Iraq for two tours and Afghanistan for one. Stands to reason."

"That there would be latent sand embedded in his lungs, yes. There was plenty of scar tissue from the old irritant. But this is recent. Like in the past few days. His mother said he hadn't been overseas. I'm having it tested, we should know more this afternoon. Did anything in your investigation indicate that he'd been lying to everyone about his whereabouts?"

Fletcher felt that familiar zing. Croswell had lied to his family, too.

"No. This looked cut and dried. I'm still not convinced it's anything other than bad timing, bad luck."

"Did ballistics come back on the bullet recovered from the scene?"

Fletcher caught Hart's eye, saw the amusement in them. He was enjoying this, damn him.

"No," Fletcher said slowly. "We're expecting the report back any time now. Dr. Owens, can I ask? What's your tie to Edward Donovan? Why did his mother call you?"

She got a faraway look on her face, brief, fleeting, then snapped back. "Donovan and I went to med school together. Georgetown. We've known each other for a long time. Eleanor just wanted to do right by him."

Fletcher wondered if that was the real reason she was here, but it was plausible enough.

"So other than the sand, did you find out anything else that might help?"

She shook her head. He liked the way her hair swirled around her neck when she did it. She was a deceptive package. On the surface, so strong, smart, capable. But broken inside. Fragile. She needed protecting. And boy, how he'd be happy to be of service.

Hart coughed, and Fletcher realized he was staring. He closed the file.

"Thank you for coming by, Dr. Owens. If we find anything, we'll be sure to let you know."

"That's it?" Her eyebrows arched. "Seriously?"

"What would you like me to say? This is good information, and we'll hold it in consideration as all of the facts come in."

She shook her head again, her eyes becoming frank and assessing. "Don't even think about blowing me off. Something isn't right here, and we both know it. What aren't you telling me?"

Pretty, and perceptive, too. A bad combination.

Hart spoke up, and Fletcher strongly considered stranglinghim.

"Another soldier from Donovan's unit was murdered. Yesterday."

The M.E. shut her mouth tightly, her lips compressing into a thin line. Fletcher could swear he felt shadows swirl around the room, darkening the walls with foreboding.

He needed to nip this in the bud, and quick.

"We have nothing to prove that these two cases are related."

Owens laughed, humorless and sharp. "Except your gut, telling you there's no such thing as coincidence. Did you run it through ViCAP yet? There could be related cases in other states. Have you talked to Donovan's commanding officer and gotten a list of everyone in his unit? Better yet, they keep those records at Fort Leonard Wood in Missouri—you can make a request for the files right away. You have to move fast, Detective. Tick-tock. Time's a-wastin'."

"Jesus, you sound like a cop."

"I'm a medical examiner in a city that has over a hundred murders a year. I have been for a very long time. And my best friend has spent most of her career in Homicide. We've seen a lot. She's the one who taught me coincidence doesn't exist. Not when people are dying all around you. Something else is going on here. I don't know what, but I'd like to help you get to the bottom of it."

"She's right, Fletch."

Hart. Traitor to the cause. Fletcher gave him the evil eye for a moment before returning his gaze to the pathologist. He checked his libido and really looked this time. Used his gift, his ability to read people. She let herself be read, dropped the walls. She was right. And she knew he knew it.

Someone whistled, and Fletcher dragged his eyes away. His admin, Danny Rama, stood in the door.

"Yo, Danny. What's up?"

"Lots of good news. Ballistics on the Donovan and Croswell murders you asked for. You're gonna want to see this."

Fletched snapped his fingers, and Danny brought him the file. He ignored both Owens and Hart, opened the heavy manila folder.

Son of a bitch.

"What is it?" Hart asked. Owens just sat, watching them, beatific and serene, as if she already knew what the report said.

"According to the wife, Donovan carried a 9 mm Beretta in the car, right?"

"Right," Hart answered.

"Well, ballistics confirm that Donovan and Croswell were both shot with a 9 mm Beretta. And according to this, the bullets in both cases came from the same gun. There was a match in IBIS. It's registered to Edward Donovan. Wait a second." He looked at his admin. "When did they find the gun?"

Rama grimaced. "Sorry, boss. This morning. In the Dumpster on N Street, by that new construction."

"Did anyone think to call me?" Fletcher grumbled.

"They wanted to run the tests first."

The M.E. had stopped moving, was staring at him with her big sherry eyes. "Donovan was killed with his own gun? Then whoever killed him took out Croswell, too?"

Fletcher nodded. "Most likely scenario."

Dr. Owens looked contemplative for a moment. She reached into her purse, pulled out a small plastic bag and handed it to Fletcher.

"You need to see this," she said. "Eddie Donovan gave this to his mother on Sunday for safekeeping."

Fletcher read the words on the tattered page.

DO THE RIGHT THING

"What is this? And why didn't she give it to us immediately?"

"It slipped her mind. She's not as young as she once was. And obviously it's a threat of some kind. I'd assume whoever killed Donovan didn't feel like he'd lived up to the bargain. Was a note sent to Croswell?"

"Not that I know of. Lonnie, would you be so kind as to ring Mrs. Croswell, and see if she's seen anything like this?"

"Sure." Hart stood, and nodded at their interloper. "Dr.Owens."

"Detective Hart," she replied.

Fletcher waited for Hart to leave, then turned to the M.E. angrily. "What else have you left out?"

"Nothing. Eleanor truly had forgotten the note. She didn't hold it back from you on purpose. If anything, she needed it to make me believe Donovan's shooting wasn't a random carjacking. But it's not the end of the world. If anything, it should give you more to go on. A handwritten note is better than nothing, right?"

Fletcher wanted to snap at the woman, but refrained. She was right, it was a clue. He couldn't help but feel embarrassed that she'd brought it to him, instead of the victim's mother. That meant he wasn't trusted, and if the victim's family didn't trust him, regardless of whether they should or not, his job was ten times harder. That was why the old biddy had asked Dr. Owens to come to town. She didn't believe in Fletcher.

Hart came back in the room. "Mrs. Croswell is looking through her husband's things. She thinks she remembers seeing something like that."

Fletcher nodded and swallowed his burning pride.

"I'd appreciate your help with this, Dr. Owens."

You wanted it? You got it, sister.

CHAPTER SEVENTEEN

McLean, Virginia
Susan Donovan

Susan pulled into a parking spot in front of St. John's Academy. Just seeing the edifice made her sad. Eddie had been so excited when Ally was accepted.

Would she ever be able to look at the school again without his face popping up, sitting next to her in the car, staring at the school? "Do you think she'll like it?" he'd asked, and Susan had assured him that Ally would love it. She'd love anything her father did. That was how Ally rolled.

Susan huffed out a sigh and got out of the car. She walked along the sidewalk to the school's entrance and slipped inside. The headmaster's office was to the right. His administrative assistant, Gloria, had stepped away—there was no one else around. Susan tamped down her annoyance. She didn't like that her kid was all by herself, in trouble, scared and upset.

Ally was sitting on an adult-size chair in the reception area, her legs swinging over the edge as she fidgeted. Being still was always hard for Ally. She twiddled with her hair, bounced her little legs, chewed on her lip, tapped her fingers on the table. She was a restless child. Another thing she had in common with her father.

Ally spied Susan and her face crumpled. Good God, what had the girl done?

"Ally? Are you okay?" Susan knelt on the floor in front of the chair and gathered her eldest child in her arms, smelling her still-babyish scent. Clean. Ally always smelled so clean and fresh.

"I'm sorry, Mommy. I didn't mean to." She began to cry, tears building up like water drops from a leaky sink.

"Didn't mean to what?"

A throat cleared. Susan looked up to see the headmaster, all five foot six inches of him, rattling with displeasure.

"Why don't we discuss that in my office, Mrs. Donovan?"

"I'd like to hear it from Ally." She turned back to her girl. "Sweetheart, what did you do?"

"She's broken the honor code. Cheated," the headmaster pronounced. "And you know the penalties for cheating. Don't you, Alina?"

"My kid? No way in hell."

"Mrs. Donovan. Language."

Ally broke into fresh wails, and Susan stood and looked the headmaster in the eye. *Language, my ass.*

"Hey. Threatening her isn't the way to handle this." He took a step back. Susan pulled a tissue from her purse and knelt down to wipe Ally's eyes.

"Sweetie, tell Mommy what happened?"

"I didn't cheat. I saw someone in the window. I was looking outside, not at Rachel's paper. I swear."

Susan watched her daughter for a moment. Ally wasn't prone to lies. Yes, she'd gone through a stage, like all children do, testing the boundaries of what was allowable, but that had been last year. She'd broken one of Susan's small Swarovski crystal figurines, and hid the evidence in her sock drawer. When Susan found it and asked her, she'd calmly said she didn't have any idea what had happened. Ten minutes later, she'd appeared at the laundry room door, face streaked in tears, and admitted her fabrication. Ally had been put on restriction for a week. Her first real grounding. It had made an impression. Now she was forthright and up front about everything, almost to the point of embarrassment.

"Who did you see outside, baby?"

"I don't know. It was a stranger."

Stranger danger. Drilled into their precious heads along with SpongeBob and Cinderella.

"A woman or a man?"

"I don't know. It was fast, like they were peeking. Like a ghost." Her little face began to waver again. "They had a baseball cap. Like yours, Mommy. The red one from the football game. The one you were wearing…"

The day Eddie died. Susan had thrown the hat in the garbage, not wanting anything that would be such a ready reminder of the day they'd lost him.

Susan glanced at the headmaster, who had his arms crossed and was looking dubious.

"Mrs. Donovan, please. Can we talk in private?"

Susan nodded and kissed Ally on the forehead.

"Hang on just a second, sweetie. I'll be right back. Do you want to color?"

Susan reached into her rapacious handbag for a pad and crayons, but Ally shook her head. "I'm fine, Mommy. I'll just wait and think."

A budding Zen master, her child.

She followed him inside the cool office and sat heavily in the chair across from the headmaster's desk.

"I don't believe she cheated, Headmaster. Ally is many things, but she's not a liar."

He shook his head, his glasses swinging on the cord around his neck in time, a little metronome of disapproval. "Mrs. Donovan, no one else saw this phantom at the window. And she and Rachel Bennett both misspelled *misconstrue* the same way."

There was irony for you. "Isn't it entirely possible that Rachel cheated off of Ally's paper?"

The headmaster frowned. "Anything is possible, Mrs. Donovan, but I'm afraid that we have to take Mrs. Werlin's word for it. She feels she saw Alina looking at Rachel's paper. She's the adult here, with no reason to obfuscate the truth."

Susan's back stiffened. "That's not enough proof for me. You can't expel Ally. I will raise holy hell if you even try. My daughter is not a liar. If she says she saw someone outside, she did."

He sighed heavily. "I understand things are difficult right now. I don't want to add to your burden. But this can't go unpunished. I'll have to suspend Alina, at the very least, for causing a disturbance in class."

"Fine," Susan said. "I'll take her home now. Will a week of suspension suffice?"

The headmaster finally looked uncomfortable. "Yes, Mrs. Donovan. And a permanent note in her record."

Susan bit her lip. It was utterly and completely unfair, but she just wanted to get out of there. She rose from her seat and nodded, then left the office.

"Come here, baby." She took Ally's hand and stood her up.

"Are you mad at me, Mommy?"

The headmaster had just come out of his office and was watching them.

She raised her voice a bit. "No, honey. *I* believe you. Let's go get some ice cream."

As they left, her cell phone began to chime. Six missed calls. The school had interrupted cell service inside the building to encourage a focused learning environment. She pulled it from her bag and saw the caller ID.

All six calls were from Betty Croswell.

CHAPTER EIGHTEEN

Washington, D.C.
Dr. Samantha Owens

Sam watched Detective Fletcher's face closely, looking for signs he wasn't giving her all the pieces of the puzzle.

"All right. Let's look at this in parts. On the surface, it looks like Donovan was carjacked, and shot from outside the car, with his own gun?"

"That's what the report says." Fletcher's eyes were hooded. He was skilled at not letting himself be read, but Sam was good at looking past the surface. He was holding something important back from her.

"But the gun was found in Georgetown."

Fletcher sighed. "Yes. Serial number matched the weapon he had registered in his name. According to this—" he shook the file in the air "—ballistics matched, too."

"I think we can safely say that this wasn't a random carjacking."

"I agree," Fletcher replied. "So if you'll get me that

report on the sand in his lungs as soon as you can, I'd appreciate it."

He was dismissing her again. Damn it, she wanted to help. Why couldn't he get that through his thick head? She needed all the details if she was going to do any good.

There was another way she could stay involved. She smiled, friendly and open.

"Of course. As soon as I have it, I'll be in touch. Do you have any information on the other victim from Donovan's unit? I thought I heard you say they were doing the post today?"

"Nocek's doing it, I think." Fletcher stopped and eyed her. She saw a glimmer of respect, and the knowledge that he'd just been trumped. Now she was in.

"You wanna post him yourself?"

"I'm happy to lend a second set of eyes, if you'd like."

Fletcher pursed his lips for a moment, then nodded.

"That would be a help."

Sam smiled. "I don't know if they'll let me attend, but I can ask. I'll call Dr. Nocek now."

Dr. Nocek was, of course, happy to have her attend the postmortem. They'd forged a connection over Donovan's body, professional to professional. She liked him, he liked her. They were a good team, something no M.E. sneered at.

An hour later, Sam found herself back at the OCME, scrubbed, gloved and standing by as a tech got ready to make the Y-incision on Harold Croswell. Fletcher was established two feet to her left, a slight grimace on his face. He reminded her of a greyhound ready to bolt after a stuffed squirrel. Miserable, and desperate to run.

Croswell had been shot at close range twice, once in the chest, once in the forehead. Sam listened with impatience, rubbing her hands together under mental water—*one Mississippi, two Mississippi*—as Nocek danced around the body with a small ruler and read off the specifics.

"Body is that of an adult male Caucasian measuring seventy-one inches and weighing two hundred ten pounds. Normal presentation…a rectangular ink tattoo in black and yellow with the word *Ranger* on the upper left biceps… Multiple scars on various aspects of the torso and legs, with darkened areas consistent with old shrapnel wounds… Corneas are cloudy… Three-sixteenth-inch penetrating gunshot wound to the supraorbital ridge… Quarter-inch-diameter distant perforating gunshot on the left side of the chest… Marginal abrasion… No evidence of soot or powder tattooing around the entrance…. Okay, Frederick, please open him up."

Frederick, a woefully misnamed brute of a man, efficiently slit Croswell from stem to stern.

There was a brief delay while the ribs were cut—the bones snapping in two with a short audible crunch—and the breastplate lifted and removed, then the mess that was the inside of Croswell's chest appeared.

Nocek poked and prodded in the chest cavity. "Let's see… Wound track A passes backward and downward through the sixth intercostal space with perforation of the lower lobe of the left lung, the diaphragm and the liver, exits through the tenth intercostal in the back."

"Shooter was taller than him," Fletcher muttered, and Sam nodded in affirmation.

Or five feet tall and standing on a box. You could never be one hundred percent certain, but sometimes, police work had to go with the logical answer. Occam's razor.

Nocek had moved on to the head wound.

"Wound track B slightly downward… Skull fracture, evident fracture of the cribriform plate… Large subarachnoid hemorrhage…"

Nocek looked up, the microscopic lens he wore to see the details inside the brain magnifying his right eye into obscene proportions. He looked a bit like a lopsided fly.

"This was the kill shot, to be blunt."

"Thank you for that, Dr. Nocek." Fletcher was looking green. Sam wondered what the problem was. He was a veteran detective, had seen his share of head wounds. This wasn't particularly gruesome. It was actually rather tidy. Like a large red Milky Way across a gray-matter night sky.

Maybe he was just hungover.

"Let's take a look at the lungs first, if you please," Sam asked. Nocek didn't hesitate; she gathered he was as interested as she was to see if they were loaded with sand granulomas.

Frederick pulled the lungs from the organ scale and set them on the dissection board. It only took Nocek a few moments to lay bare the bronchial tree.

There it was, the same old scar tissue overlaid with fresh granulomas. Just like Sam had seen in Donovan's lungs.

"That's the sand you're talking about?" Fletcher asked.

"Yes," Sam replied. She took a small swab and ran it lightly across Croswell's trachea. "There's more here."

Nocek took samples, and then broke for a moment, stretching his long arms, the wrists cracking slightly.

"I will let you know what I find with the samples, Dr. Owens. Are you free for a late dinner? I could give you the results then."

Fletcher coughed into his hand. Sam smiled at Nocek. She didn't get the sense that he was hitting on her; he wore a wide gold band on his right hand, like many Europeans. Just in case, though, she declined.

"That is a very kind offer, but I'm afraid I have already promised myself tonight. Perhaps another time."

He nodded. If he was disappointed, it didn't show. "Then I shall call you with the results. Let us finish."

Amazing, how quickly a body can share its secrets. Another twenty minutes and they were through. Frederick put Croswell back together, then began to wash the body and table, flicking away the remaining bits of blood and tissue.

Nocek washed up, taking his time before excusing himself. "If you will forgive me, I have another guest to attend to."

"Of course. Thank you, Amado. I appreciate you letting me help."

He turned and limped off. Finally, it was her turn at the sink. She got the water a little hotter and felt the warm, calming liquid spill over her hands, almost as soothing as a deep-tissue massage of her neck after a long day. Her shoulders relaxed. Her hands tingled from the heat. She did her best not to think about lungs, the water rushing into the airway, a dead-end street.

Sam took an extra second under the water, ostensibly getting one last bit of soap out from under her nails. It felt so good. So clean. Her eyes closed involuntarily, then flicked back open. Jesus, Sam. Watch yourself. You're not alone.

The second she realized Fletcher was scrutinizing her curiously, she pulled her hands from the water.

"We need to get in touch with the remainder of Donovan's unit." She ripped off a towel and blotted her palms with it. "They may be in danger."

"You think?" Fletcher was getting his color back.

"I do. Two murders in three days with the same gun?"

"They may be finished. These two may have been the target. Why else ditch the gun?"

Sam thought about that for a second.

"Perhaps Donovan and Croswell are the only two members of the unit living locally. Maybe the killer needs to go to another state. If he's flying, he can't take the gun with him."

"A good thought." Fletcher stuck out his hand. "It's been a pleasure, Dr. Owens. Are you really tied up this evening? I'd be happy to show you around town. Personally, after this day, I could really use a drink."

Unlike the innocent offer from Nocek, Fletcher's was tinged with expectation. He was a decent-looking man, not gorgeous, but handsome, in a weary kind of way. He had a square face, with dark, keen eyes. If Nocek looked like an oversize fly, Fletcher reminded her of a crow. One who was looking at her a little too familiarly right now.

"I appreciate the offer, but I'm afraid I *am* already committed. Besides, there's a great deal of work to be done on this case."

"Still gotta eat. You don't look like you do enough of that."

"Excuse me?" Sam forced her mouth closed, felt her teeth click together. How dare he?

"Relax. I'm just saying you could use a cheeseburger. You're a little thin."

"Thank you, Detective Fletcher. I do so appreciate the observation."

"What? I thought all women like to be told they're skinny."

What was it with men? Cops, especially? Sam would never get used to the ogling, the innuendo, the inappropriate language and actions. She could be bawdy with the best of them if needed, had a decent sense of humor, but she was a lady, and by damn, she expected to be treated that way.

But when things went too far, or she was feeling frachetty and sick of it, she would lash out. Like now.

"Yes, of course we do. All women love their bodies to be the focus of a stranger's attention. Now, if you'll excuse me? I have someplace to be." She shouldered past him, knocking into his arm as she went.

Fletcher looked surprised by her reaction, and grabbed her wrist in an attempt to stop her flight.

"Jeez. Wait. I'm just trying to be nice. Come on, Dr. Owens. Lighten up. If you're going to work with me, we can't be at each other's throats."

She wrenched her hand from his.

"I don't want your pity." The words were out of her mouth before she even thought them. She heard them tumble from her lips and knew she couldn't take them back. God damn it all.

Fletcher's brow creased. "What are you talking

about? Pity? I'm trying to buy you a drink and some dinner. That's all."

Oh, God. He didn't know. She just assumed he did. The way he was looking at her, watching her… She had expected him to look her up, and if he did, it would be hard to miss the news reports. Maybe he had and was simply good at charades. But no, he looked genuinely confused.

She swallowed. If he hadn't checked her out thoroughly before, he would now.

"Never mind," she said. "I need to meet Eleanor Donovan at five. I'm going to have to leave you here. Thank you for including me today. I'll let you know what the reports say."

She walked away at last, wrist tingling, embarrassment and dismay flooding her mind. How could she be so careless?

CHAPTER NINETEEN

McLean, Virginia
Susan Donovan

Susan Donovan sat in the driver's seat of the car with the cell phone planted against her ear and listened to Betty Croswell cry. Her words were strangely surreal. Susan was thrown back three days, when the doorbell rang and she knew, just knew, Eddie was gone. It was eight at night. The sun had slipped away almost an hour earlier. The porch lights cast shadows across the driveway, shadows that she could swear held Eddie's likeness. She'd allowed the police into the house, not listening to their words, not wanting to hear that he was dead. As if she ignored them, it wouldn't be true.

"Mommy, why are you crying?" Ally asked, jerking her back from the precipice.

Susan sniffed, hard. "Betty, can you hold on a minute? I need..."

Without listening to Betty's reply, she put the phone on the dashboard and pulled Ally right out of her seat into her lap. She put her arms around the girl and sank back into her thoughts.

Death comes for us all. She knew that. Understood it.

But damn it, she didn't need to accept it.

"I miss Daddy, baby."

"I miss him, too, Mommy."

Ally settled comfortably against her mother's shoulder, as if she knew they needed this physical connection to get through the afternoon.

One day at a time.

Susan took in one more deep breath and reached for the cell phone once again.

"Betty, I'm sorry."

But Betty was gone. Another call, or annoyance, or whatever. Susan didn't mind. She had a bad feeling about all of this.

She had no idea how long they sat there, mother to daughter—*bone of my bone, flesh of my flesh, blood of my blood*—holding each other. Ally fell asleep within minutes. Susan may have slept, too, even dreamed, her daughter's breath warm on her clavicle. Eventually she roused, and moved the sleeping Ally back into her seat. She pulled the seat belt across her frail body, knowing she should put her in the back, in her booster, but not wanting to move too much in fear of breaking the small spell they'd cast on each other. A spell of hope, mingled with love.

It was only two miles to the house on Spring Hill. She took the back road, up windy Georgetown Pike for the last bit, and managed to get into their garage unnoticed by either nosy neighbors or the police.

She shut the garage door, walked around the car, nestled the still-sleeping Ally against her breast and went into the house.

Something was wrong.

A smell, a dislocation of the air, a breeze...

The back door was open.

Had she left it that way when she rushed out to the school?

No. No way. She'd never be that careless.

Ally must have felt her tense, because she opened her eyes with a start.

"Mommy?"

Susan set her down.

"Ally, go back to the car. Get in and lock the doors. Okay?"

Ally's eyes grew wide, but she listened to her mother without hesitation. When Susan heard the thunk of the car locks, she turned and went to the breakfront in the corner. She reached up, high on her tippy toes, to the top, and felt the hard angles of the weapon stored there.

Even with a chair and the knowledge of the gun's existence, the girls were too small to get to it. She brought it down, checked the magazine, popped it back in, pulled the slide and felt the reassuring clink of the bullet settling itself into the chamber.

Locked and loaded, as Eddie used to say.

Susan was no stranger to guns. She's been around them all her life. This one in particular had been a gift from her father on Eddie's second deployment. "Just in case," he'd said with his characteristic gruffness.

Susan wanted to close her eyes and revel in the memory, but forced it away and started walking, slowly, carefully, into the kitchen. The house was broken into sections: the kitchen, eat-in and family room were open, the dining room was through a small swinging door and led to the wide living room. She crept through the rooms, into the foyer, the den, Eddie's office, then eyed the upstairs. She'd be the most vulnerable on the stairs. Hugging the wall, she crept up, one step at a time, thankful again for the silk runner she'd laid. It kept her footfalls silent. Stealthy.

She cleared the girls' rooms first, then the guest bedroom, her own office, then went into the large master suite.

Her discarded Redskins baseball cap was sitting squarely in the middle of the bed.

CHAPTER TWENTY

Washington, D.C.
Raptor Offices
Detective Darren Fletcher

Fletcher admired the glass-and-steel building nestled against the older, more sedate brick of the original wall of the Navy Yard. The Raptor headquarters looked inviting, but to get inside Fletcher had to travel through three security checkpoints. Defense contractors were all the same to him, hiding away inside their shiny metal boxes, fiddling with the security of the world. He preferred his criminals front and center, thank you very much, not amorphous maybes disguised in the cloaks of friends. He thought it sad that the days of gentlemen's warfare had drawn to an abrupt close—once you have the ability to sneak up on your enemy, and the balls not to care about the consequences, war inevitably became inequitable.

Of course, being on the side of might was a good thing.

Finally inside the quiet, cool, building, Fletcher approached the reception desk. A young woman with slicked-back hair and a nice sharp jawline looked up and said, "May I help you?"

You can give me your number, sweetheart.

"Detective Darren Fletcher for Mr. Deter, please."

"Of course. Mr. Deter is expecting you. Right this way."

Fletcher followed the woman, admiring the view, through a set of steel-and-glass doors. She used an optical scanner to unlock the outer door. Raptor took their security seriously.

A thin, balding man met them on the other side.

"Thank you, Veronica. That will be all."

"Of course, sir," she said, turning and exiting through the doors. They slid closed behind her, a brief pneumatic hiss. Fletcher felt terribly secure, and somewhat sorry the lovely Veronica wouldn't be accompanying him onward and upward.

"I'm Rod Deter. Come on in."

Deter led Fletcher through a warren of halls, stopping briefly in front of a small stainless kitchenette. "Coffee? Soda?"

"I'm fine, thanks."

"Good. This is us."

Using another optical scanner, Deter unlocked a nondescript door. Fletcher was impressed; the doors along the white hallways seemed devoid of marking. Maybe he just counted his way down from the kitchen.

A standard office space spread before them, cubicles in the middle, offices along the walls. They walked east, toward the bank of silvery windows that overlooked the river.

"I take it you have some sort of news? Your people

already went through Eddie's computers—did they find anything that helps explain his death?"

"No," Fletcher answered. "There was nothing on them that pertained to anything other than his daily work with you. I just have a few more questions."

Deter motioned toward an open door, his gleaming office. The man took his MBA training to the max: there was nothing out of place. The desk was clean except for a single piece of paper. His schedule, no doubt. It seemed almost prosaic in this advanced building—surely they were paperless, all electronic, with their schedules printed on the insides of their arms each morning in binary code.

Fletcher settled into an elegant Eames chair, just a few strips of leather and metal defying gravity. It was surprisingly comfortable.

"When was the last time Mr. Donovan traveled to Afghanistan or Iraq?"

Deter took his seat at the desk.

"He hasn't been in quite some time. One of the stipulations in his contract, actually. Eddie's mandate was personal protection for our visiting dignitaries. He traveled extensively in North America, Europe sometimes, but not back to the Arabian Peninsula. The colonel told me once that it was a deal breaker for Eddie. Of course, we wanted his skill set, so we were willing to make concessions. And when we weren't entertaining, so to speak, he had other duties. Mainly because of his medical background, he was working on several of our global health initiatives. We're not just defense anymore. Raptor has a broad outreach into Africa and other developing countries to provide both medicines and security for *Médecins Sans Frontières,* and other organizations."

"I saw that in the literature. Who's the colonel?"

"Our CEO. Allan Culpepper. He's retired now, of course, but that rank has a tendency to stick. He's the one who brought Eddie to us in the first place. They are, were, very good friends."

"May I speak with him?"

"Unfortunately, no. He's been in Fallujah for the past two weeks, overseeing a new CLS contract we've just been awarded."

"CLS?"

"Sorry. We live in a world defined by who comes up with the best acronyms. Contractor Logistics Support. We had a new global deployment team, GDT, set down last month, and they're having issues with some of the ground vehicle systems. But that's totally irrelevant to Eddie's murder."

"Nothing is irrelevant in a murder investigation. I know we talked about this before, but Mr. Donovan's wife insists he got a call from work, and that's where he was headed when he was killed."

"I know. I've asked around, and no one here remembers calling him in. I polled everyone on our team. Veronica spoke with all of the analysts, the operators. Nothing."

Time for a little pressure. "Our investigation showed it to be a general number here in the building."

"That is very strange, because all of the calls out are attached to the phone the call is made from. All calls in are either direct dial or through the general number, but it's technically impossible to call out from the main number."

He would have to double-check that info, but from previous investigations, he knew that's how most major corporation phone systems worked. Oh, well. It was worth a try. The call Donovan had received was a ghost number, anyway, most likely from a disposable cell. The paperwork had been started to find out its origin, but with disposables, it could take weeks, months even, to trace. There was no direct tie to Raptor's offices. Susan Donovan had assumed the call came from Donovan's office because of Donovan's snap-to reaction, but they had no way to prove it without a doubt. And Hal Croswell's phone records showed nothing that linked him to Raptor, either. But they paid Fletcher to ask...

"Have you ever employed a man named Harold Croswell?"

"Croswell, Croswell... Yes, I seem to remember that name. From a few years ago." Deter clicked a button and his computer's flat screen rose from inside the desk. Okay, now that was cool.

He typed a few words. "Yes, here it is. Harold Croswell, First Sergeant, U.S. Army, retired. Employed as a freelance contractor... Oh."

"Oh?"

Click, click, click.

"Mr. Croswell was on one of our quick-reaction global deployment teams." At Fletcher's blank look, Deter continued, "He was part of one of our private security forces."

"A mercenary, you mean."

"Private security. Which means private. But he separated from the company over two years ago. Inadequate performance reviews. It happens, sadly too often. These poor men and women come back from war, we hire them, but they are gripped by their time in the service. Psychologically gripped, if you understand my meaning."

"What you're saying is he had severe psychological issues that forced you to fire him."

Deter smiled, a thin smirk. "Something like that."

"Let's get back to Mr. Donovan. Any enemies? People around here who disliked him, resented him? Did he get someone else's promotion? Screw someone else's wife?"

Deter laughed. "You don't know Mr. Donovan very well. He was universally liked. A dedicated member of the Raptor family. And very much in love with his own wife. I have to say, Detective, there's nothing here that indicated a problem. Just like I told you before."

Fletcher knew when he was being dismissed. He wasn't accustomed to people he was interrogating blowing him off. "One last thing. How did *you* feel about Mr. Donovan?"

Deter smiled sadly, and this time, the look seemed genuine. "I'll miss him very much. He was an excellent operator. I thought the world of him. He's truly irreplaceable."

"You can say that again," a voice boomed from the doorway. Fletcher turned to see a tall, silver-haired man step into Deter's office with a single stride, effectively sucking all the air from the room. "Allan Culpepper, at your service."

Deter had jumped to his feet. "Colonel, hello. We didn't expect you back until next week."

"I know. Caught a ride with Hassanal Bolkiah."

"The Sultan of Brunei," Deter explained to Fletcher, pride ringing in his voice.

"That's right. He was coming over to check on his new plane. Offered me a lift. I wanted to be at Eddie's funeral. Owed it to him. To Susan. You're the detective working his case?"

"Yes, sir. Darren Fletcher." He nearly saluted. God, Hart would laugh him out of the bar tonight for that one. He couldn't help himself, though. Culpepper's very air commanded respect.

"You know who killed him yet?"

"No, sir. I'm working on that right now. We've had an additional murder we believe may be tied to him. The victim's name is Harold Croswell. Used to work here."

"Hal's been murdered, too?"

Culpepper looked startled, then his face dropped. "Oh, that's terrible. Just terrible. Rod, why didn't you let me know?"

"I wasn't aware of it until just this minute, sir."

"Have we done anything for his family?"

"Not yet, sir, but I'm on it."

"Good man. I'll head over there tonight and talk to them personally. Hal Croswell was one of my men, just like Donovan. We take care of our own. That's just horrid news. Detective, if you're done with Mr. Deter, walk with me."

He turned and stalked from the room. Fletcher nodded at Deter. "Thanks for your time. If you think of anything…" He left his card on Deter's desk and followed the old soldier out into the hall.

Fletcher caught up with Culpepper at the kitchen. The man had already poured a cup of coffee. Fletcher imagined working with him was something like constantly guzzling 5-hour ENERGY shots—he seemed a man always on the go. Despite that, Fletcher couldn't help himself, he liked him. He always respected people who knew how to get things done, didn't just talk about it. Separated the amateurs from the professionals, that did.

Tossing back the remains of the cup, Culpepper dropped his voice and asked, "You really don't have any leads?"

"A few. But it's early. With Mr. Croswell's death..."

"And they're definitely linked?"

"They seem to be, sir."

Culpepper rubbed his forehead, blue eyes cloudy with sorrow. "Donovan was one of the finest soldiers I've ever had the privilege of knowing. His FitRep said it all—he was a natural leader, fearless, smart, able to think on his feet. I recruited him hard for this job, because I knew he'd bring that same commitment to Raptor. And I was right. He was the one who fired Croswell. He didn't think he was pulling his weight. That's what I mean about his leadership. Sometimes, it's about making the hard decisions, the right decisions. But he made sure Croswell was taken care of, gave him a severance package that allowed him some real freedom."

Culpepper got quiet, as if deciding something.

"That's neither here nor there. There's two things—one, I'd like to put up a reward for information leading to the arrest of whoever killed Eddie and Hal. Will twenty-five thousand dollars do?"

"Yes, sir, that's fine. Very generous of you."

"Good, good. Also, I'm starting a scholarship in Eddie's name. Worked it all out on the plane. When they told me he'd been killed..." The man's voice became gruff with unshed tears. He cleared his throat, a great wet rip. "Boy was like a son to me. Find who did this, Detective. I don't care if you have to tear down the walls here to do it. Anything you need. Do you understand?"

"I do."

"Good. I appreciate it. And now, if there's nothing else you need from me, I must go see Susan Donovan."

Culpepper walked Fletcher to the front doors. "I'm heading back over tomorrow night after the funeral. Until then, here's my private number. Call me if you need anything. Or if you find anything out. Okay?"

"Sure." Fletcher took the card and shook the man's hand. As he left the building, he wondered if there was anyone in the world who thought as highly of him as Culpepper did of Donovan.

He had a sneaking suspicion the answer to that was no.

CHAPTER TWENTY-ONE

Georgetown
Dr. Samantha Owens

Eleanor needed her car for an errand, so Sam took a cab from the precinct to Eleanor's house in Georgetown. Afternoon traffic in D.C. was normally murderous, but the cab sailed smoothly from Fletcher's office on M Street straight up into Georgetown proper, hitting all the lights as they turned green, practically a miracle.

Georgetown hadn't changed much since she'd haunted its streets fifteen years earlier. Still full of high-end fashion stores and fabulous restaurants, there were a few concessions to consumer-driven modernity—a cupcake store that had been featured on a reality TV show always had a line forty people deep, for instance—but for the most part, the staples, the meat of the hamlet, were still there. Clyde's. Chadwicks. Filomena's. Paolo's. F. Scott's.

Her very existence in Georgetown had revolved around food.

God, it made her sad. Life just continued to flow

around her, never stopping. You excuse yourself from the world, and so long as your heart continues to beat, after a time, no one even notices. It's only when you die that you take a place in people's mythologies. She had friends here once. Girls who called three times a day wanting to get together, who showed up at her apartment door unannounced with sangria and tequila, who cried on her shoulder, and on whose shoulders she cried in return. She couldn't remember half their names now. She'd gotten so caught up in her own life, her work, her family, herself, that they were fleeting images: a flash of blond here, a brown eye there, a laugh. Ghosts.

It was her fault. D.C. was so very different from Nashville. Though she'd loved her time here, she'd been desperate to get back home. Especially once she and Donovan were over. Nashville fit her like a glove. Where life was slower, and less complicated. Where, waiting patiently, there was a man who loved her, and would never leave.

At least that's what she'd always believed about him. She'd been wrong.

Simon.

She allowed her mind to say the name. Just once. A breeze through her cerebral cortex. Those two simple syllables were like the first rush after the needle prick—all-consuming, warm, happy. His face floated before her eyes: the untamable cowlick, the glasses, the crooked front tooth that gave his smile such boyish charm.

"Hi," she whispered.

Even a whisper is enough to scare away a spirit. His face started to fade, and Sam bit her lip to keep from crying out after him. The rush was gone as quickly as it came, and pain was all that followed. The vision was gone. The massive, gaping hole in her heart began to ache.

For with Simon, and thoughts of home, came the sweetly cherubic voices of the twins.

She couldn't believe they were all gone. If only she hadn't—

"That'll be $6.70, ma'am."

Sam started. The cabbie was looking at her strangely. "You okay? This the right place?"

She glanced out the window, surprised to see a familiar red house and black shutters. Eleanor's. Where she was meant tobe. At least temporarily.

"Oh. Yes. Yes, of course it is. Thank you."

She fished a ten out of her wallet and passed it through the plastic window. The door handle stuck, she had to give it a shove.

She couldn't get enough air.

One Mississippi. Two Mississippi.

She fumbled with the keys, the cheerful vermilion door mocking her.

Three Mississippi. Four Mississippi.

"God damn it," she yelled, giving it another try. The door swung open freely, and she rushed straight to the kitchen and turned the water on full.

Her breath came in little panicked grunts. She scrubbed her hands together so violently that her nails scratched the beat-up skin and blood dripped into the sink.

Simon. Matthew. Madeline.

Simon. Matthew. Madeline.

One Mississippi. Two Mississippi. Three.

If she could just allow herself the pent-up tears that

stayed stubbornly stuck in her eyes. She understood the psychology of letting go. She just wasn't ready to let them out of her heart. Something told her that if she cried, her loves would escape down her cheeks, drip into a tissue, and the memories of them would vanish forever.

Reality slowly seeped back in. The water was burning hot, her skin fire red. Shaking, she reached for the tap and turned it off with a twist. She'd wrecked her hands. Wrecked them completely. They were cracked and torn, bright as a well-boiled lobster, blood oozing from barely healed fissures. She wouldn't be able to hold a scalpel properly for days.

Is that what this was all about? Punishment? That she'd been doing an autopsy while they died?

Sam sighed and carefully dried her hands. Eleanor had some grapefruit lotion from Williams-Sonoma on the countertop next to the sink. Sam carefully got some in her palms and spread a thin layer over the torn skin. It stung sharply for a moment, then calmed.

She turned away from the sink and jumped.

Susan Donovan was sitting at the kitchen table.

"Better?" Susan asked.

Sam fought back a tart reply. This woman had lost her heart the same way as Sam had, unwillingly, by force. She should have compassion for her, empathy. Instead, Susan grated against her psyche.

"Not really," Sam finally answered.

"Want a drink?"

An olive branch? Not exactly what she expected. But she was willing to play along.

"Yes. Yes, I do."

Susan got to her feet unsteadily, and Sam saw that

she'd gotten a head start. She retrieved a crystal-cut lowball from the glass-fronted cabinet next to the stove, then wove back to the table and poured Sam three fingers of scotch. She dumped another splash into her own empty glass, set the bottle down carefully, then raised the drink.

"Sláinte."

"Cheers," Sam replied. The Laphroaig was all peat and iodine, curling around Sam's mouth like smoke from a campfire. She let it dribble down the back of her throat.

"Mmm. That's so good."

"So much better, you mean." Susan set the glass down on the table with care.

"How many of those have you had?"

"Enough."

"Did something happen? Are your girls with Eleanor?"

"Did something happen?" Susan began to laugh, a harsh, discordant sneer. "Did something happen, she asks. I don't know, Dr. Owens. What do you think? My husband's dead. Gone. Forever. Someone decided to end his life, and no one seems to have a clue why."

"I'm working on that."

"You're a doctor, for God's sake. Not a cop. Not a private investigator. Just a flunky who cuts up bodies for a living. And a wreck of one, too, it appears. How are *you* going to figure it out?"

Sam set her glass back on the table with exaggerated care. She watched Susan, knowing she had an opportunity here.

"Susan, you're drunk."

"So the fuck what? Like you didn't get drunk after your husband died? And your kids?"

Sam felt the anger boiling inside of her, and took a breath. She still hated the venom in her voice.

"You don't know the first thing about my life, so don't you dare to presume anything about me."

Susan focused on her. "Oh, of course not. Perfect Samantha. *Dr.* Samantha. He never stopped loving you, you know. He kept all your letters. All the pictures of the two of you. He hid them from me. But I knew. I found them."

Susan got to her feet, and Sam instinctively took a step back.

Susan saw it, saw that she'd scared her perceived rival, and laughed.

"As if I'd bother." Susan turned to the stairs and shouted, "Come on, girls. We're going home."

"Susan, you can't drive."

"Get out of my way, *Doctor.*"

"No. Sit down. You are a hot mess. Let me make you some tea."

Susan spoke through gritted teeth. "I said, get out of my way."

Sam was two inches taller than Susan, but no heavier. She squared her body, tightened up, prepared for the blow and stepped closer, trying to use her body as intimidation.

"Sit. Down."

Susan got wild-eyed and coiled for a second, like she was going to punch Sam and make a run for it, then shook her head and reached for a chair. She collapsed in it heavily, sank her forehead to the table. Her voice was wavering with tears.

"Why do you even care how I feel?"

That took Sam aback. My God, did she come across as a callous, unfeeling bitch? Who wouldn't be moved by this situation? And Sam especially, having gone through this kind of heartbreak, the rending apart of the soul. Maybe it was Susan Donovan that was the bitch.

"Why wouldn't I? You've just been through a terrible loss. Grief plays tricks on the mind. I know that. I know what you're going through. I also know getting drunk isn't going to fix anything."

Susan's voice was still sharp. "You don't know me. You don't know the first thing about me."

"I know enough about you to know that you're wishing none of this had happened. That all you want is for him to come back."

"I didn't get drunk to bring him back."

"Then why did you?"

"Because I'm scared."

Sam sat at the table. She was tempted to take Susan's hands, to lend physical comfort, but Susan was still weaving like a drunken cobra. She settled for soothing words.

"I know. I know exactly how you feel. Like part of you has died, too. That you're missing something vital, your arm, your leg, and if you stand up too quickly, you're going to topple over on the floor, and never want to get up. That it would be so much easier to just take a bottle of pills and lie down in your bed, and not have to feel this pain. That you don't know why you haven't done that already."

Her voice softened. "I understand, Susan. I truly do. What you've got is much worse than a broken heart. It's something utterly irreparable. I won't lie to you. You will never be the same. Your life will never be the same. And after the funeral, especially then, you will be completely lost. But you have two gorgeous daughters who need you. They can't lose everything. That wouldn't be fair."

Susan was looking at the table. Her hand flexed in and out of fists. She took another sip of her drink and met Sam's eyes for the first time.

"Is that how you felt? Like you wanted to die, too?"

"Yes." Dear God, she had. She'd felt that so many times she'd gone to stay with her friend Taylor to make sure she didn't do anything stupid. At least if she was in someone else's house, she'd worry about them having to clean up the mess.

"It took me months, Susan. I'm still not where I want tobe. Look at me. I've developed…problems. The job I used to love seems more like a prison sentence. I can't sleep, I barely eat. I drink too much. I don't know if I'll ever get there. But you have to. You have the girls. They will be your salvation in all of this."

"Don't you throw my girls at me."

Sam sighed. "God, would you stop? I'm trying to help you."

"They're in danger."

"No, they're not. You are a wonderful mother—"

Susan brought her head up. "No, seriously. They're in danger. Someone broke into our house today."

Sam felt the muscles tense in her neck. It was one thing to threaten the adults, but if this freak started messing with Donovan's kids…

"Tell me," Sam commanded, and Susan gave her the story. About the stranger at the school, and the open door at the house. About the baseball cap she'd thrown away being dug out of the trash and left on her bed.

"Did they take anything?"

"No. From what I can tell, nothing else was disturbed, either. But I got out of there pretty damn quick."

"We need to call Detective Fletcher and inform him."

"I already did. He and his partner went out to fingerprint the house. That's why we're all here."

Susan's eyes were rimmed in red, and Sam could see she was faltering. The alcohol had caught up.

"Can I have that tea you offered earlier? Or better yet, a cup of coffee? Eleanor doesn't have any decent black tea around. I looked earlier, before I found the scotch. Eleanor doesn't usually drink this brand." There was a note of accusation in her tone. Sam ignored it. Susan was just going to have to put aside this petty-jealousy nonsense. They had to work together.

"She bought it for me. It's my favorite," Sam said, rising automatically and going to the sink to get the water for the coffee. Her mind was spinning. The break-in was unexpected. What were they looking for? What was Fletcher thinking? She hated being on the outside of the investigation like this. At home, she was always welcome to offer her opinions and insights. Here, she just felt like she was getting in the way.

Perhaps Susan was the target, after all, and not Donovan?

No, that wasn't right. What could a stay-at-home soccer mom do to draw down the ire of a murderer? It was much more likely that Donovan had come across something he wasn't supposed to see, mentioned it to the wrong person and had been killed for his trouble.

The scent of roasted coffee filled the kitchen. From

the corner of her eye Sam watched Susan try to re-group. She was brushing away tears, straightening her hair, pulling her shirt down in the back so it covered the top of her pants. Her movements were clumsy, and Sam turned without thinking and finished the job for her. As if Susan were a child who needed neatening.

But the attention didn't rile her, as Sam thought it might. Instead, she leaned into Sam's hand, and whispered, "Thank you."

CHAPTER TWENTY-TWO

McLean, Virginia
Detective Darren Fletcher

Fletcher and Hart watched the crime scene techs print the doorknobs of the Donovan home.

"You think she's just losing it?" Hart asked. "It's not that hard to misplace a hat."

"It's possible," Fletcher replied. "Then again, anything's possible. She seemed pretty adamant that she threw the hat out. Trash comes on Tuesday in this neighborhood. According to her statement, she put the trash out Monday night, with the hat in it, so that leaves a good ten hours for someone to go sneaking around."

Hart hid a yawn behind his palm. Fletcher pretended not to notice, but had to admit he shared the sentiment.

"Eh, there's nothing we can do here. Let's go talk to the neighbors, see if any of them saw something."

Hart's face lit up. The man was a ball of energy. Sitting and thinking wasn't his style.

They split the street, Fletcher taking the north side, Hart taking the south. The Donovans' house was the end house of a cul-de-sac, with eight houses on either side leading up to it. It was a pretty neighborhood. Safe. Sturdy. The houses were two-story, brick on four sides, fenced yards, with gaily-painted shutters and matching front doors.

Suburbia. The perfect place to raise a family, and feel safe doing so.

No wonder Donovan lived here. From what everyone talked about, the man was overly concerned with safety, and this was as safe as he could get without putting bars on the windows or digging a bunker.

Even though Fletcher recognized that Susan Donovan's intruder story could easily be that of a grieving widow hoping for attention, something felt off about this whole case. He had put a uniform on the Croswell house, just in case, and was waiting for the Army to give him the list of everyone who'd served in Donovan and Croswell's unit. The wives could only give them so much information—the Ranger battalion had nearly six hundred soldiers in it. It was probably a long shot at best, but Fletcher wasn't about to take any chances. Two good men were dead already. He didn't want to have a third killed on his watch.

He had a short list of men who were in the immediate group that Donovan and Croswell hung out with. There were two names both Betty Croswell and Susan Donovan had mentioned—Billy Shakes and Xander Whitfield. But he hadn't been able to find addresses on either man yet.

Betty Croswell had given him the names of the men her husband was supposed to meet in Denver. Fletcher had talked to them all—and hit another dead end. Croswell had stood them up, and while they were his friends, they'd been furious about it. Fletcher got the sense that most everyone was exasperated with Hal Croswell. Of course, once they found out why he hadn't shown, they'd grown quiet, teary and apologetic. Death was a pretty good excuse for missing a job interview.

Fletcher felt like he was overlooking something. As he made his way down the tree-lined street, knocking on doors and striking out, that lack of knowledge nagged at him.

It took an hour for him to meet back up with Hart, who'd managed to get a rock in his shoe, and was looking rather pained over it. He leaned against the car and started to unlace.

"Did you have any luck?" Fletcher asked.

"I don't know if you want to call it luck. Chick in the gray brick house remembers seeing a truck she didn't recognize over the weekend. But all she could say was that the truck was blue. There're teenagers on this street, it could be a friend of any of them. A bunch of people aren't home from work yet. We'll have to come back and recanvass later tonight."

"Did you ask if the truck had four wheels?"

"And a bed in the back, too, dickwad."

Fletcher grinned. "Fuck you. A blue truck. That's all we got. Let's go see what the print guys found."

The crime scene techs were also miffed—they'd finished half an hour before and were champing at the bit to get to their next case. The lead tech—Fletcher couldn't remember his name—shook his head.

"We scanned what we could, but don't be expecting much, if anything. The maid came Monday. Wiped everything down. She's thorough, I'll give her that. All we got was a couple of partials upstairs in the bathrooms."

"Great. Anything else?"

"You said the maid told you she didn't see anything, or anyone, unusual, and that jibes with what we're seeing here. No alarm bells from us."

Great. A clean house and a mysterious blue truck. Exactly squat.

"Thanks, guys."

The team trudged down the driveway and loaded themselves in their van, then drove off.

The neighborhood's natural noises surrounded Fletcher. Crickets, a child shouting in the distance, birds twittering. He gave the place a last glance, then shrugged.

"Might as well go on back to the Croswell site, re-canvass there, see if anyone remembers a blue truck. Maybe stop by and talk to Mrs. Lyons again."

Hart groaned.

"If you have a better suggestion?"

"No. Who knows, we might actually catch some of the folks who'd gone off to work right about now. Let's stop at the 7-Eleven. I need a Slurpee."

"A Slurpee?"

"Pure energy, my friend. I think you need one, too. Cheers what ails ya."

CHAPTER TWENTY-THREE

Georgetown
Susan Donovan

Susan had sobered up by the time Eleanor came home from her bridge game. The girls were playing quietly in their room. Ally seemed less traumatized by her morning, though Susan doubted that would hold true during the overnight hours. Sam Owens was on the computer in the den, tapping away. She was writing up the secondary autopsy notes, making everything she'd seen and heard official.

Susan wanted to hate her. She wanted to demand that Sam leave and never come back. And yet she found herself, well, *liking* was too strong a word. Understanding the woman. Feeling sorry for her, even. Losing Eddie was bad enough. If she'd lost the girls, too, she would go completely mad. The simple fact that Sam Owens was walking, talking and somewhat functioning gave her hope that, one day, she might do the same.

Susan took one last swig of coffee, then sought out Sam. She stood in the door to the den for a minute and watched her type, a pencil in her mouth. She looked like a journalist, not a doctor.

Susan guessed they must be about the same age, at least within a year or two of each other. Eddie was a year older than she was. Susan had hit thirty-eight on her last birthday, and vowed to stop counting after that. Eddie thought that was hysterically funny.

Maybe in another world Susan and Sam Owens would have been friends.

Susan cleared her throat. "Having any luck?"

Sam looked up, staring through her as if she didn't recognize her for a moment. "Oh. Yes. Somewhat. I'm done now, I was just proofing the report. What's up? Are you feeling better?"

"I am. Listen. I was wondering… I think you should come out to the house and have a look through Eddie's things. I started thinking about that note that was left for him. I don't know if you're aware of this, but Eddie kept a journal, religiously, every day. But it's in Latin. You took Latin to prep for med school, didn't you?"

"Four years. I double majored in Classics and Biology."

"Then you could read it, couldn't you?"

"I should be able to, yes." Sam sat back in the chair, a longing smile on her face. "He used to do that in school, you know. Everyone thought he was being a pretentious jerk. We gave him such a hard time. A journal, sure, that's cool. But in Latin? He always was a show-off. I can't believe he kept it up all these years."

Susan burst out laughing. The idea of her serious, capable, *humble* husband being teased for showing off just hit her funny. Sam joined in, the tension from earlier dissipating a bit. They weren't ever going to be friends, but maybe, just maybe, they wouldn't be constantly at each other's throats.

"Eleanor just got home. She can watch the girls for a bit. What do you say? Are you game to take a ride with me?"

Sam nodded. "Sure. My Latin wasn't ever as good as Donovan's, but I can give it a whirl."

She stood, and Susan noticed again how thin she was. She thought back over the day and realized that she hadn't had anything to eat. How easy it was to forget. She had no appetite. She'd gotten the girls fed and off to their respective schools, meaning to stop somewhere and grab a coffee and Danish, and had completely spaced it. All she'd had today was coffee, and for an afternoon treat, quite a bit of scotch.

She was going to have to make a better effort to take care of herself. If not for her own sake, then for the girls.

"Do you mind driving?" Susan asked. "Just in case. The last thing I need is to get pulled over."

"Of course. Just let me grab my coat."

Georgetown
Dr. Samantha Owens

Sam was glad Susan finally seemed to be accepting her. They needed to work together to figure out what Donovan was involved with that might have killed him. Sam wanted to get into his office, into his things, but hadn't known how to approach Susan about it.

Susan drove a Volvo station wagon, the backseat filled with toys and dolls and books. Sam glanced once, then forced her eyes away. Forced away the nasty

thought that followed—*this could have been my car*—
and tried her best to refocus. They got settled in the
seats. Sam checked the mirrors, then asked, "What's
the best way to get there?"

"I normally go GW Parkway, but we're going to
hit traffic this time of night, so let's go Canal. We're
on Spring Hill Road, so you can get to it from Chain
Bridge or Georgetown Pike. Your choice."

"That's a pretty part of town."

"Perfect for raising a family." Sam didn't miss the
bitterness in Susan's tone. They really were castaways,
the two of them. Sam started the car and navigated
through the streets of Georgetown to Key Bridge, turning right and following the Potomac River out of town.

Her cell phone rang a few minutes into the drive. She
didn't recognize the number, but it had a 202 area code,
so it was either Fletcher or Nocek. She apologized to
Susan and answered it.

"Dr. Owens? Sam? This is Amado Nocek. I have
received the results from the lab about the chemical
makeup of the granulomas found in the lungs of both
Edward Donovan and Harold Croswell."

"Oh, wonderful. What did you find?"

"The irritant is indeed sand, but it is not from the
Arabian Peninsula. It is indigenous to western Maryland. Specifically, to the Savage River. I cannot pinpoint
it better than that, unfortunately."

"The Savage River. Isn't there a state park up there?"

"Yes, there is. It is a beautiful area, if you like to go
camping or fishing. Or hunting."

The word hung in the air, pregnant with meaning.
What was cold-blooded murder, if not the culmination
of a hunt?

"What did Detective Fletcher say about the results?"

Nocek gave a warm laugh. "I will call him right away."

"You told me first?"

"Yes. You seem to have the victims' best interests at heart. Not that the detective does not, as well—it just seemed you have a deeper connection to this story."

"You're a very astute man, Amado. I owe you dinner. Maybe not this trip, but sometime soon."

"I would enjoy that very much. When do you return to Nashville?"

When, indeed? She'd gotten drawn into this case, into their lives, so seamlessly that she'd nearly forgotten she needed to go home tonight. "I'm not sure," she answered. "I was supposed to fly back this evening, but I think I'll be missing the flight."

"Understandable. It is difficult to leave loose threads unraveled. Let me know if I can assist you any further. It has been my great pleasure to work with you. Perhaps one day you will desire to work with us again, under better circumstances."

"Perhaps I will. Thank you, Amado. For everything."

She hung up and realized Susan was staring at her.

"The sand we found in Eddie's lungs was from western Maryland, not Afghanistan. The same for Hal Croswell. Do you have any connections to that area? Know anyone who lives there?"

"You said the Savage River, right?"

"Yes."

"That's weird."

Sam felt a little thrum in her chest. Her adrenal gland was throwing a party in her brainstem.

"What's weird?"

"We vacation there. It's great for the girls. We camp,

hike, go fishing. It's one of…was one of Eddie's favorite places. But we haven't been since last summer."

Susan got quiet and Sam knew she was thinking about something.

"What. What is it?"

"One of Eddie's old Army buddies lives up there. I haven't met him. According to Eddie, he's a bit of a recluse. Saw too much in the war. Usually when we go up there, Eddie will take a morning and go fishing with him. I don't know the last time they spoke, though."

Bingo.

"What's his name?"

"Xander. Xander Whitfield. They served together during Eddie's last tour in Afghanistan."

Sam left a message for Fletcher, asking him to call when he had a chance, then finished the drive to the Donovans' house in silence. She didn't like what the evidence was saying. Someone connected to the Savage River was involved in the murders. She hated the thought that it could be someone from Eddie's unit, but knew that was the most likely place to look.

The intersection of Old Dominion and Spring Hill Road appeared ahead. She took the right turn, realizing she wasn't entirely prepared to roll up on Donovan's house. She'd never seen where, and how, he lived before. Left. Left again. The final turn came up before she'd fully steeled herself, and then they were there, in a perfect little cul-de-sac, facing an elegant two-story whitewashed redbrick house, with black shutters, a red door and a fenced-in backyard.

It was so unlike anything she pictured Donovan in, and yet it was exactly right. A perfect place to raise children, away from the hustle and bustle of downtown. Another *what if* strolled through her mind to poke at her, and she abruptly slammed on the brakes in response. Susan shot her a glance.

"Sorry. Shall I park out here on the street?"

"It looks like all the police cars are gone. You can pull rightin."

Sam drove around the side of the house and left the car in the drive.

They walked in through the mudroom, which exited into the family room. It was a beautiful space, honey oak floors and built-in bookshelves, with an indoor-outdoor glass conservatory hidden in the back. The family room led to the kitchen, the heart of the house.

Sam could smell Donovan. God, it was like being thrust back fifteen years. He obviously hadn't changed his cologne since she'd dated him. She wondered if this was the case in her own house, and she was so used to the way it smelled that she never felt Simon and the twins there.

"Oh, my God," Susan said. Sam focused and saw the mess. There was fingerprint powder everywhere, a fine black dust that coated everything like soot after a fire. Susan ran her finger across the kitchen counter, leaving a snail's trail in the dust.

"Yeah, crime scene techs aren't known for their neatness."

"I can tell. What's the best way to get this up?"

"Clorox wipes work great. Just be thankful you don't have carpets. Stuff will never come out properly."

"I'm going to need a gallon of them. Can I get you something to drink?" Susan asked.

"Water would be nice, Susan. Thanks."

"The refrigerator water is filtered."

"That's great. Tap is fine, too. Good old Potomac never messes me up."

Susan got the water from the refrigerator, anyway, then handed it to Sam. "It's colder this way."

Sam took a sip, fortifying herself, then set the glass on the counter. Now or never.

"Why don't we take a look at his office, Susan."

Susan was delaying, Sam knew that. It was one thing to invite a stranger into your home, but when that stranger used to sleep with your husband, it became a whole different matter. Sam was about to go someplace Susan hadn't been allowed, into the very private mind of her spouse.

Sam would be stalling, too.

Susan took a deep breath.

"Just promise me one thing, Sam."

"Anything within reason, Susan, of course."

"If he didn't love me, but couldn't tell me, I don't want to know."

CHAPTER TWENTY-FOUR

McLean, Virginia
Dr. Samantha Owens

Sam's first impression of Donovan's office was dark wood, very unlike the surrounding rooms in the rest of the house. It screamed Man. The doors to the office were glass, so the owner could keep an eye on things while still having the privacy of a closed door. There were floor-to-ceiling bookcases to the right stuffed with books of all shapes, sizes and colors, and two windows to the left. The large desk sat in the middle of the room, perpendicular to the bookcases, with a classic leather nailed desk chair behind it.

Empty.

So empty. This wasn't good. Old emotions paraded around her, laughing at her hesitation. Sam could picture Donovan sitting there as clearly as if he'd appeared before her.

Sam entered his office with trepidation. It didn't feel right being here. This was Donovan's world, even more so than the rest of his house. To walk in his footsteps, to see how he'd arranged his life just so—that was profane. She wasn't meant to be a part of Donovan's life. She'd known that for years. Hell, he'd known it when he broke things off that night, giving her that damn mix tape with all the songs they'd identified with. On the insert, he'd written a line from a Dire Straits song, "Romeo and Juliet."

I love you, Sam. It was just that the time was wrong.

She'd taken one look at that and allowed her heart to run back to Nashville, back to her previously meted-out life. Followed the path that was expected of her.

That fucking voice was niggling in the back of her mind again. The voice she'd drowned out all those years ago.

You could have fought back, Sam. You could have won him over. He wanted you to stay. To accept his decision, support him, wait for him. If you could have just forgiven him, allowed him to do what his honor told him was right. But you let your pride get in the way.

If she hadn't listened to him, had fought for him to stay, to love her, then what? Would he still be dead? Would Simon? And what would have happened to Matthew and Madeline? If they'd never been born, how could they die?

She couldn't undo any of it now. They were all dead because of the choices she'd made.

She struggled against the rising tide, but the stress of the past few days finally overwhelmed her. A sob wrenched free from her chest. Here she stood, in the middle of Donovan's office, his wife a few feet away, crying like a damn schoolgirl over an old lost love. Over all her lost loves.

Silently, Susan appeared at her elbow. She handed

Sam a tissue and looked at her curiously. Sam wiped her eyes and tried for a smile.

"I'm sorry, Susan. I am a fool. A first-class fool."

"I don't know if I agree with that statement. You loved him, didn't you?"

"Once," Sam whispered. "Yes, once I did. But it wasn't meant to be. He was meant to find you, and have those two beautiful girls. As they say, everything happens for a reason."

"Too bad neither one of us believes that. And now he's dead. I can't help but wonder, if he'd stayed with you, would this have happened?"

Sam shook her head. Those thoughts were meant to be hers alone. Susan wasn't supposed to be digging into that morass, not when she hadn't been responsible for her husband's death.

The tears stopped, as suddenly as they had started. She felt empty.

"You can't do that to yourself, Susan. Trust me, I've tried that path, and it's one better not taken. Besides, Eddie would have never stayed. He was too married to the idea of going back into the military. It was just something he had to do. I hated him for it. I hated him for leaving me. And now I'm never going to have a chance to say I'm sorry."

Susan put her hand on Sam's shoulder. "He knew. It was his way. That was Eddie for you. He always found a way to understand. That's why I married him in the first place. He never once looked at me as a daughter of a general, but instead, he looked at me as me. I fell for that in the first five seconds."

They shared a moment of companionable silence,

not friends, but acquaintances on a journey neither one could face alone.

Sam pulled herself together, and moved around the room, seeking. She was able to look at the details now. It was a good office, full of light, even this late in the day, with the windows overlooking the gardens out back by the conservatory. The desk was a wide plank of polished wood, hand-carved by the look of it, with a smaller, thinner credenza behind it. The way it was situated in the room, with his back to the wall, he could see out both the windows and the doors, and have a good view of his books. Typical of the bloody man, wanting to see all the angles.

On closer examination, Sam could see the appeal of the setup. Squirrels ran up and down the branches outside the window, and a feeder covered in cardinals hung from the nearby tree. There would be hummingbirds in the summer, flowers in full bud. It was quite the bucolic little scene.

There were a few framed pictures on the wall: Donovan with his army buddies, a recent family portrait—the girls didn't look too much younger than when Sam had seen them for the first time—and a picture of Donovan with four other men in fatigues, arms around one another, cigarettes dangling from lips, wild-eyed and grinning, under which was a plaque that read The Ranger Creed.

Sam digested the words, and gained a tiny bit of understanding for the man she'd lost. As she read, she could *hear* Donovan reciting the pledge, spine straight, shoulders back, forefinger crisply to forehead, believing every single word. More than believing. Becoming.

Recognizing that I volunteered as a Ranger, fully knowing the hazards of my chosen profession, I will always endeavor to uphold the prestige, honor, and high esprit de corps of my Ranger Regiment.

Acknowledging the fact that a Ranger is a more elite soldier, who arrives at the cutting edge of battle by land, sea, or air, I accept the fact that as a Ranger, my country expects me to move farther, faster and fight harder than any other soldier.

Never shall I fail my comrades. I will always keep myself mentally alert, physically strong and morally straight and I will shoulder more than my share of the task whatever it may be, one hundred percent and then some.

Gallantly will I show the world that I am a specially selected and well-trained soldier. My courtesy to superior officers, neatness of dress and care of equipment shall set the example for others to follow.

Energetically will I meet the enemies of my country. I shall defeat them on the field of battle for I am better trained and will fight with all my might. *Surrender* is not a Ranger word. I will never leave a fallen comrade to fall into the hands of the enemy and under no circumstances will I ever embarrass my country.

Readily will I display the intestinal fortitude required to fight on to the Ranger objective and complete the mission though I be the lone survivor.

RANGERS LEAD THE WAY!

Hoo-rah, Sam thought. Damn hero. No wonder this appealed to him. He'd never given anything less than one hundred percent, be it school, the military or his heart. And when he knew he couldn't give everything to Sam, he'd walked away rather than shortchange her. Donovan was a Ranger to a T, always had been.

"That's Hal Croswell there." Susan pointed at the picture above the plaque. "And Xander. I think the other is Billy Shakes. That's not his real name. It's William Everett. No one went by their given names, always nicknames. Hal was Jackal—Eddie always said he was crazy. Xander was Mutant, because of the X-Men thing, and Billy Shakes was a Shakespeare fanatic."

"What did they call Eddie?" Sam asked.

"Doc, mostly. Since he'd been to med school, even though he dropped out. Or MH. For Mother Hen."

Oh, how that fit.

"Since he'd been to med school, was he a medic?"

"No. Eddie was an infantry officer who happened to have medical knowledge. Medics are usually enlisted men who are recruited and go through specialized education for combat medicine. He went through a bunch of the training, but he was a special case. If one of the guys got hurt, it wouldn't be out of the ordinary for him to work on them himself if the medic was otherwise engaged.

"That crew went out on nearly every mission together. They spent weeks marching through the mountains looking for Bin Laden, trying to keep the Taliban from killing everyone—Eddie found them particularly brutal. They didn't seem to care if the enemy died, or their own people. So long as things went boom."

Sam couldn't help herself; a small laugh escaped her lips. Susan arched an eyebrow.

"Honestly, I didn't sleep while he was gone. Iraq I could wrap my head around. That was just sheer hell, knowing every time the phone rang, it might be the call that he'd been blown up. He used to tell me stories about the IEDs they discovered. Every day the roads would be swept, and every night, the Iraqis would find ways to lay the bombs down again. But Afghanistan—I didn't know anything about their mission, and *that* was harder to deal with. His silence. It was all very hush-hush. I still don't know. He never told me. But he came back different afterward. Got out and never looked back."

"Bin Laden?"

"Perhaps."

"Glad we finally got him, at least," Sam said.

"Eddie was ecstatic. Not riot-in-the-street happy, but he truly thought that might be the real beginning of the end. Al-Qaeda may be a hydra, but Bin Laden's face was on all of the heads."

Sam stared at the picture. She'd never noticed that Donovan and Simon had the same smile, half-crooked, devilish and devastatingly cute.

"Who was the fifth man? The blond over on the right, kneeling?"

Susan's face changed. "Oh. That's Perry Fisher. King, they called him. He's…passed."

"Killed?"

"Yeah." Susan reached to the picture, straightened it, though Sam hadn't noticed it was crooked. "King was larger than life. Handsome, funny, the jokester of the crew. His wife, Karen, and I had our babies the same week. This was Vicky. Eddie and King came home together for the births. Those two were inseparable, crowing about the kids, smoking cigars in the hospital, getting in all sorts of trouble. Lord, that was a fun week. Then they went back over, and King was killed a month later. Eddie wouldn't talk about it. Every time I brought it up, he got tears in his eyes and walked off. They were so close, it just about killed him."

"Three dead," Sam murmured. "What a shame."

"Yeah. What a shame."

"You said Eddie came back from his last tour different. Different how?"

Susan shrugged. "Angry. That's really the only way to put it. He used to tell me things—nothing compromising, but the little details, the intimacies that he had with his men. He missed them. He was a good leader, well, you would have seen that, even back then. He missed having them around, the camaraderie, the responsibility. The adrenaline, too—being a Ranger was one thing, but being an officer in a war zone is pretty intense. Constant concern and worry for your men. But after King died in the field, it all changed. Eddie was angry with the government. He was sick of 'nation building.' He felt like they were treading water, and losing good men and women for no good reason. He almost seemed relieved to be away from them."

"So something might have happened?"

"I'm sure a lot of things happened."

"You know what I mean. Something was different on the last tour."

Susan tapped her fingers against her closed lips, a nervous tick Sam had noticed her doing before.

"I just always assumed it was about the mission when they lost King. That he disapproved of what they were doing and lost his best friend at the same time. But Eddie would never say that. Hell, I may just be making it up. Looking back, I can read a thousand different things into a single gesture."

"Looking back is dangerous, I know. But we're going to have to. Two members of the same unit being murdered isn't a coincidence. Did Fletcher ask about any of this?"

"All of it. I even printed him out a copy of the picture from our computer. He's trying to find the rest of the guys, make sure they're aware of what's going on. Though Xander is going to be hard to find. That man's been off the grid for a while now."

"I'm glad Fletcher's on top of this. He seems like a decent guy. All right. Where's Donovan's journal?"

Susan looked sheepish. "In the locked drawer. I put it back after I looked at it this morning. I'd never gone in there before now. It was his private place, and I respected that. But I knew the journal was there. He'd lock it up every time he wrote in it. The key was on the key chain found with his car. They gave it to me, after... Here." Susan pulled the keys from her front pocket, went around the desk and unlocked the drawer on the left side.

"He has several more of these in his boot locker up in the attic. I just didn't bother going through them. I figured if there was anything relevant, it would be in this year's journal."

The book Susan handed over was red leather, bound with a thin cord. Sam accepted the weight in her hands almost reverentially. She felt wrong about this, delving into the private world of her ex-lover. This was the kind of stuff her friend Taylor Jackson, a lieutenant with the

Nashville homicide unit, did for the force. Sam didn't investigate crimes, didn't go digging in people's private worlds. She wasn't used to it, to seeing the most cherished personal moments laid bare for the scrutiny of strangers.

Well, how different can it be than seeing their heart? Or their brain? That's where it all comes from, anyway. Stop dillydallying.

"You may be right. Let's look through this, see if it tells us anything. We might want to get the ones from his last deployment, too, when King died. But I can start here."

She opened the journal. Donovan's distinct scrawl leaped out at her, the edges of the words dotted with ink. She choked out a laugh. "He still uses that leaky fountain pen?"

"Yeah. He's had it for years. I can't get him to give it up."

Sam met Susan's eyes. "I gave it to him."

Susan bit her lip. "Oh."

The tension crowded back into the room. Sam shouldn't have said that, damn it. What was she doing?

She distracted herself with the opening page of the journal. It was dated I.I.MMXII. The first of January, 2012. All in the elegant scrawl, all in Latin. Sam sighed.

"Do you have a pad of paper I could use? And maybe something stronger than water? It's going to be a long night."

CHAPTER TWENTY-FIVE

Capitol Hill
Detective Darren Fletcher

There is a moment in every murder case when things begin to coalesce. Whether it's within the first hour—when a witness spills their guts, the idiot criminal has been identified and you're off to apprehend him—or twenty years later, when the piece of the puzzle that's been missing for decades suddenly drops in your lap, there's always a moment.

A smoking gun.

Fletcher thought he might be looking at his.

There was a dizzying array of papers spread out on his coffee table. The analysis of the sand from Donovan's and Croswell's lungs, identified as coming from the Savage River. The ballistics report, showing they'd both been shot with Donovan's personal weapon. A photograph of five men in uniform, arms interlinked, intently cheerful, as if proving what a good time they were having. The autopsy reports on Donovan and Croswell. Financials, phone records, personnel files.

And two notes that read "DO THE RIGHT THING," both of which had been given to the dead men prior to their murders.

Do the right thing.

So what had these two men, who served together in a very sticky, rampantly political war zone, done wrong? These guys were heroes. Heroes didn't do bad things, they did good things. And yet someone felt otherwise. Someone who thought Donovan and Croswell had done something so bad that they'd been threatened. And, when they didn't respond to the killer's satisfaction, murdered.

Something in these papers had the answer. He'd combed through everything multiple times. The problem was, as much as he knew in his bones the smoking gun was right here in front of him, he wasn't seeing it. That intangible connection between the facts just wouldn't come to him.

He'd made a list of all the things that didn't fit—the blue truck, the baseball cap, the fact that Croswell had been murdered in an empty home not his own. Made a list of things he needed to find out—whether Croswell and Donovan had been in touch recently, what Donovan was working on, why Croswell was supposed to go to Colorado to interview for a job, who made the 9-1-1 call, a warrant to talk to Croswell's therapist, another call to Donovan's boss, why someone had broken into Donovan's home. It hadn't been trashed, and there was no trace evidence found. Nothing was missing. Only the baseball cap left behind.

All this, and now the sand from the Savage River, plus two names of men he needed to find and warn, or, perhaps, arrest: Alexander Whitfield and William Everett. Mutant and Billy Shakes.

Fletcher had no doubt that one of those men was most likely the killer. He shuffled the papers around until he found the picture. Five healthy young men. Three of them dead in a year's time frame. Two by the bullet of one's gun. All but one had survived the war, only to be gunned down in their homeland.

The odds were astronomical.

He sat back on the couch and took a sip of his beer.

Maybe he was wrong. Maybe he was missing something bigger than all of this. And that piece of information he didn't have in front of him.

He needed to call in a favor.

He thought it through long and hard. Favors in this town were, on the surface, a dime a dozen. But in reality, a real favor, the kind he was talking about, that wasn't exactly illegal, but barreled off into the murky gray area of ethicality, was what D.C. was built on. He didn't like to become indebted to people, because there would be a serious quid pro quo involved.

But his gut told him to do it. There was something more to this case than met the eye. And he had a feeling the information he needed was going to be locked away where prying eyes couldn't find it.

He had two choices. Make the call, lose some sleep and maybe find the answer. Or sleep well and work harder tomorrow.

Hell, she might still be so pissed at him that she hung up when the phone rang. Or, she'd have mellowed, and look back on their time together fondly.

Hardly. But a man could dream.

He sifted through the papers one more time, already knowing what he was going to do.

It would have to be the favor.

He picked up his cell and dialed a number he knew by heart.

One ring. Two. Three.

Fletch, this is probably the worst idea you've had in a very long time.

He started to hang up when a quiet voice answered.

"What do you want, Fletch?"

"Hey, Felicia."

CHAPTER TWENTY-SIX

McLean, Virginia
Dr. Samantha Owens

Sam read and translated as best she could, pausing only to accept dinner and another drink from Susan. The food was simple fare, tomato soup and crusty bread that only partially filled the empty space in her stomach. They sat at the kitchen table in silence, each lost in her own thoughts, spooning the warm soup into their mouths absently. The tension hadn't dissipated after Sam's comment about the fountain pen, and she felt bad about it.

The soup was nourishing, but not filling. The scotch, on the other hand, a sixteen-year-old Lagavulin, curled up in the remaining empty holes and lit a merry fire, making Sam cozy from the inside out. It wasn't a cure, but a damn good intermediary medicinal.

After the first twenty minutes of frustrated page flipping, Sam set the journal on the desk thoughtfully and looked to the bookshelves for a primer she knew Donovan would have close by. It didn't take long to find.

His battered copy of *Wheelock's Latin* was on the third shelf, happily nestled between Pliny and Vergil. She took it reverentially and went back to the desk. "Never come between a man and his Wheelock," Donovan used to crow.

Better equipped, she set back to work.

Sam hadn't talked to Donovan in years, but the tenor of the entries told her something was definitely wrong. His words were melancholy at best, downright miserable at worst. But it didn't say why. He wasn't thrilled with his new job, she did gather that. They had him hopping, and while he enjoyed the work, she got the sense his boss wasn't his favorite person. There were a number of references she couldn't decipher; her Latin translation skills were a little rusty.

The first thing Sam had done was flip to the page dated the day before Donovan's murder. It seemed like the most logical place to start. She'd gotten horribly choked up—he mentioned the day off from work, how he was looking forward to spending some quality time with his family. The girls featured prominently in his missives to himself, he was tickled with them both. Especially Ally, the one he saw himself in so clearly.

Sam understood that.

A child, a creation, something made of love, and desire, and passion, and fear, became the best, and the worst, part of you. To have them stripped away was inhumane punishment. Just as it was for a daughter to lose her father. Sam had been lucky, her parents had lived to see her graduate and become a doctor before they passed. In marrying Simon and having the twins, she'd found a family again. And now even they had been taken from her. Punishment, surely. But for what? Why? She would never understand.

One Mississippi. Two Mississippi. Three.

She shook herself slightly, to refocus, and the journal's pages flipped of their own accord. The book settled open to April 10. Sam glanced at the page, a vivisection of Donovan's all-day meetings with a representative from NATO, and started to turn the page back to where she was already reading when she felt the slightest bit of resistance.

She flipped the page open and saw April 4.

The journal skipped several days. That was unusual for Donovan, a natural chronicler. He had a fresh entry for each diurnal and, as Susan had said, wrote up the happenings of his day religiously, no matter how short or mundane.

Five days in April, missing.

She looked closer, pulling the binding apart as far as it would stretch. The resistance she'd felt was from tiny slivers of paper, left over from where the pages had been cut out of the journal. It acted almost like a bookmark.

Sam went into the kitchen. After dinner, Susan had respread the financial papers on the kitchen table and had her glasses on as she perused something. She heard Sam come in, looked up and raised her eyebrow.

"Need a refill already?"

"No, thank you. Did you see this, Susan? The pages have been torn out here, or cut out. From April 5 to April 9. What happened those days?"

Alarm colored Susan's face. "I don't know…. Nothing I can think of offhand. Let me go get my calendar."

"Did Eddie keep his own calendar?"

"Top right drawer. But he carried most of that info on his BlackBerry. His admin at work would probably have a better idea of his work schedule. The calendars we keep here are for family stuff. That's why he doesn't have a work laptop at home anymore—he was trying hard to keep work at work, but had his BlackBerry on all the time, for emergencies."

Sam went back to Donovan's office, pulled the drawer open and found a cocoa-colored leather day timer. The leather was well broken in, but the pages inside were crisp and white, barely used. She opened to April 5, and saw nothing. All the pages were blank, actually, except for one. The previous Tuesday had a small notation on it. A cross, with the letters *BS*.

Susan came back into the office with her own day timer, a pink Filofax stuffed full of coupons and receipts and checkbooks. Sam used to have one just like it. When she had a family of her own to manage.

"There's nothing in here that's out of the ordinary. We had a babysitter on the night of the sixth. We went to the movies. Date night. Other than that, it's the usual kid stuff. I didn't notice anything weird or strange then… I've been racking my brain. Maybe the fountain pen exploded and ruined the pages? It's done that before."

"When it did, would he just rip the pages out?"

"No. He'd just fold them together and keep going. He hated to waste paper." Her eyes went wide. "Do you think the person who broke in took the pages? That something on them is why he was killed?"

"I don't know, Susan. You said he got called into work the day he was killed, even though he'd taken a vacation day?"

"Yes. It doesn't add up. I know his boss says they didn't call him in, but Eddie reacted so quickly, and said it was going to take a while. Work is the only thing that would make sense. He always left when Raptor called. What else could it have been?"

The pressure of the day, the enormity of the situation, was suddenly too much for Susan to bear. She broke into tears. "I was angry with him, Sam. The last emotion I felt toward my husband before he died was anger. I am a horrible person. I'll never be able to forgive myself."

Sam took the woman in her arms, let her cry. When she started to quiet down, Sam stepped back, her hands on Susan's shoulders.

"Look at me. You can't do that to yourself. There's nothing to be gained in the guilt. He knows you were upset because you loved him and wanted to be with him. That's the right kind of anger."

"But I should have been better about it. I should have understood—"

"Susan. Trust me. He knew you loved him. It's kind of hard to miss."

Susan gulped a choking laugh, the hysteria of loss. She pulled away from Sam.

"Thank you," she managed. "That helps."

"Good. Take a look at this for me, would you?" She showed her the page on the calendar with the notation. "Do you know what that means?"

She traced her fingers across the letters as if forging a connection to the dead.

"No. I have no idea. It looks like a doodle more than anything. That's weird."

"Yeah, it is. I'm going to look at the journal a little

more. I think we need to get the ones from his last deployment, though. Can you manage yourself, or do you need help?"

"I'll do it. I need…well."

Sam understood. Susan would have to open a part of her soul that was already cloudy and worn to go through more of Donovan's things. If she broke down again, she'd rather do it privately.

"I'll be here," Sam said, then went back to the desk. She fingered the journal, thinking.

CHAPTER TWENTY-SEVEN

Washington, D.C.
Detective Darren Fletcher

Fletcher and Hart had taken over one of the conference rooms and spread out the papers pertaining to the case so they could sort through all the angles and see what they were missing.

Fletcher told Hart the story about the phone call, to which the younger man whistled silently.

"I can't believe you called Felicia for help. That took balls, man. What did she say?"

"To go fuck myself. What do you think?"

Hart stood with his hands on his hips. He looked like a disapproving schoolmarm.

"Fletch, you actually sound surprised. You call your ex-wife, a woman you haven't spoken to outside of custodial legalities for four years, and ask her to help you break the law?"

"Jesus, man, keep your voice down. There's nothing illegal about it. It's a shortcut, that's all."

"And now you've alerted a civilian that you're wanting to look into the private records of several troops. DOD will chew you up and spit you out before you can laugh at them. Nothing illegal, my ass."

Fletcher stopped stacking papers and sat back in the chair. "Lonnie, get off my back. It was just a thought. I was trying to move things forward. I don't see you grinding out any brilliant solutions."

"Well, gee, sorry, Batman. I thought we were working on this together."

"We are, Boy Wonder." Fletcher sighed deeply. "I was just trying to play a hunch."

"He does that, you know." A female voice startled them both. Fletcher turned and couldn't believe his eyes. A gorgeous blonde stood in the conference room doorway, legs up to her chin, and obviously pregnant.

His ex-wife.

"Felicia. I thought… What are you doing here? You're… That's…"

Hart shot him a look, went to the door and gave Felicia a hug. "Come on in. Don't mind him, his ass is taking a vacation day, and the rest of him doesn't know how to speak."

Felicia laughed. "Some things never change. How are you, Lonnie?"

"Better than I deserve."

"Good. Give Ginger my love. I hope she's doing well."

"She is, she is." Hart looked to Fletcher, who took a breath and shut his mouth, then back at Felicia, who was staring at the nails on her right hand. "Listen, I was just about to go get a cup of coffee. You want anything?"

"I'm good," Felicia answered.

"Uh, guess I am, too." Fletcher nodded at Hart,

though he wanted to cry out, *No, don't—don't leave me alone with her.* Hart went to the door, ignored the admonishing glare, instead smiling a bit at his angry partner. Fletcher had to restrain himself from shooting the man the bird. The door closed, and he was left alone with Felicia. He was going to fire whoever had let her in without calling him to say she was on her way up.

"So," they both said at the same time.

"Sorry. You first," Fletcher said.

"Thanks. Mind if I sit?"

"Have at it."

She settled into a chair, barely fitting in it. He remembered how stunning he thought she was when she was pregnant with Tad—glowing and ripe with the fruit of his loins. They'd barely been able to keep their hands off each other. His balls shrank a little looking at her now, knowing that whatever was inside her was not his.

She saw him staring at her belly. "I thought I should tell you in person."

"Flee, you don't owe me anything."

She smiled, almost a little sadly. "I know that. But still… Did Tad tell you I was seeing someone?"

"He might have mentioned it," Fletcher said, coloring. Tad had mentioned it, and Fletcher had responded by getting head-over-heels shitfaced drunk and losing half his precious weekend time in bed with a vicious hangover.

"We're getting married after the babies come."

"Bab*ies?*"

She laughed, and Fletcher saw a little of the girl she'd been when they first met. "I can't believe I'm going to tell you this. Ryan, that's my fiancé, had a vasectomy when he was in his twenties, thinking he never wanted kids. He changed his mind and had it reversed, but there were still problems. We did in vitro. Ended up with twins. Two girls."

She looked happy, and Fletcher was torn between raising a stink and trying his damnedest not to fuck up the fact that she was actually here and talking to him in a tone that didn't sound like nails on a chalkboard. He stowed away all his pride, all his hurt and anger, all the animosity that had been fueling his thoughts of her for the past several years, and smiled.

"I'm really happy for you, Flee."

"Dear God, Fletch. I think you actually mean that."

"I do. You deserve better than me. You always have."

She pursed her lips and cocked her head to the side, as if weighing his sincerity on some sort of internal scale, then started to get to her feet.

"Let me help you," Fletcher said, giving her a hand. She laughed ruefully, rubbing her back.

"If I'd known what a pain it is to carry two…"

They stood there staring at each other until she finally blinked and looked away, smoothing the elegant maternity dress across her belly. She always did know how to dress.

"So you came all the way down here to tell me you're having babies and getting married?"

Felicia reached over and smoothed his hair back from his forehead.

"You think I'd come all this way just for that?" She laughed, then got serious. "I'm having lunch with Joelle."

His heart began to pound.

"Are you sure?"

"Yes. I never could resist your gentleman-in-distress act."

"Felicia," he started, but she put her finger to his lips.

"Thank me later, if I can talk her into doing it. I'm going to ask her to be their godmother first, soften her up a bit."

"I owe you one. A big one."

"And I'll collect sometime. Right now—" she shook her head ruefully "—I just need to pee."

Fletcher gave his ex-wife a genuine smile.

"Serves you right."

CHAPTER TWENTY-EIGHT

Georgetown
Dr. Samantha Owens

Sam was dreaming. She knew she was dreaming, because the twins were in dark blue graduation gowns, and Simon's hair was shot through with silver. He held the hand of a younger girl, a serious-faced teen who had sherry-drowned eyes, just like Sam. She watched them from afar, not a part of the day, not able to straighten Matthew's cap, where it had gone askew over his thick dark blond curls, nor retie the bow that held back Madeline's lighter blond waves, like a field of wheat in a steady breeze. Not able to touch the ghost child under the chin to make her smile. Where had they gotten such gorgeous hair? She didn't have good hair, it was thin and needed constant brushing, and Simon's was straight as a stick. They were both dark-headed, too, yet they'd created two stunning blondes, and one mini-Sam.

The sight of them all together, laughing, made her happy. She wanted to join them. She started their way but ran into something, a barrier, clear and intractable, barking her shin and elbow so hard that tears sprang to her eyes. She hammered on it with her fists, hoping that they'd hear her and invite her to be with them, something, anything, to get their attention, but they turned away and walked off the stage. The scene became black, dark, empty.

She realized she was looking inside her own body, on the table at Forensic Medical, where she'd cut herself open to perform her own autopsy, and instead found that she'd been full of nothing but the dimmest air.

No lungs. No brain. No heart.

There were mighty red gashes up her arms and across her stomach. Everything had leaked out through the wide slices of flesh.

She was screaming.

She knew she was screaming.

But she couldn't seem to stop, and the sound swallowed her whole.

She bolted upright, eyes wide, breath coming in little pants. Her hands grasped her stomach. She could feel the rough, raised scars under the fabric of her T-shirt. Her subconscious was punishing her. Punishing her for not fighting harder. For asking too much. For not loving them all enough.

Every moment of the dream played out again and again in her head. She fought to hold on to it: the way Matthew's eyes crinkled when he smiled, and Maddy's wide grin spilled sunshine as she played with her father. And the last child, the one that never was, the one Sam hadn't gotten a chance to know, watching them, so serious and sad. Tears rolled down her face, and as they did, the dream faded, until she was grasping to remember the details. What color were the gowns? How tall was Matt? When did Simon's hair go gray?

She covered her mouth with her hand and bit down, trying so hard not to lose it. Not to crawl right back into the dream. It wasn't real. None of that had happened. It never would.

Despair, as bleak and unforgiving as the inside of an ice storm, rained down on her.

These were the moments she wondered why she bothered. She had no one left. No one who needed her. Her job was meaningless. Her life wasn't worth living.

God, she missed them so much.

She curled into a ball and let the tears come, hard and insistent. She tried to focus on what might have been, instead of what had really happened. That was a place she couldn't allow herself to go.

There was a soft knock on the door. She ignored it. Maybe whoever it was would go away.

No such luck. The door rattled and opened, and Sam felt the warm, soft arms of her old friend Eleanor, who crawled right into the bed and spooned Sam, holding on for dear life.

"I know," Eleanor said. "I know."

Sam didn't know how long they stayed like that, only that it felt like a great deal of time had passed and she had finally, finally stopped crying.

Eleanor gave her a last squeeze, then sat up.

"Come on downstairs, sweetie. Let me make you some breakfast. They just called to let us know they're releasing Eddie's body today. We have a funeral to plan."

Sam stayed on her side for a moment, then rolled onto her back with a great, gusting sigh.

Oh, my darlings. I miss you so.

* * *

Sam showered while Eleanor cooked.

She'd driven back to Georgetown late last night, Susan in the seat next to her nearly asleep, afraid to stay alone in her own house. Sam hadn't blamed her a bit. She'd had that exact same reaction at the beginning, not wanting to be alone, begging friends to stay over so she wouldn't have to face the immense emptiness by herself. Only she wasn't being stalked, and *her* husband wasn't harboring secrets…

She was going to have to sell the house.

The thought jumped into Sam's mind so suddenly, so strongly, that she gasped a little. She didn't know why she hadn't thought of it sooner. It wasn't a home anymore, but a mausoleum. A prison. One that, until this very moment, she'd wanted to keep herself in.

But her rational mind had finally poked through. She was hurting herself more staying there than selling it. As soon as she went home, she was going to put it on the market.

An inexplicable feeling floated through her as she washed the shampoo out of her hair.

She almost didn't recognize it. She hadn't felt it in so long.

Sam used to be a decisive person. Strong. Capable. Not just nominal, but forward and somewhat brash, though never forceful.

The feeling she'd had was one of decision, and with it, she felt the first tiny brick being laid, just at the bottom of her feet. A new foundation. It was small, and the structure was going to take months, if not years, to rebuild. There would be cracks, huge, gaping holes, but there would be mortar, ready mix, wattle and straw. Somehow, she would hold the miniature slabs together.

She toweled off and blew her hair dry. Put on her fresh clothes, grateful that Eleanor had done the wash for her unasked. She'd forgotten how nice it was to have someone take care of her.

She could hear the delighted screams of Susan and Eddie's children down the hall, some game that they'd devised to keep themselves amused. They all needed to keep a closer eye on them, just to make sure they were managing. But children were resilient. They would never forget, but they were young enough to actually heal.

How Susan would cope, Sam had no idea. She didn't know what the relationship between her and Donovan was really like. He'd been unhappy, that much was clear from his journal, but whether that stemmed from his work, his time overseas, PTSD or his home life, she couldn't be sure. She'd lay bets on the military issue, but it had been so long.... Donovan was always so gung ho, it would have taken something huge to change his feelings.

An act of God.

As she brushed her teeth, she thought about the entries in the journal she'd had trouble deciphering. They were misuses of the Latin language. In someone less versed, she'd call them mistakes. But for a scholar of Latin like Donovan, little mistakes were a red flag.

What looked on the surface like mistakes were, she felt sure now, codes. Messages meant to be read.

Now she just had to figure out what he was trying to say.

PART TWO

"We few, we happy few, we band of brothers..."

—WILLIAM SHAKESPEARE, *HENRY V*

CHAPTER TWENTY-NINE

New Castle, Virginia
Detective Darren Fletcher

The Blue Ridge Mountains run from Maryland to Tennessee, leaking across the borders of North Carolina, South Carolina, Georgia, West Virginia and Pennsylvania in the process. A blue haze hangs in the sky along the mountaintops, giving them their name, making them look like the keepers of long-lost secrets, hill ghosts from epochs past. It is an area full of mystery and distrust. The people along the knolls and rivers forever take care of their own. Generation after generation of settlers, wary and resistant to the rules of law enforcement, of anything that wasn't theirs, fight against the encroachment ofcivilization. They have their own rules, their own language, their own food, traditions, even their own liquor.

They do not look kindly on outsiders.

Darren Fletcher observed the long shadows where the trees of the mountains hung across the road, keeping it cool and dark in the brightest of sunlight, and felt a chill crawl up his arms. He felt like he was being watched, but not by a person. No single human being could cause the shivers he felt running through his spine. This was something older, ancient even, something he didn't belong to. He was an interloper, unwelcome, seen as nothing more than a threat.

He shook himself. *Good grief, Fletch, what was in that barbecue you ate for lunch?*

He glanced over at Hart, who also seemed uneasy. They were standing at the foot of the porch that led to the doorstep of a house that belonged to the mother of one William Everett, and the sheriff's deputy who'd driven them out here had backed away from the door after knocking once and calling out their intentions.

No one charged out with a shotgun, so that was a plus.

The deputy had been clear that Mrs. Everett didn't like to be surprised. Still, everything felt wrong. All three of them were seasoned professionals, though the deputy was young. They'd all seen their share of the surreal. So the fact that all three had the hair on the backs of their necks standing on end was something to pay attention to. Something was off, and Fletcher was pretty sure he knew what that was. He squared his shoulders, went up on the porch and knocked himself, three hard raps with his balled-up fist. "Police, Mrs. Everett. Open up."

There was still no answer.

"Force it," he said to the deputy.

"But…"

"No buts. We have a warrant. Get it open, Deputy."

The young man just shrugged his shoulders and went to grab the battering ram from his trunk.

The Department of Defense had cooperated fully with the "official" inquiry into the deaths of Edward Donovan and Harold Croswell. They'd provided name, rank and socials, all they were required to by law, and very little else outside of the men's discharge papers.

DOD had also cooperated with the "unofficial" inquiry made into the records of five soldiers from the 75th Ranger Regiment, Bravo Company, though the powers that be probably weren't aware of that fact, and Fletcher hoped to God they never would be. He liked living as a free man.

Felicia's lunch with her oldest friend, Joelle Comprant, had been fruitful to the extreme. Giddy with the knowledge she was going to be a fairy godmother, not once, but twice over, Joelle had been more than happy to dive into the personnel records—it was her job, after all. She'd broken just about every rule she'd promised to uphold by making printouts of all the records she could get her hands on, but Fletcher was a man of his word. He'd guaranteed Felicia that Joelle would never, ever be compromised, that he would resign without his pension before her name would ever leave his mouth in conjunction with this case.

He and Felicia had formed some sort of new bond, as well. On the plane down to Roanoke, when he told Hart that she'd actually offered to increase his visitation time with Tad, his partner had grinned.

"All she ever wanted was to be a part of your life, Fletch. You kept the job so separate from her that she felt unwelcome, and left out. By asking her for help, you thawed a long-frozen icicle. Learn from it."

"Why didn't you ever say that before?"

"I did. You just never wanted to hear it. Ginger and I were talking—"

"You told Ginger?"

"Dude. Unlike you, I plan to keep my wife around for a while. Of course I tell her. I tell her everything. That's why she loves me. And puts up with my bullshit."

Fletcher had just shaken his head, wondering what in the hell he was going to do with everyone in his life. Maybe he'd been too dumb and too blind to listen to them before, who knew. But he was determined not to fuck this up again. Tad was everything to him, and if he could get more time with the boy, he'd move heaven and earth to do it.

Just as soon as they figured out what the hell was going on with Edward Donovan and the men from Bravo Company he served with.

There were two people left alive from the picture in Donovan's office. The illicit DOD records confirmed the obvious: the five men had served together in Afghanistan.

But the man they were here to see, William Everett, hadn't gone gently into that good night upon his return home. A little extra digging showed he was on a watch list the Secret Service kept of possible threats to the executive branch. Mr. Everett didn't like the fact that American lives were being lost in an unwinnable war, so he availed himself of his considerable skills as a writer to let the President know exactly what he thought about the current administration's foreign policy agenda.

Homegrown terrorists, the folks at Homeland Security liked to call them. Ironic, really, that the government would turn on the very men and women they'd relied on to keep them safe. Still, Everett had been low on their totem pole of possible threats. He was just an angry soldier who liked to send letters.

Except that now he was a suspect in the murders of two of his fellow soldiers, on home soil. He became the subject of record by default—their other possible, Alexander Whitfield, was a ghost. He'd come back from the war, mustered out and literally dropped off the face of the earth. It was going to take considerably more time to dig up his whereabouts.

And so they'd caught a flight to Roanoke and driven northwest. The last known address for William Everett had led them directly to this little cabin, outside of the small, picturesque town of New Castle.

The deputy approached the rickety porch again, this time with the cylindrical metal ram in hand. The door didn't look too stable, would probably only take a kick, but Fletcher wasn't in the mood to pull splinters out of his shin should it collapse too easily. No, make the locals work for it.

He and Hart raised their weapons to cover the young deputy, who gave a halfhearted swing. The door withstood the force with only a minor shiver. Fletcher cleared his throat and the deputy rolled his eyes and gave it a good thrust. The door spun open, flashing back, and the great gusting scent of decomposition wafted out.

"Jesus," the deputy said. He dropped the ram on the porch and covered his nose and mouth with his hand. A few flies bumbled out the door, escaping into the open air.

Fletcher caught Hart's eye.

"No one smelled this when they came out last night?" Hart asked the deputy, the insinuation clear.

The deputy was still young enough to be intimidated by Hart's steely glare, and the knowledge of what he was about to have to deal with. "I doubt anyone got close enough, to tell you the truth, sir. Like I said, old Mrs. Everett can be a might tetchy. And she's got wicked aim. They probably called out to the house and, when no one answered, came on down the mountain."

Hart muttered something that sounded suspiciously like "incompetent hillbillies" and Fletcher shot him a look, glad the kid hadn't heard. It wasn't his fault. He wasn't the one who'd screwed the pooch.

He said a very bad word under his breath, then sighed and led the way.

The inside of the cabin was worse than he expected. It was hot, musty and stinking of death. Dust motes floated through the air, accompanying the flies on their perpetual journey. Newspapers were stacked up on the table, along with the remnants of a meal laid out for two. Maggots writhed on the plates. Fletcher made sure to breathe through his mouth.

The cabin wasn't very big, mostly comprised of a large room off a utilitarian kitchen housing the table, a couch, an armchair and a beat-up television set. A short hallway led to a bathroom, with two doors on either side.

"Let's find him," Fletcher said to Hart, who set off down the hall. He turned to the deputy. "Anyone heard from the mom recently?"

"Mrs. Everett was in town beginning of last week, getting supplies. I saw her myself, at the hardware store."

"But no one saw William?"

"Not that I know of, but we can ask around. Bill doesn't come home much. Once he got out… Well, who could blame him? His momma is mean as a snake. There was nothing for him here anymore."

"A dead snake." Hart appeared, face pinched. "Mrs. Everett's tucked up in her bed, single gunshot to the head."

"Aw, shit," the deputy said, pulling his hat from his oversize head and mopping the sweat off with a red bandanna.

"What's in the other room?" Fletcher asked.

"Empty."

"The bath?"

"See for yourself."

It wasn't a pretty sight. A man who matched the description of William Everett sprawled in the tub, canted to one side, the water a murky black. A straight razor was on the floor, the blood long crusted. His face was congested with blood, the skin turning a dark puce.

"Suicide?" Fletcher asked, not really as a question. He was merely stating the obvious.

"Could be. Killed his momma, then slit his wrists."

"Why, though?"

Hart shook his head. The deputy was getting greener by the second. Fletcher barked at him. "Get out of here before you puke all over my crime scene."

The kid didn't have to be asked twice. He bolted from the room. Fletcher didn't blame him. He'd like to, as well. Billy Shakes smelled like hell, and looked ten times worse, to boot.

"Let's take a quick gander for a note, then let the

Roanoke police, or whoever handles their shit around here, deal with the scene. Damn it."

"You thinking what I'm thinking?"

Fletcher nodded. "This much decomposition? He's probably been dead too long to have killed Donovan. Definitely too long to have hit Croswell."

"Yep, that's what I was thinking. Experts will know for sure, but he's been gone for a while."

They backed out of the bathroom, took a cursory glance around the house, but didn't see anything that smacked of a suicide note. Fletcher didn't feel like digging through the mess himself. He left that job to the techs.

The deputy was sitting on the front porch with his head between his knees. Fletcher patted him on the shoulder as he walked down the stairs.

"You okay, kid?"

"My name's Brendan." A little bite to him still. He'd make it eventually. The scene inside the Everett house could have been worse, but it was none too pleasant. Fletcher took pity on him.

"Ah. Brendan. Sorry, I'm a little preoccupied at the moment. When you're feeling up to it, let's call in your crime scene folks, have them take a look. Apparent murder-suicide. Warn them about the decomp. They'll want to bring extra suits."

"Yes, sir," the deputy said, misery making his shoulders droop.

"Brendan. Seriously, you okay?"

"Yeah. Just… No one deserves to go on like that, rotting in their bed. And I just saw her last week. And him, well, I mean…he got out. Why in the world would he come back to this? And kill your own mother? That's just cold. She wasn't a nice lady, God rest her soul, but she still birthed him."

"We might never know the answer to that. Go on. Make that call," Fletcher said. The deputy rose to his feet and went to his cruiser. Fletcher turned to Hart, who was fanning himself.

"This is a dead end."

"No pun intended, of course."

"Of course. He'd been dead at least a week, right?"

"I'd say so. If the deputy is accurate about seeing the mother in town last week, that absolutely would be before the Donovan murder. But murder-suicide?" Hart rubbed his chin. "I don't know, Fletch. This case get's weirder by the day. You realize Alexander Whitfield just became our prime suspect."

Whitfield, the hermit, living up in the woods. Whitfield, the ex-soldier, who would most likely be armed to the teeth. Fletcher couldn't think of a more dangerous wild card.

A wild card who may have four fresh bodies to his name.

Fletcher heard the thin wail of sirens bleeding through the air. The New Castle folks would arrive soon enough. The last thing he felt like doing was playing patty-cake with the locals, but it must be done. He needed as much information out of Everett's house as they could dig up before they took off.

There was a funeral in D.C. tomorrow, and he planned to be there.

CHAPTER THIRTY

Georgetown
Dr. Samantha Owens

Sam didn't like funerals.

No one does, she knew that. But she'd developed a deep and abiding discomfort of wakes and processionals and graveside tears when she was a kid, at the funeral for a childhood friend who'd been hit by a car, and it had never gone away. Her job was to uncover the cause of death, not to see the person into the ground. Not experience the agony of the people left behind.

And yet here she was, one of the left behind.

With everything that had happened, she honestly didn't know if she could manage to get through the afternoon. It was too soon. She wasn't ready to face a hole in the ground. And she knew she wasn't ready to bury Donovan, either.

But she didn't have that luxury. Susan and Eleanor needed her. So instead of putting her head in the sand and waiting for the day after tomorrow, she was on

M Street, walking into White House|Black Market to find an appropriate black dress to wear.

She'd rescheduled her flight home so she could stay for a few more days. Called work and told them she was taking a week of vacation. But she only had three days' worth of clothes, and nothing appropriate for Arlington. Susan had offered to let her go through her closet, but she didn't feel right about that. She and Susan were the same dress size, but there was something really creepy about wearing your ex's wife's clothes to his funeral. Sam had demurred, and set out for a walk down the hill, knowing she would amble by plenty of shops on the way.

Sam used to love to shop. That was another thing loss did to you, it stole your pleasures. But the day was sunny, the air filled with the scent of flowers, and she was surprised to find herself enjoying the outing. She found several pieces that she liked, along with some shoes that were more appropriate than her clogs or loafers.

Walking back up Wisconsin with her bags slung over her shoulder, she ran through the case in her head. She felt like everything had stagnated. She couldn't break the code in Donovan's journals. She'd left three unreturned messages with Detective Fletcher. Her cursory search into the whereabouts of Donovan's friend Xander had turned up nothing. Short of driving up to the Savage River and asking around for him, she was at a loss for what to do next. And if this man was responsible for the death of two men, she couldn't particularly go running toward him. Instead, she wanted to back away, away from everything going on, from her cruel emotions, the hurt she was digging up like pieces of shrapnel caught deep under her skin.

Think like a detective, like Taylor, Sam. What would Taylor do?

She wouldn't back away. She'd charge forward, heedlessly even, and solve the case. But that's why she was who she was, and Sam, well, that's why she was a pathologist. Charging forward had never really been a part of her personal lexicon.

Sam was a cautious woman. To the point that she took pride in the fact that she always looked before she leaped. She thought things through, measured the cost, the impact, the consequences, before acting. Spontaneity was not her strong suit.

Yet here she was in D.C., forging through a murder investigation without a road map. Simon would have laughed at her. He was as cautious as she. It must have something to do with their chosen professions: she a pathologist, he a geneticist. There was comfort in the explained, the immutable constants of science, for both of them.

His death wasn't explainable. The death of the twins wasn't explainable. Her own miscarriage right before she lost her whole family wasn't explainable.

So why did she keep trying to find answers in that which was utterly without reason?

Sam felt her breath coming fast.

Shit.

She dropped the bags on the street in front of her and pulled the antibacterial gel from her purse.

One Mississippi. Two Mississippi. Three Mississippi. Four.

God, the urge had snuck up on her, laying her bare

in front of this street full of strangers. She couldn't help that, ignored their curious glances, just scrubbed and scrubbed until her hands were dry, then poured more gel in her palms and did it all over.

Simon. Matthew. Madeline.

Donovan.

She stopped short when she realized she'd added him into her frantic prayer.

Breathe.

Open your eyes.

Cars driving by, the construction workers on the corner, the scrambling students hurrying past on their way to class. Slowly the real world came back. She looked to her left and realized she was standing at the base of the Georgetown University steps.

How many times had she stood in this very spot? Meeting friends before a night on the town carousing, exchanging study notes, sneaking kisses with Donovan, taking a breather after a run. The memories flooded her like waves on a beach, relentlessly crashing into the hard sand.

The code in Donovan's journal.

He was referencing dates. Dates that corresponded to their time together at Georgetown.

As if he'd known Sam was going to see his journals one day.

She shook her head and sat down on the second step from the bottom. *Think, Sam. That was crazy. That wasn't it. You're being narcissistic.*

And then it hit her.

He wasn't sending her a message. He was sending them to himself.

She sat there for a few minutes, letting the pages of

the journal run through her head. She remembered....
Her breath caught. All the tumblers fell into place, and
the vault in her mind opened wide.

The code she thought she was seeing wasn't a code,
per se. They were memories. Memories. That's how he
wrote his journal, covering the parts of his days that
seemed so mundane, interspersed with memories. Now
that she had that, she could see they certainly didn't all
refer to her, though some did, especially recently. But
there were many, many moments he'd captured.

The elegance of his system made her smile. *But my
God, forty years of memories...* Whatever was refer-
enced on the missing pages could have been anything,
from any time in his life.

Donovan had never been shy about the fact that he
journaled. He used to talk about the process with their
friends. He told them emptying his mind of what was
there, regardless of topic or length, helped him sleep,
so he did it every night, even when he was drunk, or
so tired he couldn't get the pen to run along the page
properly.

That's when Sam bought him the fountain pen. She
thought it might be more fun for him to write with than
a cheap blue Bic ballpoint.

Those close to him knew he wrote in Latin, but she
couldn't imagine him telling too many people that fact.
Despite the teasing way he'd lorded it over them in
school, to share such a detail with just anyone smacked
of arrogance, and while Donovan had always had ma-
chismo to spare, he wasn't a braggart.

Someone knew that he'd written down something
incriminating, and had determined that they needed

to stop him from sharing. So they broke into the house and stole the incriminating pages from the journal.

If she was right, if that theory held together, the culprit must be someone very close.

Or...when he received the note, he tore the pages out himself and destroyed them.

God, she felt like she was running in circles. She picked up her bags and started up the street, anxious to get back and look through the journal one more time. She couldn't help but wonder again about the people he worked with at Raptor, and the men he'd served with. His death wasn't random. Whoever had killed him was someone he knew well.

Sam needed to read Donovan's journals from the time he was overseas with the unit comprised of the five men in the picture. See what story they had to tell. Susan had gone into the footlocker in the attic last night and pulled three dark red leather diaries from the pile. They were waiting for Sam back at the house.

The closer she got to the answers, the farther away she felt. But at least she had an idea of what to look for now. Leave it to Donovan to scatter a trail of bread crumbs, no matter how purposeful or unwittingly he'd done so.

CHAPTER THIRTY-ONE

Washington, D.C.
Detective Darren Fletcher

"Thank you, Deputy. I'll wait for that fax."

Fletcher closed his cell phone and leaned back in his chair. The homicide offices were quiet now, in between shifts. He had space to think.

The folks from New Castle, supplemented by some crime scene techs from Roanoke, had turned out to be a rather quick and talented group; they'd finished the post and gotten the report done in the time it took Fletcher and Hart to get back to D.C. It helped that they had a pathologist on staff who was an expert in entomology. Through the insect activity on both bodies, the doctor had been able to pinpoint the time of death for William Everett to the previous Tuesday, a full three days before Donovan's murder. That made it official; Billy Shakes was not their man.

The cause of death was listed as exsanguination. Method of death was probable suicide. They could not rule out intimidation or coercion, but there was no solid evidence to prove that scenario.

Except for one little detail. One little detail that could be used to suggest that all was not as it seemed.

The crime scene techs had retrieved a goodly amount of trace evidence, including a long dark hair from the wound in Mrs. Everett's head, a hair that didn't match either William, who was blond, or Mrs. Everett, who was steel gray. A hair with intact follicle, which would be used to find DNA. That hair, coupled with the time of the murder, gave Fletcher enough pause that he was unwilling to categorize the murder of Mrs. Everett the sole responsibility of William Everett, and instead added a possible third person to the mix. It was entirely possible that someone had killed Mrs. Everett, and when William arrived home to find his mother dead, he offed himself.

Or, which might be more logical, someone was waiting for him when he got back. Someone who didn't want a witness to their conversation. Someone who was more than willing to take out an old woman so she wouldn't get out of bed and overhear a personal tête-à-tête.

It did appear that Everett had slit his own wrists. There were hesitation cuts beginning an inch below his left palm, deep enough to bleed but not deep enough to hit the artery that would eventually let his life's blood escape into the tub. It was possible that he was forced to use the razor on himself. His BAL was nearly three times the legal limit, which meant he'd gotten very drunk before he killed himself. Drunk, but probably not passed out: his liver showed a solid dive into cirrhosis. Billy Shakes was an alcoholic, and most likely a functioning one. His employer had been found; he worked the timber forests in North Carolina. The man was genuinely sorry to hear of Billy's death, he was a good worker, one that kept everyone in stitches or tears as he acted out the great soliloquies from his favorite master, Shakespeare. Billy had been caught drinking on the job a few times, but a stiff reprimand had cured his foolishness.

No fresh granulomas had been found in his lungs, furthering the suicide theory. But there was no note. And more than that—there was no calendar, no mail with his name on it. Only a duffel bag full of clothes, enough for a week's worth of changes. It seemed Everett had come home for a visit and stayed for a few days, which jived with his boss's recollection that Billy had taken a week's vacation to visit his sick mother.

But Mrs. Everett wasn't sick.

Maybe he'd run home as an escape, thinking he could get clear of whatever trouble was hunting him down by hiding out in the holler with his mama's shotgun to protect him. Not the most manly thing for an ex-Ranger to do, but people did crazy things when they were scared.

So what, or who, had managed to scare someone who'd spent the past decade tromping through the deep sand and unforgiving forests hunting terrorists? And had he killed himself, or been forced into that good night?

Fletcher was doing his best not to get frustrated. The case was turning into a sprawling, convoluted mess, spreading across multiple jurisdictions, diving in and out of logic. He had no way of knowing if he was dealing with a single killer or more. Whether the military angle was even relevant. Where the last piece of the puzzle was. All he knew for sure was things just weren't adding up.

Hart had gone home for the day. He had a wife to go home to, a wife who wanted him there. Fletcher didn't mind. Hart and Ginger were good people. He'd never begrudged his partner the family time Fletcher had so blatantly wasted when he had his own young family.

But that absence was felt keenly, because his partner wasn't there to bounce things off of. The case was moving in fits and starts. He was missing something. He knew it was all there in front of him, he just needed to think about things the right way, and it would all fall into place. So he did what all good detectives do when they're stuck. He went back to the beginning. Back to the original crime, the Donovan carjacking.

Donovan's wife had told Fletcher he received a phone call, and skedaddled from the family outing. The number had been traced back to a disposable cell, which meant it could have come from anywhere. Susan Donovan said her husband had left her to go to work. Fletcher had been to Donovan's office, and everyone he'd talked to there had denied calling the man in. He was off for the day. He'd made it clear he wasn't to be disturbed.

That call was where it all started. So that's where he needed to go.

Fletcher grabbed the phone and rang Susan Donovan.

CHAPTER THIRTY-TWO

Georgetown
Susan Donovan

Susan was reading a book to Ally and Vicky when she heard the door chimes. Muted footfalls followed, then the bell-like voice of her mother-in-law, Eleanor, drifted up from the foyer, followed by the deeper tones of Detective Fletcher. Susan sighed and handed the book to Ally, who took it self-importantly and turned to her little sister, more than happy to take over.

"I'll be back in a bit, ladies. If you need anything, call from the landing. I bet Grammy will be up shortly."

"Okay, Mommy," they chimed in unison.

She watched them from the doorway for a moment, her perfect little angels, then took the stairs down. The terrible threesome, as she'd started thinking of them, were lined up in the kitchen, ready to dissect her words yet again.

God, she just wanted this over. Hiding out at Eleanor's house, dreading the funeral tomorrow, trying to keep the girls entertained and sheltered from the reality of their father's murder, wondering who had broken into her house, and why, was starting to take its toll. And the girls… Tomorrow was going to wrench all of them apart, but especially the children. It would tear asunder the basting stitches she'd put into their little psyches.

Susan had actually entertained the thought of not allowing them to attend, but Eleanor had talked her out of that. She made the entirely valid point that it was important for them to have some finality to the situation or else they might think he was coming back. Apparently Eleanor had lost her father at a young age and was never told the whole story, only that he'd gone away, and figuring out the truth when she was old enough to be cognizant of the realities of life and death had caused a permanent rift between her and her mother.

Susan thought the girls had a handle on things, albeit on a small scale—they'd lost multiple goldfish and a hamster and seemed to grasp the concept of death—but she wasn't altogether sure they would understand that their daddy was never, ever coming back. This wasn't like a deployment, when he'd go a few days without word, then show up in their Skype, smiling and freshly sunburned, with new shadows behind his eyes. For now, being away from home was causing more consternation than anything. They were both out of their routine, and that made for difficulties.

After tomorrow, things would have to go back to normal.

Her new normal.

At least that's what she kept telling herself.

She entered the kitchen and the conversation stopped. The detective stepped forward and shook her hand. His was warm and dry, like he had a fever. She pulled away abruptly; she didn't need to get sick, but he didn't seem to notice. Or care.

"Thanks for letting me come over, Mrs. Donovan."

"You're welcome. Do you have news?"

"Some. I've just gotten back from New Castle, Virginia. We found William Everett. It looks like he committed suicide last week, prior to Major Donovan's death."

Susan rubbed her eyebrow, where a sudden headache had sprouted. Panicked confusion ran through her mind. What did that mean?

"I'm very sorry to hear that," she managed. "But, Detective, please. Is that going to help solve Eddie's case? What's happening? Why was Eddie killed? Why were any of them killed?"

He held up his hands to placate her, which made her even more uneasy.

"Mrs. Donovan, that's exactly what we're trying to figure out. If it's all right with you, I'd like to run through everything again. And have you tell me a bit more about the last man in the picture, Alexander Whitfield."

"God, Xander's not dead, too, is he?"

"We have no way of telling. We don't know where he is. He has no address on record."

Sam looked at Susan. "You didn't tell him? About the Savage River?"

Fletcher straightened. "Where the sand came from? What about it?"

Susan shook her head. "No. We haven't talked. I…I'm sorry, Detective. It slipped my mind. Xander lives somewhere near the Savage River."

The detective's face tightened. "Where, exactly?"

"I don't know. We used to go up to the park to camp, and Eddie would go off and meet Xander somewhere to have coffee and talk. He never invited us along, said it was man time. So I've never met him, only seen the pictures."

Susan saw Sam staring at her again. "What, Sam? What is it?"

"The nicknames. All the men in the picture went by nicknames, right?" Sam asked.

Fletcher perked up, too.

"Yes, they did. Nothing unusual there. Why?"

"'BS.' Remember? The little doodle in Eddie's calendar that I thought looked like a cross? Didn't you say William Everett was called Billy Shakes?"

Susan nodded. "Yes. But if he committed suicide, and Eddie knew about it, wouldn't he tell me that one of his good friends had died?"

Fletcher passed his hands over his face as if scrubbing away his frustration. "That's one helluva good question, Mrs. Donovan. Can you ladies clue me in to what you're talking about?"

"I'll show you," Susan said. The journals and Eddie's nearly empty day runner were sitting on the kitchen table. She retrieved them and pointed out the spot on the calendar, then showed him Eddie's journal.

"I see," Fletcher said. "That's very interesting. Was William Everett in touch with your husband?"

Susan shook head. "Not that I know of. But, Detective, he was a grown man. He didn't tell me about everything. Certainly not about who called him on any given day, unless it related to the family."

"Well, in a way, he did," Sam said. "The journal. May I see it again?"

Susan handed it to Sam, who flipped back to the corresponding date. "I think I figured out what I was overlooking...."

The detective was obviously lost. Susan explained it to him quickly. "My husband keeps a journal, but it's in Latin. Sam has been translating. So far she hasn't found anything relevant to the case."

Sam shook her head. "Until now. Look. Last Tuesday has a notation that's out of the ordinary. Remember I told you Eddie had slipped in words that looked out of place? I realized earlier today that they're memories. It's his own brand of shorthand. And using the nicknames as a guide..." Her eyes skimmed the page, and even Susan felt her eagerness.

"Here it is. He's crushed by the news of a close friend's death. He's talking about them. About the day the five of them met. They were all in the same unit on his last tour. He was confident they'd work well together. When I first read it I thought it said that he was shaky about remembering the details, but I misinterpreted. He's talking about his memories of Shakes, and how much Billy Shakes's death upset him. And the section starts with 'Mutant in touch.'"

"Mutant in touch?" Fletcher asked.

"That was Xander's nickname," Susan replied.

"Yes, I know. And he lives somewhere near the Savage River?" Fletcher asked.

"Yes," Susan answered. "But there's no way he'd be involved in this."

Fletcher's eyes grew bright. "I need everything you know about this man, Mrs. Donovan. Everything. I'm afraid he's our last viable option."

"Option for what?" Susan asked.

"Mrs. Donovan, sometimes logic trumps everything else in a murder case. It's becoming rather clear that Alexander Whitfield is involved in your husband's death."

"There's no way. Xander is a good man. The way Eddie talked about him… No. I can't believe that."

Susan hated this. Jesus God, she hated this. All of Eddie's friends dead, and the one left was the one Eddie had the utmost respect for.

"Mrs. Donovan, I'm sorry. I'm not accusing him of anything, not yet. I just need to know what his connection is to the past few weeks of your husband's life. So if you'll indulge me, I'd like to start at the beginning. Let's go over it all again. Tell me about that phone call he received, the one that came on the day he was murdered."

Susan thought back, as painful as it was. Admitting to Sam that she'd been upset with Donovan, that their last words had been slung in anger, made her feel better temporarily, but the guilt was crawling back in. Having to share this with the detective, and Eddie's mother, was making it even worse.

"I thought it was work calling. He answered, said, 'Now?' then hung up and said he had to go."

"Who from work? Did he say? The last call to his cell was from a blocked number. Everyone I talked to at the Raptor offices said they hadn't been in touch. They all check out—no call was made to your husband's phone from their offices. So why did you think it was work related?"

"I don't know. He didn't say. I…I was upset with him, asked him to blow it off, and he just shut down. He did that sometimes. Especially when we talked about work. Just got cold and turned off. "

"So the call could have been from anyone. You just assumed it was from work."

"Yes, but…I'm so confused. He was killed near his office, right? Where else would he have been going?"

"These are all valid questions, Mrs. Donovan, and I'm doing my best to find out the answers. Did your husband like his job?"

"I think so. He seemed to. I wanted him to quit, but I already told you that."

"Tell me again," Fletcher said.

Susan leaned against the granite counter. She wasn't terribly proud of how she felt, but she was trying to do what was best for her family.

"He'd done his time. Three tours. And he was finally out. But then he went to work for Raptor, with a bunch of his ex-Army buddies. I felt like Raptor was too close to the military, and I wanted him all the way out. But working there, that kept his hand in the game. They send contractors over to the war zones to manage transitional training for the Iraqi and Afghan governments. Even if the war was over tomorrow and all the troops came home, Raptor's operators would still be there to help train people, rebuild the infrastructure, all of that."

"But he didn't travel overseas."

"Not to the Middle East, no. Eddie was responsible for security for the people who came over here. Allan Culpepper kept him jumping all the time. He's the heart of Raptor. That's who I'd assumed called. It would take a lot for Eddie to be pulled away. He'd promised us the afternoon. It had been arranged for weeks."

"I spoke with Allan Culpepper. He thought the world of your husband." Fletcher was getting a little red in the face, frustration setting in.

"I know. He came by as soon as he got back from Iraq. He's crushed. He's the man who brought Eddie into Raptor in the first place. He doesn't work for him directly, his boss is Rod Deter. But Allan's been his mentor for a while. They were together in Afghanistan."

Susan felt the wheels spinning in her head as something clicked. "They all served with Allan. Xander, William, Hal, King—Perry Fisher—and Eddie. He was their commander. He took care of them."

Fletcher was taking notes, and Susan shook her head. "I'm sorry I didn't mention this before. Does this help?"

Fletcher looked eager to be away. "I don't know yet, Mrs. Donovan. But I've got a few more places to look, thanks to you. Just one more thing. Did he say he had to go to work? Or that he had to meet someone? Be as specific as you can."

Susan thought about it, mind tuned to that morning. "Honestly, he didn't say. He got the call, and I just assumed they'd called him in. He wasn't specific."

"Are you sure the phone he answered was his regular phone? What did it look like?"

That brought her up short.

"A separate phone?"

"I'm just trying to look at all the angles. The last call to his BlackBerry was a blocked number, but if he had another phone… I've been doing this a long time, and this pops up more often than you'd think. We've interviewed a lot of people, all who worked directly and indirectly with your husband. They swear up and down they didn't call. He could have had a separate phone that we're missing, and the call that caused him to leave came in on that cell. If that's the case, we need to be looking for another."

She thought back. She hadn't looked at the phone. She'd just assumed it was his BlackBerry. They'd all been assuming.

"Honestly, no. I think it was his regular phone. Eddie wasn't the secretive type. And I've been going through the bills with a fine-tooth comb. I haven't seen money going anywhere unusual."

Fletcher looked disappointed.

"We didn't see anything unusual in your financials, either. Well, it was worth a shot. Thank you for your time. I, uh, my partner and I will be at the funeral tomorrow. We know it's going to be a hard day."

"You don't have to do that."

"We want to."

"I appreciate it," Susan said.

He stood and shook hands all around. "If you think of anything else," he said.

Eleanor gave him a tremulous smile. Susan felt horrible for her—she'd lost her only son, and sometimes Susan's own grief got in the way of remembering that.

"Of course. We'll be in touch immediately. Eleanor, I'll see the detective out. You stay here."

Eleanor didn't move, and out of the corner of her eye, Susan saw Sam touch the woman's hand.

Three women, all tied together through one man. All widows. All torn apart like ragged dolls by their loss. Susan just hoped, between the three of them, they could pick up all the pieces again. She shut the door behind the detective and went back to the kitchen.

Sam looked up at her.

"You know why they're coming to the funeral, don't you?"

"To pay their respects."

"To try and catch Xander. They think he'll show. Fletcher thinks he's the killer."

Susan was tired. So tired. She didn't want to think about this anymore. She just wanted a few moments alone to think about Eddie before she had to say goodbye forever.

CHAPTER THIRTY-THREE

Georgetown
Detective Darren Fletcher

Fletcher sat in the car for a moment and processed the conversation he'd just had with Susan Donovan. What stood out to him was her very innocuous statement that Allan Culpepper had been Donovan's commander. That he'd commanded all of the men in the picture. Why hadn't Culpepper bothered to mention that before? Or even Rod Deter? And why wasn't it in the DOD files Felicia had procured for him? It was a big piece of information to leave out of the conversation, and pushed Culpepper right onto Fletcher's list of possible suspects, despite the proven fact that the man was in Iraq during the murders. Paperwork could be faked, altered, falsified. And the people at Raptor had the technological know-how to do just that.

Fletcher had to locate Alexander Whitfield. Whitfield was involved, no question. And now that he knew Whitfield knew Culpepper, the possibilities were endless. He pulled out the card Culpepper had given him and rang the man.

Culpepper answered almost immediately.

"I'm sorry to bother you, Colonel. But something's come up. Do you know a man named Alexander Whitfield?"

"Yes, of course. Great soldier. Very capable. Good friends with Donovan, as I recall."

"Have you seen him lately?"

"No. It's been years. Heard he went out in the woods somewhere, and didn't come back. Sometimes war does that to a man. The regular world doesn't make sense anymore...."

"Is there any reason he might hold a grudge against Raptor? Or against you?"

Culpepper was quiet for a moment. "Not that I know of. But anything's possible. Are you saying...? Do you think he's responsible? Could I be in danger?"

"Like you said, anything's possible. I know you're leaving the country tomorrow, but I'd be extra careful with my security if I were you."

"Understood."

"Good. One last question. Could Donovan have had a separate phone that was issued to him through Raptor, outside of his BlackBerry?"

"Not issued through Raptor, no. We give them the BlackBerry, and a laptop, it's all paid for, but that's it. Now, our overseas operators have satellite phones, and if he were ever traveling outside the U.S., he'd be issued one. But he hasn't been traveling outside our borders lately. We keep the electronics on a tight leash, as you can imagine. The Pentagon would be pissed if we let something like that slide."

They shared a strained laugh. "I can imagine. Okay. There is one last thing."

"Anything, son."

Son. Disarming. Personal.

"You didn't mention that you'd commanded Donovan overseas."

There was a beat pause. "I thought you knew that already. It's not a secret."

"I see. And the rest of the men from the unit? They were all your soldiers, correct?"

"My soldiers. Yes, they were. We were like a family—and even though many of us had gone our separate ways, they all feel like sons to me. So you can imagine how upset I am at their senseless loss. Will that be all, Detective?"

"I'm sorry to have to share this news with you over the phone, but we've found William Everett's body. He appears to have committed suicide."

"Oh, dear God. Another?"

"Yes, sir. My condolences."

There was silence on the other end of the phone, and Fletcher waited a few moments before speaking again.

"Colonel? I'm sorry, but I need to go. Again, please accept my deepest condolences on your loss."

"Yes. Thank you. Please, if you find anything…"

Fletcher could swear he heard tears in the old soldier's voice. He didn't know why that felt wrong, somehow.

"Of course," Fletcher replied, and hung up. He called Hart next, told him the developments and asked him to come back in. Hart didn't mind. He said he'd meet him in an hour downtown.

Fletcher made a few calls, initiated some checks on

Culpepper's background, but still had some time to kill. And he was right around the corner from the Croswell crime scene.

That whole thing seemed hinky to him. The 9-1-1 call on Croswell's murder was done anonymously, from a prepaid cell phone. Croswell's cell phone also had a call from a blocked number, at 6:50 p.m. on the day of his death. And Donovan had received a call, too. If Fletcher was a betting man, he'd say the same disposable phone made all three calls, but it was going to take time to prove that theory.

And so far, they'd been unable to tie Croswell to the Emerson house. Calls to Mrs. Emerson had yielded exactly squat. She'd never heard of Harold Croswell. She was horrified that a murder had happened in her house, was winging her way home to deal with the crime scene cleaners and the rest of the craziness that ensued. She was being incredibly cooperative. Fletcher's instincts said she was telling the truth.

So why there? What was so important about that house?

Someone must have known that it stood empty.

Yesterday, when Fletcher and Hart had recanvassed the neighborhood where Harold Croswell was murdered, there were more people gone than home. Maybe at this time of day, there'd be a few folks around who might have seen something.

It only took five minutes to drive to the scene of the second murder.

The sun was going to set shortly. Pink clouds edged in gold billowed through the sky, and the street was bathed in a rosy glow. Children played on the sidewalks. Parents stood in front of the town houses, keeping a close eye on them while catching up with the neighbors. It was a cozy little scene, one that immediately became curious. Stares followed him as his car rolled down the street. By now, everyone who lived nearby knew that a murder had been committed just a few houses away. It had to be unnerving. He was counting on that to loosen some tongues.

He pulled up in front of a knot of people two houses away from the Emerson place.

A slightly overweight man with a noticeable monk spot walked over to the car as Fletcher exited the vehicle.

"Oh, good, you're here. That was quick."

"Detective Darren Fletcher, Metro Homicide. There's a problem?"

"Uh, yeah? We called about Roy."

Roy?

"I'm sorry, sir. I was coming to the neighborhood on another matter. What seems to be the issue?"

The man pointed across the street. Fletcher recognized the house—he and Hart had talked to the woman the morning of the Croswell murder. Oh…that's right. He searched his memory for the name, but the neighbor jumped in and gave it to him.

"Roy Lyons. He's camped out on poor Maggie's porch. Roaring drunk, from the looks of it, and he keeps yelling at the door. We told him she wasn't there, but he won't listen. *This* has happened before." The tone of righteous indignation almost made Fletcher smile. Almost.

"Well, let me go talk to him and see what his problem is. Thanks for the heads-up."

"Certainly." The man turned back to his friends, and

they all watched Fletcher walk across the street. He could feel their eyes on him.

Fletch could smell Lyons from five feet away. He reeked of old booze and damp cigarettes. Sweat mingled with the miasma. His hair was disheveled, his eyes bloodshot. He had the look of a former athlete gone to seed.

"Mr. Lyons? Is there something I can help you with?"

The man's eyes rolled Fletcher's way. He didn't move from his slump. His words were slurry. "Get the bitch to open the door, that's what."

Fletcher pulled out his badge. "Sir, I'm going to have to ask you to step off the porch. Can you come down here so we can talk for a moment?"

"I ain't going nowhere. I gotta talk to Maggie."

"The neighbors say she isn't there."

"They always say that. She's there. I saw the cake on the table. The brat had a birthday. I can't believe she lets my sons near that bastard."

Fletcher felt a moment's alarm. He remembered Maggie Lyons now. Lawyer. Said her husband was a deadbeat, and her kid was having a birthday. But that was three days ago.

"Near who, sir?"

"Jennifer Jill." He sneered the words, the anger in his voice palpable. "I ain't paying jack shit for that brat. It ain't mine. Bitch cheated on me. Wants to go to law school, she says. Wants me to pay for it. Raise the brat. Fuck that shit."

The logic of the very inebriated was sometimes hard to follow. Fletcher tried again. "Mr. Lyons, could I ask for you to start at the beginning? I'm afraid I don't have the background information on your ex-wife."

Lyons closed his eyes for a moment, then opened them. They were still relatively unfocused, and his words were even more slurred.

"Fine. It's a short enough story. *I* was here taking care of our family. Our house. Keeping the roof over our heads. *She* came back knocked up. Simple as that. I divorce *her* sorry ass, can prove adultery, but *she* gets the kids. And they make *me* pay *her*. I told 'em, hell no. I ain't paying for some other dude's kid. So they garnishee my wages. Now I'm out of my money, and I'm about to be out of a job. I need to talk to her, make her see reason. I can't pay for my own apartment."

Fletcher felt comfortable enough to take his hand off his weapon, and leaned against the porch. The man was blindingly drunk, enough to fall if he stood, and Fletcher was reasonably confident that wasn't going to happen any time soon. He'd had enough practice with drunks to recognize one about to keel over. And this was interesting information. A less threatening stance might yield more.

"Sir, could you be more specific? Mrs. Lyons returned home from where?"

"Afghanistan, dumb ass. She's rolling in dough, gets that military pension and shit."

Fletcher's mouth dropped open.

"Your wife was in Afghanistan?"

"Yeah. She was in charge of present...present... presenting... 'Scuse me." Lyons pulled himself to a semistanding position and vomited over the side of the porch. Fletcher pulled the collar of his shirt over his nose in disgust. Good grief.

When he'd finished, Lyons straightened and held on to the railing for balance. "So you shee, I need to get in and talk to her. She's rolling in dough, and I got nothing. And she needs to know I ain't paying jack for that brat."

And with that last valiant proclamation, Lyons's eyes rolled back in his head and he went down in a heap on the porch. Passed out cold.

Fletcher checked his pulse, put a cushion from the chair under his head and knocked on the door.

"Mrs. Lyons? Metro Police. Open the door. It's safe."

Nothing. Crickets. Literally.

The people down the street were watching him with interest now.

He tried the door. Not surprisingly, it was locked. He reached down and felt for Lyons's pulse, found it strong and steady. The man wasn't in immediate danger, then. He called in to dispatch, explained what was happening, asked that an ambulance be sent to the address to cart off Roy Lyons, and a backup patrol officer, then walked around to the rear of the house.

There was a nice garden back here, with a pretty little deck covered in potted plants. He walked up on the deck, peered into the kitchen and witnessed exactly what Roy Lyons had alleged: four plates on the table, surrounding a half-eaten birthday cake.

Except Fletcher knew that cake was three days old.

Exigent circumstances. He used a branch to break the glass pane near the knob and opened the French door from the inside. He didn't smell anything noticeable, which slowed his heart rate only the slightest bit. He made a pass through the house. Prayed he wasn't going to find Maggie Lyons and her three kids lying dead in their rooms.

They weren't. The house was clear. He didn't know

whether to be relieved or angry. He chose anger. It looked like someone had left in a hurry. Probably right after they'd rolled away.

"Son of a bitch!"

Fletcher went back out on the deck and kicked the potted plant closest to the door. What an idiot he was. Maggie Lyons had lied right to his face, and he'd seen it. He'd seen her flinch when he mentioned Harold Croswell's name, even as she denied ever hearing of the man. Damn it. He'd even made himself a note to check her out, then gotten dragged off in a different direction. Now, three days later, he finds out she was in Afghanistan, too? No way that was a coincidence.

He returned to the front of the house. The ambulance was coming down the street. Fletcher caught the eye of the man he'd been talking to when he first arrived, signaled for him to come over. Monk Spot hurried to him, happy to be of service now that the situation had gotten more interesting.

"What's your name, sir?"

"Frank Wright."

"Mr. Wright, you said you told Roy Lyons Maggie wasn't home, is that right? You knew that definitively?" *Wright, right. Is that right, Mr. Wright?* Good grief, he was starting to sound like Dr. Seuss.

"Yes, sir. She and the kids left the same day you were here for the murder across the way. Like she was taking them to school, but they had bags. Bags bigger than what the kids normally carried. They were brown. Looked military. And her little girl was crying."

Fletcher eyed the man. That was an awful lot of detail. "And you just happened to notice this why?"

Frank Wright blushed. "Well…Maggie's a hot piece of ass. You know how it is."

"So you're stalking her?"

"No." Wright had the audacity to look upset. "Not at all. I just like watching her. She's pretty, that's all. I was out on my porch watching the brouhaha and noticed her leaving. She's a friend. Don't make it sound so dirty."

"You didn't talk to her, did you? Ask her where she was headed?"

"No."

Fletcher just shook his head. "Thank you for your help, sir."

"You aren't going to mention this to my wife, are you?"

Fletcher tossed a glance over his shoulder at the man and didn't answer. Let him sweat.

He flipped open his phone and called Hart.

"We're going to need a warrant for 67435 N Street. Computers included. And everything we can find out about Maggie Lyons."

Hart was quiet for a moment. "The chick from the Croswell scene?"

"Lonnie, you've got a memory like a steel vault. The very one. I stopped by to see if some more people were at home, had a nice chat with her very drunk ex-husband. She served in Afghanistan. House is empty, but no signs of a struggle. That's too close for comfort. She's moved pretty high up my suspect list now. I'm going to go talk to some more of the neighbors, see what I can get about her. Hurry, okay?"

He hung up and realized he was smiling. Two hours ago, he had no leads. Now he had two, and maybe three. Sometimes, he really did like being a cop.

CHAPTER THIRTY-FOUR

Arlington National Cemetery
Dr. Samantha Owens

White marble gravestones marched in perfect unison for thousands of yards across the undulating green hills of Arlington. Sam had never been inside the gates before. She'd seen it, no one could drive by without seeing it, but being there was more than overwhelming. All these men and women, dead in the service of their country. All of them dead and lost, and so often, their sacrifices simply forgotten. It boggled the mind, especially when she thought about the fact that this was simply a fraction of all the deaths. She wondered what they would do when they ran out of land, and then quickly prayed that day would never come.

The noises that accompany a military funeral are different than those of civilians. Clicking, tapping, the unified march of soldiers' feet as they escort the horse-drawn limber and caisson that carries the flag-draped coffin. The snap of the ceremonial flag as it's raised from its last spread and precisely folded into a crisp triangle. The three-volley shots fired in the ultimate last salute, cracking through the still air. The haunting, solitary loneliness of the bugler in his red cap, the song of the night, of the dead, "Taps," mournfully flowing from his pursed lips. The sobbing, accompanied by soft, inadequate words of comfort. Through all of that, the meticulousness and timing were flawless. As if emotions could be contained by perfection, tradition and stoic discipline.

Seeing the world Donovan had left her for—the pageantry, the unassailable honor—for the first time was eye-opening, and did help assuage her grief, in a way. It was nice to see them show him such respect. To see the throngs of people out to honor their fallen comrade. To get a glimpse of the ceremony with which he served. The vast majority of the men in uniform around her had the distinctive yellow-and-black Ranger tab on their left shoulder. A line from Shakespeare floated in her head: "We few, we happy few, we band of brothers…"

Brothers in arms.

She knew Eddie's life in the military had been hard. She knew how much pain and suffering went into his preparation, and how even the difficulties of the elite training for Ranger school couldn't have possibly prepared him for the realities of war. That was something you had to experience to fully grasp. Words on the page couldn't do it justice. PowerPoints and lectures from combat veterans couldn't do it justice. Training that left you sweating, delirious and starving in a Florida jungle or atop a north Georgia mountain couldn't do it justice. Only truly being in the fight—seeing blood spill from a wound, feeling the dead weight of an unconscious man on your back, watching a leg or arm be blown off, or watching a Bradley fighting vehicle catch on fire after being hit with an RPG, its occupants stuck inside, feeling hot bullets whizzing by your head turning your guts to water, screams of pain and fear—that, that could give war its due. As could putting those soldiers in the ground.

And as a leader who also had medical training, Donovan was faced with the worst of the worst. He had to charge forward and pass by the dying and wounded on both sides as the battle raged around him, focus on keeping his men alive and accomplishing the mission. Sam imagined that's why he sometimes disobeyed protocol and worked on his own people; being a doctor, even one who dropped out of school, the desire to help was ingrained into your being.

The reality of war was this: men and women laid down their lives. Willingly. Knowing that each day might be their last. It was a kind of courage that was unfathomable to most people. And it never seemed to end. Sadly, Donovan's interment was one of twenty-seven scheduled for the day, on the low end of average for Arlington. And they were just one military cemetery.

Some asked what was the point? There is no real reason for our soldiers to die in foreign lands.

Sam was no apologist. She'd tell them straight out that the sacrifices made allowed us the freedom to demand those answers. That liberty wasn't universal, and that all free men and women deserved the same power to question as we do. She believed in what Donovan did. Believed it in her soul. Maybe that's why she never fought for him, never tried to get him to stay. He was a good and honorable man who would make sure to defend his country with all of his being, even if it meant laying down his life to do so. She didn't fight the breakup because she respected his cause too deeply.

The honor guard who acted as the pallbearers committed themselves well. Sam couldn't imagine how taxing it must be for those young men, knew they competed long and hard to become the deads' witness. Even the horses had a certain dignity, as if they knew how vital they were to the process. The Donovans' priest stood to the side as people Sam didn't recognize spoke words of glory and humility, all of them bathed in a white glow from the sun's reflection. Sam couldn't get "The Battle Hymn of the Republic" out of her head; stood there silently singing "Glory, Glory, Hallelujah" over and over and over instead of washing her hands.

The red roses on the wreath by the coffin were like drops of blood against the white marble and green grass backdrop.

Sam had stepped back from Eddie's family when they arrived at the grave site, was out of eyeshot, watching. Trying to cope with the tearing grief that coursed through her veins as the ceremony proceeded. She wiped tears from her eyes and pushed her sunglasses higher on her nose. She wanted to be anywhere but here. She thought Susan was handling herself beautifully. She had Vicky in her lap, was holding Ally's hand. Her head was high, the pride in her husband and his accomplishments visible. She was strong. Sam envied her that strength.

Fletcher and his younger partner, Lonnie Hart, were on the opposite side of the grave from her. She watched them standing straight, their shoulders back, their sunglasses on, as well, knowing they were like hawks soaring over the trees, waiting for a vole to show its naked nose to the sky so they could swoop down and grab their tasty meal.

She'd disassociated herself from the situation. She had to. She had cheated. She took a full Ativan before they left, knowing she couldn't make it through the day without chemical support. She didn't think anyone would hold it against her.

Things were wrapping up, it seemed. Susan had been presented with Donovan's medals. She clutched the flag and the letter from the Army's chief of staff and stared blankly at Donovan's elegant, now-bare coffin. Eleanor was pale and breathing hard, trying to keep herself in check. Without their mother to hold them, the girls were lost and uncomprehending. Ally cried when the guns went off.

And then it was truly over. Susan touched her hand to the coffin, encouraged the girls to do the same with a whisper, then turned and walked away, her back straight, her shoulders square. The daughter, and the wife, of a soldier.

She knew what was going through Susan's mind. She'd done the same thing with Simon, after the memorial service. Sam bit her lip and tried not to embarrass them all by crying out.

She walked twenty paces away, stopped by a huge old maple tree, and gathered herself.

"That was beautiful." A soft voice to Sam's right pulled her back. A tall man with dark hair and soulful eyes was standing next to her.

"Yes, it was," she said, voice still shaky.

"You a friend of the deceased? Or a friend of his wife?"

"I'm sorry, who are you?"

He slipped a card into her hand. "My name is Gino Taranto. I'm with the *Daily News*."

"And why is the media here?" Sam asked.

"Paying respects. You ever hear of friendly fire?"

"Of course."

"You ever hear of Major Donovan involved in a friendly fire incident?"

"No. Why?"

"You might want to clue in the cops over there to take a look at the records from Jalalabad, 2007. Might help them figure out who killed Major Donovan."

Sam turned to the man. He had a beard, and long shaggy hair. The exact opposite of all the buttoned-down soldiers showing their respect to Donovan by being perfectly squared away. His juxtaposition was almost violent, and Sam felt anger bubble inside her. *You could have at least dressed and combed your hair to show your respect. Jerk. Probably one of those assholes who protest at soldiers' funerals.* She turned a cold shoulder, let her words cut.

"You should tell them yourself. If you have information about the murders—"

"And get fired? My bosses would shoot me on the spot for giving information to a cop. That's not my job."

"Then why tell me? Why not write about it?"

He put his finger to his lips dramatically in a hush sign. "Let's just say someone gagged me. And I know you've been working with them. You'll tell them to look deeper, and keep me out of it."

"I won't do any such thing." But he was already moving away from her, getting lost in the throngs of people moving back toward the road. She watched him go, confused. Why come to her? Why not go directly to the family? What the hell kind of journalist was Gino Taranto, anyway?

She realized that she was one of the few people left near the grave, and her heart sank. This was the part she couldn't handle. Walking away. Leaving them behind, alone. But there was no choice. This was what had to happen. She pushed the slovenly reporter from her mind and turned to Donovan's casket.

She whispered a prayer, a poor substitute for saying goodbye, and turned away, the cracks in her heart opening wide. Everyone she had loved, had given her heart to, gone.

To distract herself, she glanced down at the card the reporter had put into her hand. It wasn't a normal business card. It had *Gino Taranto—Daily News* handwritten on the front. No address. No phone number. No way of contacting him directly. Weird. She flipped it over and saw more writing on the back. Numbers, to be specific.

39-40'58" N 079-12'25" W

What in the world?

"Who was that you were talking to?"

She'd been so absorbed in what she was doing that she hadn't noticed Hart walk up beside her. She saw Fletcher over his shoulder on the phone.

She carefully put the card into her purse. For some reason, the first thought she had was not to tell Hart everything. And that was insane. She knew better.

"Some reporter. Said his name was Taranto from the *Daily News*. He said something about Donovan being involved in a friendly fire incident while he was in Afghanistan."

Hart knitted his brows. "We haven't heard anything like that. Fletch! Heya, Fletch!"

Fletcher held up a finger, the universal gesture for just a minute. He finished his call, then walked over.

"No one seems to have seen Whitfield. Damn, I really thought he'd be here."

"Some reporter talked to the Doc over here, said Donovan was involved in a friendly fire incident. Taranto, from the *Daily*. You know him?"

"Yeah. You know him, too, we talked to him about that jumper last month. Remember? Writes that column on DOD every week. He's not a friend of the military."

"Wait a minute," Hart said. "What did he say to you, Doc?"

"Nothing, really. Small talk."

"Do you see him anywhere?"

Sam looked around. There were still people milling about, but no one who remotely resembled the man she'd talked to. She shook her head. "No. He dropped the bombshell and walked away before I had a chance to ask more. Why?"

Hart looked at Fletcher. "Dude that was talking to her wasn't short and bald like Taranto. He was six-one, built, with a full head of hair and a beard."

"Fuck me!" Fletcher threw his phone down, drawing the disapproving stare of a uniform-clad passerby.

Hart got on his walkie, taking off at a jog toward the visitor's center. She could hear him yelling into the mouthpiece: "He's here, he's here."

Sam realized what they were talking about at last. She blamed the Ativan for making her dopey. She hadn't been talking to some beatnik reporter or war protestor.

She'd just had close and personal contact with their number-one suspect.

CHAPTER THIRTY-FIVE

Arlington National Cemetery
Dr. Samantha Owens

Fletcher was very unhappy with Sam. She'd apologized about fifty times, but he was still rigidly upset, the lines of his face tight and drawn, his shoulders combatively forward as he towered over her.

"Why didn't you signal, or call out? My God, Hart was right there."

"I'm *sorry.* I told you, I didn't know it was him. He looks different than the photo. He wasn't wearing sunglasses, to start, and he had a beard and long hair. He wasn't dressed like the other soldiers. And I wasn't... I was... Well, hell, Fletcher, I loved Donovan, too. I was saying goodbye to him, not looking for a killer. That's *your* job."

That calmed him down. Fletcher ran his hands through his hair. "I know, I know. I understand. Run me through it again. Anything you can think of. What exactly did he look like? What was he wearing? Did he smell like cigarettes?"

She went through it again and again, leaving out only the little bit of information that he'd handed her a card. She was being an idiot. She knew that. But she wanted to see what the numbers meant before she shared with them. Whitfield, if that was him, had approached her for a reason, and as much as she wanted to see Donovan's killer caught and punished, something told her there was more to Whitfield's involvement than met the eye. Donovan trusted Xander. His feelings on the man's character and integrity were clear in the journal. She decided she would honor those thoughts until Whitfield proved himself a villain, beyond a reasonable doubt.

Fletcher stowed his notebook in his back pocket. "All right. You did good. I know you want to get to the reception."

"Not really," Sam said. "But I don't think I have much of a choice. I'll be at Eleanor's if you need me."

"You need a ride?"

Sam looked at the string of cars leaving the cemetery and realized that, yes, she did need a ride. She'd come over with a friend of Susan's, not wanting to intrude on the family in their limousine, and the woman had obviously forgotten her, or figured she was catching a ride with another, and left.

"Come on," Fletcher said.

She followed him to the nondescript unmarked. Hart was already leaning against the car, waiting. Fletcher barked instructions as he walked around to the driver's side.

"We're going to give Dr. Owens a ride to the reception. Then I'm going to go talk to Taranto. You stick around the reception, see if Whitfield shows his face again, comes back to show his respects to the wife privately. And get someone you trust to watch this grave site overnight."

"Got it."

They climbed in, Sam in the back feeling strangely like a fugitive, especially considering her white lie to the detectives. She debated telling them about the card again, then stopped. She was breaking every rule she knew, but something told her to hold off.

Donovan, you're going to be the death of me.

Fletcher got on the phone to someone named Danny, asked him to track down the real reporter and get Fletcher on his schedule ASAP. He hung up after a few minutes and looked in the rearview mirror.

"So, Doc. We have another piece of the puzzle. Want to hear?"

"Lay it on me," Sam said.

"Woman who lives across the street from the scene where Hal Croswell was killed? Name's Margaret Lyons. Goes by Maggie. Three kids. Disappeared off the face of the earth the same day we found Croswell's body. Hasn't shown up for work, kids haven't shown up for school. Turns out she served in the same region in Afghanistan as Donovan's crew. What do you make of that?"

Sam didn't hesitate. "There are two possible scenarios that come to mind. Either she's the killer, and you got too close and she split, or she's a victim, like the rest of them."

"Mighty convenient that Croswell was killed in a house that Lyons knew was empty. She was the one who told us the owner travels all the time. She'd be in a position to know."

"That's true. But I thought you had Whitfield pegged as the main suspect?"

"We have several leads we're pursuing right now." He emphasized the *several,* which made Sam think he still wasn't sharing everything he knew. Either not sharing, or at a loss and not as good a detective as she needed him to be. She tucked that into her head while he continued.

"It's possible that Maggie Lyons is in it with Whitfield. Her husband, drunken lout that he is, claims she came back from Afghanistan preggers, and insists the kid isn't his. He divorced her over it. We got a brief look at her financials last night, and she's got a steady stream of income that's unaccountable. Just a little extra each month. It helps keep her afloat."

"Being paid off?"

"That's a distinct possibility. Maybe being paid to keep quiet about something? Or her ex is right and the kid isn't his, and the real father is making some sort of off-the-books child support payment?"

Sam looked out the window. They were driving over the Key Bridge, the Potomac River murky below them. She saw the fine square outline of the Kennedy Center reflected in the waters, the elegant white marble structure perched on the eastern bank of the river, and wished things were easier. She used to spend a lot of time at the Kennedy Center.

"Detective Fletcher, maybe you need to listen to what this Taranto guy has to say. Maybe the key to all of this is an incident that occurred in Afghanistan, and has nothing to do with Donovan and Croswell here in the

States. Did you ever speak with that Culpepper man again? His mentor? I didn't find a lot in Donovan's journal referencing him, outside of the fact that he was one of his favorite commanders, though I can go back and look some more. I'd need his nickname—that's the biggest problem. Donovan's shorthand used the nicknames for his compatriots."

"You didn't see Culpepper? He was at the funeral. The tall gray-haired man wearing a chestful of medals who spoke at the end. We've talked a couple of times. He's been…very helpful. Donovan didn't have a second phone issued by Raptor."

She watched Fletcher for a moment. "Culpepper is a suspect, too?"

"He was their commander in Afghanistan."

"But I thought he was out of the country when the murders took place."

"He was. Doesn't mean I don't have my eye on him. He might not have held the gun, but the man does own a firm that employs mercenaries. He certainly knows enough killers to arrange a murder. I've already been lied to once by a suspect in this case. Right now, everyone is in play as far as I'm concerned."

When Sam returned to Eleanor's, the post-burial reception was well under way. The house was full of people. Some cried, some gawked, some got quietly drunk in the corner. Eleanor was shell-shocked, too busy keeping everyone in food and drinks to grieve with them, and Susan had stepped out onto the back porch with the girls to have a private moment.

Hart walked Sam around to each guest personally, but unless Whitfield was a master of disguise, he wasn't there. Finally excusing her from her manhunt duties, he went to the kitchen for some coffee, and Sam took the opportunity to escape upstairs. It was quiet in her room. Blissfully quiet. She shut the door and it seemed the whole world disappeared, leaving her alone for the first time in hours.

She'd been a solitary being for so long that she forgot what it was like to be around people all the time. Work was a different story—there she was focused on the task at hand and the people were fully under her control. She could close the door to her office and be assured no one would bother her, go home and turn off the phone, revel, or wallow, in the silence. Here, in D.C., she was at their mercy, and she was starting to get frachetty. Between Susan and Eleanor and Fletcher, someone was always calling, or wanting to feed her, or ask questions or talk earnestly, and it was wearing her out.

Despite that weariness, Sam realized that something had changed. She hadn't had the urge to wash her hands at all today. Something in her deep and abiding grief had altered, and she wanted a little time and space to figure out what was happening.

She pulled her laptop from her bag and opened it. It booted quickly, and she went to Google immediately. She typed in "Friendly Fire Edward Donovan Afghanistan."

There was nothing that stood out. She surfed through to a few sites, but none of the references were about her Donovan.

Then she pulled the card Whitfield had given her out of her wallet and looked at the numbers. Typed them into Google, as well.

A fraction of a second later, up popped a map with

the header "Savage River State Park and National Forest."

Coordinates. The numbers were latitude and longitude. She couldn't believe she hadn't seen that before. Blaming grief for making her senseless, she brought up several more maps and looked through them all. The coordinates seemed to be rather general. The closest thing to them was probably the forest ranger station.

Sam resisted smacking herself on the forehead. Well, of course it was. Donovan was an Airborne Ranger, and so was Whitfield. With a bit of cunning, he was telling her where to look. Where to find him.

"See anything interesting?"

Sam jumped, turning toward the voice. Hart. Standing in her open door, his arms crossed nonchalantly.

"Don't you knock?" she snapped, hitting the screen saver so the page disappeared.

"When I'm trying to sneak up on someone, generally not. Shoulda locked your door. I saw Whitfield hand you something, and you didn't tell us. Naughty-naughty. So, give—what was it?"

Busted. Sam didn't even bother pretending. What was the point now? She had the information she needed. So Fletcher and Hart would, as well. She'd insist on going along, that's all. She would find a way to talk to Whitfield without their overbearing presence making him disappear. She hoped.

She held out the card. Hart turned it over in his hands.

"Lat and long? For where?" He sounded genuinely curious.

"Savage River State Park. A ranger station."

"Clever." Hart pulled out his cell phone, hit a single number. Calling his partner, of course. The tattletale.

"Not answering. I'll leave him a message. Fletch, we got a little trip to take. Probable location of Alexander Whitfield. Call when you're done talking to Taranto." He hung up and looked at Sam disapprovingly. "I thought you of all people knew better. Withholding vital evidence? There is a better than fifty-fifty chance that this man is a killer."

"I know that."

"So now you cope with loss by being stupid?"

"Hey," Sam shot back. "Mind your own business."

"Sweetheart…" The look on her face must have been terrifying. "Dr. Owens," he began again. "You know better than this. Three people are dead. One whole family is missing. For all we know, you've read something in the journals that Whitfield thinks can tie him to the murders, and this is a well-planned trap to get you off on your own, away from our protection. Out in the wilderness, where no one will know where you've gone. It's pretty easy to hide a body in the woods, you know. Takes a while for us to track it down."

Sam hadn't considered that she might be a target. That thought was sobering, to say the least. She hadn't felt threatened by Whitfield in any way at the funeral. Of course, as Hart pointed out, that was probably the idea. Spider to the fly. Coaxing her into a web of deceit. Sadly, she found herself unafraid. She didn't have any reservations about putting herself in harm's way. Not anymore.

"I'm coming with you," Sam said.

Hart's phone rang. He opened and listened, then nodded curtly and said, "Yeah. On our way." He shoved the phone in his pocket and said, "Yes, you are. Pack a bag. We'll be gone overnight. But first, we need to make a stop. You want to play detective? Now's your chance."

CHAPTER THIRTY-SIX

Washington, D.C.
Dr. Samantha Owens

Sam edged her way into the Old Ebbitt Grill. She stood by the hostess stand for a moment to get her bearings and quickly felt her ears start to ring. It was incredibly loud. Thursday night happy hour, and the place was packed. When she'd lived in D.C., Thursday was the night to go out. It was meant for singles, and new couples, a night to cast inhibitions to the wind and get gloriously, achingly polluted. Thursdays lasted well into Friday, the lines between the two blurring after too many pitchers accompanied by too many shots, and she'd spent more than one Friday morning in class hosting a wicked hangover. It had been well known in D.C. that Friday morning was not the time to schedule important meetings. She assumed that held true even now.

Back then, this bar had been filled to the gills with people both important and wanting to be, and cigar and cigarette smoke hung thick in the air. It was a stone's throw from the White House and political operatives had graced its hallowed halls for decades. Deals were cut in the red leather booths, leaning onto one of four long bars, on the stairs down to the marble bathrooms. Deals and assignations and every other kind of vice— Old Ebbitt's was more than a legend. It was a king maker.

And now, the crowd was even larger and infinitely more hip: every third person was staring at their palm, where tiny devices connected them to the world beyond. The Information Age. Sam found it sad. There was no real sense of being anywhere anymore. Whatever world you were in, the world you could reach through your screen was much more enticing. Why bother going out with friends at all if all you wanted to do was talk to the people who were absent?

She'd had a friend like that once. A girl who was only around Sam when there was nothing better to do, no cooler, hipper places to go or people to be with. That's exactly what this technological phenomenon reminded her of.

Sam miraculously found an empty stool halfway down the front bar and watched the women around her flirt with the men, and they in return, with interest akin to horror. It was lost on her, this sly byplay between a man and a woman: the slitted eyes with heavy-lidded, lingering glances; the engaging half smile, lips pouting so their fullness was accentuated, showing just a little teeth in a brief flash of white; hanging on every word as if it were the most important thing said on earth; the well-timed touch on the shoulder that screamed, *Tell me more, and remember, I'm stunning,* without making it seem too desperate.

She didn't know how to do that anymore. The idea

actually made her skin crawl. Which was sad, considering. She'd always been a sexual creature, at least until Simon died. Now she was shriveled up, completely uninterested in sex. Clinically, she wondered how long that would last. The body was biologically designed for pleasure, for the comforts of intimacy. In denying herself, what was she accomplishing?

No, she wasn't really denying herself. She'd been in a fog for two years, a fog of grief and loneliness and horrifying emptiness. Sex was about the last thing she wanted, or needed.

But she was a realist. Eventually those urges would come back. Just thinking about it made her ache with longing, and disgust. She couldn't even imagine being with someone other than Simon. Hadn't, since he died. But being here, thinking of Donovan, she was increasingly unable to separate the memories of them out of bed from those of them in bed. Eight out of every ten conversations she and Donovan had were horizontal. It was part of the allure.

It had been a long, long time since she'd thought of another man's body. And now, memories of both of the men she'd loved mingled in her head, each vying for attention. She'd done a psychiatry rotation, she understood what was happening. Acceptance. Accepting the fact that her grief was changing, becoming something less sharp to hold in her hands, to shield her from the world.

Her bed was cold and unforgiving now, but she missed being touched. She missed the soft caresses, the lingering kisses, the warm familiarity of sleeping next to someone.

Feeling lonely was a long way from wanting to flirt.

She wasn't ready. She didn't even pretend that she was. Yet sitting in the bar at Old Ebbitt's, she quickly understood that if she were ready, she'd have no shortage of choices. Men from three sides leaned in to see her, and a couple of women did, as well. The knowledge gave her the tiniest bit of comfort, even as she prayed to Simon for forgiveness. These weren't appropriate thoughts for a widow.

She felt a hand on her shoulder. A short, muscular man, his mustache and eyebrows incredibly full and dark brown, with no hair on his head, was standing next to her, eyes darting around the restaurant. He looked like a miniature G. Gordon Liddy, who she'd seen plenty of times in this establishment back in the day. This must be the real Gino Taranto.

"I got a table over there," he shouted. He jerked his head toward the back of the restaurant, started walking. Sam got up and followed him. He let her slide into the booth before he joined her on the opposite side. The din was manageable back here, a cicadalike buzz replacing the meat market's squalling racket.

A server rushed over to greet them. Sam ordered a Lagavulin. Taranto looked impressed and asked for a Yuengling. The waiter dropped some bread on the table and scurried away. Now they were alone.

"So," Sam said. "Why am I here? Why couldn't you just meet Detec—"

"Shhhh!" Taranto glanced over his shoulder before leaning across the table. "You hot?"

"Not really. It's a little stuffy in here, but I'm all right."

Taranto rolled his eyes. "Lady, I ain't talking about the temperature. Are you *hot*. Wired."

It took Sam a second. "Oh. No. I'm not wearing a wire."

"You'll forgive me for not believing you. Slide the shirt down a little."

She looked him straight in his beady little eyes. "I'll do no such thing. I told you I'm not taping you. Either you believe me, or we're done." She started to stand and he grabbed her arm.

"Okay, okay. Just don't use my name."

"Why, exactly, can't you talk to—"

"'Cause I can't be seen out talking to cops. It ain't safe. I ain't safe. I'm meetin' you against my better judgment. But Mutant said you could be trusted, thought Chevy could, too. Remember that. No names."

Chevy? Who the hell... Oh, Chevy Chase. Fletch. Chevy was Fletch. Clever. Mutant, she knew, was Alexander Whitfield. She wondered when she was going to get a code name. What would it be? Bones? Legs? More like Ass, hers was getting big enough for its own zip code. She hadn't been working out a lot. She knew she was too thin, but all her muscle tone was gone. She'd gotten flabby. Things were spreading in all the wrong directions.

Sam, really.

She tried to refocus.

"I'm sorry, Mr. Taranto. Cloak and dagger isn't exactly my strong suit. I'm a medical examiner, not a spy."

"*Jesus,* I told you not to use my name. 'Scuse my language. I know you're a doc. That's why I'm talking to you, and not them. You have no authority here." The waiter sidled up with their drinks. They stayed silent, waiting for him to clear out before resuming.

"Okay. You're a part of this now. So, listen up. I ain't got all day."

Sam took a sip of the scotch, let the nose expand. She closed her eyes for a second, then opened them to find Taranto looking at her in scowling amusement.

"Are you ready now?"

"Yes," she said, then smiled with her lips closed. She knew her dimples showed that way. Flirting practice. It worked. Taranto loosened up a bit, his shoulders dropping an inch.

"All right. Here's the scoop. Last month, chick comes to me, says she thinks her hubby was KIA by a friendly over in Jalālabād. We'll call him King."

Sam immediately sat straighter. King was the nickname Susan Donovan had used for Perry Fisher. One of the five men in the photo, the one who died in Afghanistan.

"What made her think that?"

"Apparently, she ran into a *shaky* guy at a mutual friend's funeral. They had a few drinks, told a few stories. This guy got into his cups and let this bit of news slip. When she questioned him, he clammed up. She pushed and pushed until he said to talk to another guy. We'll call him Orange. She did. Orange denied everything. Said that was crazy talk, that the shaky guy was a worthless drunk. Now, this lady knew her hubby liked the shaky guy, so she thought maybe there's something else going on here. She happens to read my words, regular like, comes to me and tells me the story. I go digging. One thing is consistent with the military. The brass don't like to share when they fuck up. 'Scuse my language. Orange pushed back, and hard. So I back off him, all nice like. But I do what I do, and sure enough, what that shaky dude said rings true. You got me so far?"

He sat back in the booth and took a long sip of his beer.

Sam tried deciphering that load of information in her mind. Karen Fisher had seen William Everett—Billy Shakes—at a funeral. Billy was drunk and said some things he shouldn't. Karen, concerned that she'd been denied the true story of her husband's death, followed up, talked with someone named Orange. Sam made a mental note—*find out who Orange is.*

Then it hit her. Orange must be this missing Maggie Lyons Fletcher had mentioned. One piece of the puzzle solved.

Regardless, it didn't seem like news worth killing over. She knew this wouldn't have been the first time a soldier died by friendly fire, but maybe Sam was being naive.

"All right. I'm following. So according to Shaky, who killed King? And why hide it?"

"Sister, people are getting dead against their will. That's good enough for me. I got my suspicions, but soon as I dove into it, I got some pretty nasty threats to back off. Normally I don't listen to that kind of shit—'scuse my language—but the threats weren't directed at me. They were directed at her."

Sam thought this through for a minute. "So King's wife was threatened by Orange to get *you* to back off the story."

"Exactamundo. If I didn't back off, she'd bleed. And the kids. Story wasn't worth getting someone dead for. This time, I backed off for real."

"But let me guess. She didn't."

"No. Didn't know what was good for her. She starts talking to anyone she can find that might know what went down. Gets a coupla different stories, little details changed here and there. Realizes someone's gotta be lying. Next thing she knows, people start dropping like flies."

"Why didn't she go to the police?"

He drank some more of his beer. "Well, see, that might have been the smart thing to do. But this chick, she's grieving. And she's angry. Angry she got lied to, and angry she's being pushed. You know how bees will leave you alone if you leave them alone, but you start trying to fight them off and they just dive-bomb your head? She's a real fucking bee. 'Scuse my language."

"Where is she now?"

"I can't say."

Sam sighed deeply and took another sip of the scotch. Let it roll around on her tongue.

"You don't know? Or you have her hidden?"

"Hidden, for her own damn good. She finally got the message after Jackal bit it."

Hal Croswell. Apparently Donovan hadn't been a strong enough message. "And you're certain she wasn't the one doing the killing?"

"Hundred percent. No way. This chick is looking for answers, and she knows her questions are what got a bunch of people in trouble. She's scared to death she's next."

"Have you ever heard of a woman named Maggie Lyons?"

Taranto crossed his stubby arms on the table.

"What if I had?"

"Do you know where she is?"

"Nope. Pinky swear. But I know where she's been."

"And that would be…?"

"Not that. Who."

"Who? Oh. Wow, you really have been into this story. You must have spoken to the husband. He claims the child isn't his. Do you know who the father is?"

"Think so. Which is another reason I need to keep King's old lady away."

Sam took a moment to think, finished her scotch. It all started to make sense.

"King is the father."

Taranto snapped his fingers.

"Mr. Taranto—"

"Again with the names. Jesus, lady, you trying to get me killed?"

"Sorry, you never told me what I should call you."

"Ralph."

"Ralph. Of course. Silly of me not to draw that conclusion on my own. So, *Ralph*. You really expect me to believe that you're not working this story now?"

It was his turn to smile. "Maybe I got a few things cooking. Be crazy not to at least make a few nudges, take some notes. Thing is, something like this, I get the feeling it's big. Real big. And there's heroes to think of. Dragging names through the mud, fucking with benefits—'scuse my language—with awards and stars and all that jazz, isn't my cup of tea. I may hate why they're there, but I respect the gig."

Sam didn't think the two were necessarily mutually exclusive, but now wasn't the time for a debate.

"Who's your contact inside?" she asked instead.

"Whoooooo, I ain't telling you that, girlie. Nice try, though."

Sam stared at him for a few moments. "I think you've got more than a few notes. I think you're about to bust something wide open. Why play with us like this? I'm sure De…that Chevy could help. He could bring to bear the full might of the D.C. police on your clandestine investigation."

Taranto laughed, a choking, chortling sound. "As if. Thing is, I'm not ready to go out wide yet. But you and your buddies started poking around, and suddenly my pan's too hot and I gotta scramble some eggs instead of making the omelet. I just need the fire turned down a bit, so I can get some more info together."

"I doubt I can do anything to help, but I'll pass along your request." Sam had a thought. If Taranto was pushing to find out the details of the story… "You didn't happen to be anywhere near McLean in the past week, have you?"

"Time to go." He stood briskly. Sam grabbed his arm.

"If you try walking out now I'll announce who you are in front of this whole bar."

He stopped. "You wouldn't," he whispered in horror.

"I most certainly would. I've got nothing to lose. Sit down." She used her best get-to-work voice, one she learned as a resident, corralling med students, and used on the techs when they started screwing around.

It worked. He sat.

"Now. Tell me the truth. Did you break into the house? And leave the baseball cap on the bed?"

He started to hum, and look at the nails on his right hand. Okay. Plausible deniability. He wouldn't tell her, but he wouldn't stop her from guessing.

"Who went to the school?"

He just raised his eyebrows.

"Oh, that was Karen. She was the decoy. Get Susan to the school, so you can go in and check things out. What were you looking for?"

"You got a devious mind, ya know?"

"Yes. Too much time spent among people like you. What were you looking for?"

"Words."

"The journal."

He tapped his finger to his nose. Now that she'd caught on, he gave her more to work with.

"The missus she said she got in touch with Doc a few weeks back. Thought her questions might trigger his imagination. But the pages were already gone. Someone beat me to it."

Donovan, you sly dog. You did tear them out yourself. So where did you hide them? You knew you were in trouble. The note—"Do the Right Thing"—was… She stared across at Taranto. Manipulative little shit.

"Hey. You sent that note to Doc and Jackal, didn't you? Trying to get them to give you information for your story. That's low, man."

"I… Yeah, I did. So what? They needed a push."

"You pushed them, all right. Right into a grave. They're dead because you pushed them so hard."

Taranto had the good sense to look abashed. "That was never my intention. Those fuckers—'scuse my language—are the ones who did it. They're to blame, not me. I'm just trying to figure out what in the world went down then that's worth dying for now. And why the situation wasn't mopped up over there, before they took it home."

Sam wanted to know the answer to that, too. "Your

actions, Mr. Taranto, are unforgivable. What do you expect me to do now?"

"You don't take instruction well, so just keep them all occupied. You can tap dance, right?"

"Not for very long. As soon as we're done here, I'm heading to see Mutant. I hope."

"Good. Take this." Taranto slid a folder under the table. She felt it knocking at her knees, took it in her hand. "Be careful with it. I'm calling *you* my insurance, now. They come for me, I tell them someone else has the info. They come for you, well, try not to give me up, okay?"

Sam nodded. She was dying to see what the folder contained.

"You go first. I'll see you around, Scotch."

She slid out of the booth and headed toward the door without a backward glance. She finally felt useful. She had earned a nickname, after all.

CHAPTER THIRTY-SEVEN

McLean, Virginia
Susan Donovan

Susan hadn't expected the outpouring of love she and the girls had received today. She knew they were going to be taken care of, of course. She'd done her share of funerals at Arlington and elsewhere, knew exactly what to expect. What surprised her was how strong she felt, considering she'd just put her beloved husband in the ground. It wouldn't last, she knew.

But for today—she was just so proud of Eddie. She heard so many stories that he'd never shared: about lives he'd saved, the strategic thinking that protected his men time and again, the real truth about the picture of the camel he had in his office, which had made everyone at the service laugh. Eddie wasn't the kind of man to brag on himself. Susan knew in theory how well respected he was, but hearing about his deeds and adventures and close calls from the men and women who'd served with him made her miss him even more, but in a different way. Perhaps it was having grown up in the military.

Knowing he had touched so many helped cushion the blow the day could have thrown.

She'd gotten the girls to sleep at Eleanor's and, with her mother-in-law's blessing, sat in the backyard until the remaining guests had left.

She was exhausted. And she hadn't had a minute to herself in two days. When Eleanor suggested Susan take a drive to clear her head, she jumped at the chance. She'd driven right back to the house, poured a glass of wine and stepped into Eddie's office, where she felt his presence the strongest.

And there, in the darkened room, she started to say her final farewells. She allowed herself the tears she'd held back this afternoon to keep the girls in check. She sobbed looking at their wedding photos, until the last one in the album, where they were walking under the tunnel of sabers, and Eddie's best man, Perry Fisher, had swatted her on the butt with the flat of his saber and said, "Welcome to the Army, ma'am."

She relived the moment through the photo. She knew the brief spanking was coming; it was tradition. But King had smacked her a good one, and her flesh stung under her dress. She'd burst out laughing, and the camera caught her, turning to scold King, face lit up in glee, her mouth wide open. Eddie hadn't realized she'd stopped and was a foot in front of her, holding her arm, so she looked like she was being pulled in two directions, the train of her gown flying up in the air as if a breeze had blown it from below.

It was a perfectly timed photo, the kind of spontaneous shot that made the unscripted moments of the day come to the fore. How Eddie had tripped getting down on his knee to pull the garter off her thigh. The band playing the wrong first dance song. Her father, sick but still kicking, leading a bunny hop. It had been a perfect wedding.

She didn't want to say goodbye to that man, the one who loved her unconditionally, who sang to their babies, who fretted about his ties and brought home her favorite ice cream as a surprise. All of the little things that made their marriage tick.

Lightning flashed in the distance, briefly brightening the office. She realized she was sitting in the dark. She counted off until she heard the thunder. Not too close, not yet. She knew it was supposed to rain this evening. She was just glad it held off until they'd gotten the burial over with.

She wondered how Betty Croswell was doing tonight. After Hal's murder, she'd taken the kids and gone south to her mother's. She would be back next week for Hal's inurnment. She'd sent Susan a beautiful email this morning, expressing her sorrow at missing the funeral, hoping Susan would understand. She asked if there was news about the shooting. Susan had written her back and shared what she knew, which was precious little.

Stop and start. Start and stop. Every time it felt like Detective Fletcher got some momentum on the case, things would screech to a halt.

Sam had ridden off with Fletcher earlier, escaping the throngs of people at Eleanor's for the reception. She was working on Eddie's case. She was trying to find his killer.

Susan wasn't sure how she felt about Sam being privy to more information than she was.

That wasn't true. She knew exactly how it made her feel. It sucked. Eddie was hers. They'd built a life together. Sam hadn't waited breathlessly through every deployment, started at every ringing phone or chiming doorbell. Sam didn't know what it was like to worry that your husband wasn't coming home.

Check yourself, Susan. She lost her husband, too. And her kids. You can't be angry with her. She's just trying to help.

And face it. You feel helpless. That's why you're so angry with her.

Susan went to the kitchen, poured another glass of wine. The chardonnay bottle was empty now. She set it on the counter and went back to Eddie's office.

What were they missing?

Something hugely important, that's what. And she had no idea what that might be. Another flash of anger toward Sam—Susan couldn't even decipher her own husband's journal.

Susan started moving through the room, trying to look at things she may have neglected. She went through the pile of paper on his desk: bills. Just bills. She ran her fingers over his bookcase, remembering him sitting in the family room in the chair closest to the fire, reading.

She thought about how he'd run his hand up the back of her neck, under her hair, and let his palm rest there. How he'd use that leverage to pull her to him, settling his mouth on her with the intensity he brought to everything.

She would never feel that kiss again.

She collapsed in his chair. The tears flowed steadily as she said goodbye.

CHAPTER THIRTY-EIGHT

Washington, D.C.
Dr. Samantha Owens

Sam left Old Ebbitt's, crossed the street and walked toward the White House, then turned into Lafayette Square. It was strange not to have cars passing by. Pennsylvania Avenue had been turned into a walking mall several years before, a security measure probably long overdue. She crossed the park, pausing only once to glance over her shoulder at the luminous building that hosted the leader of the free world.

That symbol of freedom was the very thing Donovan and his friends were fighting for. So why did she feel an ominous chill looking at the building, beautifully lit against the darkened sky? Was it the shadow of a sniper on the roof, one of many who kept vigilant watch over the White House environs? Or the knowledge that Donovan had done the very same thing, securing points of importance or interest, trying to spread the message of freedom and democracy to an inhospitable place through force and cajoling? The pen was mightier than the sword, but it wasn't mightier than an M16 wielded by a very capable operator. A sledgehammer to the process, perhaps, one that got the point across rather bluntly, but it was much quicker than diplomacy.

She felt eyes on her and sped up her pace. There were still homeless who slept in this park, though they'd be rousted and moved if they got in the way of sightseers. But this felt more aggressive, and she walked as fast as she could without looking obvious, the heels of her shoes tapping across the concrete. She heard another set of footfalls behind her, and glimpsed a shadow gaining on her position. The steps grew heavier, closer, and she broke into a run.

Taranto wasn't kidding. The information he'd given her must have been inflammatory. She passed the Hay Adams Hotel at a sprint, saw the doormen giving her a look. She reached K Street and turned left abruptly, her heels skidding a little on the concrete sidewalk.

Fletcher and Hart were waiting, engine idling. She scrambled into the backseat of the unmarked and said, "Go. Someone's following me."

They didn't move, just slid their weapons from their holsters and started checking the mirrors.

"Lay down," Fletcher told her.

"Shit," Sam said, sliding down in the backseat. "Do you see anything?"

"No one that looks suspicious. Hart, you got anything?"

Hart shook his head. "No. Nothing unusual. Just some folks out enjoying the night air. You sure you were followed?"

Sam thought about that shadow, growing closer, felt

the chill move through her body again, and crouched lower in the seat.

"It certainly felt that way. When I sped up, so did he. The silhouette was big, definitely a man. That's all I saw, though, before I took off. I'm afraid I may have panicked a bit."

Fletcher reached over the seat and patted her arm.

"That's all right. We knew the risk we were taking sending you in to talk to Taranto instead of one of us. Didn't think you'd be followed, though. That makes it kind of interesting, don't you think?"

Hart said, "Check your six."

Sam saw the shadow from Fletcher's head move slightly. She realized she was holding her breath.

"Big guy, moving north?"

"Yeah."

"Nope. He just met some chick coming up from the Metro. They're heading out arm in arm."

Fletcher looked over the seat at Sam, who was still crouched down out of sight, and smiled.

She shot him the bird and he laughed, a sound she was surprised to hear was incredibly joyous. She didn't see that they were in a position to celebrate, not just yet.

"Let's loop back down to the restaurant, though I'm sure Taranto managed to get himself out of there just fine. You certainly had him on edge. I may have to hire you as a full-time stool pigeon. *Scotch*." Fletcher steered the car away from the curb, doing a wide U-turn. Sam felt her breath begin to ease.

"Can I sit up?"

"Give it a ten count, so we're clear of the park, then yeah. Go for it. You can get that mike off, too."

Sam waited a few moments, then raised herself off

the seats and smoothed back her hair. She felt foolish for panicking. The footsteps and shadow were most likely just another reveler cutting through the park on his way to the Metro stop.

There was a reason she worked with the dead, under the cold gleam of fluorescent lights, a sharpened scalpel and a set of Henckels knives her only weapons. Wait until she told Taylor this story. Her best friend would laugh her out of the room.

Fletcher glanced back at her. "So Taranto gave you something, outside of the golden nuggets we heard? Great job getting him to fall for that, by the way. You really did well."

Sam shook the folder. "Thank you."

"Welcome. And careful, be sure you turn the mike off before you untape it. Don't break it. They'll have my head."

She untaped the transmitter and battery pack from the small of her back, and the mike from between her breasts. The transmitter wasn't bigger than a deck of cards. Very discreet.

That was a close one. She imagined the audio would have a clear recording of her heartbeat going absolutely wild at the beginning there, when she played dumb. She finished and got her shirt wrestled back down, caught Fletcher eyeing her in the rearview.

"Enjoy the show?"

"I did."

She shook her head. "File doesn't feel too thick. Gino is scared, though. You heard the end, right? He was the one who broke into Donovan's house. He's been working with Perry Fisher's wife, Karen. He has her hidden away until he thinks things are safe."

Fletcher asked, "So what's in the folder?"

"Let's see. He said I was the insurance policy, so it must be something inflammatory." Sam flipped open the folder, pushed the overhead light above her right shoulder. The pages inside were blank, but something thin fell out into her lap. A CD in a clear sleeve.

"There's a disc in here." She flipped it to and fro. "No writing on it. We need to get to a computer and take a look, see what this is."

"Hart's laptop is in the trunk. Just hang on a second while I pull over."

Fletcher steered the car to the curb, and Hart hopped out before the car had come to a complete stop.

Fletcher turned to Sam. "So whaddaya say we—"

Sam heard the strangest noise. A dull thunk. The car moved slightly.

"Did you hear that?" she said, just as Fletcher's head swiveled and he screamed, "Get down!" His door flew open and he dived sideways from the car. She saw him land on the sidewalk, roll and start firing behind them, his weapon discharging again and again. She could hear him shouting, calling for Hart, and she huddled in the backseat, her heart beating a mile a minute, praying. There was a sudden burst of fire behind them, what sounded like an automatic weapon, and the car shook from the volley. She couldn't be safe in here. And they couldn't be safe out there.

Sam started to move, to where she didn't know, and heard Fletcher shouting, "Radio, radio—Sam, get on the radio. We need backup!"

She slithered over the front seat and, lying flat against the leather, grabbed for the radio mounted on the dash.

"We need help!" she yelled. She didn't know the codes, all the cop speak, so she went for logic instead. "Detectives Fletcher and Hart and Dr. Samantha Owens. We are on KStreet, three blocks south of Lafayette Park, under fire—I repeat, we are taking fire. Someone is shooting at us, and the detectives are returning fire. Please send someone."

Sam unkeyed the mike, heard a torrent of words and static. A woman's voice said, "Repeat, repeat," and Sam shouted all the information again, looking over her shoulder. The shooting had stopped, but that didn't mean the danger was over. She saw Fletcher run to the passenger's side of the car. He came to the passenger window and yelled, "Ambulance," through the glass. He had blood on his shirt, she didn't know from whom, him or Hart. *Oh, my God. One of them had been shot.*

Sadly, that call was one she knew how to make. She keyed the mike again. "Officer down. We need an ambulance sent to the shooting on K Street. I repeat, officer down."

She dropped the radio and flew out of the car. Fletcher was at the back bumper, kneeling over Hart, who wasn't moving.

The fear left her immediately. Finally, something she could do to help. Sam pushed Fletcher away from Hart's body. "Let me see him. Where's he hit?"

"I don't know," Fletcher yelled. "He has on a vest, so the blood's coming from somewhere else."

She dropped to her knees, pulled Fletcher away from his partner. Hart was canted to the side facing her, like he'd taken the shot upright, then slid down the car. There was blood everywhere.

"Fletch, take a breath. Get me your Maglite." She

started running her hands over Hart's body, feeling for an entrance wound.

Fletcher grabbed his Mag from the front seat, then scrambled back around the car and shone the beam on his partner, waving it frantically up and down his body.

Sam pointed at Hart's head, and spoke as calmly as she could. "Fletch. Slow. Start here, at the top."

The wound was in the base of Hart's throat, an inch above the notch where the bulletproof vest cradled his collarbones and an inch to the right. Sirens sounded, drawing closer. But there was so much blood… She didn't think there was time. He wasn't breathing, and his pulse faded out under her fingertips. His airway was constricted from the bullet's explosion. She didn't think it had severed his windpipe, just that the trauma was causing swelling and blood was filling the field.

Regardless, they had to get him started again.

Sam laid Hart down, tilted his head back and gave him three quick breaths, happy to see his chest rise from her blows. She started chest compressions. "Do you have a defibrillator in the car?"

"Yeah." Fletcher was white as a ghost. He didn't have to be asked twice, he ran to the trunk and grabbed the portable unit. Fletcher had calmed, his training taking over, and as Sam lifted her hands off his partner's chest, he unstrapped Hart's vest. It only took a moment, then they both ripped at his shirt. Fletcher handed Sam the unit and she got it going, attaching the leads while it charged. She bent and gave him three more quick breaths, then two long ones.

"It's ready. Clear," Fletcher said, and hit the button.

A shock wave of electricity coursed through Hart's body, making his heart jump in time. Sam put her fingers on his carotid. There was a single pulse, then it stopped.

"Again," she said, hitting the button herself this time. The unit whined as it charged and Sam felt the moments slipping away. Jesus, this was why she didn't work on live people, she was afraid to lose them.... *Breathe, you dummy, breathe.*

"Ready. Clear."

Fletcher hit the button and Hart's body rose, his back arched. When it settled, Sam sat with her eyes closed, willing his heart to start. It did. She felt the pulse skip under her fingers, and then the paramedics were there. She stepped back and let them work. They slapped a mask on him and hyperventilated his lungs. When they stopped Hart's chest rose of its own accord.

She stepped back and directly into Fletcher, who clutched on to her. "It worked?" he whispered.

"Yes. For now," she answered.

"Thank you."

She turned away from Hart, looked up at Fletcher. "What the hell?"

Fletcher shook his head, pointed at the car. They'd been hit at least six times, with Hart taking a shot, as well.

"If we hadn't stopped..."

"They were behind us. He, I think, I only saw one. If we hadn't stopped, they might have hit all of us, driven right up beside us and shot... Fuck."

Fletcher weaved for a second, then sat down abruptly in the street crossed-legged.

Sam kneeled next to him. "Are you hit?"

"Yeah, I think so. No. I don't know."

"Where does it hurt?"

He pointed to his left arm. Sam thought that blood was Hart's. She lifted Fletcher's left hand gently, saw the tear in the fabric just above his elbow. He was wearing a white button-down—it was soaked nearly black in this spot.

"Hang tight, I've got to cut your sleeve off."

He nodded and she went to the paramedics, who were sitting back on their heels over Hart, looking quite satisfied with themselves.

"He gonna be okay?" she asked.

A skinny guy with a flattop turned to her and nodded. "Yeah. You did good, getting him back in sinus. Where'd you learn that?"

"Georgetown Med. His partner's hit, too. Can I borrow you?"

"Sure, Doc. Lead the way."

She took him back to Fletcher. He was talking blankly to a large African-American man with a holster on his hip. As she drew closer she realized he was listening, not talking.

"The fuck you doing, Fletch? Why the hell didn't you tell me you were gonna get shot tonight?"

"I'm shot?"

"He's in shock," Sam said to the man, rather unnecessarily. The paramedic excused himself and barreled in between the two of them, dropping to his knees and tearing Fletcher's sleeve open. The wound was raw, but didn't look life-threatening.

Sam turned to the newest addition to the scene. "And you are?"

He looked at her in surprise. "Captain Fred Roosevelt. Who are you?"

"Dr. Samantha Owens. You're Fletcher's boss?"

"Yes, ma'am. What in the hell is going on here? He tried to tell me, but you interrupted. Good thing you did, idiot didn't say he'd been hit."

Roosevelt looked both worried and like he wanted to boot Fletcher in the ass. It was menacingly sweet.

"It's a through-and-through. He's gonna be fine. Other guy's gonna be okay, too. Good thing they had a doctor in the car with them," the paramedic chimed in.

Roosevelt's eyes closed briefly, then opened and focused intensely on Sam's. "Good. Now talk."

Sam took a deep breath. "It's a long story. We are investigating a lead from the Edward Donovan murder case."

"We." Roosevelt's tone cooled immeasurably. "*We* being you, Fletcher and Hart?"

"Yes, sir."

"And why, pray tell, is a civilian working a murder investigation in my town? Not only that, but without my authorization?"

"I'm not entirely a civilian. I'm a chief medical examiner, from Nashville. I've been around—"

"Cap, I asked her to help," Fletcher groaned from somewhere behind Roosevelt's meaty calves.

Roosevelt tore his laser gaze from Sam and directed it on Fletcher. "*You* asked her to help. Did you think you might want to clue me in that you've got some fucking chick riding along with you on a case? Or did that slip your mind?"

Roosevelt proceeded to dress down Fletcher, using some of the more colorful language Sam hadn't heard in years. She might have enjoyed the show had she not been covered in the blood of two men—men she was becoming rather fond of—one of which was being loaded into an ambulance, the other who was sitting on the hard pavement with a bloody bandage wrapped around his arm, his pants and shirt soaked in his own and his partner's gore.

Sam got right up close to Roosevelt and held her bloody, sticky hands in front of his face.

"Excuse me, Captain Roosevelt? Do you mind if I wash my hands? It's been a long night."

He took a step back and stopped yelling. Her point was made.

Fletcher tossed her a look of gratitude, and she smiled at him. He had saved her life tonight. They'd forged a bond that would be hard to tear asunder.

CHAPTER THIRTY-NINE

McLean, Virginia
Susan Donovan

Susan vaguely heard the house phone ringing. She opened her eyes, realized she'd fallen asleep with her head on Eddie's desk. She struggled upright and went to the kitchen to answer. Eddie had been planning to add the house line onto his office phone. Instead, she'd have to get that business line disconnected, put the office phone back on the regular phone number.

She didn't recognize the caller ID, but that wasn't unusual this week.

"Hello?" she answered.

"Susan? It's Karen. Karen Fisher. I'm so glad I caught you."

"Hey, Karen." Susan couldn't hide the exhaustion from her voice anymore.

"Oh, you sound beat. Honey, I'm so sorry I couldn't make the funeral. I'm… Listen, are you at home? Can I come over?"

Susan glanced at her watch. It was getting late. She

really should be heading back to Eleanor's. And the last thing she wanted right now was a trip down Karen's memory lane. When she'd lost King, she hadn't handled things well. She'd want to commiserate, and it would become all about Karen.

"Why don't we do this tomorrow, Karen. I need to head to my mother-in-law's and get the girls."

"I'm afraid tomorrow might be too late. It's important, Susan. Really important. Life or death."

Life or death. What the hell was Susan supposed to say to that?

Fine. Just...fine.

"Are you close by? Maybe I could just meet you—"

"I'm at the 7-Eleven behind your neighborhood. Oh, my God, Susan, thank you. I'll be there in just a second."

She hung up. Susan rubbed sleep from her eyes, grabbed a Diet Coke from the refrigerator. She went back to the office to close the doors, snapping on the hall light as she went. There was enough illumination to spill into Eddie's room, and Susan noticed the picture of the boys, the one the cops were so interested in, was crooked. She shook her head; she'd just straightened it the other day. She was one of those people who were driven crazy by a misaligned picture. She had that innate ability to see if something was crooked. Eddie had teased her about it all the time, sometimes going so far as to knock pictures a little off center just to watch her blood boil when she entered the room.

Her heart skipped a beat.

Eddie.

If only that were the case. Susan didn't believe in ghosts. She believed in heaven, and hell, and purgatory for those who did bad things but could eventually be re-deemed. But she didn't think the dead lingered behind, haunting their loved ones.

Seeing that picture crooked was enough to make her doubt everything she'd believed in for her entire life. But that was wishful thinking. She told herself that, even though her flesh was crawling.

She turned on the overhead light and walked to the wall. Straightened the picture. As she turned to leave she noticed it swung back down to the right, crooked again.

That was strange.

She straightened it again. As she watched, the frame slowly slid to the right.

Goose bumps paraded up and down her arms. Then she thought of that movie, the one with Demi Moore and Patrick Swayze, and shook her head. This wasn't a penny sliding up the wall. Eddie wasn't invisible in the room, using all his ghostly energy to push the picture off its center. There was a totally rational explanation for why the picture wouldn't align properly.

She took the photo off the wall and flipped it over. The backing was bulging, that's why it was listing. *See,* she told the universe. She pushed on the hard cardboard to try to pop it back in place, but it wouldn't budge. Something was making it protrude from its regular spot. The back was stuck, too. She tried and tried to get it to pull out, with no luck. Just as she decided she needed to grab a pair of pliers, it suddenly gave way. The backing came off with a rapid slide, and several pieces of paper fluttered to the ground.

She knelt and picked them up. Felt the breath leave her body.

The pages were from Eddie's journal.

The doorbell rang.

Shit. Karen was here.

Susan folded the pages in half and shoved them in her back pocket, and slid the backing into the frame. She put the picture back on the wall, saw that it now hung straight and went to the front door.

Karen Fisher looked like hell. The rain had just begun to fall, but it was picking up in earnest. Karen's dark hair was wet already, and her voice shook from the chilly air.

"Oh, my God, Karen, what's wrong? Come in, before the rain gets worse."

Susan hustled Karen into the foyer and shut the door behind them.

"Thank God you were home. I didn't know where else to go."

"What's wrong?"

Karen looked exhausted. Black circles paraded under her eyes, and she smelled the tiniest bit like alcohol. And cigarettes. When had she started smoking?

"I just… Susan, can we sit down?"

Susan felt the alarm coming off Karen. Something really was wrong.

"Of course. Of course. Come on into the kitchen. Can I make you some coffee? Tea?"

Karen followed her into the kitchen. Out of habit, Susan turned to the stove and started to fill the kettle.

"No," Karen said. Her voice wasn't shaking anymore. "But you can tell me why you never shared the truth with me. Why you didn't come straight to me when you found out Eddie killed my husband?"

Susan set the full kettle down on the stove with a

thump. "What in the hell are you talking about, Karen? Eddie didn't kill Perry. He loved Perry."

"Don't take another step, Susan. I'm warning you."

Susan heard the menace in Karen's voice. She stilled in her tracks, then turned slowly toward the woman.

Karen had a Glock pointed at Susan's chest.

Without thinking, Susan gasped and started to back away. *Holy Mary, mother of God, what in the hell was Karen doing with a gun?*

"Stop!"

Susan stopped.

"Eddie did kill Perry," she said. "And I have the files to prove it."

Susan held her breath. Karen was mumbling to herself, the gun wavering in her hand. Susan's thoughts raced. Could this be true? Could this be what got Eddie killed? Is this what was on his papers? Susan tossed all of that away and went into survival mode. She'd taken self-defense classes, and spent the past thirteen years married to a Ranger. If she could just distract Karen, maybe she could get the gun out of her hands. Or better yet, persuade her to set the damn thing down. Susan had her own weapon, stashed on top of the breakfront…but that was two rooms away, and with Karen in her path, she'd have to fight by hand.

"Karen, put the gun down. We can't talk like this. I've never heard anything—"

"Shut up! Just shut up. I've seen the proof. Eddie is the reason Perry died."

Against every instinct, Susan took a step closer to Karen.

"I've never heard anything about this, Karen. You have to believe me. Eddie never said anything about it.

And you know how they were. Confession was the only thing that kept them sane, both he and Perry. Whether they did it with God or with us, late at night, they told us everything that mattered. And Eddie never told me this."

"Ha. You think he was so perfect. He wasn't. He was just as bad as the rest of them. Just as bad as you."

Susan felt something in her shift. Everything crashed into place, and a calm came over her. She must get out of this situation. She may not have Eddie anymore, but she had her girls. And she couldn't, wouldn't, leave them.

"Karen, put the gun down, now, so we can talk about this."

"No. It's your fault. If he'd just told you, you would have warned me. I wouldn't have had to find out from Billy Shakes."

"Karen, honey, you're distraught. Let's just make some tea and sit at the table, talk this out."

The gun wavered, then Karen got a firmer grip on it. "No. You want to know the story? You want to find out what really happened in that godforsaken desert? Then you're going to listen to what I have to say and stop talking."

"Then talk, Karen. But may I make myself some tea? It's been a very long day." Karen didn't say anything, so Susan turned on the burner. She estimated she had three minutes before the water started to boil.

She swallowed down her fear and turned back to face the gun. "Now, Karen. Please, talk to me. Tell me what you've heard."

Karen shook her head, her mouth in a tight grimace. A normally pretty woman, she looked fierce and frightening, and ugly. "You can deny it all you want. I've seen the checks. I've seen the videos."

"But I haven't, Karen. I don't know what you're talking about." Susan was trying very hard not to lose her temper, but having a gun waved in your face makes you think crazy things.

The gleam in Karen's eyes bordered on insane.

"Eddie fathered a child in Afghanistan. And when Perry found out, Eddie killed him."

CHAPTER FORTY

Washington, D.C.
Dr. Samantha Owens

Sam rode to George Washington University Hospital with Captain Roosevelt. Fletcher had been transported separately, and Hart was taken directly into surgery, so Sam was left with trying to explain to their boss what was going on.

She started with the phone call Donovan received, detailed the postmortem, the granulomas, then Croswell's murder and post, the link to Savage River, the funeral, Taranto, Whitfield, everything. She knew she didn't have all the pieces of the story: Fletcher had held several things back from her. Not that she blamed him. She was along for the ride, and he didn't owe her anything.

Until now. Now, she'd saved his partner's life, and she could use that as leverage to get all the way in.

Roosevelt got quieter and quieter as she spoke. He'd harrumphed a few times, at the beginning, but the more words spilled from her mouth, the tighter his grew. He pulled in front of the hospital and slammed the car into Park.

"Lady, I don't know whether to arrest you or commend you. Guess I'm going to have to wait on both. Get out."

Sam didn't waste time arguing, just unlocked her safety belt and opened the door. She stepped out, for the first time realizing the air had cooled tremendously. She shivered.

"By the way." Roosevelt leaned over, his bulk taking up the whole front seat. "Thanks for saving my guys."

"My pleasure," Sam said, then turned and walked directly toward the emergency room entrance without looking back. She knew she'd been treading on thin ice playing with the boys on this case. She was damn lucky Roosevelt didn't cite her on the spot for interfering in an official investigation.

She wasn't an investigator. She knew that. She wasn't trying to play cop. She wasn't trying to be careless. Just the opposite, she was being incredibly cautious. But her curiosity was getting the better of her, and damn it, she had a stake in this, too.

Someone had murdered Donovan. Someone had tried to kill her tonight. And she didn't take kindly to being pushed around.

CHAPTER FORTY-ONE

McLean, Virginia
Susan Donovan

Staring into the barrel of a gun is unnerving at best.

Susan tried to work on her breathing. She didn't want to panic, not yet. She thought about Eddie, about the things he'd done to calm down when the dreams overtook him and he woke up screaming for cover fire: the square breathing—four beats in, hold for four, out for four, rest for four—putting your mind in a safe, happy place. None of it was working.

The reality of Karen's last statement wasn't sinking in properly. Eddie had an affair. Her Eddie. And not just an affair, he'd gotten a woman pregnant.

How was this possible?

Breathe, Susan. Just breathe. Goddamn it, Eddie. Is that what you wrote in your journal? Is that what you're trying to hide from everyone? When you got called in to work, was it her?

Did Sam know all of this? She'd been on the inside of the investigation practically from the start. She could be holding back, and the thought of that made Susan seethe with anger.

No, no, no. Susan shook her head. This couldn't be happening. Sam was trying to help. She was one of the good guys. Susan had to believe that. She needed to have one ally she trusted in.

Karen laughed. "You don't believe me, do you? Well, fine. I'll show you."

Karen used her left hand to pull a file from her bag, never letting the weapon drop. She tossed the file to Susan.

"See for yourself."

Susan opened the file. In it were pictures. A sunny-faced little girl, angelically blond. Running in the grass, looking contemplative over a blue balloon. There were about thirty pictures in all, spread over several years.

"Where did you get these?"

"I took them, of course."

"This child is local?"

"She lives in Georgetown. Her mother is a lawyer now, but she served in Afghanistan with Eddie and Perry. Perry used to tell me about her, her name is Maggie. She drove one of the supply trucks. They saw her all the time. She was their friend. But she and Eddie were really close. Eddie got her pregnant. Perry disapproved. He thought it was wrong, what Eddie was doing. So he was going to report him. Maggie got sent back to the States, and three days later Perry was dead. Eddie killed him to cover up his affair with Maggie."

Susan wanted to vomit. This couldn't be true. It just couldn't. But that little girl—she looked a lot like Vicky.

Don't think about that now. Keep her talking.

"Did you kill Eddie, Karen? Did you kill Hal?"

Karen laughed. "Of course not. Why would I do that?"

"You're the one waving the gun around."

"No, no. It's not me. Maggie killed them. Hal and Eddie, they were cutting her off. They couldn't keep giving her money. And Eddie refused to leave you for Maggie. She was furious. And so she killed them both."

When Susan found Maggie Lyons, she was going to kill her personally.

The teakettle began to whistle, a sudden piercing shriek. Startled, Karen turned toward the noise. Susan grabbed the empty wine bottle from the counter and swung with all her might.

She connected squarely with the back of Karen's head. There was an audible crunch, a dull, wet smack, and Karen went down on the floor. Susan could tell the blow had knocked the woman unconscious.

"Thank God."

She didn't even feel bad about it. She turned off the stove, grabbed the gun and her keys, and tore out of the kitchen to the garage. She got in the car and locked the doors, sent the garage door up and pulled out of the house.

As she drove away, she picked up the phone to dial 9-1-1, then hit the off button. What was she going to say? The police would make her go back to the house, and all she wanted was to go to Eleanor's and make sure the babies were okay. And what if she'd really hurt Karen? Then she could get arrested, and the girls would be without a mother and a father.

No, there was only one thing for her to do. She needed to take the notes she'd found in Eddie's office to Sam, let her decode them. Then they might have an idea of what really happened.

She reached for her phone again as she took the left turn that led out of the neighborhood. That's when she heard the breathing. And everything went dark.

CHAPTER FORTY-TWO

Washington, D.C.
Detective Darren Fletcher

The song was right. Waiting *was* the hardest part.

Fletcher sat in silence with Sam and Ginger, Hart's wife, plus a host of other officers in and out of uniform, waiting to hear how Hart was doing. He'd been in surgery for an hour. Fletcher was worried, but Sam had assured him it would all be fine. He sipped his coffee and said prayers to a God he hadn't talked to in years: prayers of thanks, prayers of forgiveness and prayers of revenge. He couldn't help himself on that last, it just slipped out among all the other holy speak and thank-yous, and he knew better than to try and take it back. He was a realist. He figured God would punish him more for being a hypocritical liar than speaking from his heart.

He and Sam had been interviewed multiple times by the investigating detectives, around and around the mulberry bush. He gave them everything he could think of, which wasn't much. Sam had even less; she'd been hidden in the car for the majority of the shooting, only feeling the terror build instead of facing it down. At least he'd been doing something.

Fletcher's arm ached. It had gone through so many different sensations tonight he wasn't sure where to start. Hot, cold, numb, on fire. The bullet had torn through the fleshy part just below his biceps, thankfully missing bone and artery, just hollowing out a furrow through the thin flesh. He'd never been shot before. It hurt. A lot. It was not something he highly recommended.

Thank God it was his left arm and not his right. They'd cleaned, sewn, bandaged and slinged the arm, and it was utterly useless. If it had been his right, he'd be in a damn sight of trouble.

He was in trouble, anyway. Roosevelt was furious with him. He didn't blame the man. He'd fucked up. They should have just charged in and arrested Taranto, made a scene, but the subtle approach seemed like a better idea. He'd gone and talked to Culpepper again, looked at some more files on employees, looked at the visitor logs. Nada. Culpepper was genuinely torn to pieces about his former men's deaths. The day had taken its toll. The awe-inspiring Patton-esque man Fletcher had met was gone. When he'd spoken at Donovan's funeral, he was still the commander, a forceful presence for his troops, but outside of the spotlight he'd finally broken down, turned into a brokenhearted buttercup. A brokenhearted buttercup who had the paperwork to prove he was in Iraq when both Donovan and Croswell were shot, officially taking him off the suspect list. After Fletcher's third fail out at the Raptor headquarters, Taranto seemed like the only viable lead.

He had told Fletcher a little bit about Whitfield, though. Enough that Fletcher had formed a plan of attack. He needed to squeeze everything he could out of Taranto, then head to western Maryland and see if they could put eyes, and hopefully hands, on Alexander Whitfield.

But Taranto refused to speak to them. He wanted to talk to Sam. As did Whitfield. Everyone wanted a piece of Sam Owens. And bless her, she'd been more than willing to help.

Now look at them. Bloodied, beaten, raked over the coals and impatiently waiting to hear if Hart would live or die.

Ginger caught his eye and smiled, hopeful, grateful. He didn't deserve her gratitude. Jesus, she should have pummeled him with her fists, cursed him with her tongue, shot daggers from her eyes. Instead, when she got to the hospital, the first thing she did was envelop him in a hug so big he felt lost in her arms, and told him how much she loved him, and how much Lonnie loved him, too.

It was fucking sloppy police work that had gotten Hart shot. Sloppy, shoddy and ridiculously off the book. Fletcher was going to take a major hit. Part of him was glad. Maybe now he'd get off homicide. He hadn't done enough to be relieved of duty altogether, but he might be forced to ride a desk until retirement.

He'd do it. He'd do it without raising a stink.

Just as soon as he figured out who killed Edward Donovan and Harold Croswell, and scared William Everett into shooting his mother and killing himself.

Though his mind was a bit blurry from the painkillers they'd given him while they patched him up, he ran through their remaining suspects again.

Alexander Whitfield should be at the top of the list. He had the skills, means and opportunity to pull all of this off. You don't get to be a sniper in the Rangers without a dead eye, and Whitfield had operated overseas long enough to know a few tricks when it came to communication.

But Whitfield seemed to be trying to help, not hurt. Fletcher needed to find the man and talk to him before he could cross him off the list.

The second was Maggie Lyons. According to Taranto, Maggie had a child with Perry Fisher. That would be an easier claim to prove, if she hadn't scooted out with her kids in tow. There had been no activity on her credit cards, no phone calls to her parents or ex-husband, nothing to the schools. She just went *poof.* She, too, was weapons trained, fully capable of killing a man. According to her jacket, she'd done that once already, in an ambush outside Fallujah, when she laid down suppressive cover fire while Donovan and Fisher pulled a few troops to safety. She had three kills to her name, and a Bronze Star for bravery she probably kept hidden away, where no one could be reminded of its impetus.

The third was Karen Fisher. A woman scorned is a dangerous thing. From what Taranto said, she was upset about the infidelity, and had found out her husband might have been killed by friendly fire. Now that they had Taranto's information, Fletcher really wanted to sit down with Culpepper again, but it would have to wait seventeen hours minimum—the man was back on a plane heading to the desert. Croswell had been cremated, and the inurnment in Arlington National Cemetery's Columbarium wouldn't be for another week. Culpepper was coming back for that ceremony, but Fletcher believed in his heart this case was getting close to a finale. A week would be too long.

Fletcher rested his head back against the wall. He was still missing something. The pages from Donovan's diary sure would be a help. And now he had a broken wing to hinder him further.

Roosevelt came into the waiting room. He was always a stern-looking man, but right now he looked downright forbidding. Fletcher caught himself swallowing, hoping his boss didn't hear the audible gulp. This wasn't good news. Fletcher straightened.

"Hart?"

"He's fine. Miss Ginger, they're asking for you down the hall."

"Oh, thank God," the woman exhaled, practically flying out the door. Fletcher felt the wind leave his body. Sam reached over and touched him on his good hand, and he tossed one last bit of thanks upward before facing his boss.

Roosevelt sat across from them and eyed Fletcher and Sam.

"That reporter you were talking to? Gino Taranto? Just fished him out of the Potomac, with a third eye."

"Oh, my God," Sam said.

Fletcher just asked, "Where'd he go in?"

"No idea. But he didn't last long outside your meeting with him." He turned his focus onto Sam. "We need to go over it again. Every little last detail."

Fletcher smiled for the first time all evening. "We can do you one better. We have it all on tape."

A rotund nurse with a crew cut and jangling gold earrings came into the waiting room.

"Is there a Detective Fletcher here?"

"That's me," Fletch said, standing.

"Your partner is asking for you."

"Go on, then," Roosevelt said. "We'll handle this in a minute."

Fletcher gave Sam an apologetic look and went with the nurse. Hart was four doors down, in a private room. Everything smelled oddly clean, antiseptic. A machine hissed air into his lungs. Hart was pale, but at least his eyes were open. Ginger moved from her vigil at his bedside and let Fletcher take her place.

"Fletch." Hart mouthed the words. The doctors had done a temporary tracheotomy; they had a hard time intubating him with the trauma to his throat. He couldn't make sounds, but could make himself understood.

"Dude, you gave me a scare," Fletcher said. "Did you see who shot us?"

Hart shook his head, a tiny movement. "You okay?" he mouthed.

"Yeah. 'Tis but a flesh wound."

His Monty Python impression worked, Hart smiled.

"Really, I'm fine. Don't worry about it. You just heal up. I'm gonna get whoever did this to you. I promise."

Hart just closed his eyes. Fletcher gave his hand one more squeeze and stepped away. Ginger gave him another hug.

"Be careful, Fletch."

"I will. Call me if anything changes, okay?"

"Of course. Be good."

Good.

If he found the man who shot them, and the opportunity arose, he would kill him.

CHAPTER FORTY-THREE

Washington, D.C.
Metro Homicide
Dr. Samantha Owens

Sam tried not to yawn. It had been an exhausting day, and it was now two in the morning.

The disk Taranto had given to her was confusing, at best. It seemed to be a video taken of a nighttime military raid, but it wasn't marked. She had to assume it was Afghanistan. The video had been shot through night vision from above the scene, probably from a Predator drone or Apache helicopter. The screen was grainy and bobbing, and looked something like a video game crossed with a science-fiction movie. Globs of green-shaped soldiers moved through a blackened backdrop, five of them, spreading out in a fan, converging into a single file line, then stopping. Friendlies. Two blobs headed off on their own while the remaining three stayed stationary. Then one blob stopped moving, and its partner walked off in a totally different direction, looping back to the main group. As he got close to the cluster of soldiers, there was a sudden scramble and flashes of light from the right, which Sam took to be shooting. Pandemonium looks the same through night vision as it does in daylight. People started running all over the place, traces of light shot through the air. The single blob on its own didn't move again, didn't engage in the firefight. It seemed he'd gone down before the shooting started.

The whole video took forty minutes. It gave Sam a vicious headache, trying to decipher what was happening. But she, Fletcher and Roosevelt agreed: this had to be the friendly fire incident.

It was going to take a bunch more research to find out what was going on, that was for sure. Inquiries were being made at DOD, but it was going to take some time to get people to talk. If the Army had covered up this incident, they would hardly parade out and tell what really happened, not without a lot of pressure from multiple sources. Taranto had put in a FOIA request, but DOD could take months to comply, and now that the requesting party was dead…

When the video was done, they'd dissected it to death, and Roosevelt had left for the night, Fletcher brought her a cup of coffee.

"So what do you think?" he asked.

"I have no idea, outside of the obvious. That lead soldier went down before the big firefight took place."

"Right. Problem is, this video has no identifying features. Nothing that can tell us when or where the shooting took place. It could be a complete fake for all we know, doctored, anything. Without Taranto to tell us what we're looking at so we can at least pressure DOD… It's going to be hard to get the info from them, anyway. Not like they're going to say, 'Oh, hi, you're looking for this? Be our guests, here you go.'"

"Not only that, it could be of another situation wholly unrelated to Donovan and Perry Fisher."

"You're right."

"How's your arm?"

Fletcher sighed. "Honestly? It hurts like absolute hell."

"Did you take the painkillers the E.R. Doc gave you?"

"No. I'll never stay awake."

"You need some rest. Why don't we head home and start fresh in the morning?"

"I can't let you."

"Huh? Why not?"

"You're safer here. Someone tried to kill you tonight. They managed to get to Taranto. Or had you forgotten?"

She hadn't. The knowledge was weighing on her mightily, but she didn't want to give in to the fear. She'd spent the past two years jumping at shadows, locked in her own torturous nightmare. As horrible as it was to say, she felt alive for the first time in a very long time.

"I haven't. But without sleep, neither of us will be able to function. Speaking of Taranto, do you want me to attend the post? I'm sure I can call Dr. Nocek and ask."

"No. I want you with me. We're going to Savage River at first light. We're going to go get Whitfield."

"Roosevelt's going to let me go with you?"

"You're going to have to sign some forms. Basically saying if you get killed, the department isn't responsible. But if you're willing to do that, then yes, he said you can go. It's against his better judgment, but he understands. We won't be going alone, though. We have a whole team, a couple of SWAT guys, the works. For your safety as well as the safety of Alexander Whitfield."

"Assuming we find him."

"Which is why I was able to convince Roosevelt to let you come. I think Whitfield will show for you. He chose you at Donovan's funeral. He gave you the means to break loose the real story. We roll in there guns blazing and this guy will rabbit."

"So I'm just bait."

"Maybe." Fletcher moved too quickly and winced.

"Poor baby. Let's at least put some ice on it. Where's your kitchen?"

She got him set up, then he showed her the sleeping arrangements he'd organized. There was a cot in his office, made up with a gray blanket that had a large orange safety stripe down the middle. Fluorescent orange, at that. Just her color.

"Thank you. So you're going home?"

"No. Roosevelt decreed that I stay here, too."

"Here? Where will you sleep?"

"Locker room. There are a few bunks in there, just in case one of us pulls an all-nighter and needs some rack time. I've done it before—it's not so bad. Just lock the door to my office once I leave, okay? Just in case."

"All right. I'll see you in a few hours. Take the pain medicine, okay?" She touched him briefly on the cheek. "Thank you for saving my life."

He smiled, and she noticed how that simple act transformed his tired face. "You're welcome. Get some rest."

He turned to leave, then stopped. "Sam...I..."

"Yes?"

"Nothing. Never mind. Sleep well."

"You, too, Fletch."

She shut and locked the door behind him, then lay down on the cot. As tired as she was, sleep was the last thing on her mind. She needed to call Eleanor and let her know what was going on, but she hated to run the risk of waking her. Like Sam, Eleanor didn't sleep well, but Susan and the girls were at the house. She didn't want to wake them up, either. She put it on her mental checklist to do in the morning and rolled onto her side.

Tomorrow she might meet the mysterious Xander, and find out why Donovan had been killed.

Was she ready?

Because it was looking more and more like Donovan was involved in something less than savory. And she didn't want her memories of him to be sullied.

She didn't want her memories, period.

CHAPTER FORTY-FOUR

Washington, D.C.
Dr. Samantha Owens

Sam was surprised by knocking on the door. She realized she had actually fallen asleep, despite thinking there was no way she could. She looked at her watch—it was five in the morning. A full three hours of rest. Joy.

"Just a minute," she called. She'd slept in her clothes but taken off her bra. It took her a second to find it, on top of Fletcher's cup of pens and pencils. He would have loved that. Last night, before he left, she had the feeling he was about to say something of a more personal nature than she was ready to hear. She was glad he changed his mind. Hurting Fletcher was the last thing she wanted to do. He seemed like a really great guy, but she wasn't close to being able to think like that about him.

She shimmied into the lace and wire and straightened her shirt. She had a red welt on her stomach from the tape they'd used to keep the mike in place. She must have been allergic to the adhesive.

She pulled the door open. Fletcher greeted her, looking amazingly rested, with a cup of steaming coffee in his hand.

"Drink up. It's time to roll."

She accepted the cup gratefully and took a deep sip. It was good, better than the usual police station fare.

"Did you make this?"

"Yeah. I have a stash. And a French press. Life's too short to drink bad coffee."

"Amen to that." She finished the cup. "I'm ready when you are."

She followed him out of the offices and down the stairs to the garage.

A full tactical team awaited them. Sam took one look at the group of unsmiling men bristling with weapons and adrenaline, and shook her head.

"Fletch, you've got to be kidding. This is going to scare him away."

"Sam, this is nonnegotiable. Whitfield must be treated as a murder suspect. We've had boots on the ground up there for two days looking for him, and haven't had a trace. The man's a ghost. I can't take the chance that you might get hurt. Or anyone else, for that matter. Like it or lump it, the team comes along."

The team came with a driver. Fletcher motioned to the backseat of an unmarked sedan, and Sam joined him, glad he wasn't going to try and be a man about things and attempt a cross-country drive one-handed, on no sleep and a gunshot wound. She would have been forced to drive herself, and damn it, she was tired.

The sky was still shadowed, the sun just beginning to peek over the horizon. Traffic hadn't picked up yet. It was like they had the city to themselves, an eerily empty town of half a million slumbering under their noses.

They shot out of the city, crossed the Roosevelt Bridge and headed west on the George Washington Parkway. Sam loved this road, loved its leafy canopy sheltering the gentle curves as the Potomac River undulated beside them. It only took ten minutes to hit the beltway, then they looped around to 270 heading to Frostburg. The drive was going to take three hours. Sam settled against the door and shut her eyes. Maybe she could get a few minutes of sleep on the way.

Sleep didn't come. After fifteen minutes she gave up and turned to Fletcher. He was staring out the window opposite, obviously lost in thought.

"Fletch. Tell me about Whitfield," Sam said.

"What do you want to know?"

"All Susan could tell me was that he and Donovan were incredibly tight. Donovan's journals backed that up. But who is he? Where is he from? What did he do in the Army? Did he go to school? Because I'm telling you, the way Donovan talked about him, he was a hero. Donovan worshipped him. Said he wouldn't have made it out alive if it weren't for Xander. I'm having a hard time wrapping my head around the fact that he's a killer. And to send us to Taranto, and the friendly fire incident... Just, who is he?"

"Sun Tzu said, 'If you know your enemy and you know yourself, you will not be imperiled in a hundred battles.'"

"Exactly. I'd like to know who we're really after here."

"All right. Here's what we've managed to find so far. U.S. Army Ranger First Sergeant Alexander Roth Whitfield was born in San Francisco, California, and moved to Colorado when he was two. His parents were hippies, pacifists, Vietnam War activists who, after the war ended, decided they'd had enough of the world and started their own commune in the mountains north of Dillon, Colorado. His father, Alexander Roth Whitfield II, was the heir to the Roth television enterprise. He met Sunshine Rollins at a party, fell madly in love, told his parents and their considerable fortune to take a hike, dropped out and tuned in. Alexander was their firstborn. His birth name was Alexander Moonbeam, but they called him Xander Moon. He had it legally changed to Alexander Roth III when he was eighteen, right before he enlisted. Guess he figured Moonbeam wasn't a good strong Ranger name. He has a younger sister named Yellow Sun. She lives in Modesto, California, now, runs a metaphysical shop. Clean as a whistle.

"They homeschooled the kids. Xander's army entrance exams show an IQ off the charts. He went through Basic and caught eyes, apparently he wasn't just smart, but a physical machine. He started specialized training—Airborne, Ranger, Snipers, the works— and excelled at everything. If there was a school, he went through it. He's a sharpshooter, won all sorts of awards, ran marathons and was first in line when we engaged in Afghanistan. Did three combat tours before he abruptly ended his career with the Army by voluntarily separating in 2008. He was the ultimate soldier. G.I.-fucking-Joe."

Fletcher started playing with his cell phone.

"And then what?" Sam asked.

"And then he dropped off the face of the earth. He's in a bit of hot water from Uncle Sam, hasn't been paying his taxes. There's just no record for him after he mustered out."

"Did he go AWOL? Is that why he's in hiding?"

"No. He left legitimately. Just chose not to return for another tour. He was lucky, most of the men he served with got stop-lossed and didn't have a choice. He managed to sneak out under the wire."

"So why did he leave? If he'd made the military his career, gone through all that training, why walk away? Donovan doesn't talk about it in his journal. You'd think he would. His whole team mustered out. Why?"

Fletcher shrugged his good shoulder. "I haven't a clue. All I know is Whitfield is a highly skilled killer. He was awarded a Silver Star, that's nearly as good as it gets, has a Purple Heart, two Bronze Stars. This man has bravery and courage to spare, apparently. Luck, too. Oh, and he plays piano. I forgot that. He was some sort of prodigy."

"A killer and a pianist. Interesting combination. Doesn't exactly fit with his upbringing, does it?"

"No. But we never know what goes on behind closed doors. He's a trained soldier who disappeared off the face of the earth. No job, no accounts, no accountability. And now all the men he was close to are dead. So don't let the romantic warrior full of valor creed get in the way here."

"I wasn't planning to," she mumbled. "When do we get there?"

The driver, whose name was Kip, looked over his shoulder. "Another hour."

"Thank you," Sam said. She was about to ask more about Xander when her phone rang. She recognized

Eleanor's number. Damn it, she'd forgotten to call. She answered with an apology.

"Eleanor, I'm so sorry. I meant to get in touch, it's been a busy morning."

"Oh, Sam, it's good to hear your voice. I was worried when you didn't come back last night. Where are you? Are you okay? Are you with Susan?"

"No, I'm not with Susan, I'm with Detective Fletcher. We're heading to western Maryland to see if we can find one of Eddie's friends. I meant to call last night, things just got insane, and then it was too late. I didn't want to wake everyone. I'm fine, though. I suppose you saw the news about the shooting?"

"I did. I'm so glad you're all right. I couldn't take it if something happened to you. The detectives are okay?"

"They are. Worse for wear, but they're both going to be fine."

"I'm so relieved." Eleanor sounded so old. The past week had really taken its toll. "Sam, you said you weren't with Susan. Have you talked to her this morning?"

"No, I haven't. Why?"

Eleanor sighed. "Yesterday was so hard on her. I suggested she get some air. I think she was planning to go to the house. But when I woke up this morning she wasn't here. Her car's gone, too. That's why I assumed you were with her."

"Did you try her cell?"

"Yes, and the house, as well. No one's answering."

Sam felt the first beginnings of fear flutter in her stomach, but tried to keep her voice steady for Eleanor's sake.

"Eleanor, she's probably just asleep."

"I should run out to the house."

"Why don't we save some time? I can ask Detective Fletcher to have someone check on her for you. That way you won't have to wrangle the girls or anything."

"Can they do that?"

"Sure. I'll ask him right now. I'll call you back once they get there."

"Thank you, dear. I'm just a little worried about her."

You and me both, Sam thought.

She hung up and looked over at Fletch. "Can you have someone do a welfare check on Susan Donovan? She didn't show up at Eleanor's last night."

Fletcher knitted his brows. "That's not good." He got on the cell and called Roosevelt, asked him to have the Fairfax County police do a run-by.

"Thank you," she said when he hung up. "Hopefully she's just still asleep. I know how hard it was for her yesterday."

"You're welcome." Fletcher cleared his throat. His eyes flitted to hers, then away, out the window, then back. "Sam, maybe this isn't the time.... I hate to say this, but I looked you up online. I saw the story about your husband and kids. I just wanted to say, I'm sorry. Really sorry."

Sam froze. She didn't want to go there with him. Nashville, the flood, their deaths, felt a million miles away, and then intruded back into her world with a suddenness that took her breath away.

She didn't have a voice. What would she say? *Yes, Fletch, they're all dead, and that's okay? It's great that you were doing background on me?* Instead, she opened her purse and brought out her antibacterial gel, poured some in her hands and started to rub.

"I've seen you do that a few times now.... You have OCD, don't you?"

"Jesus, Fletch. What is this, the inquisition?"

She felt sorry for the outburst immediately. He was just trying to make friends. Like a little puppy who doesn't know his boundaries and kept licking at her legs.

"I shouldn't have brought it up. My mistake." His voice had cooled. Now he was mad at her. She huffed and stared out the window. They were getting close, she saw the exit for Frostburg. They needed to work together, so she swallowed her pride and put the gel away.

"Yes, I have OCD. Yes, my family died in the floods. But neither of those things have any bearing on me being here now. They aren't affecting my judgment. So don't worry about it. Okay?"

"It's been two years. Maybe—"

"Come on, Fletch. Am I interrogating you about your ex-wife? This is private. It's my business. So please, just stop."

"I'm not interrogating you, Sam. I'm trying to get to know you. Let me amend that. I'd like to get to know you. If you'd let me."

Shit. Here it was. She knew this was coming. She thought she'd sent enough signals that she didn't want to go there. Obviously she was out of practice. But she needed to end this right now, before he actually got interested. And keep him from booting her out on the side of the road.

"Fletch, it's not you. I'm not in any shape to be known. Okay? Please, let's just dangle me out as bait for Whitfield, capture him and then I'm heading home.

I've overstayed my welcome, I believe. I have responsibilities back in Nashville."

She didn't realize until she said it that she meant every word. She had no business still being in D.C. She'd come to do a job: a secondary autopsy on a homicide victim. That job was well-past done, and where was she now? In a car with a smitten homicide detective on her way to try and help capture a possible murderer. This was ridiculous. She was not a detective. What in the world did she think she was doing?

The wall of Donovan's office swam into her mind, the picture of the five men, the band of brothers, atop the words that bound them together. They weren't forced to be strong, to exhibit their rare brand of courage. They did it because it was right, and just, and good. They volunteered to be the courage for the rest of us. They volunteered to fight so we wouldn't have to.

They weren't feeling sorry for themselves. They took an oath, and they lived by a creed. *Never shall I fail my comrades.... Readily will I display the intestinal fortitude required to fight on to the Ranger objective and complete the mission though I be the lone survivor.*

Right now, Xander Whitfield was the lone survivor. And so was Sam.

Shame overcame her. Donovan deserved better. He deserved someone who believed in him, who'd fight for him to the death. That's why Eleanor had called her. She knew, better than Sam did, the depth of emotion that ran between them. Even apart, even in death, there was a connection. A link. Eleanor knew that Sam would find a way.

Mentally, she squared her shoulders. No, she wasn't

going home just yet. She wouldn't run away from him this time. She would find the strength to see this through. She owed Donovan that much.

CHAPTER FORTY-FIVE

Susan Donovan

Susan's head hurt. She reacted to the pain, raising her hands to cradle her skull, but her arms wouldn't move.

She opened her eyes. Her sight was woozy, going in and out of focus. Where was she? What was happening?

Memories floated back to her. Eddie's casket, draped in the flag. Sitting alone at the house. Karen Fisher calling—Jesus, Karen. She'd pulled a gun, and Susan had smashed her in the head with the wine bottle.

The pages from Donovan's journal. Oh, God, were they still in her back pocket?

There was no way to find out, her arms were tied tightly behind her back. She was seated on a chair, hard steel pressed into her skin.

The girls. Oh, my God.

She started to yell and realized her mouth was taped shut. Panic set in. She started to cry, breathing hard, straining against the tape. Her nose got stuffy immediately. She couldn't breathe. She was going to die. She was going to die tied to a chair not knowing who or where or even why because she was crying so hard she couldn't breathe.

"Stop fighting, Susan."

A voice floated near her ear. A voice she recognized. But from where?

She heard a lighter, smelled a newly lit cigarette. Who did she know that smoked?

"Where are the journal pages, Susan?"

She shook her head. *Think, Susan. Who smokes?* Her brain was all foggy, like she'd been drugged.

"I know you know where they are. I need them, Susan. I need to make sure Donovan didn't screw up."

She shook her head again and closed her eyes. The pages. Everyone was after the pages.

The voice and the cigarettes, all of it clicked, and she sent a silent prayer that her person remained unsearched.

"Scream and I'll kill you." A rough hand ripped the tape off her mouth. "Now answer me."

"I don't know," she murmured, her voice thick and slow. "Someone broke into the house. Stole them from his journal." Her voice drifted away.

That worked. She heard a curse, smelled something acrid and her eyes shut again, the fear she felt leaving her drifting behind.

PART THREE

"... And could you keep your heart in wonder at the daily miracles of your life, your pain would not seem less wondrous than your joy; And you would accept the seasons of your heart, even as you have always accepted the seasons that pass over your fields. And you would watch with serenity through the winters of your grief."

—KAHLIL GIBRAN

CHAPTER FORTY-SIX

Savage River State Park
Dr. Samantha Owens

The scenery was breathtaking. Rhododendrons lined the wooded walkways, lush and full. The banked walls on either side of the path were glowing with the apex of multiple spring flowers and grasses. A riot of color overwhelmed the senses: yellows and purples and blues and greens, all vivid and clear. Something about color in the mountains was different. Sam could hear the water from the river flowing nearby, smelled the cool green sap from the evergreens. It was paradise. Paradise with the backdrop of a very serious hell.

They'd arrived at the coordinates Whitfield had slipped Sam at midmorning. They made it to the spot easily; the path was rated green for unskilled hikers. Fletcher kept looking around, as if he expected Whitfield to jump from the trees and yell, "Surprise!" Sam knew it wasn't going to be like that. He was too smart to give himself up without expecting something in return.

Was the man guilty, or trying to help? She was of

two minds. Either he was a master manipulator and they were walking into a trap, or he was truly trying to help them solve the murders. Sinner, or saint? It would be interesting to figure out which.

Sam didn't really know what to expect. Would the man meet them there? Was he waiting for them? Would there be some sort of scavenger hunt to find him? Surely the spill of armed men, two with dogs straining against their leads, would be intimidating. Right?

But Whitfield was a soldier. As skilled as this group may be, he'd faced much worse than a D.C. tactical team. And they were all on his turf now.

Fletcher directed the team to disperse throughout the woods. Sam tried to fathom how he could set up an ambush for a man who was trained to see them, and was expecting them. But Fletch seemed to have an idea of what he was doing, so Sam stowed her concerns and followed him into the forest.

Ten minutes later they veered off the path. The foliage was thick, and the men disappeared into the brush, melting away as if they'd been set for camouflage all along. It was just her and Fletcher, standing side by side in front of a seemingly deserted forest ranger station.

The hunted come to the hunter.

In the solitude, as the quiet shrillness of insects and whispering breezes and the running river became overwhelmingly loud, Sam grew nervous. They were sitting ducks. Whitfield could pick them off one by one. This had been a very bad idea.

She could feel Fletcher's unease, as well. There was no way he thought Whitfield was really the killer, or else he'd never have let the show go down this way. He must think Whitfield had the answers. Or he was trying to protect a man who didn't think he needed protection. Fletcher didn't strike her as a careless man, but maybe he was. Maybe he didn't know any better. It wasn't like he could defend them one-handed.

Breaking the interminable silence, Fletcher's cell phone rang, making them both jump. Sheepishly, he fished it out of his jacket pocket and answered.

He listened, not saying anything, until he finally muttered, "Yeah. Keep me informed," and hung up.

Something was wrong. Sam could see it in his face. Hart? Susan?

"What? What is it?"

"I don't want you to freak out. But Susan Donovan is missing. They found her car at the house, parked in the garage. There was broken glass and blood on her kitchen floor. The blood's being tested right now."

Shit. Shit, shit, shit.

Sam turned, started marching away, into the woods, back the way they'd come.

"Where are you going?" Fletcher asked.

"Where do you think? We have to go back. We have to help look for her."

"Sam, stop. We're three hours away. We already have a mission. Roosevelt's working with the Fairfax County guys and her mother-in-law. They'll find her. I promise, they'll find her."

She kept moving, ducking under branches. She had to get back. She had to help find Susan. She couldn't help but feel that this was her fault, that she'd done something to curse this family. Brought her own sorrow and misfortune to bear upon them, perhaps.

Fletcher ran after her. "Come on, Sam. We need to stick to the plan."

She didn't listen, just kept crashing away through the brush. She didn't care if Fletcher heard her cry. How could he blame her? This was all turning south. Every decision she made was the wrong one.

She heard him running behind her, but he was off-balance, fighting one-handed with the branches and undergrowth that she was able to thread through more easily.

"Sam. Please. Stop!"

She halted at last. He was right. She was being foolish, yet again.

Fletcher walked up to her and pulled her into his arms. She broke away immediately, panic flooding her system. God, she hated to be touched when she was upset.

"Don't," she said, started walking again, fast.

"Sam. Sam! I'm sorry. But you have to stop. We're off the path. You're going the wrong direction. If you want to head back to the car, that's fine, but we need to go the other way. And we're not safe out here alone."

She quit walking. This time, he didn't try to touch her, just turned and gestured back the way they'd come. She folded her arms across her chest and strode past him. He followed in silence.

They went for a minute until Sam heard a branch snap to her left. She stopped dead in her tracks, crouched, coiled, her heart pounding.

"Fletch. Fletch, did you hear that?" she whispered.

Before he could answer, the trees just to her right rustled, then parted. She wanted to run, to scream, but she was frozen.

A dark-haired man stepped out of the forest, silent, deadly. A knife was strapped to his thigh. He had the strap of an assault rifle slung across his chest, the weapon trained on both Sam and Fletcher. He gave them a sad smile.

"Detective Fletcher is absolutely right, Dr. Owens. You're *not* safe out here alone."

CHAPTER FORTY-SEVEN

Savage River
Dr. Samantha Owens

Sam stared at the gun. It looked wicked, black and hard and lethal. She swallowed and glanced at the man holding the weapon. While she knew it was Whitfield, he didn't look like the same man who'd come to Donovan's funeral. He'd shaved, for one, and was wearing dark, wraparound sunglasses. His hair was shorn, as well. He appeared much more like the man in the picture than the man she'd seen just a day ago.

She heard the whisper of metal against leather as Fletcher drew his gun from its holster.

"Whitfield. We don't need anything going south accidentally here. Put down the weapon. Put it down now."

Whitfield cocked an eyebrow skyward. "You first."

"You can't do this. You need to come in. We need to talk."

"Detective Fletcher. I appreciate your interest in me, but I assure you, I am not the one you need to be afraid of." He turned his gaze to Sam.

"Dr. Owens. Would you be so kind as to accompany me?"

Sam looked from Whitfield to Fletcher. The tension between the two was ridiculously thick. She was in the middle of two loaded weapons, and it wasn't just the guns she was worried about.

Fletcher was the first to blink. "I can't let her do that, Whitfield. You're wanted for first-degree murder. I can't let her walk into the woods with you, never to be seen again. I promised to watch over her, and I damn well intend to do that. Now, I'll say it again. Put down your weapon."

Whitfield moved his head fractionally, as if to say okay, fine, whatever. There was a flash from behind Fletcher, and he went down, hard. Sam saw a tall woman standing behind them, a handgun turned backward in her palm, stock out.

"Like he was going to let her come with you, Xander. Really."

Sam tried to stay brave. She had no way to defend herself. For all her talk, she was frightened to death, especially knowing she now had no choice but to leave with Whitfield. The first rule of kidnapping was not to let yourself be taken from the initial spot in the first place. She was about to be forced to break that rule.

"He okay?" Whitfield asked the woman. She bent and felt his pulse.

"Yeah. Gonna have one hell of a headache when he wakes up, though."

"All right. Let's get moving. Dr. Owens, give me your cell."

Sam fought down the panic. She was loath to part with her phone. This was her last link, the only way

Fletcher had to find her. But if Whitfield had it on him, they could still trace it, right? Even if he turned it off? As long as the battery was still attached...

She handed him the phone. He turned it over in his hand and heaved it as hard as he could overhand into the woods.

"You asshole," Sam burst out. "That was my phone."

He looked at her and her stomach turned to water. It was unnerving not to be able to see his eyes. But she didn't need to see them to know this wasn't a man to be messed with.

"I know it was your phone. Move out. Now."

He turned and started to walk away. Sam didn't move. The woman came up behind her and prodded her.

"Follow the man," she said, her tone brooking no argument.

Sam tried to keep her fear in check. She'd come up here to be bait, yes. So Fletcher and Whitfield could talk. Traipsing off into the forest with a killer wasn't on the menu.

She had one trick left in her arsenal. She took a deep breath through her nose and started to scream.

Whitfield turned and slammed his hand over her mouth, cutting her lip with the force.

"Don't even think about it," he whispered. "You want to get dead, too? Keep quiet or I'll gag you. Don't think I won't. I've done worse things today."

Sam shook her head. She could taste the blood in her mouth. Behind the shades, she could see his eyes boring into hers. She was trapped. Testing, he lifted his hand, and she spit the blood out. It landed on his boot. He just looked at it and sighed.

"You are not the first. Come on."

* * *

They walked for what felt like an eternity. Sam didn't exactly have the right gear—she'd worn fine leather boots and wool trousers—and the forest wasn't kind to either. She was cold. They were climbing higher, up into the mountains, but she'd left her jacket in the car.

Smooth move, Owens. Now you've really gotten yourself screwed.

She assumed the woman at her rear was Karen Fisher. She was grim, determined and forceful. When Sam started to lag, she pushed her from behind with the gun in the small of Sam's back.

She took heart in the fact that the dogs would be able to get her scent off her coat. If Fletcher woke up and was able to lead them back to the place they'd been ambushed. If. If. If.

She tried to engage them in conversation multiple times, asking questions about Donovan and Croswell and Everett, until Xander rounded back on her and said, "If you keep talking, we'll never get there. Now shut up and walk."

She listened. They were the ones with the guns, after all.

They hiked until the sun grew low in the sky. After what felt like ages—climbing through the woods, crossing streams, carefully sneaking over a barbed-wire fence—they followed a steepening path that opened to a glade. A sturdy log cabin sat in the middle, with smoke rising from the chimney. There was a huge pile of wood under a tarp, an ATV and a Jeep with the plastic pulled back. Sam saw laundry hanging from the line in the backyard. Children's clothes. They'd set up quite a nice little house up here. A sweet little family estate in the woods.

Sam heard a joyous bark and a black-and-tan German shepherd bounded across the grass toward them.

Whitfield dropped the gun and let the dog leap into his arms. "Who's a good boy?"

Big tough guy, undone by a puppy. That was it, she'd had enough. She'd been frightened, coerced, marched through the woods at gunpoint by strangers, hadn't eaten and was scared witless. She did the only thing she knew to do.

"What's his name?"

Whitfield turned to her in surprise. "Thor."

"May I?" She held out a hand. The dog eyed her warily, stiff legged and alert until Xander said a word she didn't understand. Thor relaxed and came willingly, cuddling up against her leg and giving her hand a good lick. She would pay for that. It only took a few moments for the itching to start, but she ignored it.

A little girl came flying out the cabin door, running down the porch stairs, calling, "They're back, they're back. It's okay, it's only Mommy and Xander." Two boys followed her out more cautiously, staying on the porch instead of running to their mother. The taller of the two held a rifle in his arms, the barrel pointed toward the porch floor.

The woman smiled and grabbed the girl up in a hug. The girl said, "We missed you," then turned to the stranger in their midst. "Who are *you?* Are you one of the bad guys?"

Sam's heart tugged. Good grief, he'd brought his family into this, too?

"No. I'm Sam. Who are you?"

"Jennifer Jill Lyons. I'm six."

"It's nice to meet you, Jennifer." The name registered. Lyons. Sam looked at the girl's mother. This wasn't Karen Fisher. It must be…

"I'm Maggie Lyons," the woman said. "Sorry about that back there. We didn't have a choice."

"I thought you were Karen Fisher."

"Hardly." Maggie's face tightened, and Sam felt like she was missing something. Of course, she'd felt like that for days.

The dog nudged at her hand again, then took off running for the boys. Sam turned to the man who'd kidnapped her. He'd taken off his sunglasses and was watching her with a bemused expression on his face, his eyes darkly unreadable.

"I guess we need to be properly introduced. You're Alexander Whitfield, I take it?"

"Xander. Call me Xander."

"Okay, Xander. I'm not sure what in the hell you're up to, but now that I've seen your little domestic drama, can we go back down the mountain? They're going to be looking for me."

"They can look, but they won't find you until I'm ready."

The words had a menace to them that sent shivers down Sam's spine.

"Xander," Maggie whispered. "You're scaring her."

"So? She needs to be scared. Maybe then she'll stop parading around like a fool, sticking her nose in places it doesn't belong. Go in the house, Maggie."

Sam didn't want to see the woman go. But she wasn't going to let this man know how scared she was. As

Maggie and her daughter went back across the glade, Sam bit right back at him.

"Hey. You came to me. You gave me the card with the coordinates."

"Yeah, but you weren't supposed to show up with the cavalry."

"No, I was supposed to ride off into the forest alone to meet a stranger who's the number-one suspect in my ex-boyfriend's murder. Is that more like it?"

She was pissed off now. She didn't like being scared, didn't want to be here. She was worried about Fletcher. Worried about Susan. Worried for herself.

Xander didn't budge an inch. "I trusted you. And you told the cops about me."

"I had absolutely no choice about that. I tried keeping your little visit to myself, but Detective Hart saw you talking to me. They were looking for you at the funeral. They think you killed Donovan, and Croswell. And you haven't exactly given anyone reason to believe otherwise."

"Do you? Think I killed them? The men I served with, whose lives I've held in my hands countless times? Do you think I laid in wait and shot Eddie in the back of the head? Or Hal?"

Back of the head. He said back of the head, Sam. Donovan was shot in the temple. She'd seen the bullet track firsthand. Her anger dropped a notch.

"I have absolutely no idea. All I know is if you *didn't* kill them, you should have come straight to the police and turned yourself in when you knew they were looking for you."

"And if I did? What if I did murder them? If you thought that for a moment, why on earth did you agree to come out here? Unless you don't value your own life. Or you're just plain stupid."

She looked away, taking in the clearing. He was well established up here in the forest. It was a good hideaway. But why had he run? Why had he disappeared? Why had he led them on this wild-goose chase? If he was innocent, why hadn't he said that from the start?

When she looked back, she realized he was staring at her again with those intense brown eyes. She took a deep breath.

"I'm not stupid," she said.

"Well, I'm glad we've established that, at least. I couldn't turn myself in. Among other reasons, they have my DNA at Billy Shakes's house. I'm sure they've already told you that."

"No, actually, they didn't." And why the hell hadn't they? She immediately got annoyed with Fletcher. Wasn't that something he thought she might want to know? For Christ's sake, that tipped the scales, didn't it?

"So you killed him? Made it look like a suicide?"

His eyes hardened. "You really think I had something to do with their deaths, don't you?"

When his voice got quiet, she could feel the danger in him, coiled and ready to spring. *Easy, Sam.*

"You aren't telling me you didn't."

"I didn't. There. You satisfied?"

He whistled for the dog and strode away, disappearing into the woods where it didn't seem there was a path.

"Wait," she called, but he didn't come back.

She got the strangest sense that she'd just hurt him, wounded him deeply, and she couldn't understand why

she cared. Why it even mattered. This was a stranger. A
stranger who had allowed all of them to run around in
circles, and whose games might be getting more people
killed. She couldn't possibly be feeling sorry for him,
sorry that he'd lost his friends.

And yet she was. She'd read Donovan's journal. She
knew Xander was his right arm. That he trusted him
implicitly, above all the others he commanded.

Maybe that's why she'd come up here, walked right
into his trap. So she could see what Donovan saw.

Maggie Lyons appeared by her side. Sam realized
she'd been staring off into the woods after Xander as if
thinking about him hard enough would bring him back.

"He won't be back for a while. Not when his dander's
up. Why don't you come in the house? I'm sure you're
hungry."

Defeated, Sam followed her to the cabin.

CHAPTER FORTY-EIGHT

Savage River Forest
Detective Darren Fletcher

Fletcher woke up alone on the forest floor, a knot the size of Manhattan on his head. The lovely Dr. Owens was nowhere to be seen. He managed to stand without throwing up—his head was splitting. He wasn't sure exactly what had happened, just knew Sam and Whitfield had been in front of him. So someone had taken him from behind. Which meant Whitfield had a partner. Great.

Where the hell was the tactical team?

He used the compass app on his iPhone to get himself righted. It only took five minutes to get back to the spot he and Sam had started from. He stumbled into the clearing, saw concerned eyes on him from the brush.

"Come out," Fletcher called.

One of the tac team members came out from his hiding place. "You're bleeding."

"I'm not surprised. Check it for me." He bent his head for the guy to look.

"Small gash. Probably need a stitch or two. What happened? Where did you go?"

"I got smacked in the head, that's what. Where the hell were you guys?"

"Here. Setting up our perimeter. Waiting for you to come back from your chat with the chick."

"Great job. While you were futzing around, Whitfield took Dr. Owens."

Fletcher was incredibly pissed off.

His head hurt. His arm hurt. Sam was missing, along with Susan Donovan. He was stuck up here in the woods with no suspect in sight, and Roosevelt had just chewed him out for the second time in two days.

He didn't get paid enough to put up with this shit.

The dogs had scented on Sam's trail about an hour earlier, but the track had led them back to where they'd started. A big-ass circle. Which meant Whitfield had doubled back with her to throw them off the trail. They were seven men and two dogs stuck chasing a trained survivalist through the woods. Fletcher knew they weren't going to find Whitfield without a lot of help and a little luck. But he couldn't give up. They'd called in for a forest service team to come help. At least they knew the lay of the land and could guide everyone around.

It was taking forever to get the warrant enacted to look for the GPS signal for Sam's phone. He just prayed she still had it on her. It was the only way he'd be able to find her outside of a bunch of luck.

If he lost her, if his actions got her killed, he really didn't know what he was going to do.

CHAPTER FORTY-NINE

Savage River
Dr. Samantha Owens

Sam stepped inside Xander's home and let her eyes explore the cabin. It was simple, plainly decorated, saved from being utterly Spartan by the wall of bookshelves and a baby grand piano in the western corner. It was bigger on the inside than she expected. Opposite the front door, there was a vaulted ceiling with glass windows up one wall that looked out over a ridge. The main floor was taken up by a large great room with a big fireplace, a surprisingly modern kitchen and a small dining area. There was a hallway that she assumed led to bedrooms, and a second-story loft that looked like a master bedroom. The furniture was handmade, heavy, wooden, Adirondack-style. She didn't see a television, and she didn't see a phone.

Maggie directed her to the bathroom, where she took care of the necessaries and washed her face, which was smeared with dirt and sweat from the climb. She longed to hop in the shower and let the warm water sooth her aching muscles, but that didn't feel right, somehow.

She brushed her hair back from her face, secured it with a ponytail holder she found on the sink and went back to the kitchen.

Maggie was setting the table.

"We have fresh venison stew. Would you like some?"

"Yes, please."

Venison wasn't her favorite, but she'd eat a horse right now if someone offered. Funny, she couldn't remember the last time she'd been this hungry. It must have been the hike and the clean air. Healthy stuff, especially after the grit of D.C.

Or sheer relief at being alive. She wasn't fond of guns.

Sam accepted a bowl of stew and a large glass of water from Maggie. She was starved, and didn't waste time talking, just focused on getting the food into her stomach. It was good, better than she expected, hot and full of potatoes and vegetables.

"Do you like it?"

"It's very good."

"Noah shot the deer himself." She pointed with pride at her eldest son, who hid a shy, pleased smile in his own bowl.

"Good for you." Sam turned to the boy's mother, who was looking at her son with quiet satisfaction.

"Maggie, I need to ask. What's going on here?"

Maggie poured some more milk for her kids. "It's been a hard few days, Dr. Owens. If you don't mind, can we wait until we put these three to bed?"

She didn't want to talk in front of the children. Okay, Sam could understand that. But the anticipation was driving her mad.

"Fine. But when is Xander coming back?"

"I don't know." This was said simply, with no embellishment, but Sam caught the tone. Maggie was angry with her. She'd chased Xander away with her distrust.

This situation grew more confusing every moment. Sam finished her meal in silence.

After dinner the kids played cards, teasing Jennifer with their antics. Sam honestly didn't think the time would ever come to put the kids down, but at last it did. The minute Maggie left the room, Sam scrambled, trying her best to be quiet as she looked through drawers and cabinets and on shelves for a phone, or some way to communicate with Fletcher.

She struck out.

Maggie came back into the great room. "He doesn't have a phone, if that's what you were looking for. But he does have beer. You want one?"

That wasn't good news. If he didn't have a phone, it stood to reason that he might avail himself of a disposable cell when he needed to, right?

Sam agreed to the beer. She probably shouldn't. Alcohol dulls the senses. But if they wanted her dead, they'd have killed her in the woods, where no one could ever find her. If they still wanted her dead, well, maybe a little alcohol would lessen the pain. She probably couldn't stop them, anyway; they were trained to take bigger threats than Sam down without hesitation.

She wasn't afraid of dying. Not anymore. She'd lost so many, sometimes it felt like it would be easier just to go to them. She just didn't relish the idea of it hurting to die.

Then again, knowing what Simon and the twins had

gone through, maybe she should welcome that punishment, too.

Maggie went to the refrigerator and brought back two Miller Lites. She offered Sam a cold glass. Not exactly the most threatening gesture. She demurred, took the icy beer by the neck.

"I don't drink in front of the kids. Their father, Roy, is an alcoholic. I try to shelter them from it, which means I have to be careful when they're around."

"That sounds wise," Sam said.

Maggie sighed. "I can't believe they're dead. All of them."

If you only knew.

"Please. Maggie. I am so in the dark here. I'm just a medical examiner from Nashville. I'm not supposed to be involved in all of this. My connection to Donovan is over a decade old. His mother asked me to come do a secondary autopsy, and suddenly I'm thrust into this investigation as a pawn, apparently. The reporter, Taranto, told me things that I don't understand. I've tried to be patient, but I need to know what's going on. I need to know why I'm involved."

A deep voice came from the door.

"Then we'll try to explain it."

Xander was back.

CHAPTER FIFTY

Savage River
Dr. Samantha Owens

Xander took up most of the doorway. He held a rifle in his hands. Sam wasn't good with guns, but this looked very similar to the ones she'd seen in Donovan's photograph. Which meant it was powerful, military-grade, and Xander held it like it was an extension of his body.

Dangerous. This man was more dangerous than anyone she'd ever met.

He watched her eyeing the weapon. He passed his hand over the trigger, then grasped the stock and set it carefully against the wall. He held his empty hands open as if to say, *Okay, I've disarmed myself. I'm vulnerable. Now it's your turn.*

"Where do you want me to start?" Xander asked.

That was an excellent question. But first...

"Where have you been? Did you see Fletcher? Can I call him and let him know I'm okay?"

Xander shook his head. "Detective Fletcher and the remainder of his crew are fine. They're all with a friend of mine, getting settled down for the night. When the time is right, Dr. Owens, I'll get you back with him. But now is not the time. So, what other questions do you have?"

Shit. Fletcher was going to kill her, if Xander and Maggie didn't do it first. Would Xander really give her answers? Then she might as well start with the biggie.

"Who killed Donovan and Croswell? And why is your DNA at Everett's house?"

"I don't know who killed them."

"Come on. You expect me to believe that?"

Xander settled at the kitchen table, accepted a beer and some stew from Maggie. He took his time answering. Sam realized how very measured he was: in his manner, his words, his actions, everything. No wonder he'd stalked off earlier—rather than say something or lose his temper, he walked away.

That said something about his character.

Finally, he set down his spoon and said, "You'll have to believe it, because it's true. All I know for sure is it was someone Donovan trusted, and Croswell. Someone they knew, who was intimately familiar with their lives. Neither one of them would deviate from their schedule without good cause. Once a soldier, always a soldier."

"Xander, you realize you're describing yourself."

He quirked a smile at her. "Unfortunately, yes. Who do the police think did it?"

"You."

"No, they don't. Not really. Who else?"

"Maggie."

The woman's eyebrows raised and she immediately looked scared. "Me? They think I'm involved? My God, Xander. What are we going to do?"

"Maggie, calm down," Xander said, grabbing her hand. "Hal was shot across the street from your house. The minute you found out, you blew town. Of course you're a suspect. The more important question is—do they know how you know Hal? Your real connection to him and Donovan?"

"Yeah, they do," Sam said. "That reporter you impersonated? Told us one hell of a story. About your daughter, and who her father really is. Taranto's dead, by the way."

Xander whipped his head back to Sam. "What?"

"Right after I met with him. I was followed out of the restaurant, back to Fletcher and Hart, and they shot at us. Hart was hurt badly. Fletcher took a bullet to the arm. Then the killer went and tracked down Taranto, shot him and tossed his body in the Potomac."

Xander ran his hand over his mouth. "So that's why Fletcher was in a sling. I am very sorry to hear about Taranto. He was a good man, or at least trying to do the right thing. And I'm happier than ever that you're up here now, where I can protect you."

"Protect *me*? What about Donovan's family? Susan Donovan is missing, too. For God's sake, Xander, we can't just hide away up here pretending everything's going to be okay. It's not. It's not okay—nothing will ever be okay again." Sam choked back a sob, of frustration, fear, she didn't know what else, and slammed her chair back from the table. She went to the sink, not giving a damn if they watched her.

One Mississippi. Two Mississippi. Three Mississippi. Four.

Slowly, the water and soap calmed her beating heart, helped her get her emotions back in check. She breathed deeply with each perambulation, counting off in her head over and over and over.

One Mississippi. Two Mississippi. Three Mississippi. Four.

Simon. Matthew. Madeline. Eddie.

When her mind finally felt quiet enough to stop, she rinsed one last time and dried her hands on a red checked dishcloth.

She turned back to Xander and Maggie, who were politely looking away, staring into their beers.

She joined them at the table.

"I'm sorry. I get…upset. Washing helps."

Like they care, Sam. Really. You need to stop telling people about your troubles. She'd managed to go nearly two years without anyone commenting on her failings, and now half of D.C. was aware she'd become a hopeless mess. Maybe she did need protecting, after all.

Xander met her eyes, frank and open. "I understand, actually. That's why I'm up here. I get…upset, too."

"The war?"

"Among other things. I don't know how much you know about me, Dr. Owens."

"Your background. Your parents. That you were a very brave soldier." She stopped for a moment, then started again, quietly. "I know Eddie Donovan thought the world of you. He trusted you implicitly. He talked about you a lot in his journals. He respected you, in addition to enjoying your company. That's why I'm here. Eddie trusted you. And now it seems, so must I."

"Mommy?"

A small, scared voice startled all three of them. Jennifer had climbed out of bed and come down the hall.

"Did you have another nightmare, sweetie?" Maggie asked.

"Yes. The bad one." The little girl's face was pink with the effort not to cry.

"Oh, sweetie. Come here." She gave Sam an apologetic look, and spoke sotto voce. "She's been having bad dreams since we ran." Then to her daughter, she said, "Tell me about it."

The little girl was trying hard to hold it together. "It was the house across the street. Back home. There was a man there. He had a wand. Like Voldemort. He waved at it you, Mommy, and sparks flew out, and you fell down."

She started to cry in earnest, and Maggie pulled her to her chest and held her, murmuring soothing words of nonsense to help calm her child. Sam fought the nausea that immediately blossomed when she saw the intimacy. She stood and went to the window, looked out in the dark night sky, saw the outline of the trees, their edges shimmering in moonlight.

A repeating nightmare.

The house across the street.

A man with a wand.

Perhaps a childlike interpretation of a gun?

Sam rushed back to the table. "She saw the shooting."

Maggie and Xander both stared at her.

"Ask her," Sam said. "Ask her."

Maggie frowned, but sat Jen back on her lap. "Honey, the other night, your birthday night, you read that scary book and had a bad dream, then you called for me. What was it about?"

"That wasn't a bad dream, Mommy. Across the street,

there was a shooting star in the window, and then some-one left."

She stuck her thumb in her mouth and started hum-ming "Twinkle, Twinkle, Little Star."

Maggie pulled her thumb from her mouth gently. "Sweetie, the someone who left. Did you recognize him?"

Jen shook her head. Maggie tried again.

"Was it a him? Or a her? Could you tell?"

Sam glanced over at Xander, whose face was intent with interest. He doesn't know, she thought. He really doesn't know who killed them.

The realization that Xander had been telling the truth almost made her collapse in relief. For some reason, she so wanted to believe this man. She wanted to believe him in the very worst way.

Was it Donovan? Did Xander remind her of him? Or was it the things Donovan had written in his jour-nal that made her feel like she knew Xander? Parts of him, at least.

Or was it the way his eyes probed into her like he was trying to share the universe's thoughts with her?

Flustered, she turned away, but heard Jen's answer. "It was a him."

Maggie sighed, and Xander sucked his breath in through his teeth. "You're sure?" he asked.

"Yes," Jen answered. "He had short hair and made a big shadow across the street. I thought he was coming to get me. Do you know the bad man?"

Xander glanced at Maggie, then over to Sam.

"Yes, sweetie. I think I do. And I promise, he won't ever come near you again."

CHAPTER FIFTY-ONE

Savage River Lodge
Detective Darren Fletcher

The sun was gone. Defeated, Fletcher had agreed to hunker down for the night. His sense of honor was in tatters. He was so worried for Sam he could barely breathe. As darkness had enveloped the search team, they decided a staging point would be necessary, and found the nearby Savage River Lodge, a beautiful stone-and-timber retreat that Fletcher had half a mind to check into and never come back out again.

The forest service guys were stretched out over a table to his right, looking at a topographical map, estimating times and drawing circles with their protractors, then tapping things into their computers. They were attempting to figure out how far Sam could have gone on foot, working on the assumption, however faulty it may be, that she hadn't been shoved in a car. Or put on a horse. Or dropped off a cliff.

All he could do was wait. On the streets of D.C. he knew what his place was, what he could do. Out here, in the woods, he didn't stand a chance. He'd never been much of a nature guy. Outside of the odd Boy Scout camping trip with Tad, trips that Felicia increasingly took in his stead as the boy grew up, he'd never spent any time in the woods. He wasn't a hunter or a fisher. He was a cop. A jog down by the river was as exotically outdoors as he ever got.

He'd been stupid to think he could control the situation. Alexander Whitfield was a seasoned soldier, capable of hiding in plain sight, and that knowledge made Fletcher even angrier. He'd been played. They'd all been played.

But something in his gut told him Whitfield wasn't his man. He was so far off the grid that calling attention to himself by murdering his old friends seemed out of character, at least the little bit he'd been able to profile from Whitfield's record and Sam's translations from Edward Donovan's journal.

Now, Margaret Lyons was another story. A woman scorned is a powerful thing. According to Taranto, Perry Fisher was the father of her kid. Maybe someone in her chain of command had figured that out and was using that knowledge to scuttle her career, and things got out of hand. Croswell could have found out and confronted her. She snapped, walked him across the street to the house she knew was empty, shot him and played dumb until morning, when Fletcher and Hart came knocking on her door.

A plausible theory, sure. But where did Donovan fit into that? Lyons had been at work at her law firm when Donovan was shot. Three people had seen her and confirmed.

Karen Fisher was still a good choice. Assuming she

was playing the reporter for her own personal gain...
She could have been using Taranto to ferret out the real
story, and Donovan and Croswell were trying to keep
it quiet.

Shit, if he just knew who'd been the actual shooter
in the friendly fire. That would help narrow it down.

DOD wasn't talking. Roosevelt had called three
times, pushing hard. He was about to play his last
card, which was going public with the information in
an attempt to bluff them into telling the story. Fletcher
wanted him to do it right now, but Roosevelt fancied a
few more tries to see if he could work the back chan-
nels.

Fletch even thought about calling Felicia, beg and
plead for her to talk to Joelle again, but they were running out of time.

That damn phone call. That's what got the ball rolling. But there was nothing to indicate that the Raptor
offices were Donovan's end goal—he could have been
meeting anyone anywhere. For all intents and purposes,
it looked like a fluke that his direction took him toward
the Raptor offices. Donovan's boss, Deter, hadn't called
him in. The other guy, Culpepper, was in Iraq at the
time. Fletcher had interviewed the personnel there three
times, and didn't have a single hit.

So Donovan was headed somewhere else. But where?

Fletcher paced around the room.

He thought back to the conversation Sam had with
Taranto. He brought out his notebook and went through
the code names again.

King, that was Perry Fisher. Doc was Donovan.
Shaky Guy was William Everett. Mutant was Whitfield, Jackal was Croswell.

There was another name on that list. Taranto said when Karen Fisher heard that her husband might had been killed by one of his compatriots, by one of his friends, she went to another, Orange, to get the truth.

So who the hell was Orange?

Orange was his killer. He had to be. And something about Perry Fisher's death exposed the man, or woman, who operated under that nickname, and as a result, they needed to minimize the damage as quickly and efficiently as possible.

And the best way to make sure no one talks is to permanently shut them up.

Had Susan Donovan figured out the truth? Fletcher resisted smacking himself on the head. Of course she had. She'd found the missing pages from the journal.

Could she be responsible for her husband's death?

Shit. That couldn't be. She was missing. But had she gone on the run? No. He was firmly convinced the killer was part of Donovan's unit overseas.

He called Roosevelt.

"Where are we with the DOD?"

"Third time's a charm. I've been invited to the Pentagon. Fifteen minutes."

"That is fantastic news. I've got a couple things for you, too. Knock on my head must have sprung loose some nuts. You need to go find Karen Fisher. Taranto supposedly had her hidden away. She is involved, though how I don't know. Check Taranto's credit cards—he told Sam he was keeping Karen somewhere safe, so he probably got her a hotel room. And while you're at the Pentagon, see if you can find out who was saddled with the moniker Orange while they were over there. Someone in Donovan's unit was called Orange, and that's who our killer is. I'm sure of it."

Roosevelt was quiet for a minute. "Seems I should let you get shot, lost and hit on the head more often. How would someone get saddled with the nickname Orange?"

"Fuck if I know. Maybe he likes orange juice, or is from Florida or California. Remember that show, the O.C.? Orange County? Or has red hair. Doesn't matter. We just need to find out who he or she is."

"Your wish is my command."

Fletcher laughed. "Call me back." He closed his phone and went to the table of forest service guys.

"You got anything?"

The lead kid, and Jesus, he was a kid, nodded. "Four sites they could be, sir. Spread across the mountain. All very remote. Permanent camps on private property. It's going to take a few hours to get to any of them."

"Show me."

The topographical map was just a bunch of lines and squiggles, circles and four small red *X*s. All of them were in an area within the greatest concentration of lines, scattered across the map like miniature camp-fires.

"What do those lines mean?" Fletcher asked.

"Oh, you don't know how to read a topo? That's an elevation indicator. Pretend it's in 3-D. If you can imagine the lines as rising into the air, as the concentric gets smaller, that's the higher up the mountain it is."

"I failed Boy Scout 101. How far are these from us?"

"Closest one will take two hours. Farthest is five, minimum."

"Do you know who lives at any of them?"

"No. No, sir. Very remote. We don't normally get up that way. We're assigned to the park only. That's private property."

"All right, then. There are four of you. Each of you will guide a team of my men. And we aren't waiting for morning. We're moving out right now." He turned to the tactical team guys who were happily sprawled around the lodge's great room, enjoying the fire and their full stomachs. The lodge owners had taken good care of them.

Fletcher spun his finger in the air over his head.

"Get off your asses. Lock and load. We're rolling."

"But, sir…" The kid who'd explained the map looked panicked. "Really, it's not safe."

Fletcher turned on him.

"There's a woman in danger at one of those camps. Do you want to be responsible if we get there too late because you were scared to go out on the mountain at night?"

The kid puffed out his chest. "I'm not scared. I'm just not an idiot."

"Then prove it. And keep us safe while you're doing it."

CHAPTER FIFTY-TWO

Savage River
Maggie Lyons

Maggie got Jen a glass of water and took her back to the bedroom to tuck her in. They were sharing a double bed—an inflatable air mattress. The boys were out cold on the floor in their sleeping bags. It always amazed her how hard they slept. Of course, they played hard, too, and, since they'd been up here with Xander, worked hard, as well.

This room was Xander's armory, and playroom. Weapons in various forms lined the walls, guns and bows and artillery, a variety wide enough the ATF would probably freak if they ever saw. He'd pushed a table out of the way that contained all of his fishing lures, tackle and numerous other things Maggie didn't recognize.

It was nice, having guy friends who could do some of the fathering Roy was incapable of providing. Noah and Bobby had both been up here before. To them, visiting Xander's was like a really elaborate camping trip.

She wondered if they'd remember the fun times they had up here when all was said and done.

Now that she'd finally listened to Jen, who'd been trying to tell her about the scary man across the street for three days, now that they knew for sure who had killed Croswell and, of course, Donovan, Maggie had no illusions about what was going to happen.

She and Xander were next. And once they were gone, the whole situation went far, far away.

She didn't want to die. She'd already been through hell, and come out the other side. Not unscathed, never unscathed, but whole enough to get her life back on track.

She had made mistakes. Big mistakes. Getting involved with Perry Fisher—that had been a whopper. She'd always hated women who cheated, but once Roy started drinking more and more, treating her like she was a piece of dirt trapped under the sole of his shoe, after he punched her when she was home on leave and she had to return to her unit with a black eye and lie about how she got it, something in her changed. Her allegiance to Roy was shattered. She met Perry, and was lost. Perry was a gentleman, a soft-spoken soldier with intensely blue eyes that to Maggie seemed like staring into a perfect summer sky. He was married, as well, which made her feel doubly bad, but he'd filed for an official separation before they got involved, so she supposed it wasn't as much of a sin as it would have been if he was just getting his rocks off.

He loved her. And she loved him.

When it became apparent to both of them that their feelings went deeper than just a simple physical affair, she'd gone online and found the makings necessary to file for divorce from Roy. Separation wasn't even on the drawing board. Roy would have to be a clean split, or else he'd never let her go. Not all the way.

But she had to tell him in person. She owed it to him. So they were waiting for her to get back to the States to file.

She and Perry snatched time together whenever they could, which wasn't a lot. War doesn't leave a lot of downtime. But they'd managed to finagle leave together, back at Kandahar Airfield. Compared to being out on the roads, the Kaf was the Four Seasons.

And that's when it all went south.

The fight they'd had after the "incident," as she called it, was epic. She'd come out an emotional wreck. Perry died three days later, and nine days after that, while she was still in the grips of horror, she found out she was pregnant with Jen.

She went straight to the doctor, determined to have an abortion, but couldn't go through with it. The doctors who treated her wrote her a medical discharge, and she was out of Dodge before you could shake a stick. She wasn't even going to pretend she wanted to stay. She just wanted, no, needed, to lick her wounds at home, away from prying eyes.

There was no way to play Roy, though. She was three months gone before the dust settled and she was back in Georgetown, applying to law schools. One look at him, drunk and weaving, the fire of anger boiling in his eyes, and she blurted out the truth, told him she wanted a divorce and threatened to kill him if he touched her again.

She didn't tell him the name of Jen's father, though. She didn't tell anyone.

She kept her head down, worked hard, loved her kids, all three of them, and tried to forget. Until three days ago, when Hal Croswell was murdered across the street from her house, and all she knew to do was bug out. She ran straight for Xander and told him the whole story, start to finish. Not the party line. She'd told him what really happened. He'd gotten her set up with the boys and immediately headed south, to Billy, to bring him to the safety of Xander's home. But he was too late. Billy had caved under the pressure.

They were all dead. And the man who killed them was still out there. Haunting her. Hunting her. Trying to make sure the secrets never came out.

She put her head in the pillow and let the tears come.

CHAPTER FIFTY-THREE

Savage River
Dr. Samantha Owens

Sam watched Maggie's subtle retreat to the bedroom. Xander got up from the table and cleaned the kitchen in silence. He was a big man, naturally lean and muscled from outdoor work. He took up a lot of real estate in the small kitchen space.

She considered him for a few moments. When nothing was forthcoming, she said, "Um, hey. Are you planning to share? Because I'd really like to know what's going on. You know who killed them now?"

"Yeah," Xander said. She could practically hear the gears turning in his head, but he didn't say anything more. She sighed and nudged him again.

"Are you going to tell me who did this, or are you going to keep me in the dark, like you have everyone else?"

He shut the refrigerator door.

"Let's go for a walk."

More walking. Her legs were like rubber already.

He must have realized the reason for her hesitation, because he smiled and said, "Just outside. It's a pretty night. Here." He took a thick flannel jacket off the peg by the door and tossed it to her. "Put this on. You really shouldn't be out in the woods without a coat."

She glared at him and put the coat on. She swam inside it, but the warmth curled around her and she relaxed. She'd been cold all night. He was the reason she was devoid of suitable outerwear. If he hadn't kidnapped her... God, that smile of his was like turning on a light switch in a dark attic. It illuminated everything around him.

"Come on."

Sam was getting awfully good at following orders. She stepped out the front door, waited while he shut it behind them. The darkness surrounded them, pushing in, and she suddenly felt afraid. Now that she'd heard some details, was he going to get rid of her?

"Dr. Owens. You can relax. On my honor, I promise I'm not going to hurt you."

God, he could read her like an open book.

"You can call me Sam, you know."

"I'd like that." He took her hand and led her from the porch, surefooted as a mountain lion in the pitch-dark. The moon had set already, but it would have been blocked by the chimney on this side of the house, she realized.

"We can sit here."

Xander helped Sam find a seat. She swung above the ground for a sickening moment, then settled, her feet barely touching. She felt a breeze on her butt. She realized it must be a rope hammock. She heard a sharp flick, then saw flames dancing in Xander's hands. He dropped the two matches onto the ground, and a nice fire sparked. Now that there was some light, Sam could see the fire pit clearly. Simple and clean, prepped and waiting, just like the rest of his things.

"A hammock by the fire? Is the ambiance appropriate now?"

"I like to lay out here and think sometimes."

"It's…nice," she said. She expected her teeth to start chattering, but the jacket held its warmth. And his smell. Evergreen and the tiniest hint of sweat.

Jesus, Sam. Get it together.

He worked the fire a bit, then settled on his haunches on the ground next to her. No, he wasn't on the ground. She realized he was perched on a tree stump, looking like it was the most comfortable place in the world. He set the gun against his leg.

The creaking of the night settled around them like a blanket. Insects chirped, birds rustled. She could hear her own breath, and his. It was time.

"You know what's on the pages Donovan tore out of his journal, don't you."

"I think so," Xander said. "Are you sure you want to hear the story? It's not sanitized."

"Of course I do. My God, isn't that why I'm here? To hear the truth?"

"You're here so I can keep you safe."

Around and around the mulberry bush. This man was going to drive her crazy.

"Can I ask you something?"

"Sure."

"Why do you feel the need to keep me safe?"

"Because you need looking after."

Way to state the obvious. Sam wasn't a warrior. She

was just a girl. That had been emphasized all the more back in the cabin when she was sitting side by side with Maggie, who was also of the female persuasion but could hardly be called *girlie*. Hell, even the way she strutted around with the weapons was graceful and contained. She reminded Sam of Taylor. That was funny.

"I don't disagree with that. I do need looking after. But why does it have to be *you?* The cops can take care of me. They've done a decent job of it so far."

"Ha. They sent you, a civilian, into an ambush, nearly got you killed, then lost you on a mountaintop. I'd hardly call that taking good care."

Xander poked at the fire, and the blanket of silence settled over them. She gave it a few minutes before she acquiesced. Maybe agreeing with him would draw him out more.

"Granted. But the way you say it, it's like you have an obligation to me or something. You don't. You don't even know me."

"I know you better than you think."

He got quiet again. She felt like she was pulling teeth, long, slow, arduous teeth that were cemented in a fossilized mandible. She let her breath out slowly, hoping some of the exasperation she was feeling would bleed away. It didn't.

"Eddie loved you a lot, you know," Xander said.

That she wasn't expecting. It was obvious that Eddie had mentioned her to Xander, or else he wouldn't feel the need to keep her tucked away, but she never imagined his feelings had been this deep. Not after such a long time.

"We hadn't talked in almost fifteen years," she said quietly.

"Doesn't matter. A man never forgets his first love. And you were his."

She laughed, a harsh, unforgiving sound that surprised her. "No, I wasn't. I was his second. The Army was always his first love."

"Hoo-rah," Xander said automatically.

"Exactly my point."

"Point taken. But you can't think it didn't break his heart to leave you, too. Because it did. I knew him before he met Susan. She was the best thing that could have happened to him. Because until he met her…that man was lost without you."

Sam didn't want to hear that. Didn't want to be reminded of what might have been. There was no going back in this life, no do-overs. She'd walked away, across the bridge, and closed the door on Eddie Donovan forever. Or so she thought.

The night air drew in around them, and she used the chirping crickets as cover for her shaky breath.

"It wasn't supposed to be him. We both knew that. Him leaving was for the best."

Xander tossed the stick to the ground. "He knew that. God, Sam, don't you see? He left because of the obligation he felt to you. He knew he'd put you in an untenable situation. Making you choose between the man you'd loved for years and the man you'd practically just met? He couldn't handle the thought that, one day, you'd wake up and realize you'd chosen the wrong man. He didn't want to put you through that. So he pushed you as far away as he could. He sacrificed his own happiness to assure yours."

Sam couldn't hold the tears back anymore.

Donovan, you bastard. Still making me cry. You weren't supposed to love me like that.

Xander waited patiently while she pulled it together. Finally, she took a deep breath and wiped at her eyes.

"I didn't know that. Thank you for telling me. It helps. I'm glad he was able to find happiness again. But he found you, obviously. You were his very good friend. I can tell."

"Yes, we were. We met in Ranger school. An experience like that bonds men. Of course, that's part of its intent. Then we were both assigned to the 75th, though we started in different units. By our third rotation, though, he was my commanding officer. Man could have risen through the ranks like he was on fire, been a colonel, even a general, easily. He was a *great* leader. He cared about his men. He didn't just keep them safe out on missions, he helped them with their money troubles, girlfriend troubles, whore troubles. He called and wrote letters to each parent as soon as their son or daughter joined the unit, letting them know he was watching their backs. He fought for better facilities, more rack time, safer gear, real counseling after bad missions. When we lost someone, he cried with us. He inspired loyalty. That can't be taught. It has to come from within."

She could see him tense, the line of his shoulders taut under his jacket.

"You were in charge of men, too. You must have embodied some of that."

He didn't respond right away. Sam turned away from him, listened to the fire crackle. Xander nudged a log with the toe of his boot. It shifted and settled deeper into the flames, sending sparks into the clear night sky.

When he spoke again, his voice was gruff. "You're kind to say that, but everything I learned about being a leader was through his example. He was the real deal. And he had medical training, so we were always doubly covered out on missions. He'd drop his weapon and bind up a wound while shouting orders… He was something to behold, let me tell you."

His voice trailed off. She let him sit in silence, not wanting to push him, realizing he was telling her the whole story, just in his own way.

"Have you ever heard of literal obedience?" he asked, finally.

"No, but I can divine its meaning."

"It's an important concept in the military, one that's drilled into every new recruit and officer candidate the moment they get their high and tights and become one of the masses. When your commanding officer says, 'Come stand on this line,' he means stand *on* the line. Not an inch in front of it, or behind it, or to the side, or with your knees bent or your toes sticking out. But *on* it. We were taught to be literal because when we're out in the field, and your commander gives an instruction, that inch left or right or forward or backward might mean our leg, or our arm, our life or the life of the man standing next to us. Orders have a reason. That's why they're orders. A good commander won't ever have to ask twice. Obedience and loyalty go hand in hand if there's respect, too. That's the kind of soldier Eddie was. He never had to give an order twice."

He sighed, and Sam felt like he'd made some sort of decision.

"I trust that you'll keep this to yourself."

"Of course. I don't want Eddie dragged through the mud any more than you do."

"It's not Eddie's reputation I'm worried about. You may not know this, but it's illegal to have relations within the unit. Fraternization can get you court-martialed. It could have gotten all of us in trouble. Because we knew. Shakes, Jackal and I. We knew about King and Maggie. They were trying to keep it quiet, but King needed to talk to someone about it. We were his closest friends. He was conflicted—he didn't love Karen anymore, felt she was unstable. He wanted custody of the kids. He was head over heels for Maggie. They clicked, like two magnets. I know Karen, know she's not a piece of cake to live with. So I supported him, because that's what friends do."

"So you covered up the affair for them?"

"And covered our asses, as well. Yes. We did."

Sam pushed off the ground with her foot. It was so quiet up here. No one was around. Xander could tell her this story, then toss her off the mountain, and no one would be the wiser. But Eddie had trusted this man. She wanted to trust him, too.

Xander put another log on the dwindling fire, then sat back and spoke again.

"We'd been on a week's leave at the Kaf when something happened. All was well and then boom, at the end of the week, Maggie suddenly wouldn't talk to King. Wouldn't see him. Shut him off completely. Wouldn't give a reason. He was devastated. Wrote her letters, begged, pleaded… She cut him off cold, and he had no idea why. Before he could fix things, we got sent back out, and within three days he was dead."

Xander was tense; Sam could feel him next to her,

rock still. She spoke softly, not wanting to interrupt but realizing he needed some space, that he'd slipped back in time to the moment of his friend's death.

"Taranto had a video. I saw it, but I couldn't understand what exactly happened."

His voice was like a metronome, flat and emotionless.

"Mission went south. We were all back at the base, in our racks. Got called out to provide support. Echo Company was taking heavy fire, they'd been ambushed on a ridge. We scrambled out there, everyone, all hands on deck. We got to the fight, saw things were out of hand. Doc and Orange devised a plan, sent us around the back of the firefight to flank the Taliban who'd holed up in the hills. They were taking potshots, just picking our men off as they drove up the wadi—that's the dry riverbed. Some of the most dangerous spots we had to ride through. King and I took the lead, on foot, got around the backside, running along the top of a ridge. I stopped and he went ahead of me, over the edge, into the wadi. We'd flanked them perfectly, and Doc ordered us to open fire.

"It was a seamless operation. We neutralized the threat, our guys were able to get out of harm's way. Except, somehow, King went down. He had gotten in front of us. We didn't realize it for a few minutes. He was KIA instantly. When Donovan found him he tried to resuscitate him, but it was obvious he was gone. We had to pull him off to get him to stop. We got King back to base. Once the wound was lit up, we could see it clearly. There were two shots to the *back* of his head. Below his helmet. He was shot from behind. It was one of us."

Sam heard the pain in his voice and, without thinking, reached her hand out and touched his shoulder. He didn't move, and didn't shove her hand away, but kept talking in a soft monotone.

"There are always eyes on every battle. The video you saw, hell, it could have been us, I have no idea. Powers that be hushed it all up, didn't want King's wife to know. Covering up friendly fire happens more than you could ever imagine. If Karen suspected a cover-up, decided to start making a stink, filed a lawsuit to get the records and videos, hell, it could go all the way to a wrongful-death suit, and the Army couldn't have another case make the evening news. Plus the mission was a sensitive one, and if word got out—well, sometimes they don't think these things through. Too many variables, too many repercussions. We all got asked to shut up about it. And we all agreed."

"I see," Sam said.

"No, you don't see. When we debriefed, it didn't make sense. How King could have gotten so far off track. It was almost like someone contacted him and told him to go in a different direction, to charge east instead of west, effectively cutting back in front of us. But I was the last person who talked to him, and I certainly didn't give that order.

"Once they triangulated everything, wrapped up the story, it was pretty clear Doc was the one who'd shot him. They did an autopsy and pulled the slugs from his head, saw they were from an M249. That's a light machine gun—it's what Doc favored so he could have a medical kit with him, too. He was the only one of us carrying that weapon. Brass said it was pretty damn straightforward. They confirmed that he'd shot King."

Sam realized she was wringing her hands. *One Mississippi, Two Mississippi. Three…* This time, it was Donovan's pain she was trying to wash away. Donovan's, and Xander's.

"Donovan must have been crushed."

"Yeah. Doc was torn up. Ripped. He shut down harder than I've ever seen, wouldn't talk to anyone. They sent him to Germany, got him talked to. He came back, but he'd changed. He wanted out as soon as possible. When our rotation was up, he made it clear he wasn't going to stick around. Without him, none of us really wanted to stay, either.

"But the sequence from that night, it didn't feel right to me. I couldn't get it out of my head. So a few weeks ago, I went to Orange and requested the video. I wanted to see for myself, see how we messed up. He told me to let it go. Doc was the shooter, it wasn't my fault, or my responsibility. But that's not how we work. We were a team. A good one. We didn't fuck up. And getting King killed, that was as big a fuckup as can happen."

Sam was sitting forward now, completely caught up in Xander's story.

"But you thought that wasn't the case?"

He shook his head.

"I started digging around the files, the briefings, to see what I could see. I still have friends in the Pentagon. What I found was damning, at best. The video they'd shown us wasn't our video. It was date and time stamped on the disc, like they all are, but it had been altered. It was from the year before. Some other friendly fire incident.

"I went straight to Doc. We sat down and had a long talk. Mapped everything out, I'm talking down to the fraction of an inch. As best we could figure, the shots that killed King came twenty degrees from my left. Doc was on my right. So someone else was up there, either trying to engage the Tallies, or..."

"Trying to kill King."

"Yeah. I was convinced Doc didn't do this, and it wasn't right for him to have to carry that burden. I went to Taranto, started some quiet inquiries. And then everything went to hell. Doc, Jackal and Shakes were dead. Maggie showed up here and finally told me the whole truth about what happened back when we left Kaf. She'd given me most of the story, but not all."

Xander got quiet again. Sam waited him out. A frog started up, singing in the rushes down toward the river. Finally, Xander cleared his throat and told her the rest of it.

"The night it all started, back at the Kaf, Maggie and King were supposed to hook up, their usual spot, but he didn't show. He'd gotten sent out on patrol, didn't have time to warn her. She didn't know that, though. She was really upset. But someone else made an appearance. Turns out the five of us weren't the only ones who knew about their affair. This guy told her he'd get her tossed out if she didn't have sex with him. She turned him down flat, so he raped her."

Sam sucked in a breath. *Oh, my God.*

"Rape isn't the most uncommon thing in the military, unfortunately. You look at the studies, four out of every ten women in the service say they've been raped or assaulted. Forty percent. It's one of the reasons we fight against having them side by side on a combat mission—there's serious naked aggression that goes into what we do. We have to temper ourselves, or else we tip over the edge, and that's when massacres occur. Some men get a release from forcing women, even though we're over there telling them it's not right to rape their own women....

"Anyway, she wouldn't tell me who raped her. Didn't tell me who it was until she showed up three days ago. But she did tell King. They had a huge fight about it, and she broke it off with him. Said she couldn't face being with an honorable man after what had happened. He blamed himself, of course. If he hadn't been sent off to the line, if he'd made their date..."

"Please tell me it wasn't—?"

"It was Orange," he said bitterly. "We fucking trusted him, and this is what kind of man he was all along. He assigned King that tour. He wanted to get at Maggie himself."

"Xander, who is Orange?"

It hit her then. *Orange*. She suddenly knew exactly who it was. He was so named because there was a city near Orange, Virginia, called...

"Culpepper."

CHAPTER FIFTY-FOUR

Savage River
Detective Darren Fletcher

The darkness cut across the sky like a heavy blanket. Fletcher regretted his choice to ride in one of the four-wheel-drive Jeeps the forest rangers used. He regretted insisting they set off in the dark. He regretted not waiting until morning and letting a helicopter fly him up the mountain, instead of this jolting, thumping canter up the tiny switchback roads. Each bump felt like a hot poker was being shoved into his arm, over and over and over, and his head was aching in time. Sweat had broken out on his forehead, and he felt a bit like vomiting.

But he wasn't about to admit he was wrong, so he gritted his teeth and sucked it up.

They'd been on the road for an hour. Before they decided which camp to take, Fletcher had practically knocked the teeth out of the forest ranger, making him give his best guess as to where Sam would be. He had the distinct impression the kid knew, and he threatened and cajoled until the boy chose the site they were headed to.

He could only hope his instincts were right. Whitfield had to have friends in these hills, people who would do him a favor or two, like distract a tactical team trying to find his place. Someone young and idealistic, maybe. Someone like a young forest ranger.

Fletcher's phone rang, and he fished it out of his pocket, thankful he'd remembered to charge it back at the lodge, and that he had a signal. It was Roosevelt. "Tell me you have good news."

"I do. We found Susan Donovan. Poor thing's pretty beat up, but she's alive. Guess where we found her?"

"I have no idea," Fletcher said.

"Tied to a chair in Allan Culpepper's living room. He wanted the journal pages. Smart girl, she told them they'd been stolen, that no one knew where they were, and he believed her. But she had them in her back pocket and didn't give them up."

"Wait a minute. Culpepper is in Iraq. I saw the billet. Are you sure it wasn't Rod Deter? That bastard was lying to me," Fletcher said.

"No, not Deter, and Culpepper isn't in Iraq. He's definitely in the U.S. I'm thinking probably up there running around the woods someplace close to you."

"Fuck. Son of a bitch played me."

"Apparently so. DOD gave us the info we needed at last. His passport hasn't been stamped in the past month. He's been in the States the whole time."

Fletcher resisted the urge to smack his forehead. The documents he'd seen were forgeries, and damn good ones, at that.

"Why lie, though? He gave me a big song and dance about hitching a ride with the sultan of… Just… Fuck."

"Yep, again. We got confirmation that he's your dude. Crime scene found a cigarette butt at the Croswell crime scene, in the garden behind the house. Matches the brand we found in his condo. DNA tests are under way, expedited, but it will be a couple of days at least."

Fletcher slapped the dash with his open hand.

"Son of a bitch."

"You could say that. There are weapons galore at his place. No telling if one of them will match the hole in Taranto, or you, or Hart."

"Or William Everett's mother. Jesus, how could I be so stupid. Bastard lied to my face and I took it like a man, believed every honeyed drop from his lips."

"Don't beat yourself up. You know now. Problem is, he's off the radar. We got a BOLO out on his car. The Garrett County folks are looking hard at anything that closely resembles him. Highway patrol's been alerted, too."

"You think he's up here?"

"All the last pieces of the puzzle are in those woods. That's where I'd go."

"Good to know you can still think like a criminal, Cap."

Roosevelt laughed. "If you only knew. Now, go get him, tiger. And by the way, Hart's been upgraded to stable. He's gonna be just fine. We got a guard on him just in case. Thought you'd want to know."

"Got it. Appreciate that. Now I'm going hunting."

"Fletcher. Be careful. This guy doesn't have anything to lose anymore."

Fletcher hung up the cell and turned to the kid driving, used his most frightening voice. It was the one that always worked on Tad when he was lying.

"It's time to tell me the truth. You know Alexander Whitfield, correct?"

"Sir?"

"Listen, kid. He's no longer a suspect. He's now the target. We've got a grade-A assassin somewhere nearby who's gunning for Whitfield. If you know which camp is his, now's the time to be honest with me. Because if you don't tell me, you could be responsible for his death—you feel me?"

The kid gulped. "We're heading to the right one. Xander just wanted a delay. He wanted you up there. Just not before daylight. You kind of messed with the plan."

Suckered again. "What the hell's the plan?"

"I don't know that, sir. I just do what I'm told."

Fletcher did his best not to clock the kid, and braced himself.

"Then step on it. Because we don't have all night anymore."

CHAPTER FIFTY-FIVE

Savage River
Dr. Samantha Owens

"But Culpepper was in Iraq when Donovan got killed. Fletcher told me."

"Culpepper lies. Colonel Orange is a master manipulator. He even managed to talk Doc into going to work for him at Raptor. Got Jackal in there, too, and Shakes. But they weren't able to hack it. Jackal was majorly fucked up, saw too much. He had some of the worst PTSD I've ever seen. And Shakes, well, he drank like a fish. Always did. Hard to show up for a job when you're passed out in the gutter. But Doc, man, he found a way to make it work."

The fire popped and crackled, and Sam burrowed deeper in Xander's jacket.

"Why didn't you go work for Culpepper, too?"

Xander waited for a minute, then shrugged. "I had a bad feeling about Orange. As good as he was, I just never fully trusted him. I wanted out, all the way out.

Out of the military, out of D.C. and the bullshit there, out of it all."

"So you built this place and ran away."

He glanced at her, jaw tightening. She'd offended him again. Would she ever say the right thing to him? But he surprised her by smiling.

"Yep. And it's been nice and quiet for years, until Doc and Jackal came flying up here two weeks ago, telling me we had some sort of major problem. Someone had sent them each a note saying 'Do the Right Thing.'"

"Taranto. Taranto sent the notes."

"Yes, little fuck told me that. If he'd just been straightforward from the beginning, maybe none of this would have happened."

"So Donovan and Croswell came up here two weeks ago?"

"Fighting like cats and dogs, too. Jackal wanted to have a sit-down with Taranto, Doc was dead set against it. Who could blame him—the official report says it was his weapon that fired the shots that killed King. He doesn't need that in the media. But those two, they turned on each other, got fighting down in the river, for God's sake. I had to wade in and pull Jackal off Doc. He had his head under the water, practically drowned him. We're not supposed to water-board our teammates. Doc came up pissed, madder than a wet hen, pinned Jackal down face-first. Idiots practically killed each other.

"We must have looked like fools. Thor was bounding around barking, thinking we're playing, I'm screaming at them, trying to remind them that you don't turn on your friends, that we'd figure out who was behind the notes, everything."

"The sand in their lungs," Sam murmured.

"What?"

She took a deep breath, happy to at least have one part of the mystery explained satisfactorily. "Both Donovan and Croswell presented with fresh irritations from inhaling sand into their trachea and lungs. It's what initially made you the number-one suspect. The sand's biological makeup traced back to here. The Savage River."

"Wow. That's…awful."

"What about Everett, though? How does his suicide fit into all of this?"

"He wasn't a suicide. I went down there, I told you that. He wasn't answering his phone, and after Doc and Jackal, I got worried. That's how they got the hair they matched to my DNA. I checked the scene thoroughly. They were both dead when I got there, had been for a day or so. Trust me, Shakes wouldn't kill his mother. He may be a drunk, unable to hold down a job for long, but he loved her. No, I'm betting Culpepper went to see him, make sure he wasn't going to do any talking to the media. Somehow Mrs. Everett got in the way and was killed."

His voice caught. "Shakes wasn't doing too well. He was unstable enough as it was. A push in the right direction—either at gunpoint or through serious intimidation, and he'd cave. If he did cut his own wrists, he was coerced."

"Jesus," Sam said. "This just keeps getting worse. So what's on the pages from Donovan's journal? Details about the note and y'all getting threatened?"

"You just said 'y'all.'"

"So? I'm from Nashville. It's not exactly a stretch."

He smiled at her. "I liked it, that's all. No, I think Doc finally realized what his brain wouldn't let him know. He didn't kill King. There was no way. But all these years, he's felt responsible."

"Culpepper killed King, I take it?"

"That's what I think. Maggie told him about the rape. I assume King went to Culpepper and demanded retribution. Culpepper isn't the kind of man who's easily threatened. He probably swore to do the right thing, then shot King at the first good opportunity. For all I know, he got that firefight started in the first place. There was another unit closer that could have been called in. He set us up."

She tried to absorb the enormity of what he'd just told her. "God, Xander. All of this. He rapes a woman, murders her boyfriend, then kills three more men to cover his tracks. But why now? He's had plenty of time. He could have made it look like an accident."

"No, that wasn't his way. See, Karen is crazy as a fox. When Shakes spilled the beans to her about the friendly fire incident, and she started digging, she must have found out about Maggie. She went to Orange for confirmation, and God knows what sort of lies he told her."

"And somewhere along the way, she found out that Jen is King's daughter."

"No, she's not." Maggie's voice interrupted them. She came around the fire, her long body casting grotesque shadows across the yard and onto the trees beyond. Sam saw one that was distinctly rectangular. Maggie had a weapon in her hand.

Xander shifted toward her, and Sam heard the confusion in his voice. "What are you talking about, Mags? You told me—"

"Never mind what I told you. I lied. I had to."

"Xander, she has a gun." Sam was stuck between the two of them. She saw Xander's hand go to his waist, hoped the gun wasn't visible. She couldn't believe it. All this time, she was utterly convinced Culpepper, Orange, had been the killer. She didn't think it was Maggie. Didn't want to think it could be Maggie. She liked the woman, damn it.

But here Maggie was, with her weapon pointed right at Xander's head.

Xander froze, and Maggie took three steps closer.

"Maggie. You don't want to do this."

She laughed, humorlessly.

"Xander, I don't have a choice."

And she pulled the trigger.

CHAPTER FIFTY-SIX

Savage River
Dr. Samantha Owens

Xander moved faster than Sam thought was possible, knocking her back on the ground out of harm's way, his weapon rising as he used his foot to flip it into his hands, spinning, graceful as a ballerina, toward the threat.

God, he was like something out of *The Matrix,* she thought, squeezing her eyes shut, not wanting to see Xander killed in front of her, realizing if he didn't stop Maggie, she would be next. She started to pray and blinked her eyes open once, just in time to see Xander swing the weapon toward the trees.

Away from Maggie.

Gunshots rang through the clear mountain air. Her ears echoed with their fury.

Deafened, Sam risked another glance and realized Maggie and Xander were standing hip to hip, arms up, firing into the forest. Their only communication was under their breath. Sam caught "forty degrees to your left" and "reloading" but her ears were ringing, she couldn't make out anything else.

Xander stopped shooting long enough to grab Sam's arm and fling her to her feet, shouted, "Cabin!"

Sam didn't waste any time, she took off running, Maggie on her heels, a hand on her shoulder, holding her bent over. They reached the porch door and Maggie shoved Sam down on the hard wood. She could hear Thor barking frantically. He was stuck in his pen, unable to come to his master's aide.

"Goddamn it, the light. He's going to see us go in." She shouted, "Cover me!" and Xander lit up the night with a barrage of bullets. Maggie pushed Sam through the door and slammed it behind them, knocking the light switch off as she did.

Sam could hear Xander's weapon, the sharp, staccato bangs moving now, circling the house, then there was silence. Even the dog stopped barking. Sam prayed he wasn't hit.

"What the hell just happened?" Sam whispered.

"Shh."

Maggie had her back to the wall. She reloaded the pistol with sureness. Sam realized Maggie could probably rebuild the weapon blindfolded, in ten seconds or less, or something else equally impressive. She was again reminded of Taylor.

She wished she had that kind of fearless courage.

Then Maggie leaned over and pushed the gun into Sam's shaking hands.

"Here. Anything comes through that door, shoot it."

"Wait. No…" But Maggie slipped away, creeping across the floor on her belly. Sam heard the distinct noises of the lock on the gun cabinet being freed. More weapons. Damn it, Sam hated guns.

Then Maggie was back, a thick black assault rifle in her hand. Sam could still hear intermittent gunfire.

"Goddamn it, tell me what's going on," Sam whispered, this time with enough force that Maggie complied with an answer.

"Culpepper. He was in the trees over your shoulder. Listening. I couldn't sleep, I was coming to join you. I saw him in the flash of light from the door. I was trying to be subtle. I can't believe Thor didn't let us know he was out there."

"You're about as subtle as a heart attack. Is Xander okay?"

"He'll be fine. He knows this mountain like the back of his hand. He was ready for this, as well. He'll be leading Culpepper away from the house. I have to go help. You need to stay here and guard the kids. Noah has a rifle, he knows how to use it. I told him not to shoot you."

"No. No, you can't leave me here. I—"

"Sam." Maggie put her face right into Sam's. "Focus. Listen. You have to. Protect my babies for me, Sam. If that door opens, shoot. Don't hesitate. Hesitate and you could get all of us killed. Do you understand?"

And then she was gone.

Xander had somehow kicked out the fire. Sam didn't think she'd ever seen a darkness so incredibly black before. It scared her, made her feel like she was blind. She desperately wanted to light a match, flick a lighter, anything to break its all-consuming cover, but she didn't dare.

She couldn't hear properly, and the cloying blackness made her claustrophobic. She began to count mechanically, running her mantra through her head, breathing slowly so she wouldn't hyperventilate and pass out.

One Mississippi. Two Mississippi.

A short burst of gunfire pulled her up short. She smashed her body against the wall. Damn, that was close. She tightened her grip on the weapon.

At least she finally understood what had happened, the why behind all these senseless deaths. Maggie hadn't gotten pregnant with King's child. She'd gotten pregnant with Culpepper's. Jen was the product of her mother's rape.

And now her father was out hunting down her mother, trying to silence the one person who could undo him, his career, his reputation, after all these years.

What an idiot he was. Maggie obviously didn't have any desire for anyone to know the true story behind Jen's parentage.

But pushed by Karen Fisher, Culpepper thought the truth was coming out. And he did everything in his power to stopit.

Sam's hand was cramping. She loosened her grip on the gun. She couldn't hear the children, but didn't want to call out, to draw attention to them all.

She was so tired. Getting drawn into Culpepper's game, nearly dying herself, now squatting breathless in a darkened cabin with a gun in her hand…it was all too much. She needed to go away someplace quiet and have a nice little breakdown.

Too bad that wasn't an option. At least, not right now. There were three children twenty feet to her right, and she would be damned if any harm was going to come to them. She'd lost her own children because of her self-ishness. Even if she had to step in front of a bullet, she wasn't going to let anything happen to Maggie's kids.

She heard something on the porch. A scraping, soft and gentle. Like a shoe fall.

Her heart leaped into her throat and started beating so hard she thought she might black out. She reminded herself to breathe, tried to bring air into her lungs silently. She focused on the handle to the door. She knew if it were Maggie or Xander, they'd call out to let her know.

It must be Culpepper.

She gripped the gun more securely and bit her lip. *Please no. Please.*

The doorknob began to twist. She could see the shadow under it as it moved. She swallowed hard and aimed the weapon at the door.

Could she do this? Could she shoot someone in cold blood? Even knowing he was about to come hurt her? That he might have already killed Xander and Maggie?

Yes, she could. For the children.

She steeled herself. The gun stopped shaking. A quiet calm came over her.

The door gently began to open. She used her left hand to cup her right so the gun would be steadier.

She smelled the night air, the breeze gusting through the door, setting some papers on the counter fluttering. Her finger grew tighter on the trigger.

A man's silhouette now, oddly one-sided. She remembered her training. Squeeze your finger softly back toward your body, apply even pressure. Don't jerk at it, it will raise the barrel and you'll miss your shot.

The shadow grew larger. She was about to take the

shot when a deep voice called from outside the cabin, a voice she recognized.

"Stop! Police! Put down your weapon and step away from the door."

She nearly fainted in relief.

"Fletch," she called out, voice cracking. "It's me. It's Sam. I'm inside the cabin."

And the world exploded into fragments of light.

CHAPTER FIFTY-SEVEN

Savage River
Detective Darren Fletcher

The forest service kid had driven the Jeep off the trail about a quarter of a mile down the road, so they'd had to hoof it up the hill the last bit. Fletcher had approached the house slowly, cautiously. It was dark, and he thought no one was around. Disappointment and worry crowded into his thoughts—he'd missed her. Shit, maybe he'd chosen the wrong campsite. Then he heard the distinct crackling of campfire embers. A dog's throaty bark covered the noise he made as he moved toward the house. As his eyes adjusted to the darkness, saw the outline of a man opening the front door. Surreptitiously. Fletcher announced himself, heard Sam's responding shout and then all hell broke loose.

Fletcher wasn't ready for the shots. When Sam called out he'd started to lower his weapon, and that nearly cost him everything.

The man who'd been going into the doorway began to fire. Fletcher instinctively ducked, but quickly realized the man was firing into the house, not back out toward Fletch. So he called out again, screaming this time, running as fast as he could toward the door. His Maglite showed the outline of the man, and he had a clear shot through the open door. He squeezed the trigger once, and the firing inside the house stopped. Sam was shrieking. He didn't know if she was hit or scared, but the simple fact that she could call out was good news. She wasn't dead. Yet.

Two steps closer now, and he was at the base of the steps. A shot came from his right. Fletcher swung his weapon toward the new shooter. The two other tac team guys were bringing up the rear, they'd cleared the woods around the house as they came in. It was either them, or...

A voice called out, strong and true. "Thor, *steh!*" The dog whined but stopped barking. "*Braver hund.* Detective Fletcher, this is Alexander Whitfield. I have Colonel Culpepper in my sights. Permission to fire."

"Where are you, Whitfield?"

"Eighty degrees to your east, sir. I have a clear shot in my scope. You hit him, but he's not dead. I'd like to remedy that situation."

The man's voice had a cadence to it, a bit flat on the vowels. Not local.

"I'd like to keep him alive if we can, Sergeant. You down with that?"

"I suppose I don't have a choice, do I, sir?"

"No, you don't. Come on out. I've got him now."

"I'm just gonna hurt him a little bit then. Make sure he doesn't pull any punches. Firing."

A single shot rang out, and Fletcher flinched. He

didn't like people shooting around him in the dark. Jesus. Fucking yahoo.

A screaming groan emanated from the cabin, and Fletcher took the opportunity to rush inside. He sprayed the beam of his Maglite across the room. Culpepper was on the living room floor, moaning in agony. Fletcher went to him immediately, kicked his weapon away, then looked for Sam. He couldn't see her, and felt the panic slide in. But then, in the meager light, she stumbled toward him with three children in tow. Sam was trembling, shaking, and when he put his arms around her, he felt the slick stickiness of blood on her shirt.

He stepped back, holding both her arms. "Are you hit? Are you okay?"

"No. I'm okay. It's his blood." She gestured to her right. "He's been hit a couple of times. But the kids are just fine."

"Jesus, there were kids in here?"

Sam nodded. "Maggie's."

Fletcher resisted the urge to pull her into his arms.

"Thank God you're all right. That all of you are all right."

Sam smiled at him, then turned back to the kids.

"Come on, guys. We're going to go outside and find your mom. Don't look, okay?"

She guided them past Culpepper's now-still form and herded them out onto the porch.

There were steps beside him, and Whitfield appeared on the porch, night-vision goggles around his neck. He looked utterly wrecked, hair sticking up, blood on one shoulder. He nodded tersely at Fletcher.

"Son of a bitch slipped past me. Sam, are you okay?"

"I'm okay, Xander."

"Thank Christ."

Fletcher heard a note in Whitfield's voice, one of genuine concern, genuine…something else. Anger flared up—she was his, damn it—though he shoved that right back down where it came from. She'd been pretty clear earlier she wasn't interested. Why in the hell his feelings were somehow hurt by the possessiveness he heard in Whitfield's voice… He was imagining things. That was it. He was simply overtired and hearing things.

Xander took three steps to Sam and checked her over, just to make sure, then checked the kids, too.

"Where's Maggie?" Sam asked.

"I'm here. Don't shoot." A tall, fit woman stomped onto the porch. The kids crowded around her. The youngest finally started to cry. Maggie holstered her weapon and pulled her little girl into her arms.

"Thank you, Sam. Thank you for keeping them safe."

Sam swallowed hard. "I didn't do anything. It was all you."

They heard movement. Culpepper had come to and was trying to prop himself up.

Three weapons pointed at him immediately.

"You have to listen to me," Culpepper said, the pain in his voice making Sam wince. She should want to help him, to be a doctor, to follow her code. She didn't move a foot.

Fletcher went to him instead. "Shut the fuck up, Culpepper. You're lucky you aren't dead."

The colonel looked smaller when he was on the ground, bleeding. Xander had popped him in the thigh, high and right. An impressive shot. Fletcher had caught him in the shoulder of his gun hand, which effectively ended his ability to shoot. Not a bad shot, either.

"Detective, you don't understand. I'm here to protect them. You're all in danger." Culpepper wheezed out his proclamation.

"Yeah. Danger from you. You stupid son of a bitch." Maggie edged closer, her weapon trained on her rapist. "I wouldn't have said anything. I took your money and kept my mouth shut all these years. Why did you think I'd disgrace myself, admitting I'd been tainted by you?"

She hauled off and kicked him in the side. Fletcher grabbed her and pulled her back.

Culpepper laughed, a high, tinny squeal.

"It wasn't me. I swear it. I had no interest in seeing those boys dead."

Xander had crossed his arms on his chest, across the top of his gun, was staring down at Culpepper with loathing. Fletcher was just waiting for him to draw a knife and stab it in the man's chest. He stepped closer.

"No, you just snuck up here loaded for bear to tell us you had our backs, right?"

"I did. I wanted to make sure you were safe. Xander, I've lost so many of you. I didn't want to lose you, too. This is all my fault, but no, I didn't kill them."

"And that's why you left Susan Donovan tied up in your house? Is that why you shot and killed Gino Taranto, dumped his body in the river? Is that why you shot my partner, you piece of shit?" Fletcher demanded.

Culpepper didn't respond.

"I'm sorry then, *Mr.* Culpepper, but I'm going to place you under arrest now." Fletcher read him his rights, and Culpepper lay there quietly, pathetically bleeding on Xander's kitchen floor.

When Fletcher finished, Culpepper simply said, "It wasn't me. I'd like my lawyer now."

Xander blew up. "Even now, you can't tell the truth. Even now, you're lying, covering things up. You killed King, you bastard. How could you do that? He was one of us."

Fletcher saw Sam step forward and take Xander's arm. Maggie signaled with her head toward the open door. Sam dragged Xander away, out the door, yelling all the while.

Well, that went well.

Fletcher waved to the forest service kid, motioned for him to come over.

"Yes, sir?"

"Call an ambulance. We need to get him to a hospital."

"Can't get an ambulance up here. We'll have to Medevac him. I already radioed. The Search and Rescue guys are sending a chopper up." He headed back down the drive to the Jeep.

People moved around slowly now that the threat was over. Fletcher felt strangely let down. He always did when a case was done. Honestly it was just beginning— there was so much that needed to be handled, so many loose ends that needed to be tied up. But for now, he could go to sleep tonight knowing he'd taken a killer off the streets.

But could his heart recover from the blow of seeing Sam and Xander standing together, talking together, so obviously connected? He didn't know.

CHAPTER FIFTY-EIGHT

Savage River
Dr. Samantha Owens

Sam walked Xander out to the hammock and sat him down. He was flushed, furious and about to cry. Sam could see the tears welling up in his eyes. She turned her back for a moment to let him compose himself. She knew what it was like to be frustrated to the point of tears. To feel betrayed.

Maggie came out then, sat next to her. She was vibrating, probably from leftover adrenaline.

"Kids are with a forest ranger, learning knots. Sam, thank you. I owe you."

"Don't worry about it, Maggie. I wasn't going to let anything hurt them."

Maggie gave her a quick hug. "I owe you," she said again. "Man, I hope he rots. Why can't we just drop him off a cliff?"

Xander half laughed. "Trust me. If that fucking cop wasn't standing over him like a hawk, I'd have done just that."

She was quiet for a minute. "I lied back there. I did tell someone everything about that night."

"About the rape? Who?"

"Perry. We had a terrible fight. He wanted me to report it, said it was high time some of these jerks get court-martialed for their actions. He didn't think it through, what that could mean for me. Not only was I raped, but if I went after a colonel for it? My career would be finished. Hell, it was finished, anyway, and that was before I found out I was pregnant. After that son of a bitch forced me, I went to the docs and filed a restricted report. They took a rape kit and everything. I thought that would be enough. He would be informed that an assault had happened within his unit. He'd know it was him. I thought that knowing I'd told someone would scare him into staying away from me. I had no idea that he'd go after Perry instead. Oh, God, poor Donovan. All these years, thinking he was the one who shot Perry."

"But that's good news," Sam said. "Now he can be prosecuted for your rape."

Xander shook his head. "No, he can't. Since she didn't follow through, the evidence would have been destroyed. They only hold rape kits for a year or two. It's just not something the military wants to be accountable for."

"But if we—" Sam started, but was interrupted by a flurry of activity from the road. Vehicles were pulling up, more forest rangers, it looked like.

Fletcher came out of the house. Sam watched him search the crowd until he found her. He smiled a bit, and she realized that in another world, another life, she could really like Darren Fletcher. Maybe even more than like him. But it wasn't meant to be. He knew that, too, she could tell he did. Somehow, she'd made some sort of choice. She was outside with Xander and Maggie instead of inside with him. And he knew it.

He walked over to them. "Chopper's coming."

Moments later, the *whump, whump, whump* of the helicopter was plainly heard. The rotors from the chopper blew all sorts of debris around, little twigs and leaves and the tarp on top of Xander's woodpile. A forest ranger had dropped glow sticks around the clearing, creating a temporary landing pad. The space was just big enough for the helicopter to touch down. There were several people on board. Two men hopped off with a stretcher, went inside the house without a word. A few minutes later, they wheeled Culpepper out. He was white and gasping, obviously in pain. As he passed by them, he caught Xander's eye.

"Son. You've got to believe me. I didn't do it. I swear." He raised his arm in an attempt to point, face ashen. His voice was filled with horror. "It was her."

Sam looked over to where Culpepper pointed.

There was a dark-haired woman five feet from them. She had almost magically appeared, though logic told Sam she must have gotten a ride on the helicopter, claimed she was family. In all the mayhem, she'd been able to slip up to the house, with no one noticing. Blood leaked down the side of her face and her arm was outstretched, holding a small silver gun.

"He took my Perry from me," she ranted, shaking. "And all of you wanted to hide that fact. All of you. I killed them. I killed them all because they were more interested in protecting their reputations, protecting a killer, instead of finding justice for one of your own. How could you?"

She turned to Culpepper. "How could you?" she screamed.

Karen Fisher fired at Culpepper, hitting him in the head.

Before anyone could react, she turned the gun up to her chin and pulled the trigger.

EPILOGUE

"In your presence I don't want what I thought I wanted."

—RUMI

The file was closed on Donovan's death. Karen Fisher's claim that she was the killer had credence, but it was the detailed letter in her car, a suicide note, that allowed them to piece together the rest of the story. She'd gone to Culpepper and asked about the friendly fire, and Culpepper was smart enough to know he needed to keep her close to make sure the whole truth didn't come out. He'd manipulated her, played her, gotten her turned around in circles until she started to think he was lying to her. The only thing she felt she could do was start asking the men questions. When she'd uncovered the information about Maggie's little girl, Culpepper saw an opportunity to clean up his mess for good, and Karen, in her furious grief, had complied.

They were going to have to wait for Culpepper to wake up to confirm that truth to that theory. Karen's shot had gone a little wide, putting Culpepper in a coma, though not killing him. Her last shot, though, did count. She died in the medevac helicopter before it landed at the bottom of the mountain.

Sam had stuck around long enough to look through the pages Donovan had torn from his journal, which detailed Karen Fisher coming to him in the extortion attempt. She'd sworn to tell Susan that Maggie's daughter was his, and all about the friendly fire incident. Her plan was to destroy him completely if he didn't pay her off. She knew the Donovans had money. She knew they could afford it. When Donovan said no, threatened to take a DNA test to prove Jen Lyons was not his child, she'd gone to Culpepper. And things unraveled from there. Sam realized Donovan tore out the pages for two reasons—first, for insurance, in case everything exploded, which of course it had. Second, he was ashamed. He was still operating under the illusion that he'd killed Perry Fisher, and he'd briefly considered capitulating to Karen Fisher's wishes to keep the story quiet.

Sam made sure that part was kept from the Washington media, who, through multiple exposés that would certainly be Pulitzer contenders, detailed the whole story. *USA TODAY* even gave Taranto a posthumous byline, printing his notes, his theories, embellishing the story with the help of a colleague. Sam was glad to see him honored—he'd taken more of a risk sharing his story with her than anyone had realized.

And then there was nothing left for her to do, but return to Nashville, and get her own life back on track.

Susan and Eleanor hadn't wanted her to leave. As much as she enjoyed their company, she needed to. They had a little farewell party for her, just the three of them and a bottle of scotch, toasting the man they all had loved.

The following morning, head aching, heart sore, Sam packed her things and headed to the airport.

Somewhere between Key Bridge and Reagan National, as she'd thought of the dark soulful eyes she'd come to enjoy looking at, her phone rang. A deep voice, not pleading, but filled with need, simply said, "Don't go."

She'd listened for a few moments, then hung up and told the cab to turn into the car rental instead of Departures.

She'd called Fletcher as she was driving up to the mountains. Told him what she was doing. He wished her well, though she could hear the note of sadness in his voice.

She called Taylor, and warned her she wouldn't be back for a little while. Taylor was overjoyed at that news, for all the right reasons.

She called Forensic Medical and told them she was taking a sabbatical. They, too, were happy and understanding.

It was time for Sam to get her life back together. It seemed everyone had known that but her.

When she'd arrived in Savage River for the second time, driving up the rutted road that seemed to be even worse than she remembered, she'd had a moment of panic. *What are you doing?* She felt the urge to wash and, just as quickly, turned the thought off. She didn't need that crutch anymore.

At the end of the long, unpaved driveway, Xander and Thor were waiting for her. Xander's lighthouse smile filled her, and she returned his grin as he helped her from the car.

"I didn't think you'd come."

"Neither did I. I'm honestly not quite sure what I'm doing here."

"You're healing," he said, and pulled her into his arms.

Sam and Xander had spent the last few days just hanging out, watching Thor gambol around the clearing, getting to know each other. Today was no different. Feeling especially lazy, Sam lay in the hammock, a toe on the ground, idly pushing herself. She enjoyed the motion of the swing. She liked being here, in the mountains. The sun was bright and warm on her shoulders. She'd slept like the dead, eaten all manner of male-oriented food and dispensed with her sunscreen. Freckles paraded across her nose.

Xander was a surprise. Erudite, funny, amazingly kind, he kept her either laughing or in heated debate constantly. He'd seen something in her that she had forgotten was there. A happy person. Someone who wasn't bound by guilt, by the horror of her past.

He understood loss. Simple as that.

Xander threw the stick for Thor again and leaned back on his elbows in the grass.

"We're going to have to go back down the mountain," he said.

"Why? I thought you didn't want to be around people. Isn't that why you're up here in the woods, running away from the world?"

"I'm up here waiting for the zombie apocalypse. I thought you knew."

"Ha, ha."

He grinned at her, and she felt the strangest twisting in her stomach.

"*Ha* back. Now, let's be accurate. I didn't say I was leaving civilization behind entirely. Besides, the kind of people who come to this place aren't the kind I like to avoid. They have respect for the land. Respect for our freedoms. There's a certain mentality to the woods, Sam. Out here, it's just you and your thoughts. Uninterrupted by phones and televisions and computers."

"You know, it strikes me I've never asked what do you do for money?"

He laughed. "As if money is important. I have savings. I'm not a really expensive man. I'm a guide, too. Word of mouth, only. You saw my workbench. Fly-fishing around here is some of the best in the mid-Atlantic region. I have a P.O. Box down in Frostburg. Once a month, I go down there with my calendar, get the mail, drink some coffee at this great little diner and set things up. That's what I was thinking. We could go eat some greasy food and I can check my mail."

"But they can't call you. What if they have to cancel?"

He gave her an amused smile. "Then I go fishing without them. I figure if it's important enough to them, they'll make the effort to be here. If not...it's their loss, not mine. The world doesn't end."

"How do you get the news?"

"Forest rangers, and the people who come to fish. Though, thankfully, it's not loaded down with the kind of superficial bubblegum crap you probably deal with on a daily basis. I just want to know if things blow up. That's all."

She swung a few more times. Xander was a good one for silence. She liked that she didn't have to talk all the time.

"It sounds lonely."

"No. Alone, yes. But I like to be alone. I like my privacy. I don't want a bunch of people scurrying around, telling me what to do. I did my time. Literally. Peace, quiet and alone—that's my idea of heaven. Toss in a book, my music, Thor and a beer or two, and I couldn't be happier."

"What about marriage? Children? Haven't you ever wanted that?"

"Wow, aren't we getting personal here." But he smiled at her, a cocksure grin, and she felt that funny thing in her stomach again, what she'd been feeling for the past several days around him.

"Sorry. I'm just trying to understand."

"But you do, don't you? You've wanted this, too. You've been alone for the past two years, right?"

She paused for a minute, then set her head back against the hammock and stared at the clouds.

"Alone, yes. But unlike you, I've been lonely. Very, very lonely."

"You don't have to be alone anymore, Sam. I can make room for you here. You belong. Even Thor loves you."

The dog loved her. That fit. She wasn't deserving of much else.

She swung in silence for a few more minutes. "It's my fault they're dead."

Xander came over to her, pulled her upright. He sat down next to her and put his hand under her chin. It was as close as he'd gotten to her since that first night she'd arrived at his doorstep, and he'd hugged her softly, like she was a burn victim. He'd been respecting her boundaries without even having to be asked.

"Oh, Sam. Haven't you realized by now that unless you take the life by your own hand, physically strip the body of its ability to live by *your own hand,* you aren't responsible for the death?"

"Xander, that's not true. It was my actions that put Simon in danger. My selfishness. My sense of self-importance. I should have been with them. I put the dead before the living. I've always done that. It's what I do. You need to know that."

"Tell me what happened. I'll tell you if you're responsible or not."

"No."

"Sam. Have you talked to anyone about this? Really? Do you think I'm going to think less of you? Think about the past few weeks. I've admitted that I was complicit in covering up the death of one of my team members. I lied to the government, I lied to my commanding officer, I lied to the JAG corp. I deserted every code I believed in. The very code that kept me safe, and I committed the ultimate sacrilege toward it. Don't you see? I'm in my own personal self-exile, living alone, refusing myself the comfort I could have by letting go of my burden? Until now. Until you came parading into my camp and demanded the truth. And I gave it to you. Sam, won't you do the same? Won't you allow yourself that small comfort?"

"I thought you said that you were only responsible for a death if you committed it by your own hand?"

He just looked at her.

"You didn't kill King. Culpepper did."

"Maybe. If he doesn't wake up, we might never know for sure. But I was right there. I should have known what was going down. I could have saved him. All of them. So yes, I feel like it was as much my finger on that trigger as his."

"Xander, you can't have it both ways."

He looked her in the eyes, made her acknowledge him.

"Can't I? I'm a man, Sam. I've forsworn all that I swore to uphold. You're different. You didn't drown Simon and the twins any more than I did. That isn't enough for you, though, is it? You want to feel responsible. That way you can avoid moving on. All because you made a choice. The universe isn't kind, Sam. It's indifferent. You can't punish yourself because of bad timing."

She was crying. Again. She hadn't cried for nearly two years, then the second she got to D.C., she'd turned into a fucking puddle.

Xander didn't say a word. He sat back in the hammock and watched her, wary and hungry, like a wolf deciding its victim's fate, then came to some sort of conclusion. Even with the raw grief tearing her body apart, she could sense the change in his body, in his posture, then felt his arms go around her. He put her head against his chest and didn't say a word, just held her, let her cry.

She had no idea how long they stayed there. Eventually the tears stopped, and she started to talk. It got dark. Xander built up the fire. The flames warmed her feet, and Xander warmed the rest of her. He listened patiently, never interrupting, letting her tell the story. And finally, at the end, he cried with her.

Nashville, Tennessee
Dr. Samantha Owens Loughley
May 1, 2010

Sam was in the middle of a tricky dissection of an aortic rupture when the morgue phone began to ring. Her assistant, Stuart Charisse, answered for her.

"Dr. Loughley? It's Kris, she says your husband's on the phone."

"Finally. Thanks, Stuart. Can you put it on speaker for me? I don't want to lose my place here."

"Like that could happen," he said with a smile, then clicked the button. A small fog of static filled the room. Good luck for her she was at the station closest to the phone.

"Hi, Simon. What's up?"

"Hey, are you guys keeping an eye on things?"

"The only thing I've got my eye on is a serious buildup of plaque. Why, what's happening? Is it getting worse?"

The rain had started the day before, sheets of it, thrumming incessantly. Nashville had already gotten eight inches in twelve hours, and the panic was setting in. Simon had suggested she not go into Forensic Medical, but they were understaffed, and behind, so far behind. If things got as bad as the weather forecasters expected, she would be on duty for the next few days. They were saying this was a hundred-year flood. A flood of epic proportions. Memphis had gotten twelve inches the day before, and the rainfall totals for Nashville were expected to be even higher. For a city that had a large river running through its downtown, and tributaries spreading through the suburbs, that could spell disaster.

"It's getting much worse." She could hear a strange tone in Simon's voice. Her husband was a scientist, a rational man. Nothing rattled him. Even the miscarriage she'd suffered several months earlier didn't shake him. His ability to move on had actually caused major friction between them—she thought they might split up over it. He wanted her to move on and try for another baby. She couldn't face it again so soon. She didn't know if she'd ever be able to face the idea of getting pregnant again.

Eventually they found a happy medium—not talking about it. It had saved their marriage, at least temporarily.

"Simon, hold on, just one second."

She made the final slice and laid bare the culprit, a large piece of calcified plaque that had caused the aortic rupture. Now she could stop for a moment.

She slipped off her gloves and went to the phone.

"Sorry about that. I was right in the middle of something. How bad is it getting?"

"They're doing water rescues in River Plantation."

That caught her attention.

"Seriously? That close to us? The Harpeth is up that far?"

"Yeah, it is. We're getting water in the basement already. I don't want to be an alarmist, but I think I should get out of here."

"And leave the house?"

"Sam, there's three inches of water in the basement. I don't have sandbags or anything to keep it at bay. And if the river gets any higher—you should see this. It's unreal. Wait, I'm going to send you a picture."

She grabbed her cell from her back pocket. A few seconds later it vibrated.

She couldn't believe what she was seeing. They lived on a tributary of the Harpeth, but up on a hill. There had never been any concern about flooding. But the water was in their front yard.

"That's got to be, what, thirty feet above flood stage?"

"Thirty-four right now. But we just lost electricity. I can't stay here with the twins like this. What if it gets higher? Sam, I'm getting Maddy and Matthew out of here, right now."

"Where are you going to go? The base of the driveway is underwater."

"Which is why I have to go now, while I can still get out. Jesus, the furniture, all the stuff."

She heard real fear in his voice, and that in turn scared her.

"Don't worry about any of that. Chances are it won't be that bad. Just grab my laptop, but that's it, Simon. Go on. Get out of there."

"Okay. Listen, I'll call you when I get to high ground. I'll go to Taylor and Baldwin's place. There's no chance of the water getting that high, their neighborhood is up on that huge ridge. You stay there, you're completely out of harm's way. Love you, Sammy."

"Love you, too, honey. Be careful, and call me the second you stop. You want me to call Taylor and let her know you're coming?"

"I'm sure she's mobilized, Metro called everyone in. Activated the emergency plan. I have the key, anyway.

They won't care if a few drowned rats show up on their doorstep. They're only ten minutes from here. I'm gone, sweetie."

"All right. Call me as soon as you get there."

"Will do."

Simon hung up. Sam turned to Stuart, who'd caught enough of the conversation to look incredibly alarmed. He'd gone white.

"My mother lives in River Plantation. I just tried calling her, I can't reach her."

"Go turn on the television in my office. It's going to be okay."

Sam felt the oddest sense of dislocation. Suddenly the aortic rupture on the table didn't seem terribly important. But she couldn't leave him open.

She regloved and started working swiftly. She had cause of death, the rest was perfunctory at this point.

Stuart came back. "Sam, it's awful. They've got bodies. We're going to be getting fatalities coming in."

She adopted her calmest voice, though she was suddenly feeling panicked. "Okay, Stu. It's all right. Get Taylor on the phone for me. We'll have her check on your mom."

It took Stuart five long minutes to get Taylor Jackson, just enough time for Sam to finish up with her guest and get things put back together. She'd have to notate the disruption in protocol, but the man was ninety-four, she hardly thought the family would be searching for more answers. She wasn't one for cutting corners, but she felt something in the air, a strange sense that this needn't be her priority at the moment.

"I've got her," Stuart shouted, and Sam repeated the earlier movements, taking off her gloves and going to the morgue phone. She left it on speaker. Homicide Lieutenant Taylor Jackson's voice came strong through the air.

"Sam. What's up? I'm slammed. The whole city is going to be underwater by evening. The businesses along the Cumberland are already taking on water and you should see it out here in Bellevue."

"God. Sorry, but Simon called, and we're getting water in our house, too. He's taking the twins to your place. I've been here at the morgue all morning, but he just told me about the water rescues in Bellevue. How bad is it?"

"It's bad, Sam. I've never seen anything like this. Call Simon back and tell him to stay put. The Harpeth's rising too quick, he'll never make it. He's better off going to the second story of the house and waiting it out. I'll make sure the rescue units know that the water's already up to your area. They'll send someone to the house."

Sam felt a horrid sense of foreboding come over her. "Taylor. He left more than five minutes ago."

"Oh, shit. Okay, call him. Call him right now."

Sam already had her cell out and was dialing. Simon's phone rang and rang, then went to voice mail. She tried again. Same result.

"He's not answering, Taylor." Her voice had gone up an octave. She could hear Taylor barking commands in the background.

"Okay, honey. Relax. Cell service is spotty at best. The power lines are down in Bellevue, and so are the phones. The cell towers might be affected, as well. We'll send someone his way. He's probably already at my house."

"But you said…"

"I'm sure I was wrong."

Taylor wasn't wrong. Fire and Rescue found Simon's waterlogged car two hours later, wedged up against the concrete abutment by the Publix. The windows were down.

The car was empty.

Nashville, Tennessee
Dr. Samantha Owens
Current day

Sam stood at the base of her driveway. The red-and-white For Sale sign had a new addition that read Under Contract. The rooms were empty; the moving company van had just pulled away. She watched the truck turn the corner, and looked back to the house.

So many memories. Good. Bad. Sublime. Surreal.

It was time to say goodbye.

This was easier than she expected. She'd lived in Nashville her entire life, except for the years in D.C. while attending medical school. She'd lived there, loved there, married there, given birth there.

Stood vigil over the ashes of her family, her life, there.

Leaving wasn't something she ever thought of doing.

But with the loss of her family came a fracture from her city, one so deep that she didn't know if she could ever recover. She would visit. She would come back on holidays. But she could never live here again.

Her BMW was packed full of precious items she hadn't wanted to entrust to the movers. Most especially, the black marble urn that held the remains of her family.

Simon's will had stipulated that he be cremated. Hers did, as well.

But the twins. She couldn't bear to put them in the ground. For them to be alone.

Ashes to ashes. Dust to dust.

It had been the kind man at the crematorium who'd made the suggestion.

You can't tell anyone we did this, but we can bury them all together, if that's what you want. They're small enough….

Small enough, the two of them, to fit inside the thin cardboard coffin of their father. To be reduced to ash along with him, forever mingled, forever together.

It was illegal, but they'd done it, anyway. And deposited all three into the urn, sealed, like her heart, until she chose to open it and scatter their remains to the winds.

Simon wanted to be thrown into the air off the top of a mountain. Sam now had that place picked out.

A strong arm went around her waist. Bolstering her, just when she needed it. He knew. He always knew.

"Sam, are you sure? There's no going back now."

No going back. How true the statement was. You don't get do-overs in this life. She knew that better than anyone.

She turned to face Xander, the sun in her life. He'd grown in his beard, let his hair go a bit. He looked wild, untamed. His dark eyes met hers, and her heart constricted.

She touched him on the cheek and smiled softly.

"I've never been more sure of anything in my life. Let's go home."

They got into her car, Xander driving. He pulled

away from the curb slowly, so she could watch the house fade away in the distance if she wanted to.

She didn't. She shut her eyes, and thought of the clean, cool air that awaited her. The green trees. The clear blue streams. The arms of the man she loved.

She had finally found her peace.

* * * * *

Acknowledgments

My village. I couldn't do this without them. Thanks to:

My dear agent, Scott Miller, who really believed in this project from the get-go, and helped me believe in it, as well.

Alex Slater, who *handles* me.

My editor, Adam Wilson, who helped this story along so much.

The MIRA/Harlequin team, who do an amazing job top to bottom with my books, and everyone who has spent time making *A Deeper Darkness* a reality, especially Margaret Marbury, Valerie Gray, Miranda Indrigo and my awesome publicist, Tiffany Shiu.

The fine folks at Brilliance Audio, especially Sheryl Zajechowsk, Natalie Fedewa and the amazing Joyce Bean.

My tribe: Laura Benedict, Jeff Abbott, Erica Spindler, Allison Brennan, Toni McGee Causey, Alex Kava, Jeanne Veillette Bowerman, Jill Thompson, Del Tinsley, Paige Crutcher, Cecelia Tichi, Alethea Kontis, Jason Pinter and Andy Levy.

Joan Huston found all my mistakes, as always.

Special thanks to my research brethren who spot-read this one: Sherrie Saint, Dr. Sandra Thomas, David Achord and Andy Levy. Kelly Kennedy's *They Died for Each Other: The Triumph and Tragedy of the Hardest Hit Unit in Iraq* gave me insights into the war-time soldier's mind, and Craig Mullaney's *The Unforgiving Minute: A Soldier's Education* taught me what being a Ranger is all about.

The underlying story in this novel, the friendly-fire killing of Perry Fisher, was inspired by a real-life incident. My favorite teacher in high school, Dave Sharrett, who is, oddly enough, also a third cousin, sent his wonderful son, David H. Sharrett II, a boy we all knew as Bean, off to war in Iraq. He was killed by friendly fire, and the Army initially covered up the details. With the help of one of my former classmates, James Meek, Dave and Vicki Sharrett exposed the whole story, and found justice for Bean.

The grief we all feel cannot compare to their loss, but I hope that in some small way this book might help. God bless all of our soldiers. Their bravery and selflessness overwhelms me.

Finally, I must say thank you to my wonderful family. My long-suffering and lovely parents talked me through this one, and my divine husband, Randy, put up with so, so much. Without you, I would be lost.

REQUEST YOUR
FREE BOOKS!

2 FREE NOVELS
FROM THE SUSPENSE COLLECTION
PLUS 2 FREE GIFTS!

YES! Please send me 2 FREE novels from the Suspense Collection and my 2 FREE gifts (gifts are worth about $10). After receiving them, if I don't wish to receive any more books, I can return the shipping statement marked "cancel." If I don't cancel, I will receive 4 brand-new novels every month and be billed just $5.99 per book in the U.S. or $6.49 per book in Canada. That's a saving of at least 25% off the cover price. It's quite a bargain! Shipping and handling is just 50¢ per book in the U.S. and 75¢ per book in Canada.* I understand that accepting the 2 free books and gifts places me under no obligation to buy anything. I can always return a shipment and cancel at any time. Even if I never buy another book, the two free books and gifts are mine to keep forever.

191/391 MDN FEME

Name	(PLEASE PRINT)
Address	Apt. #
City	State/Prov.	Zip/Postal Code

Signature (if under 18, a parent or guardian must sign)

Mail to the **Reader Service:**
IN U.S.A.: P.O. Box 1867, Buffalo, NY 14240-1867
IN CANADA: P.O. Box 609, Fort Erie, Ontario L2A 5X3

Not valid for current subscribers to the Suspense Collection
or the Romance/Suspense Collection.

Want to try two free books from another line?
Call 1-800-873-8635 or visit www.ReaderService.com.

* Terms and prices subject to change without notice. Prices do not include applicable taxes. Sales tax applicable in N.Y. Canadian residents will be charged applicable taxes. Offer not valid in Quebec. This offer is limited to one order per household. All orders subject to credit approval. Credit or debit balances in a customer's account(s) may be offset by any other outstanding balance owed by or to the customer. Please allow 4 to 6 weeks for delivery. Offer available while quantities last.

Your Privacy—The Reader Service is committed to protecting your privacy. Our Privacy Policy is available online at www.ReaderService.com or upon request from the Reader Service.

We make a portion of our mailing list available to reputable third parties that offer products we believe may interest you. If you prefer that we not exchange your name with third parties, or if you wish to clarify or modify your communication preferences, please visit us at www.ReaderService.com/consumerschoice or write to us at Reader Service Preference Service, P.O. Box 9062, Buffalo, NY 14269. Include your complete name and address.